LOVE IN A MIST

SARA SARTAGNE

*Having one book under your belt doesn't always make the next one easier. So I'd like to thank JP and JW for always being around when I'm knocking my head against a wall. And Meabha Magerr, for the Irish translation! You're galánta, girl.
And finally, I'd like to thank Fiona, my rock.*

Copyright © 2020 by Sara Sartagne

All rights reserved.

No part of this book may be reproduced in any form or by any electronic or mechanical means, including information storage and retrieval systems, without written permission from the author, except for the use of brief quotations in a book review.

This is a work of fiction. Names, characters, places and incidents are the product of the author's imagination. Any resemblance to actual persons living or dead, business establishments or events is entirely coincidental.

Amazon Print edition:

ISBN

Thank you for buying the second book in the **English Garden Romance** series and for supporting independent authors.

If you'd like to know when I'm releasing the third book in the series, sign up to my mailing list and I'll be able to send you all sorts of **freebies, many of which are not available commercially.**

See back of this book for details of the sign up and the freebie, and in the meantime, enjoy *Love in A Mist!*

Sara

1

"Do sit down," Ella gestured to the comfortable chairs in front of her ancient, mahogany desk and perched on the edge, her calm smile belying her inner alarm. If Tony Smith and Gregory Wainwright were visiting together, it was unlikely to be good news. She drew a breath. "What can I do for you?"

There was silence as the men exchanged glances. Gregory opened his mouth, but Tony Smyth jumped in.

"We've come to complain about all the contractor trucks and vans on the estate," he said. "It's well-nigh impossible to move my machinery when bloody designers and their kit are snarling up all the roads across the estate! As if they weren't in a bad enough state!"

It was as though someone had fired a starting pistol. Gregory and Tony spoke over each other with complaints about the state of the roads; "Choked wi' mud!", late-night working with floodlights which disturbed livestock, and lots and *lots* of contractors messing up the estate.

Ella listened with a sinking heart but kept her face neutral.

"That sounds dreadful. Are the roads near you in a mess, Gregory? I toured around earlier this week, and I agree there's a lot of mud around, but I didn't believe it was that bad."

"Well, since we had the rain... and then they've started bringing the diggers in..." Gregory started almost apologetically.

"You don't see the half of it!" Tony growled, his face pink with indignation. Ella smothered her irritation. There was very little she missed on the estate; she made sure of that. But the garden build – and specifically, the garden build keeping to budget – had been a worry since it started. Not that the two tenants in front of her would realise that.

"Shall I come out and have a look?"

"Aye, looking is all very well – but what are you going to *do* about it? I've got livestock to move, and maintenance work to do! And we all know this is a barmy project that her ladyship has started."

Ella stiffened. Tony faltered at her glance, and Gregory took up the story.

"What Tony's trying to say is that we don't quite understand why Lady Susan feels it so vital to build this new garden when the estate's already very successful. You've worked wonders on it since you came here, so why this new venture?"

Privately, Ella was sympathetic. The estate was firmly in the black, finally, after years of barely breaking even. Ella vividly remembered her sense of bewilderment and almost immediate panic when Lady Susan had revealed the plans for the garden. Her heart still ached as she imagined the gardens she loved, had depended on for her personal solace, massacred by the new design. After all her work to make the estate profitable, it had felt a bit of a slap in the face.

But again, those were her own thoughts. In front of Tony and Gregory, she had to appear a loyal employee.

"You know her ladyship wants to make Ashton Manor a place for generations to come. The new garden will help do that. We can't just be a stately home in acres of pretty parkland – we won't survive long term," she said.

"I don't agree," said Tony, clenching his fists on his knee while Gregory sighed. "The farms are well run, we have a cracking line in organic produce, and the house attracts thousands of visitors!"

Yes, but not enough younger visitors, thought Ella, reluctantly.

Too many of the older generation, with beige macs, sensible shoes and an eye for a scone and tea at the café. But they wouldn't live forever. All heritage organisations had the problem of visitors literally dying off. Ashton Manor was no different.

"You'll need to show me the issues," she said thoughtfully, running her hand over her ponytail. "Then I can speak to Lady Susan about it personally, rather than talking about it third-hand."

"We guessed you'd say that," said Gregory. "The morning is when the disruption is worst, as the contractors come on to the estate. Blarin' radios too!"

Ella stopped herself from wincing. Loud music early morning was one of her own pet hates. Her thoughts about the garden designer and the army of contractors and hangers-on, darkened.

"Let's have a look and then I can suggest something," she said instead. "We need to accommodate the garden work and the estate work."

Gregory grinned.

"I reckon this will take some doing, even for you, Miss Sanderson. We tried talking to the contractors but all they do is talk about their schedule, their deadlines. As if *we* don't have any deadlines ourselves!"

Ella knew all about the garden schedule. It looked ridiculous on paper, even with the number of contractors around. Driving it, of course, was the big society wedding of Jonas Keane, which would launch the garden to the great and the good in August. The guest list would look, according to Lady Susan, like a who's who of the FTSE 100.

Inwardly, she sighed. Outwardly, she stood up from her perch on the corner of the desk and gave the two men a smile that was as reassuring as she could manage.

"Will one of you pick me up, or shall I meet you?"

"I'll call at seven and go round with you," Gregory said, shaking her hand in farewell.

They left, leaving Ella chewing her lip and winding her dark ponytail around her fingers.

Bloody Connor McPherson, she fumed. Lady Susan had kept her away from the architect of this monstrosity ever since they'd disagreed on the plans in the early stages.

'Disagreement' was putting it mildly, she reflected. In retrospect, perhaps she could have been less outspoken, more like her usual mild, diplomatic self. But the changes planned to some of her favourite parts of the estate had made her incoherent when she'd met the designer. She couldn't explain her thoughts about what the garden and the estate meant to her, they were too personal to share with a stranger. So she hadn't been able to talk about her impending sense of loss of a place that had brought comfort to her battered soul. Had helped her, in short, to rebuild. To add fuel to her fury, Connor McPherson had been arrogant and dismissive.

And if the physical changes weren't bad enough, she was also concerned that the reserves she'd been building up for the estate would just be sucked into the bottomless pit of the new project.

She sighed. It was too late now, but she cursed her loss of control, which meant she had no voice in the garden build. Lady Susan was managing the contact with the designer herself and had suggested Ella might focus instead on keeping the rest of the estate intact. Ella had no knowledge of the figures and had to hope Lord Ralph would be able to check his wife's wilder impulses.

It could only have been worse, Ella mused, if she'd been asked to help with the wedding. She suppressed the shudder across her slender shoulders. Yes, she wanted to steer well clear of *that*.

But now the garden plans were affecting the tenants and that, she thought, was definitely her area. Though before she waded in, she needed to see it all for herself, otherwise her employer would dismiss her opinion as sour grapes.

Ella drew a deep breath as she stopped the Land Rover, pulling the handbrake up with uncharacteristic viciousness. She sat for a few minutes, working out what she would say to Lady Susan, and how to say it. The October sun glinted at her through the changing leaves and gradually, as the mellowness of the landscape penetrated her mood, she calmed down.

She knew every inch of the estate; she'd made it her business to get to know the roads, the buildings, and the tenants and their peculiarities, over the years. Surely Lady Susan would give her a hearing?

She glanced in the driving mirror before climbing out of the vehicle, smoothing her hair. Slate grey eyes regarded her steadily. Her brows, perhaps a little thick, had drawn together, and she attempted to stop frowning. No need to go in looking like thunder, she thought.

The heavy door to the manor opened and a very tall man stepped out, laughing mid-sentence. He ran a hand through his thick black hair and stooped to hear the little bird-like woman who followed him to the doorstep. He laughed at something she said and then, to Ella's surprise, kissed her employer on the cheek. Her ire, which she'd damped down, roared into life again.

As she reached for the door handle, he waved a careless hand to Lady Susan and strode to his car, a ridiculous, low-slung sports affair. Before Ella's foot hit the ground, he had gunned the engine and disappeared in a spray of gravel. Lady Susan was still smiling when Ella joined her.

"Morning, Ella. How are you?"

"I'm very well, Lady Susan, thank you. Could I speak to you for a few minutes?"

Lady Susan's warm brown eyes were rueful.

"Oh, dear. What have I done?"

Ella shook her head.

"It's about all the garden contractors on the estate."

"Ah. You'd better come into the drawing room then."

Ella followed Lady Susan into the room, appreciating as always its beauty and the cheerful log fire that chased away the chill from the autumn morning. There were two cups on the low coffee table, both empty. Connor McPherson was certainly making himself at home, she noted, adding to her irritation.

"Now – what's the problem, Ella?"

Lady Susan sounded slightly defensive. So, mused Ella, she knows. But she doesn't want to talk about it.

"I rather think we might need to mend our fences with some tenants," Ella started quietly. "They're concerned at the upheaval from the garden project. Having been around the estate, I agree with their concerns."

Lady Susan sighed.

"A bit of mud? Surely not."

"It's not just the mud on all the roads coming off the main road – although that's pretty bad. It's the number of lorries and workers blocking the principal access routes to the farms at Downey, Steen and Hartsford. The contractors park all over the place, and the farmers can't move livestock or machinery easily. Which, at this time of year, is important as they move cattle off the open land."

Lady Susan sat silently.

"I've been out all morning with Gregory Wainwright and Tony Smyth, and I'm astounded that they haven't shot anyone yet. The contractors don't seem to understand that this is a working estate, which is making things a bit... tense," Ella added.

She paused, watching Lady Susan, who pursed her beautifully shaped mouth.

"I know you're on a schedule..." Ella offered tentatively.

"Yes, we are, and it's already under a lot of pressure because of the dreadful weather we had at the end of September!"

Oh dear, thought Ella, dismayed at the sharpness of her employer's tone.

Lady Susan absently picked up her coffee cup with thin fingers, realised it was empty and put it down again. She reached for the still warm pot and poured another cup, looking enquiringly at Ella to see if she wanted one. Ella shook her head and waited.

"You know how important it is to complete the garden by next August, and Connor's brought extra hands on board. Perhaps they're not fully informed... But really, Gregory and Tony came to you to complain?" A note of anxiety had crept into Lady Susan's voice.

"And George, later."

"Ah."

"It may just be a matter of sorting out some clear working practices," Ella said. "If we can get Mr McPherson to understand the issues that his workmen are causing the farms, I'm sure we could find a solution. Perhaps you could referee a session between Gregory et al. and the contractors?"

Lady Susan threw her a glance.

"As it's estate business, it would be better if you did it, Ella. You're much more diplomatic than I am."

Inwardly, Ella groaned. "I'd be happy to."

"And Connor, of course."

"If you consider his presence necessary?"

Ella's stomach curdled at the prospect.

"Naturally, it is! And in some respects, if the contractors are getting on everyone's nerves, then it's a very good job that he'll be spending more time here." Lady Susan beamed at her.

"He will?"

"Yes, we spoke about it this morning. I've offered him Daffodil Cottage for the duration of the project, rather than him travelling backwards and forwards from London."

"Daffodil?" Ella said faintly, thinking of the worker's cottage adjoining her own.

"Yes, I know you were about to search for new tenants for it, but it can wait until next year given how important it is to get the garden completed. Are you all right, my dear? You look a little pasty."

Ella waved her hand and managed a smile.

"No, no, I'm fine. When will Mr McPherson be moving in?"

"Connor, dear. Mr McPherson sounds rather formal, given we've been working with him for four months. He needs to sort out some things in London, and then he'll be with us next week. It's what the project needs, really, don't you agree? The designer on site to tackle some of the problems you're now having to deal with?"

"Yes, of course."

"And after all, it will be nice to have a neighbour, won't it? I know you like your privacy, but I do occasionally worry about you with so few people around you."

"Really, Lady Susan, I'm fine. You don't need to move Mr McPher... Connor next door!"

"Well, that *is* the cottage that's most convenient for the house and main garden, isn't it?" Lady Susan peered over the edge of her coffee cup, a shrewd expression in her eyes. "Unless you've a *violent* objection?"

She had. *Violent* objections.

"No. No, of course not," she managed eventually. Lady Susan looked politely sceptical. Carefully she placed the cup back in its saucer and gestured to the model which covered the whole of the enormous table by the window.

"I know you're concerned about the design, Ella, but this is part of my vision of the future for Ashton Manor."

Not *just* the design, Ella thought, crossly. It was a double whammy – ripping out the heart of my favourite parts of the garden and potentially bailing you out with my precious reserves if it all goes wrong! She wandered over to the model of the garden. Curves, straight lines and triangles all clashed together in her opinion, although she acknowledged grudgingly that the water features looked interesting. But was it worth destroying the existing garden? No. Not in her view.

Ella could hear Lady Susan sigh from across the room.

"I hope you and Connor can come to some compromise between you about the work – and the cottages, for that matter. But be in no doubt, Ella – we need the garden to open on time and I'm counting on you to facilitate that."

Having Connor McPherson next door would be the equivalent of him parking his tank on her lawn. Ella forced a smile.

"I'll do my best."

2

Connor flexed his shoulders and the fabric of his jacket pulled against him. He stretched his elbows out and just caught the mug (thankfully empty) before it toppled. That wouldn't have done. Not while Ms Sanderson was in full flow.

He'd received the invitation – or was it a summons? – to this meeting at the *very* last minute. If he had been of a suspicious nature, he might have thought she was trying to wrong-foot him. Her deep voice, although not loud, filled the room. He popped a jelly baby into his mouth from the packet in his pocket and wondered idly if she bothered with men at all, with that contralto voice, severely cut jacket and snowy shirt. It was her uniform, he saw her in it every day. Almost like a banker. He suppressed a wince. No, not a banker, thank God. He saw her hand reach for her glossy ponytail, her hair as usual scraped back tightly from her head. She turned to him and said, "Well, Mr Mc... Connor? What do you think?"

He stared at her while his mind went scuttling in two directions – one back to the conversation before he lost his concentration daydreaming. And the other to the dreadful formal corporate world he'd now left, thank God. Focusing, his brain filled in some gaps. He hoped.

"I'm sure we can come to some arrangement," he said easily. He turned to the grumpy faces of the tenants whose feathers his team and contractors had ruffled.

"Yes, I'm also sure you can, but are you happy to start the work later in the day? Particularly where it would interfere with the movement of livestock, machinery and feed?" Ella Sanderson put on a 'patient' face and his irritation, never far from the surface, flared. God, she really was objectionable.

"No bother, if you can provide the dates. We have a schedule to keep, and delays cost money, Ms Sanderson. And the budget is tight, as I'm sure Lady Susan has mentioned."

Her lips closed firmly. Ooh-hoo! He thought. Perhaps Lady Susan *hadn't* drawn the estate's manager into the finances?

"We're sorry if you've been inconvenienced by the work, and I'd be appalled if any of my team has been rude to you – whatever the reason," he continued. "I'll speak to the contractors about how we conduct ourselves on the estate. However, if you have any future issues, please come to me."

"You're never here!" cried the man called Tony.

"Well, as of tomorrow, that will change," Connor said pleasantly. "I'm moving into Daffodil Cottage for the duration of the build which means I'll be around twenty-four seven. This is a trickier job than either Lady Susan or I had anticipated—"

"And that's not counting the weather," commented a portly man with an open, kind face.

"You're not wrong there, George!" said another tenant, and the group murmured in agreement. Ella Sanderson said nothing, but he noticed she closed her fists.

Powerful passions? That surprised him.

"Oh aye, we rarely get this amount of rain in London," Connor continued with a rueful grin. "Donegal, now, that's a different story... It's a wonder I don't have webbed feet!"

There was laughter, and he smiled at the group. Only Tony continued to glare. Connor spread his hands in mock surrender.

"I'm an intruder, I know that. But I'll be leaving soon enough after the garden opens. I'm really sorry if we've been a pain lately. It won't happen again."

He saw Ella look around as the men accepted his apology. She rose to her feet and addressed the group.

"Okay, I'll speak to you about the next couple of weeks so... Connor... can plan his work," said Ella, hesitating over his name. "And obviously, this works both ways. The garden team has a deadline to meet, and Lady Susan is anxious about it. I would like her to be reassured by our cooperation. So if you can work and move your livestock at other times to help the garden crew, they'd appreciate that and so would I."

Connor ran his hands over his jeans, hiding his surprise. He wasn't expecting even-handedness.

"I believe we're done," she said, turning to him. "I'll coordinate with you a week in advance – will that be enough?"

It'll have to be, Connor thought. "That would be great."

The men left the room, leaving him with Ella. There was silence as she returned to sit behind her desk, covered with neat piles of paper.

A place for everything. He remembered his own desk back in London.

"You look amused... Connor. What's funny?"

"You're having real problems with my name, aren't you?"

"I'm used to more formality with tenants and suppliers."

"Ah no, it's not a criticism. Call me what you like."

Or perhaps not, he amended, seeing the ghost of a smile flash across her grey eyes. He might not like what she would call him, given free rein.

"And might I call you Ella? Ms Sanderson is a wee bit of a mouthful."

"By all means, call me Ella."

"I'll be getting along then. Ella."

He tried his most roguish smile on her. Damn, she was a hard nut to crack. Still, she hadn't liked – no, actually she had *hated* the garden plans, hadn't she? He recalled that angry conversation about the initial design, where she had suggested all the tired, old-fashioned ideas about garden design that he despised. She'd been genuinely horrified at his approach. He'd been a bit surprised at her reaction. Almost as though it was her garden, rather than her employers'.

He focused his gaze on her again. She had amazing skin, pale, and flawless, like china, he noticed, absently. As he watched, he saw her vulnerable, less confident.

"R-i-ght," she said slowly. She drew a deep breath. "I suppose I ought to give you the keys to the cottage."

She rose gracefully and walked to a slim cabinet and took out some keys with a yellow ribbon. She handed them over as though they were radioactive.

"Anything I should know about the cottage? Temperamental boilers? Intermittent water pressure? Creaky doors?"

She put her head on one side.

"I'd appreciate some warning if you're planning a housewarming party."

He laughed out loud.

"Would you be looking for an invitation?"

"No, I'd probably make arrangements to be out for the evening," she said sweetly. Her unexpected smile, even laced with irony, made him pause. "I'm your next-door neighbour."

Ella dropped the keys onto the bureau and walked into the cottage, ducking her head to miss the beam from the hall. She kicked off her shoes and headed towards the living room, noticing a flashing light from the answerphone as she passed it.

Jeanette, she thought. Probably about the netball.

She poured herself a whisky and sank into her favourite armchair, only to get up again a moment later to build a fire in the burner. When the flames caught, she closed the doors and sat down, cradling the drink in her hands.

"Well. *What* a bloody mess!" she said to herself before taking a deep swallow. The tang of the whisky hit the back of her throat, and she leaned her head against the back of the chair, closing her eyes.

Blue eyes laughed at her from her memory. Black hair, curling too long over his collar and a somewhat bushy beard, giving him a slightly disreputable, piratical air. And an energetic presence, all bustle and broad shoulders. Living in one tall package in the cottage next door. Damn it, she could even hear him moving stuff about next door.

Something soft and heavy landed on her lap and she jumped.

"Oh! Monty, it's you. You gave me a fright, you little monster."

Her tabby cat purred and treadled her knees.

"Yes, yes. I'll feed you in a minute."

Monty settled and for a moment, the stress of the day faded under the rumble of his purr and the crackle of the fire. Ella sighed and stroked his ears absently as she sipped the whisky.

When she'd arrived at Ashton Manor more than seven years ago, she'd been a bit of a wreck, she thought wryly. It might not be too much of an exaggeration to say that learning to manage the estate and the gardens had helped put her together, piece by piece. Her deep love for the garden had grown with her expertise and her knowledge about the estate, fresh as she was from university. God alone knows where she'd be, had she not been successful at interview...

"And then I got you! I was lucky, wasn't I?" she said to Monty, while his purrs vibrated against her legs. Monty slanted his gaze at her, looking satisfied, and she smirked at him.

She thought about the garden design. Even looking at the model for a long time, from many angles, she still couldn't see any merit in it. She knew a bit about building work and that the rain was playing havoc with the schedule; and that meant more money. If the estate was asked to fund it, Lord Ralph would naturally agree, and her plans for the rest of the estate – the renovation of the elaborate gates, repairing the major roads – would be screwed.

She'd tried to make the argument with Lady Susan that such a modern design would impact visitor numbers to the house. It had already drawn the fury of the heritage groups.

But Lady Susan had been adamant in her choice. She had seen something in the designer's vision that had totally bypassed Ella, who considered it rather ugly – brutal, almost. Like the designer. Not that he was ugly, she amended in her head. She couldn't obstruct the build, exactly. But she could be less than helpful. Forget to ask McPherson to meetings, not pass on information, that kind of thing. Even though that wasn't really her style…

The sound of music seemed to soak through the walls. Was that a *fiddle* she could hear? She'd lived in the estate cottage for nearly three years, and the adjoining cottage had been vacant all that time. She'd thought the walls were thick enough to muffle any noise, but she'd been wrong. God, she hoped he didn't like loud music in the morning.

She sighed, finished her drink and stood up, turfing Monty from her lap. He squeaked and landed gracefully, staring at her with disdain before stalking off in the direction of the kitchen. Ella's lips tweaked, and she brushed down her wool trousers. She clicked the answerphone.

"Hi Ella!" Jeanette's cheerful tones boomed round the room and Ella swiftly turned down the volume. "Are you going to play next Thursday, against Southton Village? We could really do with you as centre! Can you let me know as soon as you can – I need to put the team sheet in to the association. See you at practice on Wednesday night? Hugs!"

Ella laughed softly. Jeanette had left another version of her message in a text to her mobile. She typed a text to say she would play and yes, she'd be there on Wednesday.

"Would I miss it?" she murmured, as she clicked send.

She went upstairs to change and attempt to come to terms with the idea of a neighbour. A loud, handsome, Irish neighbour.

3

His project manager Mike Stewart was at the end of his patience. Connor sympathised, having sat in this dingy, underheated room for the past hour and a half. It surprised Connor he couldn't see his breath in front of him. Lady Susan was looking cold.

"But you must see that the house *demands* that the garden should be treated similarly!"

This was from the lady with the thick jacket who'd obviously been to these offices before. Connor glanced at his scribbles. Her name was Louisa Forsyth, and she was chair of the historical society for the county. Next to her was some chap from the National Conservation Trust, who'd looked down his nose at them all since they arrived. What was his name...? Jonathon Skillington-Bland. There were other people in the room, who brought tea and took notes. But the two in front of him were the current bane of his existence.

By God, Jonas would bloody owe him for this. He exhaled. Never take a job out of sentiment, his father had said. His mood darkened as his father came into his mind, and he shifted in his seat. Lady Susan shot him a glance.

"I'm sure, Louisa, that you recognise that I would no more damage

Ashton Manor than I would throw my dogs on the fire, but there are literally dozens of ancient houses with 'appropriate' gardens," she said, using her bony fingers to create the air quotes. "I wanted this to be a *landmark* garden, one that would be called a classic in fifty years, a century from now!"

"I'm not sure what we would call it, dear Lady Susan," drawled Jonathon Skillington-Bland. "The current design bears no resemblance to Ashton Manor, there's simply no connection."

Connor's hackles rose, his father forgotten.

"I'm sure I need not remind you of my family tree. It has hordes of forward-thinking engineers, philosophers, economists and thinkers," smiled Lady Susan sweetly as Connor drew breath. "This is just my contribution to that family tree."

Mike Stewart gripped his pen more firmly.

"If you would tell us if there is anything minor that might make the design more acceptable?" he said. Louisa threw her hands up.

"Mr Stewart, I wish I could! But there is nothing! The whole design is completely incongruous to the house!"

"And without major re-design, the National Conservation Trust is unlikely to contribute," said Jonathon, with a smile which Connor thought was meant to be regretful. Mike gulped, and Connor could almost see him re-drafting the budgets.

Lady Susan sat back, beginning to look irritated.

"Well, to be sure, it's hard to alter the design when the work's already begun," he said mildly. "It's possible for us to change the design to fit your requirements..."

Louisa leaned forward in anticipation.

"...but that won't work for me as the designer, and it would desecrate the vision that her ladyship has for the garden. So I believe we're at an impasse. It's a shame that the National Conservation Trust is so focused on the past – although the clue's in the name, isn't it? But Lady Susan wants to create something for future generations, something a little less rooted in the outdated historical notions of what gardens should be like."

Lady Susan beamed at him. Louisa swelled, as though someone had pumped her with air. Jonathon went silent.

"We were hoping for a financial contribution, but to the *existing* plan – isn't that right, Lady Susan?"

"Yes, changes to the design now would not only impact its integrity but also mean that we've done a lot of work that might be for nothing. And I have two pet hates. I abhor waste. And a lack of imagination," she said crisply.

Her chin rose slightly, and Connor hid a grin. Wonderful woman, he thought, pleased and even a little relieved. He'd not been mistaken – she was as determined – or stubborn – as he was.

"Are you saying you refuse to listen to our advice?" Jonathon said thinly.

"Advice?" Connor said, with a smile he knew showed his teeth. "Is it advice? Or is it just you holding the money over our heads so we sing to your tune?"

Louisa clasped her hands together.

"Lady Susan – *Susan* – please don't do anything rash."

"I'm not doing anything rash. I'm following my instincts and, if we're getting sentimental, *Louisa*, I'm following my heart. We need to leave a legacy for the future that appeals to people who are much younger than our existing visitors. And these plans do that exactly. My twelve-year-old godson told me it was... what did he say? Ah, yes – *awesome*. His sister, sixteen, going on twenty-five, considers it 'sick'. So I'm fairly confident Connor's design will fulfil the legacy I want to leave."

"The National Conservation Trust, not to mention the Historical Commission, will have a view on this," Jonathon said.

"Mr Skillington-Bland, they can have all the views they like. I'm determined that this garden will be a classic for the future and I'll be happy to fight for it."

Jonathon steepled his fingers.

"The work has begun, but I'm led to understand that you haven't yet obtained planning permission?"

Connor's temper rose.

"The works underway don't *require* planning permission," he said shortly.

"But the next stage most definitely will. And the local authority is famously conservative – with a small 'c'." He smirked at his little joke.

"The plans have been submitted and so far, the local authority has been nothing but supportive," Lady Susan commented tightly. "They agree with me that some kind of third-rate restoration would add nothing to the area. They want new and different and this garden delivers that in spades. Pardon the pun."

"Well, perhaps the local councillors are unaware of the opposition to the plans."

"Well, I daresay you'll be changing all that, but in the meantime, we'll be getting along." Connor stood up swiftly, noting with satisfaction that his tall shadow fell across Skillington-Bland's face, making him flinch. He offered his arm to Lady Susan, who smiled gratefully. Mike packed away his papers, looking gloomy.

"You won't have heard the last of this," Louisa warned. Lady Susan smiled sweetly.

"Of course not. Aren't we both due at the WI next week? I imagine you'll be incapable of letting it drop."

Connor snorted with laughter, and they left.

Connor gave his tall, dark friend a hug, and then turned to the pixie-like woman by his side.

"Sam! How the devil are you? Still designing gardens for this eejit?" He wrapped his arms around her, and she protested, laughing.

"I'm great, thanks, but enough of the insults about my future husband!"

He released her, taking in her short blonde hair and faint tan. It had been a while since they'd last worked together, designing gardens on one of Jonas' housing developments in Cambridgeshire. Even though Sam had her own gardening credentials with a brace of awards which had put her on the horticultural map, she had been a little overawed when they began to work together. In their first meeting, she had treated him as a guru for all of an hour, before disagreeing violently with him. They'd been firm buddies ever since.

Jonas smiled and Connor reflected again on the change Sam Winterson had wrought on his dearest friend.

They clattered into the little cottage, which shrank even smaller with two six-footers in it. Sam exclaimed with delight and wandered around, examining pictures, picking up books and generally making herself at home. Connor busied himself with drinks; wine for his guests, tea for him.

"You not joining us?" Jonas asked, gesturing at the glasses.

"Ah, no. Tea's grand for me. I barely have a tipple even at Christmas these days – I seem to have lost the taste for it after so many years."

"Well, you're looking grand, even with the beard," Jonas said, after giving him the once-over.

"Aye, I'm good." Connor poured milk into his tea, ignoring the last comment. His beard had a purpose, not that he'd share that with Jonas. "Mind you, that might change with this bloody commission! I'm wondering what on earth possessed me – oh, yes. It was you, wasn't it?"

Jonas grinned. Sam turned, homing into the conversation.

"Oh Lord, surely it hasn't got any worse? I swear to God, I wish we'd decided to get married in the registry office, rather than cause all this chaos!"

Jonas held up his hands.

"I offered to go back to that idea—"

"No bloody use after Connor's started work on the garden!" she scoffed. "What's happened, Con? More problems with the estate tenants? Or is that supercilious estate manager getting into your hair?"

Connor spat out his tea.

"Shh!" he hissed, dragging a handkerchief from his pocket to wipe his beard.

"Why? Is the place bugged?"

"No, she lives next door!"

Sam gaped.

"No! What – *right* next door? Behind this wall?"

He nodded, and in a lowered voice, told them about the meeting with the tenants.

"So you check diaries together?" Jonas smiled.

"No, I get Mike to send the schedule of work, and she liaises with him. We don't see each other that much, thank God. The temperature drops every time she walks in the room!"

"Surely she's not immune to your famous Irish blarney?" Jonas grinned.

"Falls on deaf ears, it does. Perhaps she's got something against the likes of me. Although it's only the likes of me who design the way I do."

Sam frowned.

"She *still* doesn't like the garden? God, the woman has no taste – it's *brilliant!*"

Connor leaned over and gave her a hug. Strangely, he felt the need for human contact, and Sam's comments – even delivered with her usual irony – were balm to his tender ego.

"Ella just wants to keep it as it was, and is worried about the money. But Lady Susan is squarely behind it, and Sir Ralph is behind whatever Lady Susan does. Which is probably a good thing after this week."

"What happened?"

Connor sank into one of the squishy armchairs that had come with the cottage and told them about the meeting with the National Conservation Trust and the local historical society.

"They just don't get it," he sighed. "They don't see that the design reflects the Capability Brown landscapes that they're all fixated on, they only see how modern it is. They'd like me to replicate Chatsworth, or Hampton Court."

Sam pursed her lips.

"I don't disagree with their remit in the normal course of events, but making enemies of the National Conservation Trust may land you in endless hassle," she said.

"They can't stop you, but I agree, they can make it difficult. And I take it they're withholding funding?" Jonas guessed. Connor nodded. "Damn."

"We're still on schedule, but if the local authority dig their heels in on phase two, that'll go to pot. Ah, it's a bunch of shite, really."

Sam's face lit up with mischief.

"I know – they don't understand your genius, do they?"

Connor threw a cushion at her.

"Thankfully, Lady Susan has a lot of influence in the council – she gives loads of money to all kinds of good causes, most of them dear to the local councillors."

"Let the record state that I am heartily opposed to the influence of money in the making of planning decisions!" Sam said, her eyes twinkling at Jonas.

"Now let's not rake up old history," he grinned, and Connor reflected again how very comfortable the couple were with each other. Jonas was almost unrecognisable from the workaholic he had been.

Was that jealousy nibbling at him? No, he liked his life as it was.

"Seriously, though, what are you going to do?" Asked Jonas and Connor brought his attention back to the room.

"Lady Susan has a plan, apparently, and I'm lining up the lawyers to fight our corner."

Sam blew out a breath.

"Who'd have thought a bright idea to create a garden for our wedding would have turned into this?"

Connor shrugged, rising to his feet. He rubbed his chin. "It'll turn out. Let me take you to the pub for dinner. It does a great pint, people tell me."

As he was trying to lock the door, Ella's car rolled up. He cursed as the key wouldn't turn and heard her feet crunch across the shared drive.

"Good evening," she said to Jonas and Sam, who murmured greetings. "Are you struggling, Connor?"

He could hear the mockery in her voice, damn her. He glanced up.

"Aye. As you see."

"It's stiff, I ought to have got it fixed before you moved in. Let me."

She waited until he stood aside, gripped the door and pulled. The key turned in the lock like silk.

"It's just a knack." She gave him a brief smile.

"Thank you." Connor pocketed the key, and there was a short, awkward dance to pass one other. In the end, he grabbed her shoulders and put her to one side of him.

She turned on her heel and went into her cottage.

"At least she couldn't have overheard us talking!" Sam giggled quietly.

Small mercies, thought Connor.

4

"You know how I hate to disagree with you, dear, but are you *sure* this is the right way to go about things?" Lord Ralph asked gently.

They were sitting in the cosy sitting room, and it was past nine o'clock at night. The rain rattled the windows, not completely muffled by the thick drapes. Connor cradled a porcelain cup in his hands, registering that his tea was growing tepid. Lord Ralph was nursing a brandy.

Lady Susan raised her brows at Connor and he nodded, smiling, while she topped up his cup. She waved the letter from the National Conservation Trust at him. It stated their opposition to the garden plans and informed Lady Susan that they would refer the plans to the Historical Commission.

"Ralph, I didn't ask for this kerfuffle. But now you ask, if you expect me to weaken the vision I have, so a bunch of tweed-clad historical zealots can have their small minds satisfied – does that truly *sound* like me?"

Lord Ralph smiled fondly at his wife of forty years.

"No, it doesn't. But is it wise to antagonise so many people in the process?"

"I'm trying very hard not to! But when the likes of Skillington-Bland are telling me what to do on my own land – it's beyond the pale, my love." She screwed up the letter and threw it towards the fire. Connor lazily rose to his feet to pick it up and examine it.

"Hmm," said Lord Ralph and Connor turned. "Connor, as you and I have done our fair share of negotiation when we were in the City, I wonder if there's *anything* – something that means nothing substantial to the design – that you could offer as a sacrifice to their altar of garden heritage?"

Connor stared at the letter, ignoring the comment about the City.

"Well, according to this letter, something piecemeal wouldn't do for them. They want the entire thing re-designing."

Lord Ralph sighed, and Lady Susan reached across the sofa and squeezed his knee.

"Ralph – it's all going to be a lot of bother, but you *are* with me, aren't you? I can face any number of arguments with Skillington-Bland and the council, and even Louisa, but not without you."

He raised her hand to his lips.

"Silly puss. Do you want me to involve Simon in the details of the planning application?"

"I don't think we need to bring in the lawyers just yet." Lady Susan smiled as she sat back, her eyes warm.

"No. Connor and I have a charm offensive planned for the local councillors and their children and also some schools in the area. The new garden will be perfect for young people and I think they should be able to comment on the design."

"And we're also asking our sculptor if he's happy to be nominated for the National Contemporary Art Award," Connor added. "That will draw attention to the garden as a public space and fits perfectly with the vision that Lady Susan had for it."

"You're going for a nomination to the NCAA?" Lord Ralph said in slightly awed tones.

Lady Susan nodded.

"The publicity will be perfect if we get through to the shortlist – it barely matters if we don't win."

Connor murmured agreement. Entering the award had been his idea, a reflection of his own estimation of the sculptor's talent. Ceinion Bryant, the artist, was original and his stone and steel artworks deserved a wider audience.

"I suppose the only thing is that I will be frightfully busy – and I'd like to use the house to host the events," she added, peeking at her husband. He smiled ruefully.

"Naturally. It is your home too, Susan."

"I'll liaise with Justin, of course," she said, referring to the groomed, handsome manager of Ashton Manor. Connor had met Justin briefly and wasn't sure he liked him; he was almost *too* good looking, and edged towards arrogance, Connor thought. But undoubtedly, Ashton Manor's eighteenth-century house ran on oiled wheels with him in charge.

"You can use the orangery if you like – it's a brighter space in the winter."

"What a splendid idea."

Lady Susan beamed, and Connor had an odd twinge in his gut. They were comfortable together, like a chair and its cushion. He'd not seen that while he was growing up, his father was often away, beating a stiff upper lip into his men. His mouth curled.

"A penny for your thoughts, Connor? You look awfully disillusioned."

Lady Susan's voice was gentle. He blinked and forced a smile.

"Ah, Lady Susan, I was just remembering Jonathon whatsit's face when you told him to stuff his money. It was a joy to behold."

She snorted in an unladylike way and clapped her hand over her mouth at the sound. Her eyes gleamed in the firelight.

"He's just a victim of the banal vision of the organisation. To them, design stopped a hundred years ago. I suppose, thinking about it, we were never going to win approval from them."

"So we're in for a bit of a scrap, hmm?" Lord Ralph looked directly at Connor. "But from what I understand, you're no stranger to that?"

It was a question; he didn't have to respond. Connor glanced down at his empty teacup. After a pause that seemed to last hours, he sighed.

"Aye. I've seen my fair share of scraps," he said under his breath. Lady Susan leaned in to catch his words.

"You were in the City, weren't you?" Lord Ralph pursued. Connor nodded reluctantly. It was better to speak about it than have them trawl the more lurid stories on the internet, looking for information.

"I was. I made a mistake, no one forgave me, and I left." He listened to the sentence as it came out of his mouth and decided that it more or less covered everything. Lord Ralph leaned forward.

"Yes, I know about that. I wondered how that had affected you."

Connor said nothing, and Lady Susan shifted uneasily. She reached out a hand and patted his arm.

"Don't feel obliged to answer, Connor. My husband is endlessly nosy about other people's lives. You should know better, Ralph!"

Connor shook his head.

"It's fine. I had some time away from my role as an FD and then decided I didn't want to – couldn't – go back. Not that the firm wanted me back – I think they thought the goose that laid the golden egg had turned into a bit of a turkey. I re-trained as a gardener and the rest, as they say, is history!"

"A string of awards, and an international reputation." Lady Susan beamed at him. Connor waved her comment away.

"I'm content with my life, I sleep well and in truth, that's enough for me. I command high fees, I enjoy seeing the designs come to life as we build them. I no longer need the quick hit of the deal and then lots and lots of drink..."

"You've given up?" Lord Ralph looked into his glass, appalled at the idea.

"Not entirely but I'm so unused to it, I'm a menace to society if I have more than one. I'm such a cheap date."

Lady Susan laughed and made to top up his cup, finding the pot empty.

"I think we need to get a bigger pot for when you come to visit," she said.

"Well, I'll be taking my leave," he said, glad that the lack of tea had curtailed their conversation. He gathered his long waterproof coat from a chair.

"Do you need me to meet with Justin? Or shall I leave that in your hands?"

She regarded him thoughtfully, and he wondered what was going on in what he was coming to see as a rather Machiavellian mind.

"Yes. Yes, I think you should. Can you come tomorrow morning? He might not be your cup of tea, precisely..."

Oh, she's already clocked me there, he realised.

"...but he's truly a mastermind of all things organisational. He does for the house what Ella does with the rest of the estate. How are you getting on now with Ella, by the way? She's in Narcissus Cottage, next to you."

"Oh, we barely see one another – although she helped me lock the door the other night."

"I know you didn't hit it off with her on the garden design, but she's wonderful with the tenants. You're comparing schedules, I hear?"

"Oh yes," Connor said, trying to keep all emotion out of his voice. Not so much comparing as she was dictating to him. Lord Ralph's amused eyes rested on him.

"Giving you the runaround is she?" Lord Ralph chortled, finishing his brandy. "Put your foot down with her if you don't agree with her. Otherwise she'll walk all over you."

Lady Susan made a noise of protest, but Connor loped towards the door.

"I'll bear that in mind," he said.

The orangery was lovely in the unexpected October sunshine. The oranges and other citrus trees stood to attention in enormous pots, their glossy green leaves and last fruit of the season a bright splash of colour in the limpid morning light.

Five to nine. Connor longed to get into the garden while the weather's surprise gift lasted. The rain had held them up long enough, and they were in danger of falling behind so far, the deadline would truly be beyond reach, regardless of how he cracked the whip.

The delicate chimes of the clock struck the hour and on cue, the doors opened and Lady Susan, dwarfed by Justin, walked in.

Connor felt immediately untidy for a second, comparing his dirty nails and garden boots, still showing signs of dried mud, to the tall, immaculate manager of Ashton Manor. Justin never looked hurried, or hassled – he glided, his footfall soft.

"Good morning, Connor!" Lady Susan beamed, and automatically, Connor stooped to kiss her cheek. Justin eyes widened, but he smiled and held out a hand.

"Mr McPherson. How nice to see you again," he said.

His grip was smooth, but surprisingly firm, and as he had done on the previous occasion they'd met, Connor was reminded that as well as being tall, Justin had muscles beneath his exquisite tailoring.

"Now, Justin, we don't know how many people will accept the invitation, but it could be anywhere between twenty and a hundred, and while we'll know in advance, twenty people would rattle around in here," Lady Susan said, looking around.

"But we can screen off parts of the orangery if we need to," Justin replied thoughtfully. "I suggest we start by opening the west of the room where the afternoon light is best, and we can move the pots to act as a kind of cordon."

"There'll be children coming, so we can tell them about the garden and get their thoughts about what they'd like in the final design," Connor said, his eyes taking in the expanse of expensive glass in the roof and windows, and the early-nineteenth-century tiles on the floor. "Is it okay that they're let loose in here? There's a lot of stuff to break."

"I'll put more staff on," Justin said, making a note on his phone.

"Hmm, but we could do with a slightly more welcoming feel – I wouldn't want anyone to fall on these tiles! Can we use rugs, and

Love in a Mist

some beanbags rather than the chairs?" Lady Susan turned to gesture to the far end of the room and didn't see Justin's eyes flick upwards. "Although we'll want some chairs for the parents, obviously."

"We don't have beanbags on site, but I'll buy some and you might donate them afterwards to the local kindergarten?" Justin suggested tentatively.

"What an excellent idea!" she said warmly. "How many will we need?"

"Or, you could hire them?" Connor intervened. "That might be cheaper than buying fifty beanbags for one afternoon."

"Mmm, I have just the contact," Justin said. Lady Susan smiled.

"Good. Now, what should we do for food? I hesitate to say jelly and ice cream because although that would have been a genuine treat for me, I think times have rather moved on." Justin grinned.

"Lady Susan, can I make a wee suggestion? I've got what seems to be hundreds of nieces and nephews, and they like nothing better than a burger..." Connor put in.

Justin nodded enthusiastically.

"And hotdogs? With milkshakes alongside the usual tea and coffee for the parents? And perhaps some simple sandwiches?"

"Perfect. I think we'll have the model here..." Lady Susan pointed to the end of the room, "...and we'll have people sat facing us."

"If I might make a suggestion, why not have the model in the middle of the room and you can present by walking around it. This way, you can point to particular parts of it where the children's attractions will be," Justin suggested.

Connor stroked his beard.

"Now *that's* a grand idea. Otherwise it all looks a bit boring and flat on the plans."

Julian nodded.

"Brilliant, Justin! Now, I have the list here somewhere..." Lady Susan patted the pockets in her dress and drew out a crumpled piece of paper with her black, spidery writing. She held it out to Justin in triumph, and he took it carefully as though it might explode.

"Do you have the addresses as well as the names, Lady Susan?" he asked, hopefully.

"Oh, you'll be able to find them out!" she responded blithely. "They're fairly well known in the area. If you get stuck, I'll hunt through my address book and my computer files."

"Very good, your ladyship."

Connor hid a smile and then caught sight of Ella as she hovered at the door.

"I'm sorry, I didn't mean to interrupt," she said, and Connor's stomach gave a kick at the low tones of her voice.

"Come in, Ella. Were you looking for me?" Lady Susan asked.

"No, I'm after Justin. When you've got a moment, can we have a quick word about the utilities? I've negotiated a deal and I want your view before I agree to it."

"No problem. In about half an hour?"

"Great, I'll be in my office."

Connor followed the interaction between the estate's manager and Justin. He glanced away, uncomfortable. Ella walked away, tall and elegant, her dark ponytail bobbing as she went. Justin looked – hungry. His eyes followed Ella until she closed the door.

Oh, so that's the way the land lies, thought Connor, and his stomach gurgled with nausea. Obviously, he needed breakfast. It was damned early for a meeting.

He glanced at his watch, and Lady Susan caught the movement.

"I think that covers it, Connor, so if you can liaise with Justin about the date and moving the model, you can escape back to the garden," she smiled. "I'll talk to you a little nearer the time about the presentation."

"When did you have in mind for the event, Lady Susan?" asked Justin with exaggerated patience.

"What are we doing for Halloween again?"

"Ghost stories in the Grand Hall," he responded.

"Then could we get everything organised for the week before?"

Justin considered.

"I... *think* so. If we can get the invitations out by the end of this

Love in a Mist

week, with responses not too long after that, we might make something like... the twenty-second?"

"Excellent. Does that suit you, Connor?"

He flicked through his calendar on his phone.

"Yes, that sounds grand." He pocketed his phone. "I'll be off then."

He shook hands with Justin and pecked Lady Susan on the cheek and strode towards the door. As he opened the door, he heard Justin say with a laugh in his voice,

"People will talk, Lady Susan!"

He didn't hear her response, but his temper rose and he almost turned on his heel to speak to Justin, when Ella's deep voice said, "Ignore him. He can be a bit sharp sometimes."

He saw her, sitting quietly in the window seat just outside the orangery, a slight frown on her face, her hands clasped together tightly.

"You know him well?"

"We've worked together for the past seven years. He was here when I arrived."

You didn't answer my question, he thought.

"I've no idea what I've done to him," he said.

"He's very protective of Lady Susan and Lord Ralph. We all are."

Point taken, Connor smiled.

"He considers her virtue is in danger?"

"He may be worried that you're exerting too much influence. She's an elderly lady, after all."

It was Connor's turn to frown.

"I treat her much like I treat my own mother! And I think you're wrong – she's very much her own woman. The design process showed me she can't be swayed by much!"

She put her head on one side and twisted her ponytail around her fingers.

"Hmm. But this is the first time she's done something like this. And the design is all *yours*, isn't it?"

He opened his mouth and then thought about it. Ella smiled.

"Yes, I thought so. I imagine you can be very persuasive," she said.

"So understand that those around her want to make sure she's okay. Especially with the amount of money involved."

Connor paused. Her eyes were clear, dark grey. And hostile.

"Yes, there is a lot of money involved," he said slowly. "But you don't know what it is, do you? Lady Susan hasn't shared the budget with you, has she?"

Her jaw clenched.

Gotcha, he thought.

"So as far as I can see, she's not looking for protection – she's strong and determined and wants to do her own thing in her own way. I'm happy to help her. "

He left, humming to himself.

5

"The man's a bit of a boor." Justin sighed, moving a vase a centimetre to the right on Ella's sideboard. Ella said nothing, irritated that Justin was touching her things. "I almost asked to check his boots for mud on my precious parquet floor."

She made a non-committal noise.

"Although I think his design will draw in the crowds," he continued, sitting down in front of her desk. Ella looked up, startled.

"You like the design?"

Justin straightened his tie.

"I can see it'll cause a stir and regardless that will be good for visitor numbers. You hate it, don't you?"

"I don't *love* it, no."

Justin grinned.

"You're so diplomatic. Have done and say you hate it."

Ella found herself strangely unwilling to be as critical to Justin as she had been to Connor and Lady Susan. She shrugged.

"I'm not sure it goes with this Georgian house, and I'm worried the estate will be landed with some of the costs. But anyway – it's Lady Susan's land, so that's the end of it. Here's the deal I've come to with the gas company." Before he could say anything else, she thrust the papers at him. He took them, reluctantly, and the subject dropped.

They agreed on the price and Ella was shuffling her papers together, when Justin said,

"He's a force of nature, isn't he?"

"Who?"

"The Irishman, Ella! And Connor McPherson is quite a sight for the ladies. The kitchen staff fight over who delivers the *tea*, for God's sake!"

Ella laughed.

"Is he poaching on your territory? And anyway, don't you have enough women flocking around you?"

He preened slightly.

"It's a gift."

They both laughed, and then he continued. "I thought you'd be more involved in the scheme, to be honest. Lady Susan is keeping the project close to her chest, isn't she?"

Was Justin baiting her? His face looked innocent. So she ignored his words, and the tiny sting they caused her.

"What attracts you to the design?" she asked him instead.

Justin steepled his fingers and his eyes found hers across them.

"Oh, I don't know – something about the sweep of it, I think. Something about the devil-may-care approach of it – crashing through previous ideas and sacred cows, you know? I particularly like the new walled garden."

Ella raised her eyebrows.

"Really? Which won't follow any of the traditional elements of the original garden?"

"Well, I can see you don't care for it, but it's rather splendid to have something that hasn't been designed by committee," he said, getting to his feet and brushing an imaginary thread from his trousers.

"Indeed, it is *all* Connor McPherson," she murmured. God, what a bitch I am, she thought.

Love in a Mist

"Perhaps we could be thoroughly unprofessional and discuss his worst points over a drink tonight?" Justin smiled. Ella hesitated. Ella had shared the occasional outing with Justin and enjoyed his company. He was charming and funny, if occasionally a bit malicious, and he was so handsome, it did her ego no harm to be seen with him.

Then she remembered.

"That sounds great, but I'm at netball practice this evening. Later this week?"

He shook his head.

"I'm due in London talking to recruiters about a new sous chef and yet another housekeeper. I'm staying on for a show and won't be back until Sunday."

Ella grinned sympathetically. Ashton Manor had been through four housekeepers in two and a half years, in part because of the antiquated kitchen (now completely refurbished) and in part because of something in the water which caused them to fall in love with unsuitable people and leave. Ella remembered the two housekeepers before Antonia. One fell in love with a publican in the village and left to run the pub. The other became fixated on Justin and lasted three months before he lost patience. The exchange had been brutal, Ella recalled uncomfortably, and the housekeeper had left that day, sobbing. Antonia, the present incumbent, was leaving for another job nearer an ailing mother, with much less drama.

"Another time then. When is Antonia off?" Ella asked.

"The end of December," Justin said gloomily.

"Ah well, at least you'll have some help over the Halloween and Bonfire Night events," Ella's eyes wandered to her diary and the pile of to-do notes.

"Hmm. Actually, could you pitch in with the Halloween event?"

"Of course." Ella caught sight of an urgent phone message she had to deal with. "What do you want me to do?"

"Greet guests, top up glasses and help with the games, that sort of thing. Help people get into the swing of things. Nothing too arduous."

"Sure, no problem." Ella focused her attention with an effort and smiled brightly. Justin gave her a slow smile and got to his feet as she tried to hide the glance at her wristwatch.

"Thanks for your thoughts on the quote, I'll call them."

"Anything for you, Ella."

"Yeah, right," she said, and he twinkled at her. She remembered the languishing barmaid at their local pub – another of the many women captured by his golden, handsome spell. He left, leaving her, at last, to the mountain of tasks facing her for the day.

∾

Ella heard the whistle blow with something approaching relief. They'd won – but only by one goal. She rested her hands on her knees to get her breath. A hand clapped her on the back.

"You okay, El?"

Jeanette peered into her face, looking irritatingly cool and as though she'd been out for a brisk walk, rather than sixty minutes of netball. Must be the walking she did as a nurse, up and down the wards.

"I think I'm getting too old to play centre," wheezed Ella, feeling the running she'd done in her position through the match.

"Nonsense! And anyway, we can't do without you. I've got enough problems getting players who can bloody catch, let alone run *and* catch."

They shook hands with the other team (who reassuringly looked as hot and sweaty as Ella felt) and then trailed towards the showers.

"Drink?" Ella called to Jeanette as she pulled her sweater over her head.

"Oh, yes – we love a drink!" Jeanette's voice was muffled as she wrapped her head, with its wiry, ginger locks in a towel. "But just one at the pub for me. I need to get home. I have a new kitten and frankly, I don't trust the flatmate with her for long!"

"A new kitten?"

"Yes, called her Pixie. She looks like one."

"How sweet! Can I see her?" Ella wheedled.

"Was about to suggest it, I know what a sucker you are for small and furry."

Ella shook her head, folding her kit carefully into the damp towel and rolling it up.

"*Small* and furry, yes."

Jeanette laughed.

"I take it there's something *large* and furry that's giving you grief then?"

Ella slung her rucksack onto her back and pressed her lips together.

"Ooh, what a scowl!" Jeannette hooted as Ella sighed dramatically. "I want to know *all* the details when we're alone!"

The drink with the rest of the team was fun, and Ella relaxed, tired after the exertion of the game. She took a rueful sip of her sparkling water. She never drank when she was driving, but for some reason, she needed a proper drink and longingly remembered the malt whisky in her cupboard.

"How's the shoulder, Rosie?" she asked.

Their team's wing attack rubbed her shoulder gingerly and grimaced.

"God, their wing defence was built like a tank. I was afraid for a moment she was going to rip my head off when we got that last penalty pass. I barely came out alive!" she said, taking a deep swig of her lager. The rest of the team chuckled sympathetically and Jeanette talked tactics for the next game.

Ella enjoyed her netball, but she was seriously wondering if she should take up a more sedate pastime. Golf might be a relatively safe bet. She drifted away from the conversation until she heard her name.

"And we need to give Ella more support across the court," Jeanette scolded. "She's being run ragged, poor lamb, and we need to remember she's not as young as she used to be."

"Hey! I'm only *just* thirty!"

Jeanette waved her protest away.

"She's working as hard as she can, but we need to be *with* her, not trailing behind her while she looks for the next pass!"

The team nodded guiltily. Team members next to her patted Ella on the back reassuringly as if she was a hundred and eight. Ella scowled at Jeanette, who smiled sweetly at her. Ella finished her drink and placed her glass firmly on the table.

"Right, well, I need to be off to show off Pixie to Ella," said Jeanette, leaping to her feet. "Don't forget practice at seven next Wednesday!"

It took only ten minutes to reach Jeanette's house and in less than twelve, the kitten was in Ella's arms, being cuddled and admired. When Pixie had had enough of being cooed over, the kitten tumbled off the sofa and staggered to its bed, where she amused herself by tearing the stuffing out of a toy rabbit.

Jeanette surveyed Ella over the rim of her outsized coffee cup.

"How's things?"

Ella grimaced.

"Good, thanks. Apart from the blasted garden."

Jeanette hummed, sympathetic.

"How is it progressing? Is it on schedule?"

"The weather hasn't helped, but so far, yes it is."

"How are the tenants reacting? I heard that there was a bit of a to-do..."

"Yes, the mud was making the roads dreadful to drive on, and then the garden contractors were always in the way when the tenants were moving livestock."

Jeanette nodded.

"Sorted now?"

"Eventually. We had to reach an understanding, the wonderful Mr McPherson and I."

"And?"

"He's said all the right things, and to be fair to him, he's been doing a lot of them too. I'm the go-between for him and the tenants, and we're existing in a rather tense harmony so far."

"But you're still worried about it?"

Ella hesitated. Jeannette knew her well and recognised what the garden meant to her, regardless of who was building it. She sighed.

"I'm in the dark about it, other than what McPherson tells me," she admitted. Jeanette stared. "I know precious little about the schedule other than how it impacts the tenants, and nothing about the money side of it at all."

"You don't know the budget?"

"Nope. After that first meeting when he showed his final design, Lady Susan cut me out of the conversations. She said she didn't want me to have a conflict of interest, given that I was so anti the design. She suggested I should focus on the wider estate. She's been dealing with the finances ever since."

Jeanette was silent, and Ella forced herself to relax, as she realised her shoulders were suddenly tense.

"You hate that."

"I do, but that's the way it is. I have to trust that Lady Susan knows what she's doing, and that Connor McPherson isn't going to take her for a ride or empty the coffers."

"Do you think he would?"

Ella considered, reflecting on her conversation with Connor outside the orangery.

"Well, I told him she has many people looking out for her, including me. I don't think he'd cheat her. But gardens like this cost a fortune, and he's very persuasive – we don't want her selling the family jewels to fund it."

Jeanette cocked an eyebrow.

"We like a persuasive man... I understand he's devastatingly good looking."

Ella snorted.

"You shouldn't believe all you see on Twitter! Blue eyes and a charming manner don't outweigh a bushy beard and unkempt hair. And anyway, what do I care what he *looks* like? He's the garden designer who's making a monstrosity on the estate, and I'm on his case. End of."

Jeanette held up her hands at the challenge.

"Whoa! Just saying. I thought you might be interested in a lively, decent looking man after Duncan!"

Ella wrinkled her nose, thinking of the dreadfully dull but perfectly nice man who had been a feature in her life until about six months ago.

"Also, Mr McPherson keeps popping up in conversation with you a fair amount!" Jeanette added, wickedly.

"Only because you ask me!" Ella's response was hot.

"Really? Who brought up 'the blasted garden'?"

Ella waved away the point.

"Bah. He's just a royal pain in the arse."

Jeanette hid a smile, and the subject dropped.

∼

Ella could see the lights in Daffodil Cottage as she parked. For a minute, she sat motionless in the car, pushing down her exasperation that she was having to share her space – *her* precious space – with anyone else, let alone the Irishman who resembled a mountain from a distance.

She thought back over the past week and a half and had to admit that Connor had been a considerate neighbour. She heard the dulcet tones of Radio 4 through the wall from about six in the morning, realising with a shock that their bedrooms were adjacent. Radio 4 disappeared when he went downstairs, to be replaced by pop music in the kitchen. He left promptly at seven fifteen and returned at all hours. Sometimes he parked his car up when she came back at six, sometimes she heard his front door much later. One night, she was pretty sure he hadn't been there at all. And one thing she hadn't expected – the sound of a fiddle being played in the evenings. He played surprisingly well.

Ella shook her head, tutting to herself. Time to think about dinner, not bloody Connor McPherson.

To her dismay, the door to Daffodil Cottage opened as she was pulling her kit from the back of the car. Connor stood in the light spilling from the door, a rubbish bag in his hand. He paused, stared at her, and called a greeting.

"How are you doing?"

She took a breath and slammed the car door, hoisting her kit bag over her shoulder.

"Good, thanks. How are you settling in?"

She could see his grin as he came towards the bin at the top of the garden, swinging what she knew was a heavy lid with ease.

"Just grand, thanks. It's very comfortable. I've even mastered the art of opening and closing the front door."

His tone was wry, and she smiled reluctantly.

"Excellent. Good to hear."

She caught his eyes flick over her and she tightened her grip on her bag, feeling self-conscious of her hoodie and tracksuit bottoms. She stopped herself from putting a hand to her loose hair with an effort.

"Been to the gym?"

"Netball match."

"Did you win?"

"We did – but not by much."

"Grand..."

While he searched for more words, she almost leapt towards her front door, patting her pockets for the keys.

"Well, I must get inside and into a shower before I stiffen up."

He kept with her pace for pace on the other side of the low fence as she walked to her front door.

"Do you play every week?"

"Fortnightly. One week it's practice, one week a match." She put her key in the lock.

"Time to recover a bit, then?"

She shot him a glance, seeing his blue eyes crinkle at the corners.

"Yes. At my advanced age, I need that."

He stared, dismayed.

"I didn't mean..."

"No, I was just teasing," she said quickly. "I must go. Goodnight."

"Goodnight, then."

Once inside the cottage, she tutted again to herself as Monty snaked around her ankles. Catching sight of herself in the mirror, she almost groaned – hair all over the place, flushed cheeks. She sighed and reached for the kettle, trying to put the large garden designer out of her mind, while she ran a long, deep bath.

6

"Bloody kids," mumbled Justin, as he paced the orangery. Connor hid a smile and stroked his beard, as the tall house manager tried not to guard the woodwork too closely while the councillors and their children were still there.

Lady Susan had been at her charming best all afternoon. She had been wonderful with the children. They had ranged from four to nearly sixteen, and her ladyship had invited their ideas on the spaces in the garden specifically designed for them. Connor lurked in the background and scribbled notes furiously, as the suggestions – not all of them unreasonable – came from the children, at first slowly, and then tumbling over one another. Slides down the walls, treetop walks, musical steps... His eyebrows knitted together as he redesigned segments of the garden in his head as the ideas formed, reformed, and found a place in his mental blueprints.

He heard Lady Susan's fluting laugh and turned towards it. She was beaming at a portly man, whose grandson was tugging at his hand.

"Yes, *yes*, Adam, I'll be along in a minute when I've finished speaking to Lady Susan," said the man, raising his eyebrows to Lady Susan, who laughed.

"Tell you what, Adam, shall we walk over to the model and you can tell us where the dragons should live while your grandfather and I finish our discussion?"

The trio walked to the model and Adam pointed with a stubby finger to a corner containing some mature ash trees, marking a border between one area and another. Connor listened closely.

"They would live here!" Adam declared. "In the trees where any hunters couldn't catch them!"

"But wouldn't the trees be damaged when they breathed fire?" Lady Susan asked, serious when discussing a six-year-old's vision.

"They normally breathe fire when they fly. They don't breathe fire when they're sitting *down*!" Adam scoffed.

"Ah," Lady Susan nodded. "I didn't realise that. So what you're saying is that we should build some roosts for the dragons, so they can stay here?"

Adam nodded.

"Connor, can we incorporate this into the design?"

Connor's mind went blank. He knew little about pyrotechnics, and not much about dragons, but the clear hazel eyes of the child turned on him and so he smiled.

"I understood dragons were nocturnal – is that right?"

Adam considered.

"I think so."

"Have you ever seen one in broad daylight?"

Adam shook his head and Connor went down on his haunches to be face to face with him.

"So we need to make sure they can find the roosts at night, to know where to land?"

"And have nests to sleep in during the day!" Adam pointed out.

Connor nodded.

"Well, yes, I think we could provide that, but how big are these beasts?"

Adam put his arms out on either side of him.

"*Huge!*"

Love in a Mist

"As big as me?" Connor drew himself up to his full height of six foot three.

"Maybe not quite as big."

"Aye, that will help me get the right size nest. So at least as big as you, and not as big as me?"

Adam nodded solemnly.

"Then I think we should shake on it." Connor put out his hand, and Adam, nudged by his grandfather, put out his own hand. Then the little boy turned and ran to the windows, evidently well pleased with the day's negotiations.

"Are you really going to give him a home for his dragons?" the grandfather asked Lady Susan.

"Cedric Robertson, when Connor shakes on it, the thing is done!" Lady Susan laughed. "I've no idea how we will do it, but Adam will have his dragon roosts and nests. I'm not sure about actual dragons..."

Connor turned it over in his head and wondered how many favours he could pull in at the film studio where he had shares. But even as the boy had been speaking, his mind had been turning over and he couldn't wait to reach his sketchbook.

"If you can give Adam dragons, you have my support," Cedric said. "And here's *my* hand on it."

Lady Susan shook and said how grateful she was.

"It's the most creative enterprise I've ever seen – you'll be pulling them in for miles!" Cedric said, and walked away to rescue one of the orange trees from Adam before Justin had to intervene.

"Thank you," Lady Susan said to Connor. "How on earth are we going to deliver it?"

Connor grinned.

"Ah, I have a few things up my sleeve. Leave it with me. And don't look so anxious, Lady Susan. There's the design award to consider, after all! It won't be too Disney or tacky, I promise you that."

With another beaming smile, Lady Susan glided away to sweet talk support from another guest.

The hairs on the back of Connor's neck prickled and he turned to see Ella watching him with a frown on her face, as though she was confused. He returned her stare, and her face became neutral again.

"Have you only just arrived?" he said, walking towards her.

"No, I've been here a good hour."

"Lurking among the plant pots?"

A faint flush coloured her cheeks. So you were sneaking around, he thought.

"I was listening to the children's ideas. Some of them were fantastic."

"Aye, they were. I'll be able to use a lot of them in the design."

She pressed her lips together and Connor waited, seeing her fingers curled into her palms.

"You can't play with promises to children. They never forgive you."

"What makes you think I'm playing with them?"

She shrugged.

"*Dragons*? Where on earth would that fit into a garden in a country house? Won't it just look... fake?"

His temper rose.

"Have a little more faith, Ms Sanderson. I'm a garden designer with an international reputation, did you not know? I realise you don't like my designs – they're a wee bit too *modern* for you, aren't they? But my garden will turn this frankly mediocre estate into something fun, encouraging dreams in its visitors. My designs come from my heart and soul, so they will not be *fake*."

His voice had become a hiss, and she stepped back, startled.

"Everything all right?" came the cool tones of Justin over his shoulder.

"Ms Sanderson is just insulting me, as usual," bit out Connor. "Nothing to worry your pretty little head about."

"Goodness," murmured Justin. "Shall I have your raw meat brought around, Mr McPherson?"

Connor turned on his heel and left the orangery, his pleasure in the afternoon destroyed.

Love in a Mist

Ella scowled at her reflection in the mirror and tried to pull the edges of the bodice of the witch's costume together to cover more of her breasts.

"Not that they're spilling out!" she muttered as she surveyed her slight figure.

Mind you, the push-up bra that Jeanette insisted she wear with the black dress *ga*ve her a bit of a cleavage. Being slim, she'd never had one, and she decided she rather liked it. She really wasn't sure about the Titian wig, which was making her scalp itch, and that was without the hat. She sighed and bent to tie the laces of her trainers. Wild horses weren't going to make her wear heels if she would be on her feet all night.

Her phone buzzed, and she saw it was Jeanette.

"You are in *so* much trouble!" Ella said as a greeting. "I must have been insane to let you choose my costume."

"You look fabulous, don't you?" was the gurgling reply.

Ella looked at the mirror again.

"I look like a hooker."

Jeanette's laughter pealed down the line, and it was such a sound of sheer joy Ella had to smile in response.

"I'll be there in about twenty minutes and I'll be the judge of that! Don't forget the hat!"

After disconnecting the call, she stood for a moment and considered her reflection as dispassionately as she could. She supposed her appearance wasn't that dreadful.

"For God's sake, it's one night! Practically no one will recognise you!" She swept the long skirts over her arm and skipped down the stairs. She paced around, not able to settle as she waited for Jeanette to arrive.

'Pitching in' to help with the Halloween event had turned into something slightly more than greeting guests. It had required a costume, and games, and helping with menus and serving drinks. She was suddenly on show rather than fading into the background, and the very thought almost had her reaching for a glass of whisky. Catching sight of the clock, she decided against it.

As if she didn't have enough to contend with, Connor McPherson would be there. She forced her shoulders away from her ears. They hadn't spoken since that dreadful afternoon in the orangery nearly two weeks ago, avoiding each other by what seemed like mutual consent.

She pushed the memories away. He'd been so angry. And reflecting on it, perhaps she had been wrong. She had seen him with the children, and it had startled her. He had seemed so comfortable with them, so in tune with their thinking... She closed a door firmly in her head on a pang of longing and was thankful to hear a car pull up outside, followed by Jeanette, dressed as a vampire, banging on the door. She tumbled into Ella's hallway.

"Oh, wow!" Jeanette said, her black-lined eyes widening as she walked around Ella. "And I was *so* right with that wig! You look like a Renoir painting!"

"Oh, do shut up!" scoffed Ella, reaching for her bag and the ridiculous witch's hat.

"No, really, Ella! You don't dress right! You should wear that neckline all the time!"

"What, with *this* amount of cleavage on show to all Lady Susan's tenants? I don't think so."

"We love a bit of cleavage, darling! And if you think that's revealing, you should have seen the costume I decided *not* to bring!"

"In which case, I can only be grateful for small mercies!" Ella glanced at the clock. "We need to get going, otherwise we'll be late."

"Okay, okay. But, for God's sake, don't slouch! You're slim and with that bra, you've got a fabulous décolletage, so flaunt it! Teeth and tits, darling!"

Having never felt less like flaunting anything, Ella clucked and pushed her dearest friend towards the door.

∼

Connor sighed as he parked outside Ashton Manor. He fumbled in his holdall for the cloak that went with his costume and reluctantly climbed out of the car. He pulled the lantern from the back seat, slung the pole over his shoulder, checked the battery, and then walked to the double doors of the manor. The doorman took his invitation, and he walked to the great hall.

Fake cobwebs hung everywhere, with black spiders dangling to scare the unwary. There were candles flickering, some real, others a very convincing electric version. White sheet ghosts fluttered at the top of the ceiling. All the house staff, carrying drinks or trays of food, were dressed as ghosts or ghouls. A tall, broad-shouldered man walked past him in a skeleton costume with a mask. Connor recognised the walk as Justin and turned away. He picked up the only glass of champagne he'd have all night – and mentally gritted his teeth.

He caught sight of his face in a mirror that someone had carefully tarnished and noted the slight signs of strain around his eyes. He needed to get some sleep. He promised himself a lie-in and crossed his fingers that the ideas flying around his head about the garden would let him rest.

"Connor!" said a slight woman with a white face and blackened eyes wearing a tattered dress, hung with cobwebs and ropes of pearls. He peered at her and realised with a shock that it was Lady Susan. Looking beyond her, he recognised Lord Ralph, dressed as Quasimodo. He laughed out loud, feeling slightly less out of place in his costume now and pleased he'd made the effort.

"Lady Susan, you look wonderful," he said, raising her hand to his lips.

She beamed at him, showing discoloured teeth.

"I'm so glad you came, but who have you come *as*?" She gestured to his soft suede jerkin, trousers and boots.

"I've come as Jack O' Lantern."

"Ah – that's the blighter who did a deal with the Devil?" said Sir Ralph, slapping him on the back. Connor nodded.

"Well done, Sir Ralph. Full marks for your knowledge of Irish folklore!"

"Would you tell the story?" demanded Lady Susan.

"Well, legend has it—" Connor began. But Lady Susan shook her head.

"No, not *now* – later, when the storytelling begins! It should be about nine o'clock."

Startled, Connor protested, but she clasped his arm, wheedling.

"Oh, do say yes! You've got such a glorious tone and we could do with something authentic! I know Justin has hired a storyteller, but to be honest, I can't bear his voice, it's a bit too plummy for me!"

Connor reflected for a second that a member of one of England's oldest and most aristocratic families, with her own cut-glass accent, could consider a jobbing actor as ' too plummy'. Lady Susan took his minimal pause as agreement.

"Excellent! I'll look forward to it! It's not too scary a story, is it? I don't want the children frightened…"

"No, I can tell it so it's not in the least bit scary," he said soothingly. He got another discoloured smile, and she swept away to greet another guest. Sir Ralph grinned sympathetically and followed his wife, lurching in character.

Connor watched quietly as the room filled with children and adults, with varying degrees of success in their costumes. He caught sight of a young woman dressed as a witch with flame-red hair and a lick of desire shot through him as he registered her attractiveness. She was tall for a woman, slender and graceful, with a plunging neckline and rounded breasts. He watched covertly as she turned towards the wall, put down the wine bottle she was carrying and tugged the edges of the neckline together. He hid a grin.

A losing battle there, sweetheart!

She settled the pointed hat on her unlikely hair a little more firmly, and, pinning a smile on her face, and putting her shoulders back, she started doing the rounds of the room. She was about ten feet from him when he realised that it was Ella and almost dropped his glass.

It must have been a second or two later that she caught sight of him, and her step faltered. He saw her draw a breath, pulling his eyes briefly to her breasts before he recovered. His fingers gripped his half-full glass as she determinedly approached.

"Mr Mc... Connor, good evening. Can I give you a refill?"

He shook his head, unable to say anything for a second as he took in her appearance. He saw her flush slightly, prompting him into spluttering speech.

"I'm fine, thanks."

She smiled tightly and made to turn away. Before he knew what he was doing, he put out his hand to stop her.

"Ella, I wanted to apologise." The words sounded forced from his throat, and her clear grey eyes flew to his face. "What happened in the orangery – I was furious, but my tone was out of order. I'm sorry for it."

There was a pause, and the room, with its noise and everyone else, faded away. She shook her head.

"No, I think it's me who should apologise. I was dreadfully *judging*, wasn't I? I could see how passionate you were about it all and my remarks were... very misplaced, I think. I'm sorry."

Her voice was soft but firm, and Connor was silent, not expecting her words, or the warm glow that built inside him. He smiled.

"Now then, shall we make a deal? I'll try not to lose my temper and you give me the benefit of the doubt?"

He thought she was about to smile in return, and her mouth tweaked. And then something passed over her eyes, and her tone was brisk again.

"I'm sure we'll both do our best. I must go and serve other guests. Have a good evening."

He frowned as she hurried away. What had just happened? He thought about it all evening, through the apple-bobbing and the competition for the best children's costume (won by an eight-year-old in a pumpkin costume that had obviously taken his mother weeks to craft). Then the storyteller gathered the children around the immense fireplace to listen to ghost stories, and Connor could see Lady Susan gesturing him forward.

"Aubrey, before you begin your tales, I'd like Connor to tell a story from Ireland about Jack O' Lantern. Connor?"

All eyes turned to Connor as he walked forward. He smiled at the small faces glowing in the fire's light.

"In a faraway place, a long time ago, there was a man called Stingy Jack. He was so mean, he never bought his own drinks, but tricked others into paying for him. One fine day in County Kerry, the Devil came to Stingy Jack's local pub..."

He continued, telling how Stingy Jack tricked the Devil so he would never lose his soul, but that when finally he died, his drinking and evil deeds also barred him from Heaven.

"The Devil, seeing him approach the gates of Hell, was so enraged that he couldn't claim Stingy Jack's soul, that he threw a live coal at him," Connor said, seeing the wide eyes of the children on him. "Stingy Jack caught it as it flew towards him. He placed it in a lantern, and through the years, this lights his way as he roams the earth, looking for his final resting place."

Connor flicked the switch in his pocket and the lantern flickered on, to the gasps of the children and the applause of the adults.

After receiving the thanks of Lady Susan and listening politely to the, accurately described, plummy voice of the storyteller, Connor made his way to the door. An instinct made him turn and Ella was watching him from across the room. He didn't wave as he left.

7

Ella sighed. She loved her job, but since the swing shovels had moved into the gardens to move enormous quantities of earth, there had been a steady procession of tenants coming to her door to complain. She'd just seen the last one out of her office, not much mollified.

And it wasn't just about traffic and workmen. It was about access to Lady Susan, and her laser-like focus on the build, rather than all the estate. Tenants were used to seeing her about, enquiring after crops and children, and when this didn't happen, rumblings had quickly surfaced about how she didn't care about the land any longer.

She clicked her tongue with irritation. Even if she hated the garden design, Ella could see the development for what it was – a genuine attempt to diversify the estate's income as revenue from livestock and crops steadily fell. She appreciated that Lord Ralph wanted to secure the future of the estate and what concerned Lord Ralph, concerned Lady Susan.

She tapped her pencil against her teeth, thinking. Since the Halloween party, her employers had more or less disappeared as far as the tenants were concerned. She could leave it all to fester, which would cause trouble for Connor, but it would also harm Lady Susan.

No, she thought regretfully. It was impossible. They needed to explain what the garden would do for the entire estate – not just the house. Gregory Wainwright, who had sounded almost apologetic that he was complaining, had said as much.

"It's not that we object to the garden, exactly," he considered. "It's just that – well, we wonder how much of a vanity project it is. Although of course she's got a perfect right to do what she likes – after all, it is her money."

Money that could be spent on improvements to the roads and fences, Ella completed the unspoken thought. And the gates.

Other thoughts about the Halloween party last week nudged at her, and she pushed them aside. Time to speculate about them... another time. She opened an email, typed a few words and then stopped, glancing at her watch. Nearly one o'clock. Whatever was happening in the garden or elsewhere, Lord Ralph and Lady Susan always came together for lunch. She'd find them in the manor. Her stomach grumbled. Quickly, she unwrapped a sandwich, took a bite and then stuffed it back in its paper. She'd finish it later, in the event her employer didn't invite her to sit down.

The sun was glinting through the wet trees, making the leaves shimmer. On impulse, she took a detour through the formal gardens, whose symmetry and quiet confidence made it one of her favourite places on the estate. She didn't have time to dally, but she breathed the cool, damp air as she walked, her eyes drinking in the calm of the place. As she always did when she passed this way, she patted the little, ugly statue, almost like a talisman.

A hoot of laughter came from the drawing room, and she tapped tentatively on the open door. She heard Lady Susan's voice and stepped in, straightening her jacket as she did. She stopped sharply as she saw Connor in indescribably muddy trousers, standing with his back to the cheerily burning fire. She immediately felt an interloper, and somehow slightly hurt, too, as though she'd been deliberately excluded from a party.

"Ella! How lovely! Come in, dear girl, come in!" Lady Susan beamed at her.

Her face grew warm and she guessed her colour had risen. Connor tweaked a black eyebrow. She raised her chin.

"I don't want to disturb your lunch, but I wondered if I could speak to you about a presentation to the tenants on the garden?"

"I thought you'd already done that, Susan?" Lord Ralph commented, standing and waving Ella into his chair.

"Yes, we've talked about the garden design, but it might be helpful if we talked about the *benefits* of the garden to them," Ella said, smiling gratefully as she sat down.

"Ah. Getting it in the neck again, are you?" Connor asked, with a faintly malicious grin.

"I believe it's just better for our tenants to see what the garden might mean to them, Mr McPh... Connor."

His eyes gleamed at her, and she sniffed.

"Oh dear," said Lady Susan. "I was hoping people might be a little more used to the idea..."

"It's something to get them excited about the end result. At the moment, all they can see is the process. And the mud," Ella couldn't stop herself from adding.

Connor surprised her by laughing out loud.

"And indeed, there's plenty of that! Since we've been on site, we've had the heaviest rainfall in the last decade. Lord above, I could be in Ireland!"

Knowing there was more rain to come, Ella was silent, smiling politely as Lord Ralph chuckled and Lady Susan clucked sympathetically.

"So, can we agree a date and then I can arrange something with the tenants? I thought we could talk in more detail about the business case, and potential areas of investment when the garden is open." Ella gently pushed the conversation back on track.

Lord Ralph peered at her over his glasses.

"Are you promising jam tomorrow, Ella?"

Well, given that I'm not allowed to spend anything *today*, yes, I suppose I am! Ella thought, keeping control of her face with an effort.

"Well... A lot depends on opening on time, visitor numbers – yes I understand all that. But the tenants should learn more about the intent of the garden, and they're rather in the dark about that at the moment," she said.

"*Have* they been complaining?" Lady Susan asked.

"A little. This is what this presentation is about. They'd like to hear it from you, not me."

"If you really think so...?"

"Yes, I really think so," Ella was firm. Her stomach, despite the bite of sandwich, rumbled again, and she grimaced. "If we could sort out a date, then I'll get out of your hair."

"No, no – sit. I'll fix you something to eat, and then I'll get my diary. Connor, would you like more tea?"

The big Irishman nodded, and Lady Susan bustled off. As she leaned back in her chair, Ella was acutely aware of him. He couldn't sit down because he was so filthy, Ella realised, but she didn't like him looming over her.

Lord Ralph asked her some questions about cleaning the stonework of the balustrade in the spring, and they talked about the contractors and their astronomical quote.

"I'm not entirely convinced that we should just accept the quote," Ella frowned, playing with her ponytail. "I appreciate we've worked with them for years, but this time, I think we're paying over the odds. I'd like to approach a couple of other stonemasons, with your agreement."

"Ella, in this case, it's not the money – it's the quality of the workmanship, and Taylors have been doing this for decades," Lord Ralph replied.

"Shall I get the quotes, look at references and then we can decide?" Ella replied serenely. "We've got plenty of time, and I'm well aware we need someone who knows what they're doing."

"If you wish. But it's my decision, Ella. If I decide I'm more comfortable with Taylors, that's where we'll go, and hang the cost!"

Lady Susan returned with a ham sandwich the size of a small house brick, which saved Ella the necessity of answering, but she clamped down on her irritation. The finances of the estate were her responsibility – with the exception of the bloody garden, of course – and it was only occasionally that Lord Ralph was involved in the detail. He had a personal connection with Charles Taylor, although that didn't result in "mates rates" for the work. Admittedly, the balustrade was one of the major features of the house, but Ella, always with an eye on the budget, considered their custom was being taken for granted. Inviting other suppliers to quote for the work might shave a few thousand off Taylor's price, anyway...

She found Connor McPherson regarding her with a keen blue gaze, almost as if he were reading her thoughts. Unnerved by the idea, she took a bite of her sandwich and left as soon as she could.

∼

Later that day, she closed the spreadsheet on her computer with a sigh. She was starting to feel nervous about the faith that Lady Susan had put into the project.

Of course, Connor McPherson had created many successful gardens, so there was no reason Ashton Manor would be different. Although it *was* different, she acknowledged. This would be Connor's first garden on a private estate – his work was mostly corporate and suitably avant-garde, for lawyers, accountancy firms and management consulting firms looking to impress clients and competitors. Her mind skittered away from the category of lawyers, and the memories it stirred.

She caught sight of her face reflected in the window. Her frown would give her those lines on the bridge of her nose she tried so hard to smooth, to go with the bags under her eyes. She raised her eyebrows to stretch the skin on her face, saw it was well past six o'clock and closed her computer. Time for home, and an old movie. There was nothing an hour with Cary Grant or Clark Gable, or Fred Astaire and Ginger Rogers wouldn't sort out.

Monty was sitting facing the door when she opened it. Ella thought if he could have tapped his paw, he would have done. She stepped over the mail and closed the door.

"Sorry, your highness, am I home too late?"

Monty mewed and flicked his tail before winding himself around her ankles as she picked up the post.

"Yes, yes, give me a minute to get my coat off!"

An hour later, she'd changed out of her suit, fed Monty, put one of her home-made lasagnes into the microwave to defrost and was chopping salad, humming. She thought she might develop a disaster plan, in case the garden wasn't as profitable as Lady Susan expected. She hadn't heard about any marketing yet, and that was important, even at this early stage.

Ella shook her head. She should stop fretting. It wasn't her concern, unless the estate had to bail them out. She couldn't imagine having to work with the bearded wonder, given the tension between them. She paused, staring into space, and then the microwave pinged.

Thankfully pulled back onto safe, domestic ground, she finished preparing her meal.

∽

Sinking into her comfortable armchair with a small tot of whisky, Ella sighed with real pleasure and relaxed for the first time all day. She laughed at a photo of Pixie sent by Jeanette to her phone, and Monty considered her from in front of the fire. She patted her knee, and he curled into a fur cushion on her lap.

The music was low and hauntingly lovely; a guitar concerto. It spoke of warm nights and rocky landscapes, decidedly different from the biting wind outside and the rain driving against the window-panes of an English November. Monty began to purr, his small body vibrating as she idly pulled his ears.

She took another sip of her drink and faced her thoughts. She knew she'd been avoiding this quiet time alone, instead filling her evenings with socialising. She'd seen Jeanette and other friends, played netball, gone to the cinema. During the day she focused on work, with no room for much reflection. But now – her thoughts tumbled in on one another.

Love in a Mist

Halloween had been a bit of a shock, one way and another. Not just for her, either, from what she'd seen. Her costume had made her the centre of attention in a way that she'd forgotten about. Armoured in her work suits and sensible blouses, her colleagues might have forgotten that she was female. The sight of her cleavage affected some male guests so much they hadn't looked at her face or that ridiculous red wig. She sniffed at the memory and Monty protested as her fingers curled too tightly into his fur.

"Sorry, Monty," she said, smoothing his ears again. Satisfied with her apology, he settled again.

The Irishman had also given her the once-over. Although to be fair, she amended, he held a conversation with her, not just her breasts. He had surprised her – again. First, the apology, which made her own so much easier. She still cringed at the conversation in the orangery. Whatever other traits she might have, Ella prided herself on her absolute courtesy, and her assumptions had offended him. And now she thought about it, if anyone had doubted *her* ability to do her job, she would have reacted badly too.

Although his fury had startled her and as a sizeable man, she'd felt – what? Threatened? No, she hadn't been afraid. The warmth spread up her cheeks as she focused candidly on her thoughts. Her pulse had kicked up, *excited*, as though she was on the edge of a cliff, and about to jump.

She blew out her cheeks.

Then his slow smile as he'd offered an olive branch had sent her into a bit of a panic, idiot that she was. He was a contradiction – someone who could be a ruffian, but also a bit of a smoothie. But truly, she needed to get a grip.

Yes, he had quite the reputation. But he wasn't *much* like Stephen. Connor's attitude to children showed a greater depth of kindness than could ever have existed in her ex-fiancé. And anyway, she was safe from his Irish charm. She'd seen the photos of Connor with various small, curvaceous women, dripping with glamour, all short-term relationships if the newspapers were to be believed. He wouldn't be interested in a beanpole like her, other than as a colleague he was trying to persuade to help him with the project.

Her sigh was so deep, Monty looked at her quizzically.

"I know. I'm a pillock," she agreed.

And then, there was the story he'd told at Halloween, told in his glorious, baritone Irish brogue. She'd noted how several women scurried off to the loos to check hair, wipe their teeth of black make-up, re-apply red lipstick, and re-arrange their costumes. By the twinkling eyes of Lady Susan, her employer had spotted it too.

Ella finished her drink and relaxed as the whisky trailed its hot passage down her throat. He would not be here long; eventually, the crew would complete the garden, and he'd be on his way back to London. Given Lady Susan's focus on the garden, she would have to be helpful. But at her own speed, she decided.

8

"Yes?" barked Connor into his mobile.

"Good God, who's rattled your cage?" Jonas asked. Connor realised Jonas was phoning from the car.

"Apologies. I'm having a trying day."

"Sounds it. I'm on my way to visit Lady Susan and Justin about the wedding, and I wondered if we could meet up?"

Connor was silent, momentarily panicked when he thought about the garden's progress. Then he took a breath.

"If you think you're getting out of here without a visit to the pub and a long, long chat, then you're not the man I knew, Jonas Keane."

There was a chuckle on the end of the line.

"Are you kidding? I was counting on you to stop Lady Susan drowning me in tea. See you in about an hour."

Connor pushed the phone into the back pocket of his jeans and turned his attention back to the swing shovel moving dirt in front of him. He didn't like the way the earth was shifting, in great lumps of clay. The ground had been sodden for days, the damned weather thwarting him at every turn, endless rain turning his precious schedule upside down. He estimated they were about three weeks behind now, and although Mike Stewart was working miracles, slicing half days off the back of the build to claw back time, Connor knew that they were running out of options. If the weather didn't improve soon, they'd simply not be able to finish the garden within budget, in time for the planned launch. And with it, Jonas and Sam's wedding.

As if to mock his predicament, a raindrop splashed on Connor's face and he swore. The foreman, operating the huge machine, peered out from under the cab roof, and from his lips, Connor saw that he'd sworn too. The engine stopped, and moments later, the foreman climbed down.

"If this bastard rain don't stop, we'll be able to do bugger all today," he said, spitting in disgust. Connor nodded. He knew. Perhaps he should go back to church and ask for divine intervention – his mother would be delighted. She'd been asking every time they spoke for the past fifteen years if he'd been to mass lately. He never had.

He thrust his frozen hands into the pockets of his coat and went to find Mike in the Portakabin office they shared, poring over engineering drawings and spreadsheets.

"God, it's not raining again is it?"

"Yep."

Mike put his head in his hands and groaned. Connor pulled off his coat and flung it onto a chair.

"I don't know what we can do, Mike. Unless we were going to put everything under canvas – and that's a ridiculous idea – I can't see how we'll complete the major earthworks so we can at least start the hard landscaping. We've a brave way to go to finish."

Mike leaned forward and started tapping his computer.

"I think next week should be better – it will be colder for a start," he said. Connor scowled.

"So instead of rain, I get snow? That's no feckin' improvement!"

"No, no. Just colder. No rain. Look."

Connor crossed the room to see the screen. The weather map showed no precipitation, and his spirits lifted a little. If they could get a bit of a run at the main landscaping...

"How far behind are we, again?"

Mike shot him a glance.

"You *know*, Connor. It's the same as it was this morning, we're behind by twenty working days. If we do nothing more today, it'll be twenty-one days. I'll do my best to save us some... *more* time by rescheduling, but we don't have much wiggle room." He paused, and Connor could guess what was coming. "And we're already hammering the budget, bringing on more bodies trying to keep to the *new* schedule. We can't afford any more delays."

Connor nodded tightly. He gazed at the plans on the wall and knit his brows. Mike, who had caught on quickly to his boss's way of working, kept quiet. After a few minutes, Connor nodded to himself.

"When it lets up, we need to focus on the waterfall," he said. "That way, we can get the swing shovels off the estate and stop spreading so much mud around. And I can see to make alterations to the design if we need to. And we need to get the arbour finished, otherwise, we won't have a place for the ceremony. I can't see with all this bloody machinery around me..."

He grabbed his coat and headed out, as if by staring at the sky, he could stop the rain.

∽

An hour later, Connor was sitting in the drawing room with Lady Susan and Jonas. He'd nipped back to the cottage to change his disreputable clothes. If he bumped into Ella again, he didn't want her looking down her aristocratic nose at him.

Jonas was sharing a gentle joke with Lady Susan, and she was loving the attention. Connor's lips curled upwards at the skilful flirtation in front of his eyes – not heavy-handed, just enough to assure Lady Susan that she was good to be with. And all in Jonas' glorious voice. No wonder the women fell over themselves.

The glorious voice was talking about his wife-to-be.

"Sam's gutted she couldn't come herself, but she's in the Netherlands, looking at one of our sustainable developments."

Lady Susan gave a moue of disappointment.

"I'm sure she'll be visiting before the wedding, though. August isn't far away!"

"Sam's the most organised person I know, so I suppose I'm not *that* surprised that the planning started twelve months before!" Jonas looked rueful, and Lady Susan burst out laughing.

"Oh dear! Is she having ten bridesmaids?"

"Perish the thought. Just my daughter and her niece, Lisbeth. It was the least revenge we could take on them – given they practically forced us together."

"But how? Did they set up a blind date?" Lady Susan asked, her eyes sparkling with curiosity.

"Nothing so simple! I'd been unwell and Magda asked me if I'd let her bring in a garden designer while I was off work. The designer was Sam – who I originally thought was a man, incidentally. That's how we met."

"Goodness."

"It's convoluted… are you sitting comfortably?"

Connor sat silent and smiling as his best friend told the story of his romance, and how Magda and Lisbeth had plotted to bring them together. And the new development that had almost broken the fledgling relationship before it got started. By the time Jonas had reached the end, Lady Susan was wiping tears of laughter from her eyes.

"That's wonderful! But didn't Sam want to hold the wedding in her own garden, the one she designed? Enamoured as I am with Connor's designs, I thought she'd stay closer to home."

"You haven't seen the size of my extended family. My mother is Irish, and *anyone* she knows is coming. Our village just wouldn't have coped. And I knew Ralph was looking to redevelop the garden here, and I thought we could provide you with your first booking. I just hope the weather improves!"

Lady Susan coughed, and Connor spoke up.

"It'll be fine. We're tight on time, but we will be ready if I have to bring half the country to work on it! And the weather is perking up from the end of the week, I understand."

Jonas was silent for a moment.

"Don't look so worried, Jonas, it'll be ready," Connor said easily. "My word on it."

"God, Sam'll have your guts for garters if it's not ready for our wedding!"

"Don't I know it! If absolutely necessary, we'll focus attention on the areas of the garden where you'll be, and leave the outer spaces far from the house until nearer the official opening."

"When is the official opening?"

"Two weeks after the wedding," Lady Susan said, patting his hand. "You'll be the first people to see it, to experience it. It will be marvellous. But we also need to speak about catering and numbers, and I ought to get Justin in."

As if on cue, there was a knock on the door, but it wasn't Justin, it was Ella. Connor's nerves tightened. No plunging neckline or outrageous red wig as she'd sported at Halloween, but her usual ponytail and sensible sweater. A disappointed sigh escaped him.

When she saw the group, Ella stopped short, apologising.

"No, no, come in, Ella," said Lady Susan. "This is Jonas Keane, an old friend of Lord Ralph. You know that we're hosting his wedding in August next year?"

Although it was tiny, Connor saw the flicker of emotion cross Ella's face, before her face was smooth again. He thought her smile a little forced.

"We've met briefly at the cottage. But it's nice to congratulate you in person. I hope it's all going smoothly?"

Ouch, thought Connor as Ella shook hands with Jonas. She turned to Lady Susan. "I don't mean to interrupt your planning, I just wanted to let you know, Lady Susan, that we're meeting the tenants next Thursday afternoon. I'll collect you at two thirty."

Connor watched as she walked out of the room. He turned to see Jonas watching him speculatively.

"Will Ella be much involved in the wedding arrangements?" Connor asked Lady Susan, ignoring his friend.

"Oh, good gracious, no. No, I very much doubt it. Weddings aren't her thing."

"Oh?"

"No, Ella runs the estate, not the house."

Connor thought Lady Susan's sentence was a little brusque, and his black eyebrows rose slightly. Lady Susan considered.

"Ella's happier tramping the fields than organising canapés," she added with a brief smile. "So, shall we call for Justin?" And she reached for her phone, closing down the conversation.

~

Connor sighed with relief as he closed the door to the cottage. It was wonderful to see his old friend, but he'd found his mind wandering during some of their conversations. He shook his head to clear it. Really, he needed an early night.

Taking a deep breath, he pushed himself off the door and wandered into the tiny kitchen. His mind leafed through the contents of his to-do list as he boiled the kettle for coffee. He'd just look at the plans for the Rainbow Walk trees, he thought absently. And then he'd get some sleep.

His ears caught the noise of someone moving in the next-door cottage. He rarely heard Ella except in the mornings and wondered if she had guests. The kettle clicked off and as the boiling of the water subsided, he caught the sound of a woman's laughter. That surely wasn't Ella. She must have friends visiting. "People who listen behind closed doors hear no good of themselves." His mother's voice floated in his head, and he tutted to himself. He made his coffee and made his way to the desk where a pile of papers awaited him.

Hours later, he glanced at the clock and groaned. Nearly one in the morning. He stretched and glared at the pad in front of him. The alterations had taken an age, and even now, he wasn't sure if they were exactly what he wanted. The dragon's lair suggested by Adam had been giving him a few headaches, but he'd got the better of it,

Love in a Mist

eventually. He'd finally emailed the CGI production company to say – 'give me dragons that will fly at night'.

The nests would be enormous willow baskets, hung from chains. May as well make it a bit steam-punk, he grinned to himself.

He had spent most of his time thinking about how he'd plant trees along the Rainbow Walk. The leaves and barks of the trees would create a rainbow effect in the autumn – Japanese acers, native British trees and the bluest conifers he could find. But they needed different conditions, different soil. Eventually, his solution was big steel tubs which would contain the roots and allow him to give the trees the distinct types of soil and nutrients they would need. Sinking the tubs into the ground – and getting them manufactured in the first place – might provide a few headaches, but he'd talk to Mike about that...

He rubbed the back of his neck, feeling the stiffness radiating from his shoulders. He stood and did some stretching, which didn't help much, then looked longingly at the bottle of wine that Jonas had brought him. And sighed, reaching instead for the kettle. To please his sister Caitlin, he'd bought some chamomile tea.

As he slid into bed ten minutes later, he thought he might hate the taste. But Caitlin had sworn it was calming and would help him sleep, so he forced it down. Settling the pillow behind his head, he switched off the light, and the dark wrapped round him. The gentle hoots of the owls reached him and he thought how peaceful it was in this place as he closed his eyes, waiting for sleep to claim him.

But what about the fountain? And had he emailed the sculptor about the entry into the National Contemporary Art Award?

Wide awake again, Connor stared into the darkness and after a moment, wearily pushed the quilt aside. He ought to keep a pen and paper by his bed, wasn't that what they said? Write it down, forget it and go back to sleep. He groped for the bedside lamp switch and the light made him blink. Muttering, he padded down the stairs. He brought a wad of paper and a pen back upstairs and sat heavily on the side of the bed while he wrote some notes.

With exaggerated patience, he put the pen and paper on the

bedside table, and lay down again. He carefully focused on his breathing, trying to empty his head, to swipe aside thoughts of the things he had to do, how tired he'd be in the morning, and the creeping worry that this – not sleeping – was how it began last time. The clock read three thirty before he finally slept.

9

Ella was silent, unable to say anything for a second. It seemed ironic that at that moment the sun was shining through her office window, a bright November morning. Lady Susan twisted the rings on her finger, and finally, Ella found her voice. "So how much is the project short?"

"About three hundred thousand pounds," Connor said quietly. He looked tired and strained, Ella thought."

"When did this come to light?" she asked, out of a dry throat.

"At the end of last week. Mike has cut things all ways, but unless we employ more workmen on site, the schedule – which was already tight – will be completely shot."

Ella was silent as his words sank in.

"Can you make any savings on the existing plans?" she finally asked without much hope as she pictured her reserves being decimated.

"We've at least completed the major earth moving, except for the Rainbow Walk, so most of the swing shovels can go off site. But unless I have additional workmen, we'll struggle to open in August next year, and the extra resources aren't in the budget. We just didn't plan for the wettest autumn on record. We've pushed some of the more adventurous elements into phase two—"

Ella's head rose sharply at that.

"The dragons?" she asked.

"Will still be created," Connor said stonily. "I've scaled down the fountain and water mechanisms."

Damn, thought Ella. That was the bit I liked most... She felt the weight of Lady Susan's gaze and decided to be blunt.

"Is Lord Ralph expecting the estate to contribute to these costs?"

Lady Susan shook her head vigorously and played with her rings again.

"I haven't – *yet* – taken Lord Ralph into my confidence," she said. "I was wondering about a loan from the bank?"

"But if you don't mind me saying so, that's ridiculous," Ella said crisply, losing patience. "Lord Ralph is a businessman, and if he doesn't already know the garden needs an injection of cash, I'd be astonished. And I can't just increase our borrowing without his agreement!"

Lady Susan stared.

"*Really*, Lady Susan?" Ella gentled her tone. "I can't arrange this without Lord Ralph knowing! God, he'd sack me!"

Connor opened his mouth and Ella spoke over whatever he was going to say.

"And even more important – he's your *husband*, and he'd be terribly, terribly hurt if he knew you were worried about it and not talking to him!"

"But this is *my* project and I should be able to deliver it without asking for his help!" Lady Susan's voice sounded tight. "I kept you out of the finances because you were concerned we'd overspend and be a drag on the estate's resources! Is there anything else you can suggest?"

Ella was shocked. Had she been that transparent? God, she must be slipping... Shaking her head to focus on the issue at hand, she considered, her thoughts flying.

"Sponsorship? I'm no expert, but that might give you some additional cash and an opportunity to do some marketing – something that you should have been doing, anyway."

Connor stroked his beard.

"That's a great idea. Mike knows about agencies that do stuff like that..."

"And I imagine there's a load of businesses you could talk to. For a start, what about Jonas Keane?"

Connor recoiled.

"I can hardly ask Jonas for money to finish the place he's hoping to marry in!"

"I suppose it depends how soon your budget will run out, doesn't it? Can you afford to wait until we and the agency create, pitch, and then find someone for the sponsorship deal? Or will that delay the work even more?"

He said nothing, but it surprised Ella she couldn't hear his teeth grinding together.

"And anyway, I'm not suggesting you go to him cap in hand, but I'm pretty sure Jonas Keane has a huge list of contacts he might share," Ella replied. "You asked for my suggestions. If you want money quickly and aren't prepared to involve Lord Ralph, you need people you trust to give it to you."

"I'm not asking my best friend to give us money," Connor hissed through his teeth, and then to Ella's surprise, abruptly left the room. Ella stared after him.

"Oh dear. There must be another way," Lady Susan said, although she didn't sound too convinced. "Are you sure a private loan is impossible?" Ella came round her desk and knelt by her employer's chair.

"Susan..." she paused and took a deep breath. "I love working for you and Lord Ralph. You've always been so very supportive of me, through... everything... And you know I'll do almost anything for you. But I *can't* get a loan without Lord Ralph's knowledge. It would be a betrayal of his trust and much as I love you, I can't do that."

Lady Susan looked at her for a long moment. And then smiled and nodded.

"No. No, of course you can't. It's just that I'm rather desperate."

Ella perched on the edge of the desk.

"I can see that."

"Connor calculates we might have lost as much as eight *weeks* from the schedule! Oh Ella, I'm really not sure how we'll deliver in time for the opening…"

To her horror, Ella saw a tear slide down her employer's cheek.

"Lady Susan, talk to Lord Ralph. God knows I'd rather you didn't have to, but it's the easiest way out of this problem. He'll understand – good grief, no one can be blamed for delays caused by the *weather!*"

Lady Susan fumbled in her bag for a tissue and wiped her eyes.

"Connor told me we were cutting it fine when he presented the plans for phase one. It's all my fault – I so wanted to host Jonas Keane's wedding, I've pushed Connor to keep to an undeliverable timescale."

"Enough of that. He's an experienced designer, and he must know how the weather can screw up a schedule. If he really didn't believe he could deliver in the time, he shouldn't have agreed."

"You're so severe," she sighed. "He was trying to please me. And to give Jonas a wedding he'd never forget."

Ella resolutely kept her mouth closed; she reflected the wedding might be memorable for many reasons, not all of them positive.

"Please consider approaching Lord Ralph, and he and I can sort something out," she said finally, with a sinking heart.

∞

Connor strode in, surprising Ella.

"I need to say thank you," he said, beaming at her before she said a word.

"Sorry?"

"I need to thank you for organising money to tide us over in the short term. We're bringing on more staff and if the weather holds, we'll be able to make up some time on the garden."

Ella stood up and closed her office door.

"Please take a seat," she said. Bemused, Connor did as she asked

Love in a Mist

and her random thought was that the office looked more like its normal size when he was sitting down. She sat in the chair opposite him and placed her hands carefully in her lap.

"I wanted to make my apology in person," he said hesitantly. "I was as cross as a scalded cat when we met you last week. I need to get a handle on my temper."

He smiled at her, and Ella's stomach dropped. He had a wonderful smile, even beneath that Neanderthal-like beard. She pulled herself together.

"Connor, thank you for apologising – but I told Lady Susan I couldn't organise the money without Lord Ralph being involved. Lord Ralph hasn't spoken to me, so I guess she's not spoken with him. Whatever money she's got, it's nothing to do with me."

He stared at her.

"Did Lady Susan specifically say that I'd helped her get the money?" Ella pressed. He ran a hand through his inky black hair, making it stand on end.

"No... but I assumed..." He trailed off.

Ella rose.

"This might need some tea. Do you want one?"

"Ah, thanks. But if you didn't get the additional funds, who did?"

As the kettle boiled, Ella fired questions at him. When did Lady Susan speak to him? What *exactly* did she say? Had she seen anyone else? Had she had visitors?

Connor frowned fiercely all the way through her interrogation.

"She came to the site office on Wednesday and told me that thirty thousand pounds would be transferred to the garden account the following day. I gave her a hug and then told the team to get the call out for more workers."

"Wednesday?" Ella thought a little. "She went to London on Tuesday. And I couldn't get hold of her on Monday at all. Justin told me she had been holed up in the library and wasn't to be disturbed."

Connor was silent. After a moment, he said, "I can't imagine that she's robbed a bank... but it would be nice to know that she's not done anything stupid to get the funds. But who am I to ask her where she's got thirty grand from?"

Ella worriedly stirred her tea.

"I imagine most of the collections in the house are in trust for the family, but I'll check with Justin that none of the Constables are missing..."

"She wouldn't sell her art, surely?"

Ella shrugged.

"She's an enormously resourceful woman. Frankly, I wouldn't be at all surprised if she *had* robbed a bank!"

Connor laughed.

"But how on earth do we ask her?"

Ella shook her head.

"No idea. I suppose you could tell her you came to see me – and that you were mistaken in your assumptions about where the money came from?"

He rubbed his chin.

"Yes, I could do that. See if she tells me more. And if she swears me to secrecy about the source of the mysterious cash, what do I do?"

Ella stared down at her tea.

"I suppose that would depend on how much your oath counts for, Mr McPherson."

There was a frozen silence.

"My word is my bond, Ms Sanderson."

"In which case, I imagine I'll be in the dark."

He stood up, filling the room again, putting his cup down on the table with a decided snap.

"Then let's hope she *isn't* selling off the family silver," he said before he left. "Thank you for the tea."

∼

Ella could hear raised voices as she came into the manor. She paused, listening.

"You should have consulted me!"

Love in a Mist

"Ralph, I wanted to do this on my own, and it *is* my property, after all!"

Her nose wrinkling in distaste, Ella walked slowly towards the drawing room, raised her hand to knock on the firmly closed door, and stopped. A muffled expletive reached her and she gritted her teeth and knocked. A tense silence fell inside the drawing room.

"Come in." Ella suppressed a shiver at the ice in Lady Susan's voice. She stiffened her shoulders and went in, a smile stretching her lips.

"Are you ready for our meeting?"

"Sorry?" Lady Susan stared at her.

"With the tenants? Explaining a little more about the garden?" Ella stopped herself just in time from saying anything about 'benefits' and 'investment' which would go down like a lead balloon from the look of her employers. Lord Ralph snorted and turned away to the window in disgust, and then swung back to them, as Lady Susan muttered and hastily reached for her jacket.

"I'd like to continue our conversation when you return, Susan," he said, coolly courteous.

Lady Susan inclined her head.

"Of course."

She walked to the car with Lady Susan in silence, a silence which lasted until they were in the car, heading for the meeting room at the local pub.

"I sold some of my personal jewellery. I know you're dying to know," Lady Susan said in a low voice. Ella changed gear to take a bend before responding.

"I hope I'm not so intrusive, Lady Susan."

"Oh, don't *you* be cross with me too!"

Ella took a deep breath.

"I imagine that Lord Ralph was quite upset," she said.

"Furious. And upset. And don't tell me *I told you so*, because I know!" she finished on a sob. It startled Ella enough to stop the car.

"Lady Susan, please don't cry! Surely Lord Ralph will have calmed down by the time you get back?"

Lady Susan sniffed into her handkerchief.

"I hope so. But he was furious!"

"He was angry because you didn't come to him first, when you recognised the project was in trouble, not because you sold some jewellery!" Ella was exasperated. "What did you sell? Not some ancient heirloom?"

"No, no. I sold the diamond and ruby coronet. It's one of the few things of value that's not promised elsewhere. It was Great-Aunt Agatha's, and I always thought it was ghastly in any case..."

Ella nodded.

"Yes, it was hideous, wasn't it?"

Lady Susan stared at her and then giggled. Ella laughed and patted her hand.

"What can I do to help?" Ella asked.

"I don't know – sort out an agency to get the rest of the money through sponsorship? I've bought us a little time by selling the jewellery..."

Ella nodded, feeling conflicted, and her heart sinking at the amount of work stretching out in front of her. "I can do that."

"Talk to Connor first," Lady Susan urged, taking out her gold compact and checking her make-up. Ella started the car again, sighing inwardly.

"Of course."

10

Ella watched as Connor ran his hands through increasingly untidy hair as the sponsorship agency tried again.

"Connor, we can't just go to the sponsors and ask them for money without a package of benefits! Surely you see that?" one of the agency girls said.

Ella winced at the tone, part persuasion, part seduction. The eldest of the girls couldn't have been older than twenty-three or four, and she was secretly envious of their poise and confidence, something that hadn't come to her until she reached her late twenties. She yanked her thoughts back to the conversation, and away from her life at twenty-two.

"Aye, I see that, but you're asking me to promise things I haven't even considered as part of the design. And what's this about naming rights?"

Connor, who'd been charming for the first half an hour of the meeting, was baring his teeth. The eldest girl from the agency – Melissa, was it? – explained that they could call the rainbow avenue the 'Kool Crisp Rainbow Walk' after the breakfast cereal company that might sponsor it.

"And we'd offer the picnic areas under the trees to the company's guests on the launch day and give away Kool Crisp snack bars to visitors after the garden had opened."

"There is no picnic area under the trees," Connor said.

"Oh, but you could so easily add it!" Melissa said with what she doubtless hoped was a winning smile. "Couldn't you?" she added, hesitating as Connor's face didn't change.

"Or what about the logo as part of the topiary?" piped up her colleague, even younger and thinner than Melissa.

Ella had to hide a smile at Connor's appalled face. Melissa, to give her her due, didn't give up, turning hastily in her folder to other companies, and making other suggestions about how they could put the sponsorship package together. On it went, for more than an hour, with Connor vetoing all the suggestions put to him. Eventually, Ella took control of the meeting, and suggesting a quick coffee break to revive the wilting agency staff, hustled Connor out of the office to another room.

Firmly shutting the door, she folded her arms.

"Right. I can see the agency has worked very hard to get interest from these companies. You're going to have to give *something* in return for a wad of cash, so tell me, what did you have in mind?"

Connor, who had been staring moodily out of the window, swung around to her.

"Goddamn it, I don't have a clue! I'm a garden designer, not a bloody salesman!"

"No need to raise your voice, Connor. I brought in these people, and they come highly recommended, but they can't work miracles on their own. What are we going to give them?"

He muttered something, although Ella didn't catch the words. They sounded foreign and savage.

"There's no need to swear at me, either."

He stared.

"I didn't know you understood Gaelige."

"I don't need to. Come on, Connor, the agency's lined up some reputable companies. What might they buy that *you'd* be willing to sell?"

He closed his eyes briefly, as if praying for patience. Ella knew the feeling.

"They're a feckin' breakfast cereal company! Can *you* think of anything?"

Ella paused for a moment and then took out her phone to look for something on the internet.

"Yes... yes, I thought I remembered this," she mused. "Kool Crisp has just launched a campaign to make its packaging from completely recycled paper and is doing more than any other cereal company – it says – to be carbon neutral. Could we put a standing display on the Rainbow Walk to talk about the need for trees to reduce our man-made carbon emissions? Or have their name connected with the water collection system?"

He stared at her so long, she wondered if she had a smut on her nose, or even if he'd heard her.

"That's... brilliant," he said eventually. "Will they go for it?"

"Maybe. Shall we test it on Melissa?"

As the idea hadn't come from the agency originally, Melissa was a little sullen. But as Ella continued to talk, Melissa's own imagination kicked in.

"How about we also ask them to sponsor education packs and breakfasts for school trips?" she asked, tentatively.

Ella grinned.

"Now you're talking. Who prepares the education pack?"

"Well, you'd have to do that, or your marketing agency."

No, I'm not having that land on *my* desk, Ella thought, as Connor's eyes slid to her.

"I'll speak to our marketing agency," she said, smiling. After a few more details about the proposal, Ella stood up. Melissa sighed theatrically.

"Thank goodness! I thought for a moment we wouldn't convince you!"

Connor muttered something about getting back to the site and bowed out. All the women stared after him.

"Is he always that... abrupt?" asked Melissa's colleague.

"He's an artist," Ella said smoothly. "A little temperamental."

And an arse at times, she thought.

~

Connor started as his mobile rang. He was lying on the sofa and had to dig it out from under him to answer it. The display told him it was Jonas and that it was nine thirty. Where had the evening gone?

"Jonas, what's up?"

"What's up with you? Sam's sent loads of messages about coming to stay for the weekend, but she's heard nothing back." Jonas paused. "Are you okay, or have you gone off us?"

Connor frowned. *Had* he received messages? He couldn't remember seeing any... He heaved himself from the sofa and located his headphones, so he could talk and search his emails at the same time.

"Sure, you should know I'd never ignore Sam! My life wouldn't be worth living!" While he spoke, he thumbed his screen, looking for the messages. "Anyway, to save me going through my mail, when did you have in mind? Remember, I have this damned project to sort out..."

"This weekend coming," was the brief reply. "And what 'sorting out' do you need to do? I imagined now the weather was improving it would be better?"

Connor hesitated, and Jonas pounced.

"Come on, Connor, what's happening? I can tell something's going on, so out with it."

Connor sighed as he sank back into the cushions of the sofa.

"We're just very, very late... because of the bloody weather."

Jonas kept silent and Connor realised suddenly that this wasn't only his best friend, but the man whose wedding the garden was hosting. He rushed into speech.

"We've got a bit of extra budget so we're sure to catch up with the work, it's tedious, that's all. No bother, just needs a wee bit of additional organising."

Love in a Mist

"But, Con, *you* sound worried. Or at least you did before you remembered that you're supposed to be hosting our ceremony."

Damn, thought Connor. He knows me too well.

"I'll have a better idea in a month or so what else we need to throw at it, but I can promise you, it won't affect your wedding."

"And how are *you*?"

Double damn.

"I'm fine."

"Are you? Are you getting enough sleep? When was the last time you ate?"

"You sound like my mother."

"Your mother, God love her, wasn't there to pick up the pieces the last time I was asking these kinds of questions – it was me. So I have a perfect right to ask them again. How are you? And don't even consider lying to me."

Connor slumped and stared into the fire, which needed another log.

"Look, Jonas, I'm fine."

"Define 'fine'."

"I'm okay! God, what else can I say?"

"How are you sleeping? When you're well, they need a brass band to wake you. What time did you wake up today?"

"About six – which is normal for me!"

"And you went to bed when, exactly?"

"Ah, feck off, Jonas—"

"What time, Connor? Or do you want me to get in my car and drive down and work it out for myself?"

Connor recognised that inflexible voice. He'd heard it once before when Jonas had been asking him about the pills, what – ten years ago?

"About two."

"Two. Four hours' sleep isn't enough, not over a long time. How long has this been going on?"

"About three weeks, but I've now done all the redesigns, so the pressure will be off me. So don't fret. Please."

Jonas sighed.

"Have you seen a doctor?"

"No, and I'm not going to. It's down to my team now."

Silence. Connor leaned forwards and threw another log on the embers in the fire. He poked it gently with the fire iron and it obligingly lit.

"You will make sure it's the team, not only you? And you will take more care, won't you?" Jonas' voice was gentle, and it caught him on the raw. He cleared his throat.

"Sure I will. It's just where we are in the project, and it should get better – particularly as we're about to do a pitch for some sponsorship."

"Oh?"

Connor told him about the pitch to Kool Crisp, and the plans for the education work.

"Sam will want to know how you get on," said Jonas, his deep velvet voice approving. "She's working with one of our board directors in schools, so students understand about the environment and how important the countryside is."

Connor promised to call after the meeting.

"And are you able to come over for the weekend?"

Connor considered. He should have got some shuteye by the time the weekend came and be able to get himself together. So he agreed.

"And are you away to Ireland for Christmas?" Jonas asked.

Connor hesitated again. He normally loved Christmas with his large and unruly family, but the thought of all of them, including the kids, made him shrink slightly.

"I haven't decided yet," he said.

"You're welcome at ours, if not," Jonas said. "We were keeping it small, with just Magda—"

"Lord, I haven't seen Magda for..."

"Months. She grows another centimetre every time I turn around."

"How old is she now?"

Jonas clicked his tongue.

Love in a Mist

"Your god-daughter, and you don't know that she's nineteen in January?"

"Sure, is she nineteen? I'm astonished. And appalled. This means I'm older than I thought."

"You should try being her father."

"I take it she's back from university soon?"

"In about two weeks. I *say* that it will be small with us and Magda, but Sam's family will doubtless drop in and who knows what strays Magda will drag home from university," Jonas chuckled. "But if you can bear all that, you'd be very welcome."

Connor said he'd let them know.

"Okay, we'll see you this weekend. Take care, Connor. You know where I am if you need me."

"I know. Thanks, Jonas."

∽

"For heavens' sake, don't you *own* a razor?" Ella was exasperated. Connor shrugged.

"I've got too much to do to bother much with personal grooming."

"Yes, but most days you're not asking for money, Connor!" Ella itched to get her hands on scissors and a comb, but instead, she clenched her fists. Despite a certain dishevelled appearance and the lines around his eyes, his shirt was snowy white, his deep navy jacket drew attention to the blue of his eyes, tired or not, and he'd scrubbed his nails of mud.

"Will I do, miss?"

She started, not realising that she had been doing an inventory. She could feel her face grow hot.

"I'm sorry," she muttered. "It's just that we've spent a lot of time on this, and I'm keen that we make the best possible impression."

"Why aren't you coming with us?"

"I don't have a role, and I would look a complete idiot if anyone asked me any questions. You're in expert hands with Melissa and..." she couldn't remember the other girl's name.

"Whatsername," Connor supplied with a grin, and she smiled. Their eyes locked, and time seemed to pause. The distant ching of one of Lady Susan's carriage clocks broke the moment, and she let out a breath. Ella's sharp ears caught the sound of heels on the parquet floor.

"Ah, there you are!" said Lady Susan, looking years younger than her age in a cream Chanel suit. "Are we ready?"

"Aye. Shall we go then?" Connor held out his arm to Lady Susan, who took it.

"Good luck!" Lord Ralph called from the gallery, their disagreement long since sorted out between them. His wife beamed at him.

"Thank you, darling. Back around four, I imagine."

"I hope it goes well," Ella murmured to Connor, who winked at her.

"Luck of the Irish," he said. "We'll be fine."

And in a moment, they were gone.

~

Ella spent the afternoon trying to focus on anything for more than ten minutes. She could have sworn that the clock had actually stopped at one stage, and once, she got up to check it. She jumped when the phone rang.

"Have they come back yet?" Justin asked.

"No, I imagine they'll be home around four. There's all the motorway traffic, so it may be even later than that."

"Hmm. Oh well, fingers crossed and all that. Although in my view the garden could do with the extra funds, it's looking rather bedraggled."

Ella knew. She'd walked the garden one afternoon and had been taken aback by the scale of the enterprise, and even if she didn't like the design, Lady Susan's ambition impressed her. Instead of imagining the implications of not getting the sponsorship, she asked about Justin's attempts to entice a new housekeeper.

"Well, we've made an offer, and she's talking it over with her partner," Justin said breezily. "At least this one already *has* a partner who'll live in with her, so at least she won't be leaving to get bloody married."

Ella silently winced.

"I've started the collection for Antonia," she said hastily, speaking of the existing housekeeper, and they debated the virtues of actual gifts over gift vouchers for a few minutes. Then Justin rang off and Ella was left staring at the clock again. Berating herself for idiocy, she left her office to beg a scone from the kitchen. She brought it back to the office and carefully laid out a cup and saucer, rather than a mug for her tea. Forcing her eyes away from the mantelpiece on which sat the clock, she went through the ritual of tea making, the familiar movements soothing her. She ate her scone, suddenly realising in the excitement of seeing Lady Susan and Connor off, she'd forgotten to eat lunch.

At ten past four, she heard the wheels of a car crunch into the courtyard. She stood up, knocking over her papers from the side of the desk, and almost ran outside. She arrived to see Connor helping Lady Susan out of his sports car. His face was hidden, but Lady Susan smiled despite her heavy eyes.

"How did it go?"

Connor turned to her and grinned.

"They loved it."

Ella almost forgot herself and whooped, but just stood there with a wide smile on her face. Connor stared at her.

"Don't dawdle, Connor, help me in. I need a drink!" scolded Lady Susan, and Connor leapt to attention, walking her to the front door, opened mere moments later by Justin.

"Come to the drawing room," Lady Susan said to Ella. Lord Ralph was waiting, eyebrows raised.

"Well?" he said.

"I believe the common phrase is that we smashed it," Lady Susan said gleefully. "They need to talk to the board, but they said they were very impressed."

Lord Ralph rubbed his hands together and declared that this

called for champagne. Justin disappeared without a word, returning in a few minutes with a bottle and glasses.

"Well done, everyone!" Lady Susan raised her glass. Connor turned to Ella.

"And thank you for coming up with such a cracking idea, Ella. Without you, I'd still be glowering at the agency."

The group raised their glasses to Ella. Unused to the attention, Ella's face grew hot and overcome, she choked on her champagne.

"Yes, thank you, Ella," said Lady Susan softly.

11

Her wrist ached and her writing was looking a little untidy. Ella put down the pen and circled her wrist to ease the cramp. She hummed to the song that was playing, some ridiculous record which was about fifty years old. They never seemed to release new Christmas songs, she thought, and then berated herself for sounding, even in her head, like a middle-aged woman.

She shuffled the neatly addressed cards and tapped them into a neat pile on the table. Her other friends didn't send real cards, they sent e-cards, which she privately hated. It was old-fashioned, writing Christmas cards, but her mother had done it. She was almost finished, she could afford a break. She rose from the sofa with a bit of effort – that last netball match had been a hard one, with a proper bruiser playing as the opposition's centre – and switched on the kettle.

She peered out of the window at the darkened sky. The forecast had mentioned snow. As the kettle boiled, she remembered watching at her bedroom window as a child, looking up at the sky at the seemingly endless flakes coming down, and her mother scolding her for not being in bed. A pang shot through her at the memory of her mother, and the tears stung her eyes. Biting her lip, she made tea and reached for the chocolate biscuits. It was the same every year. She should be used to it. Writing greetings cards was enough to bring back the memory of her mother at Christmas, let alone snow. Come Midnight Mass on Christmas Eve, she'd be a snivelling wreck.

Well, not quite a wreck. Jeanette would pour wine into her, read her ridiculous cracker jokes and force-feed her TV comedy shows and old movies, and she'd get through it. She smiled at the thought of Jeanette; loud, friendly and so different from her. It was a wonder they'd ever made it past that first coffee in the hospital café when Ella had applied to join the netball team.

As she stirred her tea, memories of Jeanette rolled around her; shopping trips with champagne, sessions in the local spa, arguments about suitable clothes for work ('For the love of God, are you twenty-eight or sixty-eight?') and finally, Ella had told her about her engagement. Jeanette had listened gravely and said very little as Ella choked out the story. Then she'd got out the whisky, poured a large glass, and they'd both got completely pissed. They'd never spoken about it since, but Ella knew that Jeanette was more careful, slightly more gentle around certain topics, while never making a fuss. Ella was profoundly grateful, and her friendship with the bouncy ginger-haired nurse was the most solid of her life.

Ella dipped a chocolate biscuit defiantly into her tea – she'd been brought up to eat 'like a lady' and dunking would not qualify. She popped it into her mouth and returned to writing cards.

An hour later, the cards were all written, sealed, stamped and ready to go. She leaned back on the sofa and sighed with satisfaction.

"Next, presents," she murmured, and reached for the wrapping paper, which naturally brought Monty from wherever he'd been hiding to investigate. Ella moved to the kitchen and spent the next five minutes pushing Monty off the table.

"What *is* it with cats and paper?" she asked him. Monty finally acknowledged he wasn't going to get to sit on the brightly coloured wrapping paper, and he arched his back, flicked his tail and stalked off.

The presents didn't take long to wrap; the latest crime novel for

Love in a Mist

Lady Susan and a gossamer silk chiffon scarf; a particular malt whisky for Lord Ralph; a Liberty tie for Justin, and Jeanette's favourite Dior perfume. Because it was another tradition, there was much work with bows and ribbons – real ribbons, not the horrid foil type – and finally, she sat back and admired her handiwork.

"Works of bloomin' art," she said under her breath. At that moment, she heard a car door slam. It seemed Mr McPherson was back. She wrinkled her nose, wondering if the strains of his fiddle would seep through the walls this evening. After the sponsorship presentation, she'd not seen him to speak to, although she saw him striding around the gardens with plans and even with a shovel at one point. The weather, thank goodness, had been dry. The workmen had moved floodlights into parts of the garden so they could continue to work when the winter light faded. Although, with the threat of snow, she didn't know whether that would continue.

Still, it wasn't her problem. Although strictly speaking, it *would* be her problem if they didn't open on time and all the projections were wrong. And she hadn't heard that Kool Crisp had officially confirmed the sponsorship, which made her uneasy. She wondered if this might be on Connor's mind, too – she'd been up in the early hours for a glass of water, and noticed the light from his cottage throwing light and shadows over the garden.

Another thought struck her suddenly. Lady Susan and Lord Ralph had invited all the staff for a Christmas drink next week, and Connor might be there. She didn't have a present for him. This threw her into a quandary – she didn't know him personally. What on earth should she buy him? And should she buy him one, anyway? Or should she count on him not being there?

She wound her ponytail around her fingers, thinking. She'd have to ask casually how many people were coming… Yes, she could ask Lady Susan.

Content with her plans, she stacked the presents under her tree.

Ella smiled at Lady Susan's pleasure as she handed over the elaborately wrapped presents.

"You're coming to the Christmas drinks, aren't you? Yes, obviously you are. I thought we'd announce the sponsorship to the rest of the staff then," Lady Susan said.

"Don't they already know?"

"Of course not... what are you laughing at?"

"Lady Susan, there's been talk of nothing else in the house and among the tenants for the past two weeks!"

"Oh. I thought we'd been rather discreet."

Ella hooted.

"No, that's the last thing I would call it, but by all means, I think you should make an announcement so everyone can celebrate officially. By the way, if you're announcing it, I'm presuming Connor will be there?"

"Naturally, dear girl. What makes you think he wouldn't be?"

"Because it was the staff Christmas drinks, and I didn't know if Connor counted as staff."

Lady Susan thought about it.

"Not strictly, but I don't think of the staff as employees, Ella, I think of them almost as family. And I would put Connor in that category."

Ella nodded. So, she required a Christmas present for Connor. What on earth could she buy him? Driving gloves to go with that ridiculous car? Her mind was so busy running over impersonal gift options, that she didn't notice Lady Susan's twinkling gaze on her.

"I bought him driving gloves," Lady Susan said, reading her mind. "And no, I don't think he smokes, drinks or reads much."

Ella rolled her eyes.

"Thanks. If you get any ideas, could you let me know?"

Lady Susan laughed as she rose to leave.

"Have a look in the village craft shop. They have some wonderful things which shouldn't tread on your professional relationship – if that's what you're worried about." She opened the door, and Ella couldn't contain her frustration.

"Well, it's more that I hardly know him!"

"I think few people know Connor McPherson very well," Lady Susan said seriously as she left.

~

They had certainly decked the great hall with boughs of holly, Ella thought, as a glow of something pulsed through her. Pride? Belonging? She didn't know, and she pushed the analysis aside as someone thrust a glass of champagne into her hand.

Lady Susan and Lord Ralph were standing at the end of the hall, and she could see from Lady Susan's gestures that they were about to circulate. Lord Ralph loved these occasions, flirting with younger women and swapping golf tips with anyone who played. He caught her eye and waved. She grinned and raised her glass.

Ella moved into the centre of the hall, smoothing her new dress down her hips. It was a bright, emerald green. Jeanette, naturally, had ordered her to buy it.

"You can't buy anything else! The colour makes your eyes pop and your hair look really glossy!"

"Isn't it a bit tight?" Ella had asked, feeling not much room around her thighs and knees.

"No, sweetie, that's what you call a perfect fit. Can you sit down? Yes? Then it's not too tight. Too tight and it would split at the seams."

So Ella bought it, and also the black patent shoes which now seemed stratospherically high to her. She stood, rather awkwardly, until one of the kitchen staff turned and said, "Ella! You look beautiful! And your hair and everything!"

The rest of her group turned and Ella found herself uncomfortable as the centre of attention as they asked about the dress. Ella was thankful when the conversation became more general about what everyone was doing for Christmas.

"I'm staying on the estate and I've got friends coming round," Ella said, being economical with the truth. No, she wasn't having turkey, she was having a nice piece of beef (a fillet steak for one, although she didn't elaborate), and yes, the tree in the hall was amazing, wasn't it? No, she thought New Year would be a quiet affair this year (as it always was, although she didn't say this) as she was going to lunch on New Year's Day.

There was a lull in the conversation as Connor walked in. Ella, who was in the middle of a sentence, forgot the words on her tongue as the power of the man radiated through the hall.

"Coo!" said the girl next to her. "What a hunk..."

Connor, oblivious, strode forward to clasp the hand of Lord Ralph and clap Mike, his project manager, on the shoulder. The conversation resumed its previous level.

He'd spruced up a bit, Ella noted. His beard was trimmed and his hair too. A snowy white shirt which emphasised the darkness of his hair and those blue, blue eyes. Less caveman and more... lion? She shook the fanciful thought out of her head, as she thought about the Christmas present under the enormous tree in the corner of the great hall. She suddenly worried if the gift, bought on pure impulse, would be right for him, or whether it would be just strange.

She reached for the ponytail out of habit and tutted to herself as she remembered her hair was loose, the silky strands falling around her shoulders. Dropping her hand, she caught the moment that Connor saw her. His mouth opened and shut, and he turned smartly back to Mike. Ella gulped some champagne to cover her stinging pride. She choked, and the girls with her fluttered around, patting her back.

She had just recovered and was wiping her eyes with a tissue when Connor said, "Sure, you need to take it steady with strong drink."

Internally, she groaned, but fixed a smile on her face.

"Hello, Connor. How *lovely* to see you."

He grinned and handed her another glass. She took it as if it might explode in her face, and if possible, his grin broadened even further. The girls she'd been talking to a few minutes earlier moved off when the food arrived, leaving her alone with him.

Love in a Mist

Ella took a small sip and stole a glance at the Irishman. He looked better than the last time she'd seen him, less strained and tired.

"What are your plans for Christmas?" she asked, politely.

"I'm spending Christmas with Jonas and Sam – the happy couple, come August."

"How's the build coming along?"

"Better with the additional funds, thanks. And the sponsorship should allow us to recover, I hope, weather permitting. But you're not involved in the wedding arrangements, are you? It's all Justin, I understand."

Ella smiled, but this time, moving her face was an effort.

"It's his area of expertise."

Connor's blue eyes sliced into her.

"Aye, Lady Susan said that weddings weren't your thing. I'm surprised – most women love that kind of organising."

"Your sample must be extremely narrow, Connor. Not all women simper over confetti and lace. You must learn to leave the stereotypes in Donegal."

His eyebrows rose and to Ella's relief, Lord Ralph tapped a glass and the room went quiet.

"You may already have heard – and you must have been in a cave if you haven't – but my wife, Ella Sanderson, and Connor McPherson have been looking for a sponsor to support the garden. So this evening I'd like to announce officially that cereal maker Kool Crisp will support our Rainbow Walk to the tune of *two hundred and fifty thousand pounds!*"

There were a few whistles and a lot of cheers.

Lord Ralph looked around and called Connor to the front of the room.

"And bring Ella, don't let her skulk at the back in that glorious frock!" added Lady Susan.

Ella walked forward with a fiery face as other staff thanked her and applauded, and ignored the wolf-whistles. It seemed like hours as she stood in front of the staff, receiving congratulations, but finally, she escaped from the front of the hall and everyone's stares.

Gradually, the hall emptied. She glimpsed Connor saying something to Mike, and then he headed towards the door. She called him. "Are you going?"

"I thought I'd head off, yes. Is something wrong?"

"No, you just don't have your present."

"Present?"

Ella swiftly ran to the tree and fished out the rather heavy, lumpy present. It was about the size of a milk carton and he stared at it.

"But – I have nothing for you!"

"It's only a little gift, no big deal, we buy for all the staff, almost like a family, and Lady Susan said she thought you were one of the family." The words tumbled out and Ella was almost breathless. Connor stood still, and his mouth twisted before he bit his lip.

"I'm touched, really I am. But I feel awful that I have nothing for you."

She shrugged, wondering if the sheen in his eyes was drink or emotion.

"It's not important. Merry Christmas."

There was a pause as she was pinned to the spot by his eyes.

"Merry Christmas, Ella." He bent his head and kissed her cheek. And then turned on his heel and walked out, leaving her feeling somewhat disoriented.

12

Connor dropped the wrapping paper as he lifted the object to study it.

"Oh! That's lovely!" said Magda, Jonas' daughter, from across the room. Connor's cheeks burned suddenly and he wished he'd opened the gift in private. His god-daughter didn't miss much.

He looked at the heavy sculpture.

"A moon-gazing hare," said Magda, rising from the sofa and coming to stand by him. "It's beautiful. Who's it from?"

"Someone I work with," Connor said, reaching for the wrapping paper to cover it, but not fast enough.

"Can I see?" Sam said, and Connor reluctantly passed it to her. Her slender hands smoothed over the ceramic.

"It's gorgeous. Did Lady Susan and Lord Ralph give it to you?"

For a moment, Connor toyed with the idea of saying yes, but in the end, he shook his head.

"No. It's from Ella Sanderson."

Sam was silent before a slow smile crept over her face.

"What's that? A gift from the ice maiden?" Jonas came in from the kitchen balancing a tray of full champagne glasses.

"It's a tradition with the staff of the manor. Everyone had a gift."

"What did you buy her?" Sam asked curiously.

Connor shrugged.

"I knew nothing about it, so I didn't buy anyone anything!"

Jonas laughed as he put the tray down and handed out the drinks.

"I might have known! You really do have the luck of the Irish! I spent months thinking about what to buy Sam!"

"After some incredibly heavy hints, sweetheart!" his wife-to-be scoffed as she examined the delicate antique gold watch which had been her present.

"And you don't like this Ella?" Magda probed, her green eyes, so like her father's gleaming in the light of the huge fire.

Connor was momentarily stuck for words.

"She's a difficult person to get to know," he said at last.

"I thought you described her as an 'aristocratic beanpole'?" Sam put in slyly.

Connor waved the comment away as he rose to add orange juice to his champagne, ignoring Jonas's protests that what was in his glass was vintage.

"She's very private."

"And very snooty, not very helpful, and hates your design," said Sam.

"Look, I could have been wrong about her," Connor said in desperation. "She's a rare woman – but she's been really helpful about the sponsorship – Christ, the education project was all her idea! – even though she truly doesn't like my design—"

"Rare as in strange?" Magda interrupted, clarifying the Irish slang. Connor nodded and continued.

"Even though she doesn't like my design, she'll do anything for Lady Susan. So she's not being obstructive *now*, quite the opposite, and considering this gift, I feel weird about talking about her like this. So can we stop, please?" His voice had grown sharper, and Jonas threw him an intent glance.

"Yes, of course," he said easily. "It is supposed to be the season of goodwill, isn't it? And it's a lovely gift. Can I ask who'd like apple in the stuffing?"

Sam followed this lead, talking about smoked salmon starters and followed Jonas into the kitchen. Magda grinned and said she could take a hint and took out her phone.

Connor carefully put the hare back into the wrapping paper and disappeared to his room, ostensibly to put it in his bag. But once the door was closed, he sat on the bed and examined the sculpture again.

He had been – and still was – at a loss. The piece was so perfect for him; it was as though she'd stripped his skin and peered inside his soul. The longing in the hare's face, its graceful lines, all spoke with force to him. He couldn't understand why she'd given him such a gift, and if she'd known it would affect him so strongly.

He heard his phone buzz and saw a text from Lady Susan wishing him a Happy Christmas. He sent a response and paused. He stared out of the window at Sam's glorious garden, beautiful even in the depths of winter with tall grasses glinting with frost, and the glimpse of winter jasmine. A wonderful witch hazel, its tiny yellow starburst flowers starting to appear, wafted the sweetest perfume by the main entrance to the house, and a glossy holly dripping with red berries had furnished the decorations.

He reached for his phone and hesitantly sent another text to Lady Susan. He got all the way through the message, then deleted it and threw the phone aside. Then he picked it up and started again. Finally, he had his message.

Lady Susan, I was very touched by your present and those given to me at the manor, and am horrified that I was so unprepared with gifts of my own. I would like to at least text everyone. Could you send me Justin's number and also those of Ella and Antonia?

He pressed send, and then stared again at the hare, drinking in its lines and curves, captivated by its concentrated focus on an unseen moon, heralding the spring, a harbinger of good fortune. Strangely, he felt better than he had for weeks just looking at it.

He waited for a few minutes and then decided that Lady Susan might have guests. Reluctantly, he put his phone in his pocket and headed back to the sitting room.

Magda smiled at him as he came down the stairs.

"Hidden it away? I would!"

Connor grinned and threw himself on the sofa next to her.

"Get your hands off my present, brat."

"I'll have you know I'm nineteen in January!"

"Sure, I know that – still wanting to be a garden designer?"

She nodded, her jaw tensed. Suddenly Connor was taken aback. He'd seen Magda cheeky, interested, concentrating, angry, sulky, ecstatic, in love and heartbroken, and just about everything in between, but somehow this determined, focused, intent side of her had escaped him. He knew that Sam had gently encouraged Magda to get an art and design qualification, rather than dive straight into horticulture, to give her more options, but if she was this determined, he wondered how long it would be before Magda lost patience and dumped her current course.

"How's uni?" he probed.

"Easy enough. In fact, I'm a tiny bit bored, but next term should be more interesting. I wish I'd toughed it out and gone straight for the gardening qualification, rather than a lot of stuff I won't ever use."

"Don't sound so gloomy! Won't your dad let you change?"

"Well, it *will* cost him a ton of money! But if I change to the London course, I can get to work in Kew Gardens!"

"I can't imagine your dad being concerned about the money..."

Magda glanced towards the kitchen door and lowered her voice.

"No, it's not the money. Sam thinks I ought to have a 'proper' degree. I can't see the point if I really want to be a garden designer! I think she's worried I might get bored, or fret that my nails will be a mess..." She blew the dark hair out of her eyes in frustration.

"Well, will you?"

"No! I loved the work I did with Sam and Andy and the team before I went off to uni – I'm pretty sure that if I can work through the summer we had *this* year without complaining, I won't. I really want to do this!"

"Sure, it's been a wet year all round," Connor observed, thinking back to his precarious schedule at Ashton Manor. "But you'll have told your dad how you feel, won't you?"

Magda looked a little shifty.

"Well?" Connor pressed.

"It's... difficult. Dad doesn't want to disagree with Sam, I think. Sometimes I think he worries she'll pull out of the wedding if they don't see eye to eye on everything."

Connor laughed. Jonas had kept himself determinedly single for years following the death of his first wife. And now – he was doing everything possible to get his bride-to-be up the aisle.

"Do you want me to weigh in?" he asked. Magda's face lit up.

"Oh, would you? I can't get him to see that she's besotted with him and would no sooner back out than fly to the moon! And I really would like to just *get on* with designing gardens! I want to be running my own business by the time I'm twenty-five!"

Connor's eyebrows rose. She wasn't joking.

"Ambitious, are you? Well, good for you. I'll talk to your dad."

She grinned, looking again like a teenager, and hugged him, kissing his cheek. She drew back and rubbed her fingers on his cheek.

"I've been meaning to ask you – what's this about?"

"The beard?"

"Yes, the beard! Why are you hiding your *gorgeous* face?"

He smiled. Trust Magda to cut to the heart of it.

"It's just easier," he said.

"Easier? Looks like a disguise. Or are you being stalked?"

"Don't be daft. I just don't need any hassle right now."

His god-daughter hooted.

"You don't want the women swooning after you – hardly surprising given that maniac woman last year! You're hiding, Connor!"

He was about to protest when his phone buzzed. Excusing himself, he left to look at the message from Lady Susan.

~

Ella took another tissue from the box and wiped her eyes as the credits rolled. She watched *It's A Wonderful Life* every year – along with the original *Ghostbusters* – and she cried every time. Giving a final sniff, she got up from the sofa and stretched. Strange how crying could make you feel so much better. Monty stirred from the armchair, immune to her tears.

She'd done as she normally did; went to Midnight Mass on Christmas Eve, slept in, took tea and champagne back to bed while she opened her few gifts, watched Monty play with the paper, and then gave him tuna for his Christmas breakfast. Then she laid a fire in the living room, and retreated back to bed for another hour, listening to the radio while she read a little of a novel. Finally, after an hour or so of dozing, she got up. She showered, put on fresh pyjamas, and went downstairs to stoke up the fire in the living room and eat smoked salmon blinis. She was happy, in her way.

Now, carrying her fresh cup of tea, she sank back into the sofa. She read a little more, answered some Happy Christmas texts from Jeanette and Lady Susan and cooked her steak and jacket potato, chopped some salad, and poured an exceptionally good glass of red wine, courtesy of Lord Ralph. She thought about her Christmas pudding and vanilla custard (a farewell gift from the now ex-housekeeper Antonia, bless her) and decided she'd wait until later to eat dessert, perhaps early evening, with another film. She might watch *An American In Paris*, or *Casablanca*... She crossed to the window and peered out. It was very quiet.

The sky was threatening snow, but it wasn't forecast until Boxing Day. She kept her fingers crossed that Jeanette would still make it round. She could manage one day alone – God, she did it regularly through the rest of the year! – but to spend *all* Christmas alone seemed seriously sad. It would make her... a spinster.

Shrugging away the depressing thought, she threw another log on the fire and was dreamily watching the flames, when her phone buzzed. She peered at the message, not recognising the number.

"God, surely no one would try to sell me something today?" she muttered, opening the message. When she saw it was from Connor McPherson, she almost dropped the phone in shock.

Merry Christmas! I hope I'm not interrupting your celebrations.

"Huh," she said under her breath. Another text arrived.

I didn't get the chance to say thank you for the wonderful sculpture. It's a truly lovely piece.

You're welcome. I'm glad you like it.

"God, how witty," Ella scoffed at her polite, terribly English response. "And you were lucky to get it. I nearly kept it myself!"

She put her phone aside and was surprised when it buzzed again.

Are you having a grand Christmas?

She frowned, and after a moment, wrote back.

Yes, very quiet, but nice. I have friends coming.

"Almost the truth," she said to Monty, who stretched, irritated at the buzzing from the phone.

I'm sorry, I hope I'm not keeping you from them?

She paused.

They've not arrived yet, they're coming later.

"Like tomorrow," she giggled.

That's good. I'd hate to think of you on your own over Christmas.

"Pah. As if you cared!" Another text arrived before she could respond.

I'm fascinated by the hare. What made you think of it as a gift?

Ella pressed her lips together. She herself loved sculpture and had been captivated by it. She didn't know what it had been about the moon-gazing hare that had brought Connor to mind so strongly, made her so sure the piece would be perfect for him. It had been a gut reaction.

I'm not sure I can put it into words. It reminded me of you.

A wild animal with big ears?

She giggled and received another text almost immediately.

Sorry. Me and my smart mouth.

It was an instinct she eventually wrote, struggling to clarify her thoughts. *It felt untamed. Full of emotion.*

There was a pause while she waited for his response. It seemed an awfully long time coming.

I'm honoured. Does that seem like a silly thing to say?

No more silly than me buying you a present on instinct.

This time, the pause was even longer.

Thank you. I didn't get you anything and I feel terrible about that. Shall I buy you something on instinct too, and we can see whose instinct is best?

Ella laughed out loud.

You're on! she texted.

Merry Christmas, Ella.

Merry Christmas, Connor.

~

Connor went back to the dinner party almost reluctantly. He felt... different. He paused before the door of the big dining room to hear Magda and Sam taking the piss out of Jonas for something. Jonas looked up as he came in.

"Everything okay?"

"Just grand," Connor replied as he drew out a chair.

"Are you sure?" his god-daughter asked, looking closely at him. He picked up a water glass and drank, hiding from her too-observant eyes. He nodded.

"Mammy sends her regards," he said to Jonas, naturally not revealing that the phone call to his mother had been a good thirty minutes before. He had spent the rest of the time texting to Ella.

"Is she cross you're not at home for Christmas?" Sam asked.

"Ah, no. She's surrounded by grandchildren. She'll barely notice one less in the chaos."

They talked of family in Donegal, and Connor relaxed. As Jonas heaped his plate with food, his spirits rose. By the time the huge Christmas pudding came out, he breathed a sigh of relief having escaped further questions. Contentment flowed through his veins. He was almost looking forward to going back to work.

He felt Magda's green gaze on him. Not quite escaped, then.

13

Ella was so focused on Lady Susan as she lay on the stretcher, she didn't hear Connor's car draw up in the courtyard. The snow muffled the sound of his tyres, and it was only when the car door slammed that she noticed him, hurrying over through the floating snowflakes, his frame made even bigger by the overcoat.

A man mountain was the abstract thought in her head. The paramedics pushed the stretcher gently into the ambulance and shut the door.

"What's happened?"

"Lady Susan. They think it's pneumonia."

"Where's Lord Ralph?"

"Getting his coat."

"Are you driving him to the hospital?"

Ella nodded, smoothing the leather gloves over her hands and pulling the hat over her hair.

"I'll come too."

"I doubt they'll let us all in at once," Ella said calmly. "But come by all means. Are you coming in my car, or bringing your own?"

Connor considered.

"I'll dump my bags at the cottage and make my way over."

Ella gave him directions to the hospital and turned to smile reassuringly at the shrunken and uncertain Lord Ralph. He straightened slightly when he saw Connor. His normally cheerful face was strained and grey in the dim winter light.

Connor put out his hand, and Lord Ralph gripped it. Neither said a word, but after a few moments, Ella asked quietly if Lord Ralph was ready.

The car was quiet as Ella drove with care on roads made treacherous by the weather.

"She was coughing and breathless," Lord Ralph said, apropos of nothing.

"Yes, you did the right thing calling the ambulance."

Ella saw him nod out of the corner of her eye as she concentrated on the road. Lady Susan, slight though she might be, was normally as fit as a woman half her age. The spectre of illness was not one Lord Ralph had needed to face before. Hardly surprising he was scared.

So was she.

She could feel panic rising in her and she pushed it down, indicated left, and soon they were at the hospital, the lights of the building shining into the snow-laden sky. She was hovering over Lord Ralph as he pushed himself out of the seat when Connor drew up beside them.

"God, you must have driven like a maniac!" she said as he opened the door, secretly very glad he was there.

He grinned as he locked the sports car and padded off to pay extortionate parking charges for them both.

The hospital was like all hospitals – too warm and too bright. Lord Ralph seemed uncertain, and so Connor strode to the reception. The bored-looking receptionist took one glance at his sizeable frame and bright blue eyes and almost leapt to attention. He smiled, and Ella wouldn't have been surprised to see her melt into a puddle.

"We're looking for Lady Susan..." He paused.

"Montague," Ella supplied drily.

"Lady Susan Montague. This is her husband, Lord Ralph. Could you tell me where to find her?" Connor continued smoothly. The girl stuttered the name of the ward and Connor thanked her with a wink. Ella suppressed an eye roll and took Lord Ralph's arm, and they walked along endless, pale green corridors. The flooring made their shoes squeak and silent, stony-faced nurses ambled past at intervals.

"Good God, this place is depressing," muttered Lord Ralph.

"That it is. Let's hope Lady Susan won't be here long," Connor said.

He pushed open a door, and they found the room at last. Lady Susan was lying still, small and pale, wearing an oxygen mask. Ella hadn't expected her to look so vulnerable, and before she could control herself, she gasped. Lord Ralph turned and patted her hand, while Connor looked on with narrowed eyes.

"She'll be fine, Ella," Lord Ralph said, while Ella regained her control. She nodded, unable to speak.

"I'll see if I can find coffee and a nurse," said Connor and left.

Lord Ralph sat by the bed, Ella positioned herself at the end, listening to the steady beeps of the machines.

A few minutes later, Connor slipped back into the room, having found neither coffee nor a nurse. He was very grumpy. Then there was a groan from behind the mask and Lady Susan stirred.

"How are you, darling?" Lord Ralph asked softly.

"Cross," said his wife, and she coughed. "Damn this cough! I should have known..."

"Perhaps you shouldn't try to speak," Ella said.

Lady Susan nodded and her eyelids fluttered down.

"Tired..." she said.

"Susan!" Lord Ralph said, urgently clasping her hand.

Connor said, "Let me find a damned nurse," and left again.

He returned a few minutes later with a plump, pleasant-looking woman called Becca. She checked the machines, took Lady Susan's pulse and smiled reassuringly at them.

"She's only asleep. You've tired her out, too much excitement, obviously!" She said this with a cheeky eyebrow raised in Connor's direction. "I'll find you a doctor to talk to, he should be on his rounds shortly." She bustled off.

Lord Ralph leaned back in the chair and looked slightly lost. Ella stood up.

"When the doctor comes around, he won't talk to you with us in the room. We'll hunt down this elusive coffee and bring you some. Are you hungry?"

"No, thank you – but coffee would be nice," said Lord Ralph, not taking his eyes from his wife's sleeping face. Ella nodded, and she and Connor went in search of a drink.

As they walked, she could sense Connor's blue gaze on her.

"What?" she said.

"I just thought... that you and Lord Ralph seem very close."

Ella bristled, and he hastened to add, "And close to Lady Susan, too. I'm sorry, I thought you were just another member of staff, but you're not, are you?"

"Look, a coffee machine! I imagine it's vile, but at least we can get Lord Ralph a drink. Do you want to risk it? I probably will."

Connor shook his head and said nothing.

They'd reached the vending machine and Ella was fumbling for change when Connor said, "Look, I hope I wasn't out of line. You're obviously upset about Lady Susan, and I'm sorry for that."

Ella paused, wondering what to say.

"They've been very good to me since I started working here – enormously supportive. So I'm very fond of both of them."

"Yes, you said. I was clumsy, I'm sorry." Ella got the full blast of his blue eyes and softened.

"No problem, we're all on edge." She paused while the machine dribbled brown liquid into thin plastic cups, and then said, "I'm glad you liked your present."

"I can't tell you how much. It's glorious." His voice seemed to thrum through her ribs.

There was an awkward silence and then Ella nodded towards the closed door, indicating the plastic cups in her hands.

"Can you get the door?"

Love in a Mist

"How is Lady Susan?" Ella asked Lord Ralph a week later as he stared into the fire.

"She's unwell, Ella."

Ella waited, but no more information was forthcoming. She frowned.

"I'm sorry." It was all she could think of to say. His face, normally so calm, was savage.

"And so you should be!"

Ella stared.

"My wife is worn to the bone! And why is that, Ella? Eh?"

"I don't..."

"You knew how important the development was for her, but instead of supporting her, as you *should* have done, all that you cared about was that it might impact your plans for the estate!"

Ella was stunned, watching Lord Ralph's face take on an ugly red hue.

"And because you made that obvious, instead of involving you, she took on all the work herself! She's exhausted! Did you never think about how ridiculous it was that we didn't involve our estate manager in the re-design of the garden?"

Ella's mouth worked, but no sound came out. Tears welled in her eyes.

"My wife is ill because of *you,* Ella! I hope you're pleased with yourself!"

"That's so unfair!" she choked out.

"Is it? *Is it?*"

"Excuse me, but I couldn't help overhearing," said Connor, coming into the room, to Ella's horror. She swung away, humiliated and, unable to stop her tears, ran out of the door.

∼

Connor stood very still, listening to Lord Ralph breathing heavily. He could hear Ella's footsteps echoing down the hall, and then the main door to the manor slammed shut.

"This is none of your business!" Lord Ralph snarled at him. Connor fixed him with a glare.

"I'm sorry, but it is," Connor responded coldly. "Ella may not like my designs, but she'll do anything for Lady Susan – including working on the garden. If Lady Susan decided not to involve Ella, that was her decision. And I reckon if you asked her, she'd tell you so!"

Lord Ralph swelled as though he might explode and then, like a balloon with a pinprick, he shrank, sinking into his armchair. He put his head in his hands.

"I know, I know..." he whispered. "I've just been so worried."

"We're *all* worried. And I barely know the woman."

That drew a reluctant snort of laughter from Lord Ralph, and he straightened a little.

"She's a force of nature, your wife. I doubt she'll be easily beaten by this, you know," Connor commented, coming to sit opposite him. Lord Ralph nodded.

"You're right. She is. But she's never been ill before. Nor been in hospital. I don't think she's even had her appendix out."

Connor kept quiet and watched as Lord Ralph stared at the fire again. A few moments passed and then Lord Ralph heaved a sigh.

"I'd offer you a drink, but I know you probably won't take me up on it," he said, and Connor laughed, shaking his head.

"I might keep you company for a small snifter. Just a splash, mind!" he said as Lord Ralph leapt out of his chair and towards the sideboard.

As Lord Ralph handed him a glass with slightly more than a splash in it, Connor said, "You're going to need to speak with Ella."

"I know."

"And soon. She was very upset."

Lord Ralph nodded and took a sip.

"She hates to cry in public. I'll give her some time to recover and then I'll walk over to the cottage..."

"Is crying such a weakness?" Connor asked.

"It is in Ella's mind. When she came here for her job interview, we offered her the role on the spot – she was streets ahead of everyone else we'd seen – and she burst into tears. I wasn't sure what was worse – her tears or her cringing embarrassment. She prides herself on her professionalism, you see?"

Connor nodded slowly.

"Why was getting the job so emotional?"

Lord Ralph glanced at him and shook his head.

"Some personal stuff. We were her escape. Not sure it's my place to discuss it."

Woman of mystery, thought Connor, his interest rocketing. He managed a casual shrug.

"I wouldn't dream of prying. But Ella's passionate about this place, isn't she? For such a... quiet woman, there's a lot of feeling there." Connor changed his mind about describing Ella as 'cold'. Certainly not after the last hour.

"She's worked miracles on the estate," Lord Ralph said quietly, looking a little shamefaced. "Now I think about it, it seems ridiculous to blame her for what has obviously been Susan's choice. What was I thinking?"

Connor took another tiny sip of his drink and put down his glass.

"You're anxious, that's all. Will she be at her cottage, rather than the office?" he asked. Lord Ralph considered.

"Yes. She'll have gone to make sure she looks her usual self."

"Shall we go and find her?"

~

Ella finished splashing her eyes with water and grabbed a towel to sink her face into. She drew a deep breath, willing herself to get a grip.

Had this all been her fault? The guilt swelled in her and nausea rose in her throat. She gulped. God, what a performance! she thought as she peered at herself in the mirror. Her nose was still pink. Sniffing, she went to her bedroom drawers and pulled them open, searching for some make-up.

"Camouflage," she muttered as she rooted through the contents.

She blew out her cheeks and began to apply the foundation to her skin, thinking absently that it was a while since she'd worn slap like this.

She was pulling the cover off a brush to apply blusher when she heard the bell at her front door. She wanted very much for it *not* to be Connor. That was a humiliation she could do without.

So when she pulled the door open, she was both startled and disappointed. Disappointed because Connor was indeed there, large and watchful. Startled, because with him on her doorstep, was Lord Ralph.

"Oh!" she said.

"Can you spare us a minute, Ella?" said Connor. She nodded, mutely, and held open the door.

In her living room, Lord Ralph was twisting his hands and he turned to face her.

"You have my unreserved apology, Ella. I know you must be worried about Susan and I shouldn't take out my personal anxiety on you like that," Lord Ralph said at once. His voice cracked a little and she found herself tearing up again.

She was so surprised, she didn't say anything for a moment, and then, seeing his concerned face, gave a small smile and waved away his apology.

"I should have been more diplomatic with Lady Susan about the plans – and I wasn't, I'm afraid."

"You feel very strongly about the whole estate. I know you have plans for it," agreed Lord Ralph, and she nodded.

"I do. But I'd be gutted if Lady Susan thought I wasn't on her side – and she obviously doesn't. I'm truly sorry, and if I can do anything to help, you only have to ask."

"You're wonderful. I should not have implied that you were anything to do with her illness – I know she relies heavily on you," Lord Ralph said, and patted her awkwardly on the shoulder. Then he took a deep breath. "I know you have a lot on, keeping the estate running and the tenants onside with the build, but I'm really not sure how much Susan will be able to do if she gets out of hospital -"

"*When* she gets out of hospital," interjected Connor.

"Yes, of course. *When* she gets out of hospital. It's pneumonia, so it'll be some time before she's at full strength. Would you be able to help, Ella?"

"There's no discussion. Of course I'll help! What can I do?"

She swung around to face Connor, who gave her a brilliant smile.

"Pray for dry weather? Or you might see what other sponsorship you could wring out of the agency?"

Ella nodded vigorously.

"I also thought Lady Susan had an idea for a friends' scheme for the garden? And other ideas, too," Connor continued. "You'd have to talk to her, but knowing Lady Susan, it would be a *long* list."

This raised a smile from Lord Ralph, and Ella shot Connor a grateful look.

"I'll visit her this evening, and tell that you're taking over and that she's not to worry," Lord Ralph said, beginning to look much more like himself.

Ella smiled and wondered what she'd let herself in for.

14

"But of course! We'll be thrilled to come and talk to the WI about the designs and the benefits for the area, Mrs Tennyson," Ella said with more warmth than honesty. "All we ask is the opportunity to mention the Friends' Scheme. And if you know any local businesses that would be happy to contribute in any way..." She let the sentence trail delicately.

"I'm sure my husband's building firm can support some of the hard landscaping when the garden's a little further down the line." Mrs Tennyson, who Lady Susan had once described as all fur coat and no knickers, sounded reluctant down the phone.

"We're looking for businesses in the area to get involved, so if he'd like to discuss it with our project manager, Mike Stewart, I could pass on his details? But perhaps you'll want to consult with him first, to ensure his company has the capacity and the skills." Ella was pleased with her tone.

There was a silence over the line while Mrs Tennyson's pride in her husband's firm warred with her concern about promising too much. The former won.

"I'm sure Tennyson's can meet even the most demanding of briefs," she said, a little frostily.

Love in a Mist

"Of course! And we're so eager to include as many local companies as possible. It would seem a shame if one of the area's most reputable firms wasn't on our list of suppliers. Did I mention that we're writing to the Duchess of Cambridge to be a patron, given her intense interest in gardens and young people's education?"

There was a gasp down the line and Ella put a tick next to the name on the long, long list she had. Ella disconnected the call and rubbed her hot ear. Two weeks in and she was pleased with what she'd achieved. Invitations for the fundraising ball were in the mail, she had suppliers lined up to provide drink, flowers and furniture, and she was pulling every string she could to get a live band purely for the honour of performing here. A professional one, obviously. It had to be a band – she couldn't imagine a disco in the great hall, the sound would be appalling...

She rose to her feet and stretched. Her eyes landed on the pile of postcards, with various elements of the garden design printed on them. She'd dragged a few words of explanation out of Connor for each element, and she felt smug about the result. She was also reluctantly impressed by the depth of thought that appeared to have gone into the design. Eventually, after a lot of pushing, Connor talked passionately and eloquently about the connections his very modern design had with the past. He talked about the conventions of the eighteenth-century garden that Ashton Manor would have had in the past, and how he had translated them into the current age. As he'd talked, Ella's interest in the garden had grown. After she'd got his comments for the copy, she'd crept back to the drawing room to look again at the model. To her surprise, elements of the design which had seemed outlandish, now seemed appropriate, even brilliant, as nods to the manor's history.

A knock at the door startled her out of her thoughts. Justin walked in.

"How goes it?" he asked, looking at the piles of paper on her normally tidy desk.

"Slow," she admitted. "I'm working my way down Lady Susan's never-ending list of contacts."

"Where are you?"

"About a fifth of the way down."

"Impressive. That's good going. How's everything else?"

"Piling up, but once I've got further, I'll stop and go back to the estate work. I just need to get a head start on the marketing..."

He sat in the armchair and frowned.

"Surely there's someone else who should do this? If you don't mind me saying, Ella, you're looking knackered!"

Was she? Probably no more knackered than Connor, she thought. She waved a hand, dismissively.

"I'll have plenty of time to sleep when the build is fully funded and we've got some people wanting to come to see it when it's finished."

"But do you believe it will be worth seeing?"

Ella thought.

"Yes, I think I do."

"You sound like you've had an almost Damascene conversion – have you?" Justin's grey-green eyes were curious. Ella looked squarely at him.

"It may not be to my taste. But Connor's an internationally acclaimed designer. Even if I don't like it, other people will."

Justin laughed.

"Goodness! Will we have peace breaking out soon?"

Ella laughed. "You never know! Are you here to talk food for the ball?" she asked.

"I am." He bent down to his file of papers and pulled out two sheets with different menus. "Our new housekeeper is turning out to be a gift from heaven," he said, as he passed them to her. "God knows how she'll produce this menu from the deplorable budget you've given me, but she assures me she can."

Ella cast her eyes over the menu, impressed – four courses and coffee for a cost of less than ten pounds per head.

"Looks brilliant. Do we have a veggie option?" He passed her another sheet of paper.

"I'll take the suggestions to Lady Susan this evening," Ella said.

Lady Susan would like that, an easy way to get her involved again without overloading her.

"She'll be back before the weekend, according to Lord Ralph." Justin looked rueful. "He's been following the cleaners around and wiping down the surfaces with a finger to check everything's spotless for her return. At this rate, I'll need to find a new cleaning firm as well if the housekeeper doesn't blow a fuse..."

Ella laughed and then caught sight of the clock.

"This is great, Justin, I'll let you know what she says."

"Sounds like my dismissal."

Ella smiled apologetically. "Sorry, I've got another call."

"Don't forget we were going for a drink, about a million years ago."

"I haven't forgotten, I've been busy. And knackered, as you pointed out."

"You need a break. How about this week?"

Ella thought. He was right. She could do with an evening of his light-hearted banter.

"How about Wednesday, after netball practice? We normally pile into the Golden Lion. About eight thirty?"

"I could come and cheer you on if you like?"

"The match starts at seven."

"I'll see if I can get to you by the start and if not I'll see you in the bar."

∼

"I didn't think I would have any visitors this evening!" Lady Susan said later that evening as Connor and Ella walked through the door.

"Now, why would you imagine that?" Connor smiled as he handed over a small box of very expensive chocolates.

"Oh, you spoil me! I'm sure I shouldn't..." Lady Susan exclaimed while pulling off the cellophane wrapper and opening the box. Ella blinked at the speed of her movements and then perched on the side of the bed, while Connor took the chair. A few pleasantries and then

Lady Susan fixed her eyes on Ella and asked how 'things were coming along'.

Ella smiled. She'd spent two hours sorting through Lady Susan's bulging file and the endless notes, letters, slips of paper, business cards and sketches that were most of its contents. There had been a separate plastic folder filled with printed emails, which seemed the biggest waste of paper Ella could imagine. But now she had a proper sense of her employer's vision for the garden. Lady Susan's personal stamp was all over the notes. She'd missed that sense of closeness, Ella reflected. She went through a few items, carefully chosen for maximum reassurance.

Lady Susan wrinkled her nose at the vegetarian menu but was all approving smiles at the chicken.

"I've never really understood vegetarians, I imagine they're rather lacking in vigour... you know, not getting enough vitamins," she said, while Ella, who was more vegetarian than meat-eating these days, kept quiet. A conversation about *that* wouldn't help Lady Susan's blood pressure.

"My sister Caitlin's almost exclusively vegetarian these days," said Connor unexpectedly. "Mammy was beside herself when Caitlin told the family at Christmas – when the house was chock-full with ham and beef and goose!"

Lady Susan passed the menus back to Ella.

"Really? Yes, they'll be fine, Ella, thank you. Have you got a large family, Connor?"

He grinned. "Enormous, it is, six sisters and me. And seemingly a new niece and nephew every other month."

"I love a big family, although we weren't blessed with children of our own. Still, we borrow other people's so we can give them back when we've had enough." Lady Susan leaned back complacently and took another chocolate. "Your mother must have had so little time to focus on herself! I understand your father was a military man, so her hands were likely full in supporting him, let alone seven children!"

Ella was looking at Connor when Lady Susan finished speaking, so she saw his face change at the mention of his father. She was fascinated – it was as though someone had closed the curtains on the sun.

"Before I forget, Mike sends his regards and hopes you'll soon be back at the manor. When are you escaping?" he said.

As a conversation changer, it was fairly obvious, but Lady Susan let it pass. Ella was thoughtful as visiting time came to a close and she stored Connor's bleak look in her memory, wondering what had caused it.

～

"Well, we're top of the league with that win!" Jeanette said, well satisfied. Ella took a deep swig of her lime and soda and silently catalogued her aches and pains. Jeanette still looked fresh, to her irritation. The woman barely seemed to break sweat...

"Are you okay, Ella? You look tired, is everything all right?"

"God, not you too! I've had a stream of people telling me how knackered I look!" Ella looped her damp, black hair behind her ears and scowled.

"Well, you do! I'm keeping my fingers crossed that this is you having a wild time out of the office, but somehow I doubt it. So what *is* happening?" Jeanette settled back against the pub upholstery and waited. "To be honest, you've been acting weird since Christmas... Oh-hoo! What's that blush for?"

Ella picked up her glass and took another drink before answering.

"I'm working on the garden project and it's a lot of work on top of what I'm already doing. Apart from playing netball with you, I'm doing nothing *except* work at the moment, so you stop *imagining* nonsense, Jeanette!"

"But even when I came around on Boxing Day you were a bit distracted. I wondered if you were missing your mum, so I didn't say anything, but it wasn't that, was it? So... what?"

Jeanette was her dearest friend, and knew almost everything there was to know about her, Ella reasoned. So why would she be reluctant to tell her about the text exchange with Connor?

"Working with Connor McPherson is quite time consuming and truly, I'm running around from dawn to dusk," she said.

"And Christmas?"

Ella paused.

"I gave Connor McPherson a gift before we left for Christmas," she began slowly. "You know, just like I do with all the *other* staff members? Anyway, he texted me on Christmas Day to thank me and it was a bit of a surprise."

"And?"

"Well, nothing," she evaded. "It seems to have made a difference to us working together. It's slightly less... full of friction than it was. Which is a good job, considering the amount of work there is to do!"

"I would have thought less friction would have made the work easier!" Jeanette commented, eyeing her speculatively.

Ella said nothing.

"Is lover boy joining us?" asked Jeanette, interrupting her memory of Connor's text about buying her a gift on instinct.

"Yes, he was chatting up the other side's centre when I left!"

"Really, Ella? You could do so much better!" Jeanette was scathing.

Ella shook her head.

"He's alright," she said easily. "He can be really good company when he chooses."

At that moment, Justin breezed through the door.

"I wondered if you'd got a better offer..." Ella teased, scrambling to her feet, and looking for her bag. "What can I get you? Same again, Jeanette?"

Ella went to the bar, followed by Justin. The barmaid spotted them walking across and practically pushed her colleague out of the way to serve them. Ella remembered that the young woman was one of Justin's flirts.

The barmaid smiled widely, fixed her eyes on Justin and said in a slightly breathy voice, "What can I get for you?"

Justin's eyes drifted down to the neckline of her top and then flicked back up to the barmaid's face.

"Nothing, it's not my round," he said, smiling.

Love in a Mist

The girl checked a little, and Ella stared at Justin's tone. She rushed to fill the silence.

"Can we have a lime and soda, a half of lager, and a pint of your best bitter, please?"

The girl mumbled something and, scarlet-cheeked, swung away to get the drinks. Justin leaned his elbows back against the wooden bar and surveyed the room. When Ella had his drink, she pushed it at him.

"Here, take this. I can manage the rest, you sit down."

"No, I'll stay and help," he said lazily. When the girl turned up with the last drink, her face was pale where it had been red.

Ella suddenly realised that beneath the carefully applied make-up, she couldn't have been more than nineteen. Justin took two of the drinks and walked back to the table, while the barmaid stared after him.

"Thank you," said Ella quietly.

Jeanette was disagreeing with him over something, but Ella watched the barmaid say something to her colleague and disappear.

"Didn't you used to date the barmaid? Amber, isn't it?" she asked, butting into the conversation. Justin shrugged and picked up his pint.

"I saw her a couple of times, she was a bit clingy for me."

"How old is she?"

"Not sure. She told me she was twenty-four."

Jeanette's eyes narrowed.

"She's nineteen, tops. Too young for you, surely, Justin?"

"Can I help it if women find me irresistible?"

Jeanette snorted.

"You were rather rough on her," Ella observed. "If you spoke to me like that, I'd thump you."

Justin looked bemused. "Are we going to spend all evening talking about the barmaid? I met her a couple of times, we had a few laughs, she got too clingy, we stopped. Simples."

There was a silence, and Jeanette excused herself.

"How was Lady Susan?" he asked, watching her stalk away.

Ella told him, but she was uncomfortable with Justin's treatment of the young woman behind the bar. So, it seemed, was Jeanette, who came back from the loo after a few minutes and put her coat on.

"I'll call you in the week, Ella." She stooped to give Ella a kiss.

"You're not leaving because of me, are you?" Justin smiled.

"No, I'm leaving because of the barmaid," Jeanette said and stalked out.

Justin stilled and then he attempted to laugh it off.

"My round, I think."

15

Connor's stomach flipped at the figures that Ella pushed towards him.

"Glory be, Ella, this is amazing! You've really got pledges of money from all these businesses?"

She nodded, and Connor noticed the flush of what he assumed to be pleasure spread across her cheeks. She had pale skin, almost like alabaster, he thought. If he didn't know better, he'd have thought she was Irish, with that colouring.

But he *didn't* know better, he reminded himself. She was a mystery to him. After a brief unbending after Christmas and during Lady Susan's illness, the estate manager was now back to her cool, controlled self. She was as aloof as she'd ever been. He'd swear even her accent had sharpened.

"We've been sending out the letters of agreement over the past few weeks, and so far there's an excellent return rate, signed and agreed," she said. "Not all the offers are for cash, some are for materials. Mike did an excellent job of identifying what you'll need for the build, and he seems happy with what I've pulled in so far."

"Aye, I should say so!" Connor removed his gaze from the dark grey eyes which he thought might be mocking him back to the spreadsheet. He rubbed his beard absently and totted up the figures automatically as he scanned the list.

"This is worth nearly a hundred thousand," he said quietly.

"Yes. Well, it is part of my role here," she said. "I persuade people to part with money as we normally raise the rents every few years. It doesn't always go down well, so I suppose you could call it a skill."

Connor sat back and considered her, ponytail in place, dressed conservatively as always in a navy skirt and cream blouse. The vision of her in a red wig with a daring Halloween décolletage drifted into his head and he shook it out immediately. If he hadn't seen her with his own eyes, he would have dismissed it as ridiculous that she could look that... alluring. He forced his thoughts back to the conversation.

"This will give us chance to bring forward some of the features we'd originally shelved to phase two," he said, and she nodded.

"By the way, did you see this?" Ella turned to her neat desk and picked up one of the financial pages from *The Times*.

He scanned the page, his pulse rate ticking up even reading the business headlines. He drew a deep breath and tried to focus.

"What am I looking at?"

"This!" Ella pointed a slender finger to a column which talked about a rumoured takeover of a cereal manufacturer, Elite Foods, by one of the big food conglomerates.

Connor frowned, puzzled.

"Isn't Kool Crisp owned by Elite Foods? I wondered if any takeover might threaten the sponsorship deal?" Her voice was gently impatient.

Connor thought about it for a few minutes and then put the page down.

"It might, but I doubt it. It's only a rumour of a takeover, not reported news, and anyway, the sponsorship agreement should have been identified as part of the due-diligence and honoured as a commitment. I think the lawyers got involved."

"Hmm. I'll go through the file, I missed that."

"Well, better to be sure, certainly. But the chairman seemed very keen on the idea."

She raised her eyebrows.

"I do run my own business!" he protested, stung. "Successfully. So I'm not clueless, but I assumed Lady Susan would dot the i's and cross the t's – *I'm* trying to get the damned thing built!"

He rose to his feet, his sunny mood evaporated. Ella looked contrite.

"I didn't mean anything," she said swiftly. He ignored her and was almost at the door when her hand shot out and grabbed his arm. "Connor, don't storm out!"

He paused, not looking at her, but staring at the door. He felt the pressure of her slender hand and the warmth of it through his shirtsleeve.

"I know it's been difficult, I know you and the crew have been working almost round the clock to make up the time," she said, her voice low and soft. "I'm sorry, I truly didn't mean to offend you. Please accept my apology."

He closed his eyes briefly and, unable to stop himself, rested his head on the door panel. Her fingers tightened around his arm and she pulled him gently from the door.

"Ah, I've had a few late nights, I'm touchy at the moment," Connor said, rubbing his face with his hands. "But we're getting on top of it. We've managed to scrape a few days back in the schedule."

"That's splendid news." Her voice was grave, sincere. Beneath the gaze of her dark grey eyes, something loosened in him. He nodded, and she smiled.

"I'll look for the legalities and tell you when I find them," she said. He missed the warmth of her hand as she let him go. He turned to leave.

"Hang on," she said. He paused, wondering what was coming. "Mike might want to see this, to see where his supplies are coming from." She passed him the spreadsheet.

He managed a smile and went to give Mike some positive news for a change.

Ella clenched her fists at the sight of Lady Susan, so pale, and even thinner than she had been. She stopped herself from rushing forwards with everyone else – Justin, Theresa Arnold, the new housekeeper, even Lord Ralph. Heaven knew that Lord Ralph of all people should know how much Lady Susan loathed any form of fussing. As if hearing Ella's thoughts, Lady Susan caught Ella's eye from a distance and a wry smile crossed her face. She had always used her slight figure to fool people into doing things she was perfectly capable of doing herself, but Ella knew this would be too much.

When Lady Susan was installed by the fire in the drawing room, Ella gently took charge.

"Justin, I wonder if the footstool from the library would be a good idea? Keep Lady Susan's feet out of the draught. And what about something tasty for lunch? Ms Arnold, I hear you bake a mean quiche? Lady Susan, does that sound all right? Or would you prefer soup?"

"Oh God, no. The soup I've eaten over the past month... indescribable!" Lady Susan gave a delicate shudder.

"I'll be right back," said Justin and was out of the door within seconds. Ms Arnold bustled off to the kitchen to rustle up 'something nice'. Then it was quiet, and Lord Ralph hovered over his wife.

"Why don't you sit down? Then Lady Susan won't need to crane her neck to look at you," Ella suggested. Lord Ralph was suddenly aware he was being managed and humphed a bit, but to Ella's relief, sat down.

Lady Susan, who was already looking tired by the twenty-five-minute journey from hospital, sighed and looked up at Ella from beneath her lashes.

"Thank you, Ella."

Ella smiled and took the stool from Justin as he came quickly through the door. She told him that Ms Arnold was rustling up some lunch, but would tea be possible too?

He bustled away to organise it, and Lord Ralph chortled.

"Masterly, my dear – or should I say mistressly?"

"I think it would be good to have a bit of quiet," Ella said calmly,

Love in a Mist

putting the stool under her feet. "Even with a private room, hospitals can be incredibly noisy."

Lady Susan exhaled. "I can't tell you how good it is to be home."

Ella bent to give her a hug. "It's great to have you back," she said in a barely audible voice which shook. Lady Susan patted her arm.

"Oh no, I'm not ready to shuffle off this mortal coil yet... oh, how wonderful – tea! Thank you so much, Justin."

Justin smiled broadly and put the tray down with a flourish. Ella sank into the background while cups and saucers were passed around and Lord Ralph, after a few moments, gently dismissed him on an errand to check Lady Susan's bedroom was in order in case she wanted to rest.

Justin disappeared and Lady Susan turned to Ella and said, "So, my dear, how are you getting on?"

Ella had expected this, and – as she'd done when visiting Lady Susan in hospital – had a selection of achievements to talk to her about. She spoke of Tennyson's building firm, the deal with one of the county's largest garden centres, and the growing numbers on the Friends' list. She was about to talk about the fundraising ball when Connor arrived.

He strode into the room, a look of delight on his face as he saw Lady Susan.

"Aren't you a sight for sore eyes?" he said, as Ella hid a wince. He stopped and grinned at her. "Too familiar?"

"Oh, ignore her, Connor," said Lady Susan, as she accepted his kiss on the cheek. "How are you?"

"More to the point, how are you?" Connor asked, shaking Lord Ralph's hand.

"Feeling much better now I'm home."

Lunch arrived, the lightest of golden quiches and a small salad. Lady Susan and Lord Ralph ate on their laps, and Ella watched both of them clear their plates while Connor and she exchanged platitudes. There was a pause in the conversation, and she found his shrewd eyes on her.

Finally, Lady Susan sat back with a sigh of pleasure and Ella took the tray from her. A yawn caught Lady Susan.

"Oh, excuse me! I'm sorry, I beg your pardon!"

As if by magic, Justin appeared at the door saying that all was ready.

"Perhaps a bit of a lie down?" Ella twinkled at her, and she laughed.

"Damn it, I feel about a hundred and eight! Yes, I think I will take to my bed for an hour. My dear, could you help me?"

Lord Ralph leapt to his feet and together, they moved slowly out of the room. There was a pause.

"You know her very well, don't you?" Connor said.

Ella shrugged and wound her ponytail around her fingers.

"We work closely together – except on the garden. Lord Ralph was right – I should have been more supportive, rather than flouncing off."

Connor made a dismissive noise.

"Sure, Ella, I can't imagine you flouncing under any conditions," he smiled, and Ella's stomach flipped, reminding her she hadn't eaten. "You seem very in tune with each other."

She stared out of the window and for a full minute, there was nothing apart from the ticking of the clock in the room.

"She's been like a mother to me since... since my own mother died."

Connor was quiet, a big presence coiled in one of the massive armchairs.

"I get no special treatment, but she knows how fond I am of her and I believe she's very fond of me too," Ella added after a pause.

"I can see that. Are you okay now? I knew you were worried but didn't appreciate how much."

She nodded.

"I'm feeling much more myself now she's home. I understand from the doctors that a full recovery will take a while – about six months."

"So – we'll be working together for a while?"

Ella looked up at the smile in his voice, even though he had a straight face. A spark of mischief lit up in her.

"Looks like it. How are you in full evening dress?"

He looked appalled, and she laughed.

∼

Connor knocked softly on the door to Ella's office and carefully turned the handle. It was empty. He could have emailed the latest schedule, clutched in his hand. Damn, he should have emailed it, she would *want* it on email.

Uncharacteristically indecisive, he was wondering about writing a Post-it note and leaving it on her desk when Justin walked in. Justin halted, surprised, and then he smiled.

"McPherson, looking for Ella?"

No, I've come to ransack her office, Connor thought, immediately irritated, and recognising the feeling added to his irritation.

"I'm just dropping off the new schedule – we've made up some time." Did he sound defensive?

"Excellent!" said Justin. "Thank heavens we've had better weather."

Always the weather with the English, Connor smiled to himself, his ill temper disappearing.

"I'm hopeful we'll make up more time next week if the forecast holds."

"Well, it would be nice to get rid of the floodlights. They make the peacocks very nervous."

Silence fell and the two men eyed one another.

"I don't suppose you know where Ella is? Or how long she'll be?" Connor asked.

"Not a clue, old chap."

Connor was enormously irritated when Justin sat in one of the armchairs in the office. Like he owned the place.

"I could tell her you called," Justin offered. Connor bristled.

"Thanks, *old bean*, I'll email her."

Justin grinned, and Connor wondered why he didn't like the handsome manager. Maybe it was because Justin *was* handsome? A tense silence fell.

Ella tumbled through the door, stopping short as she realised she had visitors.

"Goodness. Is there a queue?"

Justin rose to his feet.

"I'm here about the arrangements for the ball. Mr McPherson has a piece of paper to give you."

Ella tuned in to the sudden tension and Connor saw her roll her eyes.

"An updated schedule." He placed it on her desk.

"Oh! Thank you. Was there anything else?" Ella cast a glance over the schedule. Not that I'm willing to discuss in front of Justin the Jerk.

"Nothing important, I'll catch you later."

"You've made up some days! Brilliant work!"

Connor basked in her sudden smile, and they locked eyes for a few seconds.

"All we need now is to recover another six *weeks* and we'll be ready to open," Justin put in with a laugh. Connor's ears caught Ella's sigh, and he turned to leave.

"I'll email."

As Connor closed the door, he heard Justin say,

"Another admirer to add to your list, Ella?"

Connor snarled and went to wreak havoc on the garden.

16

Ella was swearing underneath her breath as she dumped the contents of the drawer on the desk and riffled through them.

"Goddamn, where the hell *is* it?" she muttered, her quick hands sorting through the documents.

She'd been searching for the last hour, since the phone call. That gently apologetic call from Elite Food's marketing department, that *courtesy* call. When she recognised the caller her initial sense of doom grew from about the second minute of the conversation.

"It *must* be here, surely..."

Another hour later, she conceded defeat. The contract between Kool Crisp and Ashton Manor, if it existed at all, was not in the paperwork she had. So God only knew who would have it. Lady Susan was not blessed with an administrative bent and Connor was frankly uninterested, so that left only Ashton Manor's lawyers. She picked up the phone to Clayton Arbuthnot, the head of their legal team.

Ten minutes later, she was staring out of the window with blind eyes. The sunshine seemed to mock her. Moving as if she had aged twenty years, she sat down and tried to think what to do. She rapidly did some calculations with the budget.

Wearily, she picked up her phone.

"Hi, it's Ella," she said to Connor's voicemail. "We've got a problem. Call me when you get this, we need to get together today."

～

"What the *fuck*?"

Ella winced at the thunder in Connor's voice and saw Lady Susan's mouth tremble.

"But we've committed time, and men – they can't *do* this to us, just pull the funding!" she said, near to tears and pulling at a lace handkerchief. Justin, who was looking grim-faced, leaned over and patted her hand.

"Look, without a signed contract, there's nothing we can do to make Elite Foods honour the commitment," Ella said loudly, to make herself heard over Connor's muttering. "We'd be better served by thinking about how we can make up the shortfall in funding."

"But how can we?" Lady Susan's voice came out like a thread. "Ella, we're down *a quarter of a million* pounds!"

Ella knew. She'd spent the last hour and a half with Mike and the budget, and they'd cut the figures they had in a hundred different ways to see if they could reduce the deficit. He was still, she noted, looking shell-shocked.

"Can't we push more of the work into phase two?" Ella asked. "We know we need to get the arbour finished because that's where the wedding will be in August. We also need to prioritise the children's area, because that will bring us revenue in the summer holidays."

"How much were we expecting from the ball, Ella?" Justin asked, his voice cool and calm.

"I'd estimated about sixteen thousand, nothing like we need. I might squeeze more out of that by adding a charity auction..."

"How about giving naming rights to some of the walks and beds?" Mike suggested.

Ella winced.

"We're trying *not* to change the garden into sponsorship city, but yes, that's a possibility."

A silence fell on the group. Connor looked... lost, Ella thought. She couldn't blame him. God alone knew what impact the loss of the sponsorship would have on the build.

"Have we sold all the tickets for the ball?" Lady Susan asked, and Ella nodded. "So what can we do to get our guests to part with more money?"

"We need television involved," Justin said. "Get a channel down here, talking to Lady Susan and Lord Ralph, following the development of the garden, interviewing some sponsors, talking to local people, to Connor—"

"No." Connor's voice was flat and definite.

"Well, think about it a little before you dismiss it completely, Connor," Justin said testily.

"I won't put my staff on display for public consumption, and if anyone so much as points a camera at me, I walk."

Ella was taken aback. She was no lover of the limelight herself, but Connor's face looked set. Given the number of photos she had seen of the designer with various beautiful women draped over his arm, his reluctance surprised her.

Ella chewed her lip while twisting her ponytail around her fingers.

"I wonder if one of the gardening mags might be a better bet?" she said tentatively and rushed on as Connor drew breath to object. "We'll have more control that way and still reach our perfect target audience."

"They won't pay you as much as the TV – if at all." Justin's voice was dubious, and Mike nodded in agreement.

"Been involved in that stuff before and publishers view it as a benefit to be in the publication. Don't think they paid us a penny."

Lady Susan blew her nose defiantly.

"I will talk to Ralph," she said. "It was good advice, Ella and I was stupid enough to ignore it. I won't do that again."

With a sinking heart, Ella thought of the fund she had carefully built up over the past two years for improvements to the estate. But those improvements had waited this long, they would wait another year ... she could hear Lord Ralph saying it now.

"I know this is the last thing you want to do, Ella, but would you discuss a loan with Lord Ralph?" Lady Susan continued. Ella had no choice.

"Yes. It's our best option, short term," she agreed. "We can also try to replace the sponsorship – we had a list of companies to approach and we can revisit. I was also wondering if bringing forward the Friends' Scheme, might add a bit to the coffers in membership?"

Nods around the room. Ella made a note on her pad.

"I'll get some ideas about the best way to prioritise the build," Mike said, gloomily. "I'll develop another schedule."

"I'll see if there are any internal suppliers that might offer sponsorship," Justin said. "Ella's approached all the external contractors we use – I'll look at those we use in the manor. And what are *you* going to be doing, Mr McPherson?"

Connor peered down his impressive nose at Justin.

"Given I've been working for nothing for the past two months, I'll carry on as I am."

Ella gaped, and Justin looked shocked. He was working for nothing? She glanced at Lady Susan, who'd gone pink.

"I'll let you know what Ralph says, Ella," Lady Susan put in quickly. "I'm not suggesting for one moment that the estate should bail us out completely, but it will tide us over."

Everyone pushed their chairs back, but Connor sat unmoving. Justin raised his eyebrows, and Ella nodded towards the door. Justin left with Lady Susan, closing the door with a click.

Ella sat down again and faced the big Irishman across the table.

∼

"This is a nightmare," he breathed, without looking at her.

"It's certainly not great, but nobody's died. Having two hundred and fifty thousand suddenly wiped from the budget isn't ideal, but we *have* a plan."

He stared at her.

"Isn't *ideal*?"

She shrugged.

"Okay, typical British understatement. Losing the sponsorship sucks, and yes, it will impact everything you're working towards, and yes, it will be a nightmare – but we'll explore every other avenue to replace the money. I imagine it will come out of the estate coffers if Lord Ralph doesn't agree to additional borrowing from the bank."

Goddamn it, she thought bitterly. But she pushed those feelings aside and concentrated on Connor as he stared, unfocused, into the distance.

Ella stopped herself from touching his shoulder. She wasn't sure how to deal with him, this prickly Irishman. Positivity might help.

"The weather really had it in for you, didn't it, at the start? But thank God the rain has eased up. And you've made amazing progress since the end of October."

He shrugged.

"But progress will come to a halt unless we get more money," he replied flatly.

"Hmm. Is that why you've not taken a fee for two months?" He stared coldly at her. "Well?" she asked again, not cowed.

He scowled, and Ella kept her eyes on his face. After a moment, he shrugged.

"I decided my fees could keep a dozen workmen on for another couple of months. Being paid's not the issue. I've enough money." Ella quirked a brow.

"Yes, I hear you're quite successful in some circles."

He stopped short at her dry tone and shot her a glance.

"I'm more bothered about my reputation than the money."

"Isn't it strong enough to survive this?"

He snorted.

"Yes, but all that might change if I screw up on this project. I've always gone my own way as a designer, and that's made me a lot of enemies in the profession. There'll be people watching and waiting, sharpening their knives."

Ella knew. She'd read the reviews, and indeed, not everyone appreciated Connor's designs. But that wasn't the point.

"But this is now not just about you, Connor. It's about *us*," Ella objected with emphasis. "*We* – not just you! Ashton Manor can't afford to screw up. This is costing a small fortune and we must get something good out of it."

"Do you not think I know that?"

"Which is why we're exploring other funding options, and whatever happens we'll have *something* completed by the wedding!" Ella continued, as though he'd not spoken. "Good God, if you can recover the schedule from the bloody weather, coping with less money will be a piece of cake!"

He gave a terse laugh.

"Ah, you're a determined ray of sunshine, aren't you?"

"I understand smiling uses less energy and muscles than frowning. And now I'm properly involved, despite our disagreements, we need to work together. So I need to forget that I hate your design and you need to forget that too and let me *help*."

He glanced up, surprised. She stared steadily back at him as his eyes searched her face, and then he laughed again.

"Surely that will be painful for both of us. But – needs must when the Devil drives?"

She smiled briefly. He was silent for a long moment and then nodded. More of her than she imagined was relieved at the ceasefire. So she screwed up her courage.

"You look tired. I suppose I understand why, but really, can't you delegate more?"

"Are you turning into my mother or a management consultant?"

His face had closed up, but she bristled at his dismissive tone.

"Well, if we *are* going to get through this, we need the principal – that's you, currently – to be standing. Call it risk management, rather than management consultancy."

For a tense moment, she thought he would ignore her.

"Okay, advice noted. Is that all, Ms Sanderson?" She pursed her lips in annoyance and watched him lope from the room.

17

Ella spat out the piece of plastic in her mouth, looked at her chewed pen and threw it into the bin in disgust. She'd better check her mouth wasn't blue with biro ink.

She sighed at the list. Almost done – with this list of suppliers, anyway. They'd been generous with the auction prizes, she thought, faintly surprised. She'd known that the manor had several loyal relationships with companies, but she hadn't realised how fondly her employers were viewed.

She stared into the small fire blazing merrily in her office grate and after a few moments, realised how distracted she was. She tutted to herself.

"For God's sake, Ella, get a grip!" she muttered to herself, picking up her papers from the desk and shuffling them into a neat pile. She sat down with another list and took another pen. Despite her best efforts, her thoughts skittered away from the job in hand.

Connor's invitation to dinner had been a huge surprise.

If you're so concerned about keeping me upright, perhaps you ought to drop by for dinner to check I'm eating, the email had said. *Would Thursday suit?*

When she'd seen him, she asked if he was serious, and his blue eyes had dared her to refuse.

She couldn't wear the black top, ran the commentary in her head; it was too low. Jeans might be too casual – after all, it wasn't a social dinner, really, not in her head anyway. She wasn't quite sure *what* kind of dinner it was if she was honest. Her principal aim was to make sure the bloody irritating man stopped work, *ate* something and stayed well enough to finish that travesty of a garden...

Ella's eyes glazed over and she bit her lip.

"What's up, Ella? You look anxious," said Justin, suddenly poking his head around the door. She started.

"Just wondering whether we'll have enough auction prizes to raise the money," Ella said immediately. Justin knew nothing about the dinner invitation from Connor and it would stay that way.

"Let's see," Justin said easily, leaning over her shoulder.

Ella stiffened as she felt the heat of his body against her back. She leaned away while thrusting the list to one side. When he adjusted to read it, she slipped out of her chair.

"Tea?" she said, as his eyes followed her. He shook his head and glanced back at the list.

"Looks like you've sucked dry my best suppliers." His voice was wry.

"I wouldn't *quite* put it that way," she protested. "But people have been incredibly generous."

"Then let's hope people feel reckless when the bidding opens."

Ah, okay. You're in that kind of mood, thought Ella. She kept quiet.

"Actually, I wondered if I might provide a bit of glamour for the event," he said, throwing the paper back onto her desk. She tipped her head to one side, enquiring.

"Before I came into this role, I trained as an actor," he continued. The statement surprised Ella; he'd never spoken of this before. "I know Cathy Mason and I was going to approach her to see if she would lend us her support by attending the ball. She's local to the area, you know?"

Love in a Mist

"I had no idea!" Ella stared at him. "God, that would be wonderful!"

"I'll call her. She can only say no."

He beamed at her. "I was wondering when we might go for dinner," Justin added. "You always seem to be busy with other things."

"Well, yes..." she gestured towards the desk full of papers.

"I was hoping we might manage this week, actually."

Ella shook her head.

"Not this week, I'm afraid. I have netball and..."

She stopped.

"And?" Justin's eyebrow tweaked.

"I'm busy."

"You're very bad for my ego! Are you avoiding me?" Justin gave a passable impression of being hurt.

"Your ego is robust enough, Justin! Next week is better for me."

He laughed. "Damn, you know me too well... How about Tuesday?"

"All right."

"Are you okay if I pick the restaurant?"

"As long as buying a bottle of wine won't require me to take out a mortgage," Ella warned, knowing Justin's expensive tastes.

He left smiling, and she was thoughtful. She'd have to watch that Justin wasn't getting the wrong idea. And keep an eye on her diary. Robust as Justin's ego was, he'd not take kindly to being one of several suitors.

∼

Ella knocked smartly on the door to Daffodil Cottage at seven o'clock the following evening. She combed her ponytail with her fingers and flipped it over her shoulder. Through the wavy glass of the front door, she could see Connor's massive frame move into the hall. A moment later, he threw open the door.

He wore a cream linen shirt and dark green corduroy trousers, and his hair was neat. She thought he'd trimmed his beard. He smiled, and she mentally shook herself for staring.

"Ella! Punctual to the minute! Come in, come in..."

Ella shrugged off her padded jacket and tried to hand over the wine she'd brought, getting in a bit of a muddle as she did so. He laughed and relieved her of the bottle.

"Sit yourself down," he said, gesturing to the two huge armchairs by the fire. "I'll get you a glass, shall I?"

She called her thanks, sinking into an armchair and sniffing the rich scent of meat and herbs. She asked him what was in the oven as he handed her the glass of red wine.

"Lasagne, so I hope you're not on any ridiculous diet," he said, flopping into the chair opposite. She laughed.

"No, thankfully! Aren't you having wine?" Connor had a tumbler of what looked like water. He shook his head.

"I'm off the sauce for a while," was all he said, and Ella was too polite to ask further questions, so she sipped her wine and knew after the first mouthful that this was not the bottle she had brought.

"This is delicious, what is it?" she asked.

"Mourvèdre. I brought some back from California last year."

"Seems a shame you're not drinking it!"

"I have a couple of cases. I'll get to it, eventually. And I like to serve my guests with good wine. I'm glad it's to your taste."

She took another sip of the silky, rich wine.

"Mmm. I should say so."

He grinned and rose from his chair.

"Can I do anything?" Ella called, watching him lope away like a big cat.

"No. Just make yourself comfy. It'll be another fifteen minutes yet."

She cradled her glass in her fingers and looked around. Connor had brought in a few things to the cottage that rendered it unfamiliar to her; brightly coloured rugs, some wonderful natural pieces of wood, polished and smoothed so that the warm grain glowed, and one or two photos. One caught her eye, and she rose and picked it up. She recognised Jonas Keane.

Love in a Mist

Two pairs of laughing eyes challenged whoever was taking the photograph, and Keane's arm was casually thrown around Connor's shoulders. She saw a Christmas tree in the background and wondered if had been the Christmas just past. Their bright smiles shone from the photograph, but she saw tiny lines of strain in Connor's face which made her pause.

A noise from the kitchen made her hastily replace it on the bookshelf and sit down again, feeling as if she had been prying. Then she realised that he was singing to himself. Strangely, she did that too.

Connor came in with a big bowl of salad and some bread. She breathed in.

"Is that garlic bread?"

"Sure it is. Do you like it?"

"I do indeed. I rarely eat it."

"Why's that?"

"Well, I try not to reek of garlic for meetings." She listened to the words coming out of her mouth and thought how feeble she sounded. Connor tweaked an eyebrow.

"Is that so?"

He said no more, but she immediately felt an idiot. She stared into the fire.

"My ma always suggested a glass of milk after eating onions and garlic to cleanse your breath," Connor said, before returning to the kitchen.

Milk?

"Come and sit at the table, and forget about your bloody meetings," Connor's voice interrupted the thoughts chasing around her head.

As they ate, Ella observed him covertly, seeing the lines around his eyes, the slight hollows in his face, the tension around the shoulders.

"This is delicious," she said, after a few mouthfuls. She wasn't joking. The food was sublime, the beef sauce thick and fragrant with herbs, the bechamel sauce creamy and with a slight tang of strong cheese. He grinned, picking up a piece of bread and tearing it with long, strong fingers.

"Not too much garlic?" he teased.

"No, just right," she said, refusing to rise to the bait, which made him grin even more. He topped up her glass and Ella thought the silence was a good one as they ate.

Conversation was hesitant, rather than stilted. They talked of his time in Argentina the previous year, of his enormous family, about his fiddling – "Just a hobby but I enjoy messing around". They talked about her role, about netball. Ella was careful about her story – just enough to keep the conversation equal. She thought he might be doing the same. She spoke in general terms of her time at university and how she came to be at the manor.

As she wiped her plate clean with another piece of bread, she commented on how nice it was to be cooked for.

"And you're doing this in a good cause, too," he said.

"What?"

"Aren't you making sure I'm not fading away before your very eyes?"

Ella chuckled.

"Protecting the principal, I think they call it."

Connor clicked his tongue in amused exasperation.

"I'm glad to have you as a dinner guest, but don't be thinking I need protection! I'm fine!"

Ella picked up her glass with a sigh.

"*All* of the garden crew have been under a great deal of pressure. First the rain, then the money – no, hear me out, Connor! The schedule is shot to bits and we're needing to scrape together cash to pay to deliver it on time. *Anyone* would be feeling it, let alone you."

"I'm grand."

"Well, I just want you to know that if you want to... oh, I don't know! Vent, be angry, be frustrated, or just burst into unmanly tears, please come to me."

"That's very altruistic of you, considering you had a powerful reaction against the design and believe that it will empty the estate's coffers. Surely it's a huge conflict of interest for you?"

"My personal preferences have nothing to do with it," Ella said calmly, aware as she did so that he was right – she was conflicted. "I just want to make sure we deliver *something*. If only for Jonas Keane's wedding."

Connor stared and then stood up abruptly, and without thinking, she grabbed his wrist.

"Connor, wait! What's the matter?"

"Have you finished eating?" he said politely, and frustrated, she released his wrist and sat back.

"Yes, thank you. That was delicious," she said, equally polite.

Connor gathered plates, and on edge, she followed him into the kitchen with the salad bowl. He turned to face her.

"I appreciate you're trying to be helpful. But I don't need your help, Ella. I've delivered hundreds of gardens. Discounting the weather, this one won't be any different. I know we're running out of lives on this build, but I have the luck of the Irish."

Ella weighed her words carefully.

"I'm not saying you won't succeed *without* my help, Connor. I'm saying it's there if you want it."

He looked at her for a long, long time and Ella sought for something to say that would convince him that truly, regardless of what she thought about the garden, she was on his side.

"I care very much for Lady Susan and Lord Ralph and I want the garden to be a success, for their sake, if not for the future of the estate."

She watched his strong face and saw his shoulders relax.

"I know. And I'm grateful for the work you're doing on the fundraising. We'll definitely need the money," he said finally. She let go a breath and smiled.

"Well – remember what I said, won't you?"

He grinned at her, and she was suddenly very aware of him and the fact that they were alone in his cottage. Her brain registered his animal-like grace and strong thighs, his presence, his magnetism. Her eyes roamed over him – broad shoulders, blue eyes, a wolfish smile. Her pulse rate kicked up and sensations she'd thought buried roared into life. To her surprise, he trailed a forefinger along the curve of her cheek.

"About coming to you for a shoulder to cry on?" His eyes glittered, and her nerves tingled. "Oh yes, Ella. I'll remember that. And that we're in this together."

18

"Well?" Ella demanded. "What's happened? What did they say?"

Even the collected Justin seemed excited.

"Cathy told me she'd be happy to attend our event, and she's also happy to recommend that *Today!* cover it, which should provide us with some publicity. God knows, we could do with some."

Ella's mind raced at the mention of the celebrity magazine. She'd never read it, but the glossy cover proclaimed it as a gossip-rich, photo-heavy read. Justin had explained that the magazine would pay for photographs of the event featuring the wealthy and titled. Now Cathy Mason was on the guest list, the mild interest they'd shown Justin at the beginning of the negotiations would firm into a definite contract. The international actress would be a massive draw.

"I must write to everyone who's coming to warn them about the photographers," she mused. "Will Cathy Mason be bringing anyone with her?"

Justin winked at her.

"I imagine she might bring her latest conquest. You know, Alexander Versay?"

Ella's jaw dropped.

"*Alex Versay* is coming with her? Good God, we must get guards on the gates! The place will be besieged with screaming girls!"

"They're bringing their own security, but yes, we'll need barriers. I've given their management my name and yours and they'll be in touch beforehand."

Ella chewed on her lip, staring into the distance as she imagined the emotional state of the serving staff when they learned that one of the most beautiful men in the world was coming to the ball.

She shook her head to clear it of all the potential problems and focused instead on the cachet that these two actors would bring to their fundraising efforts. She'd sold all three hundred tickets, and she felt pleased with the auction prizes. Or at least she had been until Justin had sauntered in. Now she wondered what the actress would think of their little prizes provided by local businesses. She needed to get something *big* that Cathy Mason and Alex Versay might bid for…

She blew her cheeks out and found Justin looking at her quizzically.

"Sorry, I was thinking," she said with a rueful smile.

"It'll be fine," he replied soothingly. "I've known Cathy since she was at RADA and her parents live about ten miles from here. Her feet were always firmly on the ground so don't think you'll need to up the ante. Don't fret about the prizes or the other diners, or anything. Although…"

"Yes?"

"She's requested an introduction to Connor McPherson, apparently. It was the one thing she wanted in return for her appearance."

"Does she know him?"

"No. Not yet. Could you speak to the spiky Mr McPherson?"

"Yes, I can't imagine he'll have any objections."

"Well, he'll need to be polite and sociable, which he might find a strain."

Ella ignored that.

"You've briefed Lady Susan and Lord Ralph?"

"Of course."

"I'll talk to Connor then. Well done, Justin! This will be amazing!"

Love in a Mist

They high-fived one another and then Justin left. Ella sat quietly for a moment. Then she picked up her phone and texted Jeanette. The little black dress she'd hoped would have done for the ball now definitely wouldn't. She needed someone to go shopping with.

∽

"Don't fuss, Ella! I'm perfectly capable of talking to the press!" Lady Susan waved Ella away and patted a silver curl into place. Ella, already driven to distraction by the phone calls and the 'dressing' of the various rooms where Lady Susan and Lord Ralph were to be photographed, gritted her teeth. Although Justin had given both their names to the publication, they always called her, as Justin conveniently never answered his phone.

"Of course," she murmured, moving away from the group. There were three people from the magazine – the photographer, his assistant, and someone who described their role as 'coordination'. Mostly, thought Ella, that meant standing around tapping an iPad.

"Could we perhaps have a photo of Lady Susan and Connor?" called David, the young photographer. "In front of the window, and I'll get a shot of the garden works too?"

"If I can find Connor," Ella muttered to herself, as she took out her phone to text.

"Mr McPherson isn't fond of the media, I'm afraid," Lady Susan commented. David ran his hands through a shock of red hair that looked as if it hadn't seen a comb in months and raised his eyebrows.

"Well, we need a little... celebrity... if we're going to find a use for these pictures," he replied urgently. "With respect, Lady Suze, very few of our readers will recognise you – but anyone who hasn't been under a rock for the last five years will know Connor McPherson."

Lady *Suze*? Ella's eyes widened, and she waited, tense, for the response.

"Well, *Dave*, all I'm trying to do is manage your expectations," Lady Susan's icy voice said crisply. "And isn't it your job to make the photos look so wonderful your readers won't care who's in them? Last

145

month I noticed you featured a complete nonentity from – what was it? – children's television? Frankly, who, other than mothers of five-year-olds would have known them? You're paid to make the pictures rich and appealing. I'm wearing a classic Chanel suit, diamond earrings that have been in my family for centuries, and handmade Italian shoes. If you can't make *that* appealing, I fear your reputation is undeserved."

David gaped, and after a second, closed his mouth.

Ella hid a smile and finished her text to Connor.

Need you in the Grand Hall.

In about a minute, she got a response.

Why?

She sighed and moved to the window, dialling Connor's number.

"Hello."

"Connor, I need you because all our precious publicity is about to go south unless you make an appearance."

"I hate photographers."

"And I hate having to find so much money to fund the build, we can't always have what we want. So I would appreciate a little help."

"You sound very cross."

"My patience is almost exhausted and a little cooperation would go a long way," Ella hissed into the phone.

"I'm filthy."

"I don't care. It will doubtless make a fabulous photo with you up to your ears in dirt and Lady Susan in a designer suit and diamonds."

Silence.

"Okay, I'll be about five minutes."

He rang off, and she breathed deeply and turned with a bright smile on her face.

"Connor's on his way and apologises in advance for his mud."

"Great! We'll take a break until he arrives," the photographer's assistant said, keeping a wary eye on David and Lady Susan who were studiously ignoring one another.

The atmosphere shifted as Connor arrived, as muddy as he'd

Love in a Mist

promised. He paused momentarily as he strode through the door, like an animal scenting danger. Lady Susan beamed at him.

"Connor! Thanks for taking the time to do this."

David turned and walked towards him, hand outstretched. Ella experienced another tense moment as she wondered whether Connor would shake his hand or ignore him. Connor grasped the photographer's hand and shook it. Too firmly, Ella thought, as she saw David flex his fingers gingerly as Connor turned away.

"Yes, thank you for coming so quickly. Now, if I could position you both against the window…"

Ella breathed more easily as the assistant arranged lights and reflectors and the shoot progressed. There was little doubt that David knew his business, and Ella had been correct – the contrast between the six-foot Connor in his work gear and Lady Susan's immaculate, tiny figure was intriguing, irresistible. Ella's mood lightened as the shutter clicked. The photos would be amazing.

"Now, our reporter is coming in about twenty minutes, is that okay? She'll want to speak to both of you, but I dare say it won't take more than an hour," the coordinator said, glancing at her wristwatch.

"Sorry? I'm not being interviewed," Connor said flatly. "I've got too much to do to hang around for an hour and a half."

The coordinator protested, and Connor just shook his head.

It was during the argument that a small, plump woman sidled into the room and stood listening.

"But why don't you want to be interviewed?" the coordinator was asking, perplexed.

"Would it help if I promise not to ask about your nervous breakdown?" the plump woman asked casually.

The words fell into an abruptly silent room, and Connor shot her a look of pure hatred. Ella felt as if the world had stopped, and Lady Susan gasped.

"No, it wouldn't help. Because I just don't give media interviews," Connor bit out and left the room.

The silence stretched out. Then Lady Susan took a deep breath and said, "I'm Lady Susan Montague. Perhaps we could move to the drawing room and have some tea?"

The new arrival clicked forward on very high heels and smiled. She put Ella in mind of a piranha scenting blood. "I'm Tonya le Clair, journalist for *Today!* I'd be delighted."

∼

Ella shut the door, closed her eyes and rested her head back against the solid wood.

After a few moments, she pushed herself off the door and walked to the chair. She toyed with the idea of tea and dismissed it in favour of something stronger. But she would need to go to her cottage for that, and it was only two thirty. There was stuff she should do in the office.

She threw herself into the chair behind the desk and shuffled her papers for a little while, before putting them aside. She wasn't thinking about their contents, anyway.

The revelation about Connor had jolted her. Not about him having a breakdown. That was almost commonplace. No, his stricken face had shocked her, and then his white-hot rage.

Maybe it was something to do with coming from an army family? All that stiff-upper-lip stuff deep in the genes, perhaps he thought it was weakness? Not that there was anything weak about having a breakdown – doctors had diagnosed her with depression after Stephen.

Tentatively, she circled around the memories of that bleak, grey, joyless time and her breath caught at the remembered pain. After a minute, she firmly swept aside her thoughts and brought Connor to mind again.

He'd looked anguished, and her anger on his behalf had surprised her, all because the journalist had wanted to look clever. She unclenched her fists. The marks made by her nails showed red. Yes, her reaction to his discomfort had surprised her.

Should she seek Connor out? She frowned. Yes, she should. She

Love in a Mist

picked up her phone and hesitated, her finger hovering over his name. No. He'd hate for her to be fussing around. And he'd also hate for her to bring up anything he didn't want to discuss. So no, she needed to be more subtle than just asking if he was okay.

What to do?

She was sorting through her potential options when a brief knock at the door heralded Justin.

"Well? How was it?"

She stared at him blankly.

"The interview? And the photo shoot?" Justin prompted.

"Oh! Yes, the photo shoot was fine, eventually. They wanted Connor in the photos, which... took more organising." Ella phrased her sentence carefully. "And the interview lasted about thirty minutes and seemed fine, as far as I could tell. Tonya Le Clair and Lady Susan seemed to get on fairly well."

"McPherson? What on earth did they want *him* for?"

"Well, he *is* a celebrity, isn't he? An international designer with a global reputation?" Ella reminded him coolly. "Lady Susan wasn't famous enough on her own, apparently."

Justin snorted in disgust.

"Plebs."

Ella shrugged.

"Hmm. Well, good. I'm glad the preparations are going smoothly. What are you doing at the ball?" Justin added. Ella was taken aback by the abrupt change of subject and for a moment couldn't find any words. She frowned.

"The ball? I imagine I'll be rushing around like a scalded cat, making sure everything goes smoothly. And I'm MC-ing the auction, thanks to Lady Susan. Why?"

"I wondered if we could go together? Like a date?"

"Aren't we going out on Tuesday?" she smiled.

"I can't make Tuesday, I'm afraid – something has come up," Justin said, his face suddenly tinged with pink. Ella's eyebrows rose.

"Oh... okay. Is everything all right?"

Justin waved away her question.

"Yes, just need to sort something out. It's a dreadful bore, but necessary, I'm afraid."

There was a tense silence which Ella didn't understand.

"Anyway, Cinderella, are you happy to come to the ball with me?" Justin asked again. She shook her head.

"I doubt I'll have much time, but I dare say we'll be on the same table, won't we? Does that count?" she said, aware of feeling slightly pressurised.

"I'll be with Cathy and Alex on Lady Susan's table, so no. Ah... I hadn't thought we'd be on different tables. Perhaps we can have a nightcap when it's all over?"

Ella looked at him for a second, wondering about his persistence.

"I imagine we'll need a stiff drink by the time it's all over," she agreed. His smile glinted at her, and then he left.

Ella sat staring into the distance, trying to sort out her head. She hadn't wanted to share her thoughts about Connor. She realised suddenly that Justin might not keep them to himself. She couldn't be a party to that. And she didn't want to examine too closely why that was.

19

Ella tried to pull the bodice of the dress higher. Jeanette tutted at her and slapped her hand away.

"Leave it alone! It's not too low, you usually dress like a nun!"

"I *don't* dress like a nun!" Ella protested. "Don't be ridiculous. But I'm not comfortable wearing this! I can't spend all night pulling my dress up! I'll try the next one..."

She pushed Jeanette out of the small cubicle and whisked the curtain across.

"Honestly, I've never met anyone so determined to hide her light under a bushel!" muttered Jeanette.

Five minutes later, she nodded approvingly at Ella in the next dress, one of a dozen gowns in the cubicle. Of midnight blue chiffon, a fine scarf draped across the throat, it left Ella's shoulders bare. The ballerina-length gown drew attention to Ella's slim waist and tall elegance. Ella twisted, looking at herself in the mirror. She hadn't completely zipped it up, and Jeanette leapt forward.

"Come here."

With the dress now fastened, Ella stepped back from the mirror. The sweetheart neck flattered her small breasts, and the drape of the scarf drew attention to her porcelain skin and shapely shoulders.

"I like it," Jeanette offered cautiously.

Ella stared at her reflection.

"I barely recognise myself," she said, almost to herself. Jeanette grinned.

"You should put your hair up and wear some killer earrings. You'd look a knockout. How does the bodice feel?"

"Like it's not going to fall down. Which is a blessing."

Jeanette laughed.

"It's not full length either, in case I need to run about," Ella mused, looking at her feet. "I'll need shoes, though."

"Heavens, don't be so practical, it's a ball, not a relay race! The store has a shoe department – we can go there next, although you should do less of the running around on the night of the ball, Ella! You've done enough to bloody sit down and enjoy it!" Jeanette was firm.

"Hmm. We'll see."

Ella stroked the chiffon and tried not to think of the price tag, which was more than she spent in a year on clothes. Jeanette watched her and then spoke.

"So — have we found The Frock? Or do you want to try on the others?"

"I don't want to try on any more. This is better than the black, isn't it?"

"Most definitely — the colour is brilliant on you, makes your eyes shine!"

"Well..." Ella took another look at the mirror. "I'd better buy it then."

∼

"I've barely had time to catch my breath!" Ella complained as Jeanette bought her a drink at the pub, a week after the shopping trip. She examined her nails, still without the manicure she'd promised herself for the ball which was on Saturday. Still, she'd been almost giddy with relief that she'd found a dress for the event – her old full-length

Love in a Mist

evening gown was just not good enough when you had theatre royalty coming for dinner. Her nails would have to do.

Jeanette frowned as she peered around the bar partition.

"What?" Ella asked.

"Oh, nothing – I was expecting to see Amber."

"Amber?"

"The young barmaid. She normally works on a Wednesday."

As the pub manager bustled towards them, Jeanette ordered their drinks and asked about the young barmaid.

"She's not well," the manager said. Jeanette raised her eyebrows in enquiry and encouraged, the manager continued. "She's not been well for a while, sickness and nausea, apparently."

"Oh dear. I hope it's not serious."

"She told me she would be all right next week," the bar manager said, shrugging.

They sat down in their usual corner. Jeannette was quiet, which was most unlike her. Ella wondered about her change in mood and searched for a topic to lighten the atmosphere.

"You've got a ticket for the ball, haven't you?" she said, stirring the lime into her sparkling water. Jeanette's face cleared.

"Yes. I might come in a man's tux to mix things up a bit." Jeanette grinned as Ella laughed.

"After forcing me into heels and a chiffon frock? Traitor! I was at least hoping for solidarity as I try to look ladylike!"

Jeanette puffed at her.

"Don't quite know how to tell you this, Ella, but you *do* look like a lady. Almost too much so. You might try not to stare down your nose at the rest of us!"

"God, do I do that?" Ella said, appalled.

Jeanette finished her drink.

"Ask her ladyship," was all she said.

Ella gasped at the sight of the great hall, full of flowers and candles, glittering with snowy tablecloths and shining silver cutlery.

"Oh, my..." she breathed.

"Ella, you look lovely!" Lady Susan said, tripping over to her in a black velvet gown which hugged her slender, petite figure. "That's a new dress, isn't it?" Lady Susan was also wearing some of the family jewels, a sparkling sapphire and diamond necklace. At her ears, stones twinkled in the soft light.

"I thought with Cathy Mason and Alex Versay turning up, I ought to spruce up a bit," Ella smiled.

"Well, it's stunning. I get so used to you traipsing around in flat shoes and wellies, it's a real treat to see you looking so feminine!"

Ella's mouth took on a wry twist at the implied criticism. Four-inch heels and chiffon frocks were hardly a sensible outfit when you were climbing in and out of the Land Rover...

She thanked her employer and asked what she could do before the guests began arriving in greater numbers. There were some early arrivals, but thankfully they were sparse, while Justin put finishing touches to the tables and the band set up.

"I believe Justin has it under control, but find the sponsors for the auction and check they're all here, together with their auction prizes. Ah, Cedric! How lovely of you to support us like this!" Lady Susan turned away to greet a plump, twinkling man, who had an equally plump, twinkling wife on his arm, impressively dressed in damson silk.

Ella recognised Cedric, grandfather to Adam who had wanted dragon nests in the trees. She smiled a greeting, murmured an excuse and walked away to find Justin, who was looking at the tables.

"All sorted?" she asked,

Staring at the table, he moved a knife a millimetre before answering her.

"Hmm... more or less. Are you free?"

"Yes, I've come to help if I can."

"Let me give you the table plan and you can put the place names out." He looked fully at her, and his eyes widened slightly. "You look... amazing. I like your hair up."

She grinned.

"Better than wellies?"

He laughed. "Indubitably, Cinderella! Truly, you look fantastic!"

"Thanks, no need to go overboard," Ella said, feeling a little strange as he gazed at her. "Okay, give me the list."

There were twenty-six tables, each holding twelve people. Many of the guests she knew; they were the great and the good of the area, local councillors, businessmen and women, and there were friends of Lady Susan and Lord Ralph. She laid out the small name cards, wondering who had written them all, and marvelling at the elegant script. There were over three hundred places, and she shook her head as she considered the effort that had gone into them.

She glanced at the menu that Theresa Arnold had put together on a ridiculously small budget, and her mouth tweaked up in satisfaction.

She caught sight of a dark-suited, muscular man hovering at the door. She raised her eyebrows in enquiry, put down the cards on the table and walked over to him.

"Can I help you?"

"I'm with Miss Mason," he said pleasantly. "I'm John."

"Ah. Hello, John. I'm Ella Sanderson, the estate's manager. Do you want to know where she'll be sitting?"

"Yes, please. And where the table is in the room."

Ella nodded and threaded her way to the right table. "We've put them here, with Lord Ralph and Lady Susan, the owners of the estate."

"Thanks. The entrance is over there, right?"

"Yes. From the front hall."

"And who else is on the table?"

She took the list of guest names and flipped over the pages until she reached those on the top table.

"Here. It's a select group — as I said, Lord Ralph, Lady Susan, various of their friends. And..." Her voice faltered as she saw the name. She grabbed the side of the table as the world seemed to tip around her.

"Are you all right?" John looked a little alarmed.

Ella dragged a chair from under the table and sat heavily in it. She pressed her lips together and tried to calm her hammering heart.

"I'm fine," she lied.

"Yes, I can see that," John said wryly as he whipped a napkin out of a wine glass and poured some water. She took the glass, and the water slopped as her hand shook.

Lady Susan bustled up.

"Ella, what's the matter? You look like you've seen a ghost!"

Ella swallowed and took a sip of water.

"Stephen Carmichael is sitting at your table," she said.

"Good God," said Lady Susan faintly. "How on earth did he get an invitation?"

"I've no idea," Ella said, plucking at her skirt. "Perhaps he was a plus-one?"

"Let me see who's on the table..." Lady Susan searched around for the list, handed to her by John. "Thank you. You're with Cathy Mason, aren't you? Welcome to Ashton Manor."

"Lovely to be here," he murmured as she ran her eyes down the names. "I'll be happy with the arrangements for Miss Mason and Mr Versay when I find out who Mr Carmichael is."

"I'm guessing he might have been invited by Terence, who's an old friend of Lord Ralph," Lady Susan said, pursing her lips and squinting at the page without her glasses.

"Is there a problem?" John asked.

There was a lengthy pause, and Ella felt Lady Susan's eyes on her. She finally pulled herself together and shook her head.

"No, there's no problem."

"Sure?" John fixed her with dark eyes.

"No, it's fine. He's an old friend." Her mouth twisted at the description. "I haven't seen him for a very long time. But if it's all right with you, Lady Susan, I'll put myself on a table a bit further away."

"Very well. Although it would be a pity to hide away. Particularly in *that* dress." Lady Susan patted her arm.

Good point, thought Ella. She began to feel a little silly at her reaction; anyone would think she was some Victorian heroine, fainting and swooning. She sat up and straightened her shoulders.

"You're right. It was a long time ago." And she'd come a long, long way in the last seven years, she thought.

Lady Susan nodded approvingly.

"Good girl. I'll tell Ralph, though. Strength in numbers and all that."

Ella took a deep breath, just as Justin arrived.

"What's happened? You're pale, Ella. Are you okay?"

She nodded and stood up.

"The dress is a little tight," she lied and saw John's face become a smooth, neutral mask. Lady Susan smiled encouragingly at her.

"I'll just freshen up," Ella said.

Taking a deep breath, she focused on putting one foot in front of the other as she walked out of the hall to organise her thoughts and put a mask of calm unconcern on her face.

20

Connor could hear the noise of Alex Versay's fans outside the gates to Ashton Manor as he walked towards the hall, and he winced. He didn't go to the theatre much these days, but even he knew of the actor's success on the West End stage. Connor's sisters, who he counted among the most sensible women he knew, had reacted like teenagers when he'd casually mentioned it.

"Connor McPherson, you'd better not be joking me, here!" Caitlin had squeaked down the phone. His other sisters demanded to know what was going on. "He's going to a dinner with *Alex Versay!*"

There had been pandemonium in the background. Then Caitlin took charge.

"Now you listen to me, I want signed photos for *all* of us!"

As he made his way through the crowds and passed his invitation to the security man on the door, Connor realised he was less concerned about wheedling photos from Alex Versay than he was about meeting Cathy Mason. He'd met her previously at some premiere or other with Jonas, and she'd flirted shamelessly with him, eyeing him like a particularly delicious morsel about to be served for dinner. A little like now. He shoved his hands in the pockets of his tuxedo jacket as he walked into the great hall and whistled softly at the sight of the enormous room.

"Connor! You made it!" Lady Susan said, arriving at his side. He turned with a smile.

"I believe I'm on the menu for one of your guests, it would have been impolite not to show up."

Her mouth twisted wryly.

"Yes. Are you truly irritated by that, Connor?" She looked at him earnestly and he shrugged.

"Well, if our finances were in better shape... but they're not, so here I am."

She gave him a brief hug.

"I'm very grateful, Connor. Hopefully, Lord Ralph and I can offer some protection..."

His eyes were raking the now rapidly filling room, and he was about to make a polite comment when the words dried in his mouth.

"Mmm," said Lady Susan, a laugh edging her voice. "Ella looks spectacular tonight, doesn't she?" Lady Susan followed his gaze.

Connor swallowed, his eyes glued to the slender figure in navy blue. Lady Susan laughed.

"I must say hello to some more guests – Jonas Keane and his fiancée have arrived, incidentally."

"What?" Connor dragged his attention from Ella and refocused with an effort. Jonas and Sam were admiring the hall from the door. Sam spotted him and waved, and Connor forced his legs to work and joined them.

"They're working you too hard, Connor!" Sam teased as she hugged him. "You'll need to buy a smaller jacket soon!"

Jonas looked closely at him, but Connor just grinned.

"It's getting my hands dirty that does it! None of this messing around in offices."

They made small talk as they weaved their way to the table plans.

"Ooh! We have the ice maiden on our table!" Sam said softly as she saw Ella's name. Connor huffed a bit and Sam grinned at him.

"Don't worry, I'll play nice. But she's the idiot who doesn't like your design, so it'll be a stretch."

"Here she comes," Jonas warned Sam, and she fixed a polite smile on her face. Connor watched Ella walk across the hall and stop by a tall, good-looking man with a platinum blonde in an indecently tight dress. The man stared at Ella, looking her up and down, which caused a wave of irritation in Connor. Her chin up, the smile never wavered from Ella's face, but Connor could see her discomfort from twenty feet away. He frowned. The man with her had dark, floppy hair and a languid grace as he gestured towards the other woman. Ella shook hands with her and stood rather stiffly while the man spoke further, his eyes seeming to eat her up. Connor thought she looked hunted, and before he could analyse his feelings any further, he was striding over to the group.

"Good evening," he said smoothly, interrupting the conversation. "I hope you don't mind me stealing Ella to introduce her to a friend of mine?" He took her by the elbow and walked towards Jonas.

"Thank you," Ella murmured as she seemed to sag against him.

"It seemed a painful set of pleasantries."

"You have no idea," Ella's voice seemed to catch. She looked stressed, on the edge of tears.

"Are you okay?"

She nodded and seemed to slot another smile onto her expression as they joined Jonas and Sam.

Sam's eyes narrowed as Ella approached and to Connor's surprise, instead of being socially pleasant, she greeted Ella with warmth.

"I'm having *complete* dress-envy!" she said. "I love it – the length, the cut – everything!"

Ella looked blank for a moment and then she laughed, a genuine sound, Connor noted.

"I was about to drag out my old black dress when we heard Cathy Mason and Alex Versay were joining us and decided I ought to make a *bit* of an effort, at least! And I can't take any credit for having any

Love in a Mist

taste – my personal shopper talked me into it!" Ella seemed to relax as she shook hands with Jonas.

"Wow, I could do with a personal shopper like that," said Sam fervently. "I'm hopeless at shopping, I have to take my niece everywhere with me!"

Ella glanced towards the door.

"I'll introduce you. She's just walked in. Jeanette! Over here!" She waved to a young woman in a glittery pink jumpsuit. "You decided against the tux, then?" she asked after she had made introductions.

"I thought I'd save that treat for another party," Jeanette smiled, flipping her dark blonde hair over her shoulder. "Oh, hello. The VIPs have arrived."

There were several flashes as the magazine staff from *Today!* took the photographs for the magazine. They'd been wandering around all evening unobtrusively. Connor had so far, he thought, avoided them.

They all turned, and Connor saw Justin lead Cathy Mason and Alex Versay to their table. Cathy Mason beamed at her hosts, and Connor hoped for her sake that she didn't consider Lady Susan to be too old to have a brain. Everyone in the room reached for their phones to film the pair, and he remembered the signed photos he had been instructed to get.

"I suppose I'd better be getting along," he said, genuinely regretful.

"Take care," Ella said lightly. "Cathy Mason has been very... *insistent*... that she meet you." Connor was surprised; she was *teasing* him.

"Who are the other guests?" he asked as he saw the man Ella had spoken to sit down at Lady Susan's table.

"Stephen Carmichael and his fiancée, Juliet."

Her voice had lost all expression, and Connor glanced at her set face and filed away the information.

"Right. See you later. Good luck with the auction."

Cathy Mason was peering through her eyelashes at Connor, to his slight discomfort. She had a beautiful face, but where he might once have found her captivating, he now found her a little too loud.

"I love the beard!" she was saying. "Makes you look almost piratical!"

He smiled politely and ate his ham terrine.

"You two know one another?" asked Justin from across the table. Justin sat between Terrence, a friend of Lord Ralph, and Terrence's almost silent wife, Anna.

"Oh, Con and I met at the premiere of *The Scarlet Heart*! You know, the film..."

"Really?" Justin looked as though he'd just found a hair in his salad.

"It was a long time ago," Connor said almost apologetically.

"I understand you're the brains behind this garden escapade?" Stephen Carmichael said. Connor allowed himself a second or two before he spoke. After a brutal introduction to banking, he'd learned to spot an untrustworthy individual within five minutes. With Stephen Carmichael, it had taken only three. Carmichael had boasted about his recent killings on the stock market as prices had tumbled and Connor had gripped his knife and fork hard, thinking of the redundancies that accompanied the fall. Lady Susan's lips tightened and Lord Ralph shifted in his seat. Juliet had admired the enormous solitaire diamond on her hand, one of the spoils of his success.

"I am." Connor concentrated on his plate.

"Is it going to be a success?" Carmichael persisted.

"I hope so." Connor put his hand over his wine glass as the waitress made to offer him wine.

"It's a brilliant design and I'm convinced it will become a classic in about fifty years." Connor smiled at Lady Susan's words.

"Sure, Lady Susan, behind my ma you might be my biggest fan."

"It's quite a risk though, wouldn't you say?" said Terrence, looking hard at Lord Ralph.

"A risk worth taking. If we don't bring new visitors – and by that, we mean younger visitors – into the house and grounds, we'll all be looking for jobs eventually!" Lord Ralph responded.

"Goodness – are you on your uppers?" Carmichael asked casually. Terrence humphed in disapproval.

"Don't be ridiculous," Lady Susan said crisply. "The dreadful wet weather has made a bit of a dent in the building schedule. We'd like to make up the time, hence our fundraising efforts."

Connor hid a bitter smile at the phrase 'a bit of a dent in the schedule' but nodded.

"It's good that all the staff are so behind it," Carmichael said as a young waitress awkwardly removed his plate, and tried not to gawk at Alex Versay. Versay smiled at her, making her night, Connor thought. Carmichael continued, "I can see Justin is leading the charge tonight, but what about Ella? This kind of do isn't to her taste if I recall. I almost dropped my drink when I saw her in a dress."

Lady Susan stiffened.

"How do you know Ella?" Connor asked quickly, before Lady Susan could speak, and was interested to see her go a little pale. Carmichael shrugged.

"We used to go out... it was ages ago."

"Yes, it's about seven years since you 'went out', isn't it?" Lady Susan said in the hardest tone Connor had ever heard her use.

"Is Ella the lady who's been helping our security?" Alex Versay said lazily, breaking the uncomfortable silence that fell. "John told me she was lovely. I haven't met her – is she here?"

Three hostile pairs of eyes swivelled to the actor – Connor's being one of them. Both Justin and Carmichael glared as the actor rose to his feet and glanced around the hall. "Ah, there she is. I'll say hello. You're okay, sweetie, aren't you?" He smiled a perfect smile at Cathy Mason and ran his fingers over her shoulders. She twinkled and waved him away.

Ella had briefed Jeanette about Stephen and his fiancée under her breath while they were still shaking out their napkins. Jeanette looked appalled and then mutinous as she glanced over her shoulder to where Stephen sat.

"I'm around all night," she said. "I won't let him near you. Are you okay?"

"Not really, but to be honest, if I was ever going to run into my ex-fiancé, I'd rather be dressed like this than in my jeans and a sweatshirt!"

Jeanette giggled and squeezed her arm. Then she stilled and her eyes widened as she looked past Ella.

"Oh, my God!" Jeanette breathed. "Don't look now, but Alex Versay is coming over!"

Ella turned her head. Alex Versay was threading his way through the tables, his eyes fixed on Ella. She blinked.

"Ella, great to meet you. You look lovely," he said, crouching down beside her so his head was at her shoulder.

"Thank you," she replied, trying not to be flustered as one of the world's most gorgeous men flicked his eyes over her bare shoulders. She hastily made introductions to the rest of the table, and he nodded and smiled at everyone. Then he turned his attention back to her. In her peripheral vision, she saw Stephen looking sulky. Her smile blossomed under the actor's gaze.

"It looks like it'll be an immense success, but I'm not just here for the magazine, I'd like to do more to raise some cash. What could I do?" His hazel eyes sparkled, and she warmed to him. And had an idea.

"Well..." Ella paused, and he leaned forward. "There are many ladies here with considerable disposable income. Almost everyone called me to check you would be here tonight, so I think we can safely assume you have a *lot* of fans here."

Alex smiled, self-deprecatingly.

"I've been very lucky," he murmured.

And being gorgeous never hurts, thought Ella.

"So I wondered if you'd be prepared to offer dinner – or perhaps lunch would be better? Lunch for the highest bidder?" she said before she lost her nerve.

He looked taken aback, but she smiled at him as though he'd been brilliant. He nodded slowly.

"I suppose whoever wins it could come to the set of my next movie in the summer. Would you accompany them?"

Ella shook her head regretfully.

"I think we'll be too near the garden opening for me to come, but anyway, whoever puts up the money wouldn't want *me* there. How about we ask Cathy to come if she's free? Or you *might* be brave and have lunch with them alone, which would be something the winner would cherish their whole lives!"

He grinned as he recognised the gentle challenge.

"Let me text my agent. Give me five minutes to check it out."

She smiled again.

"That would be awesome, but obviously I understand if it's difficult. It's incredibly kind of you to offer."

He went away, fiddling with his phone.

"That's a brilliant prize!" Jeanette said, barely waiting until Alex was out of earshot. "God, I wish I could afford it!"

"I'll get a signed DVD of his latest film for you," Ella soothed. Five minutes later, he was back.

"So, we're on. What should we start the bidding at?" Ella gulped and pulled herself together.

"How about a thousand pounds? I'll ask you to come on to the stage after... let me see. Tell you what, I'll call you up after the vintage car rally. Your next film is about a road trip, isn't it?" Ella was almost giddy, her heart thumping.

"Brilliant. Also, Cathy's offered tickets to her next sold-out West End show. It won't cost her anything, and people can come backstage after the show."

"Really? God, that's fantastic!" Ella realised that everyone in the room was looking curiously at their table. "Tell you what, shall we speak after dinner? The band will do a short set, and I'll find you before the auction begins, to iron out the details." He beamed at her, obviously well pleased with himself, and walked away. She turned back to find her dinner growing cold.

"Some new prizes sorted?" Jonas Keane asked her, and she nodded happily.

"Looks like I might have a very expensive night," he said, his mouth twisting.

21

Ella held her skirts up carefully as she walked up the steps to the makeshift stage. She smiled brightly, but her stomach was churning with unaccustomed nerves as three hundred guests stared expectantly at her. She caught Jeanette's eye and was grateful for the thumbs up that Jeanette gave her. Ella breathed in, and bending slightly towards the microphone, asked if everyone could hear her. They could, apparently.

"In which case, let me remind you of the rules of our charity auction. Please wave your card at me if you want to make a bid and shout that bid as loudly as you can. My beautiful assistants..." she gestured to Justin and three of his staff, and everyone laughed as they bowed, "...my beautiful assistants will watch for your bid. And come around for your cheques at the end!"

The laughter swelled again, and Ella relaxed. She swept her gaze over the room and spoke a little louder.

"And I should add, we have two *very* special lots, provided at the last minute – so listen out!"

Having captured the attention of the entire room, she described the first lot, a prize from the local florist for fresh flowers for an entire year. One of Justin's staff staggered out with a huge floral arrangement, and Ella spoke about it in the most glowing terms she could devise. Bidding was a little tentative and Justin had a quiet word with the waiters, who silently slipped amongst the tables, gently topping up glasses. Finally, she got a reasonable offer, and guests seemed to relax. She brought the lot to a close with a smile, and then, metaphorically speaking, they were off.

Ella saw half of the guests in the room take a drink and wryly thought the bidding might be a little brisker – and it was. There was some competitive bidding for several original photos and watercolours from a group of local artists, especially as Cathy Mason joined in. Cathy was eventually successful and seemed genuinely happy, while the artists' table were pink with pleasure that their work had been sold to such exalted company. Ella also sold a place alongside Lord Ralph at a vintage car rally for twice what they had expected. She drew a deep breath and faced the audience. The room shuffled in anticipation, and Ella began to hype up the lot.

"As you may know, Cathy Mason's run in the West End is sold out – but we have *two* tickets in this lot, fabulous seats in the stalls. I checked the ticket sites before I came up here and even returns for any performance are changing hands for astronomical sums of money! And *those* tickets don't come with the priceless offer of a glass of bubbly with this Bafta-winning actress after the show—"

"And a few introductions backstage, darling!" Cathy called from the floor. Ella grinned.

"...*and* some other members of the cast! Come *on*, ladies and gentlemen! Where else are you going to get this opportunity? Shall I start the bidding at five hundred pounds?"

"Six," called a voice.

"Six fifty," came another female voice.

The bidding climbed in fifty and twenty-pound increments, and then a deep voice which she recognised as Jonas, said,

"Fifteen hundred pounds."

Everyone gasped and then burst into applause, and Ella laughed.

"Sounds like a serious fan! Do I have any advance on fifteen hundred pounds? Going once..."

Love in a Mist

Jonas smiled as the hammer came down and Sam kissed him hard, delighted at the bid.

Ella took a drink of water and nodded at Justin to signal the next bid.

"And now we come to another surprise lot. You'll know we have two very special guests with us this evening to support the development of the new gardens at Ashton Manor, and we've heard from one of them. This is the other. Fans of Alex Versay will know him as a gifted actor, with a dozen film credits to his name. He's due to begin his next project, a film called *Lost in Provence* this summer. We're thrilled to announce that our second special lot for auction tonight will be lunch with Alex, and other members of the cast of the film, on set." Ella smiled as several muffled squeals floated out of the audience. There was some shuffling, and she saw several women in the audience reach into their handbags for their credit cards.

"This, as you will recognise, is a unique opportunity. You'll have lunch on set and then have the chance to watch the filming in the afternoon—" Ella stopped as Alex rose languidly from his seat and approached the stage. Ella blinked at the sea of phone cameras.

"I can throw in transport to and from the nearest airport," he said. Her eyes widened, and she gestured him up onto the stage and he stood, beaming at the audience.

"So, Alex has just offered to pick you up from Avignon-Provence airport, which is nearest the filming. Just think – the glory of the Provencal countryside in summer, you and a guest will be chauffeured from the airport in Alex's limousine..." Crossing her fingers, Ella threw a glance at him. She didn't know if he had a limousine, but she took a gamble and he twinkled at her and nodded. Relieved, she continued, painting a picture of the bustling set, the other actors and the hot, French June sunshine. Catching sight of Jeanette, Ella thought her friend might be drooling. Job done.

"So-o-o-o..." she paused and three hundred expectant faces looked at her. "Who'll start the bidding?"

There was a second's silence, and then there were several shouted bids.

"Five hundred pounds!"

"Seven hundred!" This was from Juliet, Stephen's *current* fiancée, she thought cynically.

"A thousand!"

Ella followed the voices with her gaze.

"I have one thousand pounds from Mrs Thompson-Jones. Any advances on one thousand pounds?"

"Twelve hundred," Juliet responded. Stephen's eyes seemed glued to her, and Ella forced herself to relax.

"Thank you," Ella said with a nod at Juliet. Alex put his hands in his pockets and posed like a charming James Bond, even tweaking an eyebrow.

"Twelve hundred and fifty," Mrs Thompson-Jones pursued. She was a handsome woman in her fifties, and Ella noted her husband was looking a little nervous.

"Fifteen hundred," came a voice she recognised, and Ella was astounded to see Jeanette raise her card.

"Seventeen hundred!" Mrs Thompson-Jones sounded a little desperate and her husband took a big swig of wine. Ella swung back to Jeanette, hoping she wouldn't top the bid; she had no idea how her friend would afford it. Jeanette chewed her lip and then gave a tiny shake of her head.

"Seventeen hundred pounds going once..."

"Eighteen hundred!" Juliet called. Ella scanned the room and knew a fleeting disappointment that her prize lot had been sold to Stephen's fiancée. She'd have to liaise with the dratted woman about dates and arrangements...

"Ten thousand, five hundred pounds!" boomed a voice from the back of the hall, and with a gasp, Ella squinted into the dimness as all heads turned to find out the new bidder. Cedric Robertson, grandfather to Adam, partial architect of the dragon's eyrie, stood up looking a little flushed. The room gave a roar of approval, and Ella saw Stephen grab hold of Juliet's hand, shaking his head. She shook off his hand.

"I am bid ten thousand five hundred pounds," Ella said, drawing a deep breath. "Going once... going twice... Gone! Sold to Mr Cedric Robertson! Thank you *very* much, sir!"

Alex applauded from the stage, and everyone cheered. Ella took another drink of water, feeling almost tearful.

"I think after that excitement, we'll take a quick break," Ella announced, wondering how a styling session at the local boutique and high tea at the manor with Lady Susan and Lord Ralph would go down after that. Alex grinned at her and offered her his hand as she came down from the stage.

"I bet Mrs Thompson-Jones was gutted," she chuckled ruefully.

"I'll go over and do a selfie with her. And send a signed copy of the DVD of my last film, shall I?"

She stared at him, marvelling that someone so gorgeous on the outside could also be so nice on the inside. Her business sense reared up.

"Make sure you get a donation!" He threw his head back and laughed.

"Introduce me, will you? And stay with me," he added quickly, and it was her turn to laugh.

∼

Ella sagged against the chair and took a sip of wine. The rush of adrenalin from the auction had passed, and combined with the stress of seeing Stephen and Juliet, she was feeling like a damp dishcloth. The band had returned to the stage after the auction, and the guests were dancing. Cathy had captured Connor and was hanging onto his tuxedo sleeve as they swayed to the music. He looked pained. Alex had asked her to dance, but with what she thought was supreme self-sacrifice, Ella had lied and claimed she had two left feet, introducing Jeanette in her stead. Jeanette's smile said she'd won the lottery and she glowed with happiness as she danced.

"I think we can call that an unqualified success!" Lady Susan said as she dropped into the chair next to Ella. "Brilliant work, Ella – especially in such trying circumstances!"

Ella shook her head.

"Now I look at him, I wonder what on earth I saw in him. He's so... *two-dimensional* somehow." She sighed, looking at the wine in her glass.

"Better late than never," murmured Lady Susan, patting her hand. Justin bustled up to them.

"Marvellous work, Ella!"

"How much did we raise?" Ella asked.

"With Cedric Robertson's bid, over twenty grand!"

Ella puffed out her cheeks.

"Wow! That's great!"

"Time for that drink!" Justin said to Ella, grinning.

"What an excellent idea!" Lady Susan said immediately. "Champagne, I think! Could you get us some, Justin dear?"

He looked a little put out to be dismissed, but smiled ruefully and walked away to find the drinks.

"I thought you could do with a bit more space. I wasn't wrong, was I, Ella?" Lady Susan asked.

"No."

Ella closed her eyes in relief and the sounds of the band and the dancing swirled over her head. She drew a deep breath and then heard Lady Susan say quietly, "Ella – don't panic but your erstwhile fiancé is bearing down on us."

Ella's eyes flew open to see Stephen walking towards them with Juliet trailing sulkily behind him.

"Don't go!" she said urgently to Lady Susan.

"Of course not. Breathe, Ella..."

Stephen checked a little as Lady Susan turned to stare at him without expression.

"Just thought we'd say how well that went, Ella," he started saying.

"Thank you," Ella responded, determined to be professional.

"How much did you raise?" Juliet asked.

Lady Susan told her, and her perfectly sculpted eyebrows rose. "Nice," she said.

"That should help the garden," Stephen said, fishing for information. Lady Susan smiled sweetly at him and nodded.

Justin and Lord Ralph arrived with a tray of champagne and there was a little awkwardness as Stephen and Juliet were left without drinks. Knowing how good manners were ingrained in her employer, Ella thought Lady Susan must be forcing herself to be uncivil, as her employer sipped and appeared unconcerned.

"Have you enjoyed your evening?" Justin asked politely. "I hope you weren't too disappointed that you didn't win in the auction?"

Juliet pinned a smile to her face so patently false, Ella had to hide her smirk behind her glass.

"Yeah, well... it's been a nice evening."

One of Justin's staff arrived with the news that Alex and Cathy were leaving. Justin put his glass down immediately and made his excuses. Lady Susan also stood.

"I suppose we ought to say goodbye too," she suggested to Lord Ralph, and she cast an anxious glance at Ella. Ella smiled to reassure her.

"You go ahead. Please let them know I'll be in touch about the details of the lots sometime next week." Lord Ralph and Lady Susan weaved their way through the tables, leaving Ella alone with Stephen and Juliet. There was a pause.

"I expect we'd better be getting along too," said Stephen. Ella's relief turned to dismay as Juliet said she needed the loo and walked off. Ella drained her champagne.

"I'd better check in with the band."

"Don't rush off. It's been years since we last saw one another," Stephen put his hand on her arm and she stared pointedly at it until he removed it.

"Have you forgotten why that was?" Ella's voice trembled with rage, and she tried to calm down.

Stephen blustered.

"Look, Ella, I tried to explain in the letter—"

"Do you think a bloody *letter* explaining why you dumped me was acceptable?"

"We were too young – I was too young..."

"Patently. Only a child would believe running away was the right thing to do."

"But—"

"Enough." Her voice cut across him like a whiplash and he stopped short. "We have nothing to say to one another. You're lucky I don't have a sharp implement to hand."

"Ella?" Jeanette asked, coming up behind her with Connor. "Need any help?"

"It's fine, Jeanette. Stephen and I are quite finished." Ella barely recognised her voice, so full of fury. She turned on her heel and stalked away.

~

"You look weary, Connor!" Lady Susan said a little later. He grinned ruefully.

"I like people, but not... all the time."

She nodded and looked at the Grand Hall, almost empty of guests now. It would be a massive clean-up operation, but it would wait until the morning.

"How are you holding up, Lady Susan?" Connor asked. He was worn out, God knows how someone who could give him nearly forty years and was recovering from pneumonia was feeling.

"I'm looking forward to a bit of a lie-in tomorrow," she confessed. "I hope Cathy Mason wasn't too demanding?"

Connor laughed.

"Ah, no. She's really in love with Alex Versay. And he with her, I think. And anyway, I must be immune, having six sisters." Lady Susan laughed, and Connor continued. "I was less charmed by Mr Carmichael and his fiancée."

Lady Susan wrinkled her nose.

"Yes, he is, to use an old-fashioned word, a bit of a cad. It was all I could do to hold Ralph back when he began asking if Ashton Manor was in financial trouble! The impertinence of the man!"

"Ella looked very tense around him."

"Ah. You saw that, did you?"

"A blind man would have noticed it, Lady Susan. What's the story?"

She stared at the parquet floor, and Connor waited.

"It's not my tale to tell, Connor, but I can tell you that Ella behaved impeccably this evening. Many other women would have gone for Stephen Carmichael with a knife. I'll only say that he hurt her badly; the rest you need to ask Ella about."

He nodded.

"Right," he said, holding out his arm. "Can I escort you to the drawing room or are you ready to retire?"

She rubbed the back of her neck wearily.

"I think I'll be away to my bed. Thank you for all your help tonight, Connor."

He grinned.

"Well, it is all in my best interests!"

She laughed and agreed. He walked to his cottage, deep in thought.

•

22

"The money's in the garden account, you should be able to draw on it," Ella said to Mike, the project manager, who looked grateful.

"Great, I'll need to draw down on it immediately. We've got the wages bill going out tomorrow."

He looked worried, and while the money situation *was* worrying for this dratted garden design, she suspected there might be more to it. Mike bit his lip and shuffled some of his endless lists and spreadsheets.

"Is everything else all right?" she asked gently.

He paused.

"I'm concerned for Connor," he said in a rush, going a little pink.

Ella nodded, encouraging him to continue.

"I think he's not sleeping well. He's always here when I arrive at eight, and sometimes it doesn't look like he's been to bed."

Ella had suspected Connor was an early bird, anyway. She often heard him at five thirty, singing in the shower. Although she hadn't listened to much singing lately, she realised.

"What's he doing on the build?"

"Too much," Mike said bluntly. "He's out there working on the structure after I get into the office and some days I see him still working when I leave, about six. It won't do, he'll kill himself at this rate."

"What – doing the actual construction?"

Mike nodded, and Ella stared, appalled.

"Isn't that what we're paying the small army of contractors and his team to do?"

"Yeah, that's what I've said. Makes no difference."

She drew a deep breath.

"What can I do to help?"

Mike smiled.

"You might get Lady Susan to speak to him? But as you two don't see eye to eye, perhaps it shouldn't be you. No offence meant."

Ella twinkled at him.

"None taken. I'll drop a hint to Lady Susan. Is he—"

"Mike, have we—"

Connor thrust open the door and Ella jumped slightly and pasted on her innocent face. He paused at the door, frowning slightly at the sight of them together.

"I hope I'm not interrupting anything?" he said in silky tones. Mike was right. Connor's face was grey with fatigue, and she wondered when he'd last had a decent meal.

"Not at all, I was just saying to Mike that I've transferred the funds raised from the ball," Ella replied, calmly.

"Right."

There was an awkward pause.

"Well, I'll be off," Ella said, smiling at Mike. "We've had an influx of people wanting to join the Friends' Scheme and I need to find things to offer them."

She gathered her papers and headed off to find Lady Susan.

*

Later that day, Ella faced her employer in the drawing room.

"But I can't do that!" Lady Susan said, aghast.

"*Someone* must!" insisted Ella. "If he falls over, Lady Susan, the impact on the build will be enormous! Even more than the bloody weather!"

She paused, recognising that if she was swearing, she must be very cross. Or worried. Or something. Lady Susan's eyebrows rose and Ella rushed on.

"Look, we're starting to get lots of positive publicity and PR about – well, everything! The auction, the build, that it's a new design... What would completely mess that up is an alternative, but much juicer story about our designer going off ill with stress and exhaustion! Surely you see that someone has to speak to Connor to tell him to take it easy! I can't do it, so it has to be you!"

Lady Susan paused and looked into the distance. She sighed.

"It seems a little presumptuous of me. I'm not his mother, Ella."

"No, but you're his employer! We owe him a duty of care!"

"He's a grown man with an international reputation. He's not in need of a nanny," Lady Susan warned her.

No, thought Ella. But he might need support or comfort. A hug. Ella shied away from thoughts of wrapping the big Irishman in a hug.

"Please, can you speak to him?" she said instead.

Lady Susan sighed and then agreed. Ella was just about to leave when Sir Ralph arrived.

"Hello, Ella, I'm glad I caught you," he said, shrugging out of his coat. "I've just secured a loan from the bank."

Ella's heart sank. She had seen the cost of the garden. It was a huge undertaking, and the project was eating money.

"Oh?" she managed.

"The loan will cover the cost of completing the arbour where the wedding will take place. I'd like you to speak to Connor and Mike and focus all the work to get that completed; then at least we won't be sued for breach of contract!" Sir Ralph said briskly.

"Right," Ella said slowly, miffed that he had arranged this without her, but relieved that so far, it was separate from the estate funds. Sir Ralph reached over and patted Lady's Susan's fluttering hand.

"Don't fret, Susan. It's just short term. It'll be fine."

Faced with the fait accompli, Ella thought she'd better try to lighten the rather sombre mood and talked about the growth of the Friends' Scheme, and her plans for the group of garden enthusiasts offering money and support. She also talked about the increase in media enquiries, following the spread in *Today!* magazine.

"There's a very tentative nibble from a private bank who would like to sponsor the Rainbow Walk," she said. "We're at an early stage, but they sound keen. And I've also had enquiries from an agrochemical firm, but I think Connor might hold views about them, and I need to double-check."

Sir Ralph nodded.

"Excellent. I'll send you the paperwork for the loan when it arrives."

"Fine. Although next time, if you could include me in the discussions, I'd prefer that. As your business manager," Ella said tightly. Sir Ralph looked at her ruefully.

"If you'd have known I was off to the bank, you'd have tried to stop me, wouldn't you, Ella?"

"I would have been there to advise you!" Sir Ralph said nothing. "And yes, maybe I'd have advised against it," she added reluctantly.

"Quite. But the estate can afford it, and any sponsorship we get in can only help. But I'm keen we complete the arbour so we can fulfil our contractual obligations. I also think it will reassure Connor, who is trying to make a silk purse garden out of a sow's ear budget."

Ella was silent. Yes, to know that the location of his best friend's wedding would be finished without cutting corners would help Connor almost more than anything else she could offer. She left, planning to check that her employer spoke to Connor.

~

Ella hoisted her sports bag over her shoulder as she headed to the car. She breathed in deeply, loving the lighter evenings and the bright cloak of daffodils which spread over the grounds. She'd be early for practice, but Jeanette would welcome the help in getting the hoops and the kit out. She was just about to drive through the gates to the house when she glimpsed the lights of the Nissan hut that served as the garden planning offices; she took her foot from the accelerator, and on impulse, pulled the car into the courtyard. Two minutes later, she knocked on the door.

"Come in!" Connor called.

Mike had already left, but the big designer looked as if he was dug in for the night, sitting at a table surrounded by sketches, plans and spreadsheets.

"Hi," she said, and then foolishly didn't know what to say next. What on earth was she doing here?

Surprised, he smiled at her.

"Hi yourself. What can I do for you on this fine evening?"

She didn't know. She shuffled by the side of Mike's desk, which she noted was tidy, all notes and files neatly stacked. He'd even lined up his pens. She hid a smile. Mike might be a man after her own heart. Connor's watchful gaze was on her, and she turned to face him, shrugging.

"I came on a whim," she confessed. "I wanted to ask how you were and how things were coming along. I know Mike said the money raised from the ball would be helpful when I saw him yesterday."

"Yes."

She waited. When Connor simply looked at her, she folded her arms, determinedly patient.

"So? What's happening with the build? I have several people from the Friends' group offering help and Lady Susan shared the budget with me, so I'm fully up to date with the costs and the phasing." And has Lady Susan talked to you? Was her silent question.

He tweaked an eyebrow at her.

"Checking up on me?"

"More trying to help."

He seemed genuinely surprised.

"What kind of help?"

"What kind do you want?"

He paused.

"I'm not sure. Can you let me think about it?"

Ella nodded, and silence fell between them. He seemed to stir himself and stood up, making the room appear smaller immediately.

"I've been revising the plans to identify if we can cut some costs, but I think we've trimmed the fat from everything we can," he said without expression.

"In which case, the phasing is the best way forward," Ella replied calmly. "We'll start fundraising on the next phases of the garden after the arbour and the – what are we calling it? The Dragon's Eyrie?"

"I wondered about a simpler name, given that we're aiming the space at children."

"Hmm. How about we get the kids to name it? Like a competition or something?"

He gave her a smile, and she was unaccustomedly warmed by it.

"Great idea. You know, I don't do this kind of thing, I'm just the designer, not the marketer."

"Well, you and me both! I'm normally involved with the estate, and I leave the sales stuff to our agency... But then again, this is a unique situation."

His smile faded, and she hastily asked to see the plans. He folded them out on the desk and she stood by him as he outlined what changes he'd made. Most were to the hard landscaping, which was the major cost, although he'd also changed some plants for the initial build which they could, he said, replace later when the project was open and making money.

"And what about the sculpture?"

His eyes met hers at the eagerness of her tone.

Ella loved sculptures, especially those she could touch. It was what had drawn her to Connor's hare. And she'd heard a great deal about Ceinion Bryant, whose pieces Connor had incorporated into the design. She might not warm to the modernity of the design, but the stone and steel pieces from the Welsh artist were an inspired addition. Vast blocks of white limestone against a lush green background, where visitors could lay their hands on them – it would be a point of real difference to other historical houses.

"Sure, I heard from Ceinion yesterday," Connor said, going back to his laptop. "He's finished three of the pieces and sent me some pictures. Would you like to have a look?"

She moved to peer over his shoulder, feeling the heat from his broad shoulders as she bent to view his screen.

"Oh, wow!" she murmured as he opened the pictures of the sculptures. Even from the photos, she itched to touch them. Ceinion had carved one piece like a pair of wings, rising from the ground, and its shape reminded her of a bird of prey, hovering in flight. Another reminded her of an ancient olive tree she had seen in Greece, twisted and graceful. The third resembled an enormous seed pod, split open to reveal its glistening interior. Ella imagined it with raindrops gathering and glistening.

"Oh, my God, they're wonderful!" she breathed, as she leaned in closer to the laptop. Connor smiled, his eyes fixed, as hers were, on the photos.

"It's a talented man we have there," he said.

She nodded and then turned her head slightly to find his mouth only inches from her own. Her eyes flew to his bright blue gaze, and for a moment, she forgot to breathe. She smelled his earthy, slightly spicy scent and felt the warmth from his body. Neither of them moved, and his pupils grew dark. His gaze dropped to her mouth, and her heartbeat sped up. She gulped and moved back so quickly, she almost lost her balance.

"Well, they'll be an enormous draw to the garden!" she said brightly and scooted to the other side of the desk. She glanced at the clock. "Oh shit, I'm going to be late for practice."

"See you later then," he said, suddenly cool.

She drove to practice, trying not to speculate on why his withdrawal had left her bereft.

23

"We still haven't arranged our night out, Ella," Justin said as Ella was taking her coat off from a visit to one of the farms on the estate. This was one of the busiest times of the year for the tenanted farmers, and many of them were looking grey-faced with fatigue after nights looking after the ewes and lambs. And now the focus was turning to the calves. She sighed as she hung her jacket on the peg and searched in the pocket for her phone. There was a missed call from Connor McPherson and one from her ex-fiancé, she noted with a spurt of irritation.

"I'm sorry, Justin, you know how busy April can be..." She heard him sigh. "But I'm sure you understand that, having worked in Ashton Manor for the past seven years?" Ella added, looking at him with her head on one side.

He seemed to do a calculation in his head, and he smiled.

"Yes, of course I do. I'm sorry, I'm feeling low and I need a bit of cheering up."

You should go to a comedy show then, thought Ella waspishly. She sank into her chair, longing for a cup of tea; it had been an interminable day. She wondered whether having dinner might finally prove to them both that they weren't suited romantically.

"I'm sorry you're not on top form, Justin," she said. "Fancy a trip to Bengal Nights on Saturday?"

"I haven't been there for years!" he said, with a quick laugh. "Do I need to book? Or do we just show up?"

"Why don't you book a table for seven?"

"Okay, I'll do that. Shall I pick you up?"

"No, I'll come to you," Ella said easily. "If you're low, I imagine you'd like a drink, wouldn't you?"

His face brightened, and he thanked her as he left. Ella stared ahead with her mind a careful blank and shaking off feelings of unease, she made tea. Stephen's message made him sound whiny.

"Ella, it's Stephen. Look, I know you think I'm a louse, but truly, I wasn't ready for a relationship all those years ago! I'd love it if we could be friends... could we meet up and talk? Catch up after all these years? I can tell you've changed a lot, and I think I have too. Let me know, but make sure you call me on this number if you would."

Ella deleted the message. She didn't have time for his excuses and didn't care. Then she listened to Connor's message.

"Ella, could I have a word about the loan for the arbour?" Connor's voice sounded as weary as she felt. "We're about to start the hard landscaping and I need to sequence the payments to the contractor. Could you call me?"

"Why are *you* doing this, Connor?" Ella muttered as she pressed re-dial. "Hi Connor, it's Ella. I got your message about the loan – should I speak to Mike?"

"Mike's had to go to see his parents," Connor said. "His ma's unwell."

"Oh dear. Will he be away long?"

"He's not sure." Connor's voice sounded tired. "It's not serious, he tells me, but you never can be sure when your folks are getting on. Anyway, I need to get it organised. Can you help?"

After Ella completed the call, she wondered if Lady Susan knew that the garden's project manager was away. This would mean even more pressure on Connor. She hoped he could stand it.

Connor knew when he was being cosseted, and however sweet Lady Susan was, he hated it.

"So, I just wanted to check how you were doing, Connor dear, and check that you realise that we're all here to help. What's this I hear about you being on site and driving an earth mover? There are some things you absolutely should do, and some that really, you need to delegate."

He folded his arms.

"Lady Susan, why did you hire me?"

She blinked, startled at the question.

"Why, because you come with a fantastic reputation as a garden designer, of course! But that doesn't include digging the ground!"

"My reputation is very important to me, Lady Susan, and at the moment, it's in danger of collapsing if we don't finish the garden on time. Because my reputation has been hard won, I will fight with every ounce of strength I have to maintain it. Therefore, if I work alongside my crew, to give them an extra hand so we can open *near* the date we agreed, that's my business."

"But people are worried about you!"

"What people? Who is worried about me enough to come tittle-tattling to you?" Connor knew his face was fierce and tried to calm down. He saw Lady Susan consider her response and decide not to reveal the sources of her information.

"*Lots* of people, Connor! As if I couldn't see from the state of you that you need some proper rest!" she said rather scornfully. "You look to me like you haven't slept in weeks and frankly, your hair is looking a trifle wild!"

"You're considering my well-being on the basis of my *haircut*?"

Lady Susan drew herself up to her full height of five feet one and frowned at him.

"Do not be ridiculous, Connor. Your general appearance is giving cause for alarm. I suggest if you want to stop people *tittle-tattling* to me about your health, you get some sleep and take better care of yourself. It will not do for you to collapse on me, Connor, I have too much invested in this project to lose you. If you won't do what I ask voluntarily, I will ban you from the site."

Connor threw his head back and roared with laughter.

"Will you, by God?"

"Yes, Mr McPherson, I will," said Lady Susan in an icy voice. "I own this land, and if you can't be trusted to take care of yourself, you certainly won't be fit to work on my estate. Please bear that in mind."

Silence fell. Lady Susan took her seat again.

"So now we've finished shouting at one another, can I ask you nicely to please take care of yourself?" she said after a few moments.

He sighed.

"I work like this, Lady Susan. But for you, I promise to take more care. Okay?"

And with that, Lady Susan had to be satisfied.

~

"Connor! You look like shit! Are you ill?" Sam demanded as they climbed out of the car in front of Ashton Manor. Connor shook his head in despair. So much for getting his hair and beard trimmed.

"I had a bit of a late night reworking the budget. Do not, for the love of God, fuss over me," he growled as he kissed her on the cheek. Jonas raised a brow as he shook hands.

"Oh, don't worry," Jonas said, putting his hands up as Connor glared in warning. "I'm saying nothing. For now, at least."

Connor knocked at the door of the drawing room and Lady Susan's voice invited them in. She glanced at Connor, taking in his neatened appearance, and rose to her feet as Sam and Jonas came into the room. After greetings had been exchanged, tea ordered, and Justin had arrived, Connor outlined what he was planning for the arbour where Jonas and Sam's wedding ceremony would be.

Sam, who'd not seen the revised plans, was quiet as he explained the planting around the paved area where they would exchange vows. Shooting a glance at her, he saw her tiny nod as he continued. Inside, he relaxed a little. If Sam was happy, Jonas would have no concerns. They would spread the seating for nearly three hundred guests over a large grassed area. Really, considering Jonas was an only child, there were a huge number of guests.

Ruefully acknowledging the foul spring weather that had followed one of the wettest autumns on record and dogged the timescale of the garden, he talked through the wet weather options they were putting in place. A dozen wooden posts sunk into the ground where they would attach waterproof sails to protect the hats and other paraphernalia normally worn at weddings.

"We also have dozens of umbrellas available for people visiting the house," Justin added. Sam nodded, but said nothing.

"Won't the ground be muddy if it rains?" asked Jonas.

"We'll spread bark between the rows of chairs and put a membrane down the aisle so you should be fine," Connor said. "I've no idea what Sam will wear, but a membrane will be a better option than bark, which might stain your dress, if there's a train."

Sam shook her head.

"No train. I'd probably fall over it at the reception."

"And the rest of the arbour will look like this," Connor said, moving to the computer-generated visuals. He spread them onto the low coffee table, and Sam gasped.

"Oh my God. Connor, this is *glorious!*"

Connor smiled at her response. He might not be able to work miracles with the timescale for this bloody garden, but his gardens were heart-stopping. He was proud of the arbour where clematis, roses and fast-growing ivy would weave into garlands, creating a cool green space where his best friend would marry the woman who had captured his heart. It featured clipped yew and holly trees, reflecting Connor's Irish superstitions about keeping evil spirits away. Hydrangeas in white and blush pink lightened the dappled shade.

"Nice work, Con," said Jonas, clapping him on the shoulder. His voice sounded gruff to Connor's ears, and Connor thought he saw the gleam of moisture in Jonas' bottle-green eyes. Sam groped for Jonas' hand and squeezed it.

"And we'll add the floral decorations at the end of the rows of chairs," Lady Susan added.

"It's lovely, Con. How soon will you finish it?" Sam asked carefully. Connor had known this question was coming – wasn't it what he himself would have asked? – so he had prepared.

"We've just got full funding for this part of the scheme so we will complete it first. We're expecting it to do the final planting at the end of June, and we'll then work as far as possible on the areas that surround it. I know we're behind on the rest of the design, but as far as you and your guests are concerned, what they'll see will be finished. We're not expecting them to hike much further than the Rainbow Walk, the fountains, and the rose garden."

"No, unlikely in heels!" Sam laughed.

The conversation turned to the tasting menu for the evening reception and Justin took over. Connor leaned back to observe Justin doing his best to charm Sam and, for whatever reason, failing dismally. Sam's normally friendly face was closed, her soft mouth a little firm. Finally, Justin left, notes in hand, and they headed back to Connor's cottage.

"Is Justin not to your taste, Sam?" Connor asked, buckling his seat belt in the back seat. He could see her nose wrinkle.

"I can't put my finger on it," she said thoughtfully. "I'm probably being very unfair."

"Not keen on him myself," Connor commented.

"But enough of Justin – what about *you*?"

Damn, he thought. He put on his best innocent face as she squirmed in her seat to get a better view of him.

"Me?"

"Yes, Connor, pet – *you*. You've lost weight, you've bags under your eyes I could pack and I want to know what's up." Connor noticed Jonas' eyes swivel to watch him in the mirror. "Or are you in love?" Sam added, her eyes narrowing.

The question stunned Connor and for a second, Ella's moongazing hare flooded his thoughts. Jonas' eyebrows flicked upwards.

"You do talk trash!" Connor said, recovering himself. "No, what's making me haggard is working out the bloody finances for this nightmare of a project!" They drew up outside his cottage and he thrust his long legs out of the car before Jonas had even pulled up the handbrake. "Come on, leave the car and walk with me to the pub for lunch. You can tell me what my god-daughter is getting up to these days."

24

"So with this walkway and this part of the terrace, we connect with the house, and the design doffs its hat to Ashton Manor's history," Connor said to Ella, waving his arms at the garden. "Do you see?" She was silent, digesting the information. They were standing on the balustrade overlooking the part-completed gardens. The estate stretched out almost as far as the eye could see. In front of the house were the formal gardens Ella so loved and beyond that, the rockery with its modest waterfall, with fountains at the bottom. Looking even further out, the fields rolled away, reaching the line of trees which marked the start of the estate's farmlands. Farmhouses were sprinkled over the hills, connected by chocolate-brown roads. The fields were a patchwork of fresh greens, golds and browns. He watched her face, seeing it soften.

"You love this place, don't you?" he said, and her eyes darted to his face.

"Yes. Yes, I do. I love the formal garden and I'm gutted it's going to be replaced, if I'm honest. I've always had a soft spot for the statues there, although I know they're not by anyone famous. It's not everyone's cup of tea, but I love the statue of the goblin – or is it a nymph? See, the one by the shrubbery?"

Love in a Mist

He nodded, recognising the piece which had one of the ugliest faces Connor could remember on a statue. Ella raised her eyes to the view of the estate and sighed.

"But I do *get* it now, your design. I think," she said, almost to herself.

Connor had a sudden rush of feeling he couldn't identify. It was as if he'd been seen. Mentally he shook himself. Ridiculous, he thought.

Ella glanced at her watch. "I think the lorry should arrive in about five minutes. We ought to go."

As they went to the stable block, they passed the statue Ella had mentioned. The figure was squat with a leering face, peering into the water caught in the lily leaf. She patted it on the head as she walked past it.

They were waiting for a lorry from Connor's technology firm which contained all the video and projection paraphernalia for the dragon's lair – or so they were calling it for now. Ella had approached local primary schools with the visuals for this part of the garden and launched the competition to name it. Entries had already started coming in, together with the children's pictures about how the dragons would use the treetop space, and brightly coloured sketches were gradually covering the walls of the project office.

"Blimey, that looks a lot of kit," she murmured as the driver threw open the doors. Connor grinned at her as he moved forward to inspect his van load of goodies, almost rubbing his hands in glee. He'd always had an interest in technology, and he was looking forward to the challenge of setting it all up in the trees and bushes. The enormous wicker cages that would be the dragons' nests were already in another of the stable blocks, and the wicker structures needed to be installed before the projectors. Connor was thrilled that Ceinion Bryant was arriving next week to help, also delivering one of the sculptures. He wondered idly, as the crew carefully unloaded the equipment, if his luck was changing. He hoped so. He sensed his reserves of energy almost at rock bottom.

"Let's give you a hand," he said to the crew, picking up a heavy box. To his delight, Ella also picked up a package and headed towards the trees.

Yes, perhaps his luck might be changing.

∼

"Goodness me, what's that banging?" Lady Susan put down her papers. Ella frowned and rose to her feet.

"Someone at the main door. Perhaps the bell isn't working, I'll go."

As Ella crossed the hall, Justin was lightly running down the main staircase.

"It's fine, Justin, I'll get it," she said over her shoulder and opened the door just as whoever was on the other side paused in their hammering. On the stone step was the young girl from the pub, her face red and blotched with crying.

"Amber? Amber, what on earth's the matter?" Ella asked gently. The girl promptly burst into fresh tears. Ella drew her into the hall, leading her towards a chair, and glancing at Justin who had pulled up short on the stairs. His face went white and then red.

"I want – I want to see J-Justin!" Amber gasped between sobs.

"Of course, but you need to calm yourself," she soothed, seeing from the corner of her eye Lady Susan hovering silently at the drawing room door. "Justin is here, look."

Amber raised her head to see Justin, motionless and looking at her with a mixture of dismay and anger. Her eyes widened.

"Justin! Why aren't you returning my calls?"

Justin's face assumed its neutral mask as he descended the stairs. His expression chilled Ella.

"What on earth are you doing here, Amber? I *told* you. You're too young for me. We've discussed all this." His voice was gentle, but Ella noted his eyes were hard.

"I thought after we got back from London and it was all sorted out, you'd still want to be with me!" Her voice was sharp and pained.

He sighed. "But I told you on the train coming back that I wasn't the settling down kind, and you said that neither were you. You also told me you were on the pill!"

"I was! I am! But I was sick before... before, and the doctor said that sometimes that can leave you unprotected!"

"But we've sorted that out, haven't we?" Justin's voice was hard and Ella's brows knitted, and suddenly it was as if a light switched on. "Sorted out"?

She suddenly realised what had happened and a dozen cogs slipped into place – Amber's sickness, her cancelled drink with Justin, the "dreadful bore" that he needed to sort out. Ella's gorge rose and she stared at him with fresh eyes.

"Yes, but I thought you'd still see me after I'd been through the operation!" Amber pleaded. "I thought..."

"Amber," Justin said, coming to lean over her. "I'm really very sorry, but nothing's different for me. You're still too young, I'm not looking for a long-term relationship, and recent events don't change either of those things." She stared longingly at him and her hands clutched his sleeves.

"Please, Justin! I love you!"

He sighed, prying her hands from his jacket.

"Yes, I know, but I don't love you and it wouldn't work, surely you understand that?" He glanced up at Ella and, as if he suddenly realised that he had an audience, grew angry. "And what do you mean by coming here, *stalking* me at work?"

Amber looked bewildered.

"It was the only way to talk to you, as you won't answer my calls! I don't understand what's happened, Justin! I thought you loved me! You *said* you did!"

"You're so naïve – little more than a child!" he said, obviously uncomfortable. "I'm sorry we misunderstood one another. You need to go, I'm at work and this is an inappropriate place for this conversation."

Amber burst into fresh tears. Ella stood irresolute, wondering whether she should leave, should have left some time ago. But when Justin's fists clenched, she decided she would stay right where she was. She placed a hand on Amber's shaking shoulder. Justin continued in a voice laced tight with anxiety and temper.

"Just so there's no misunderstanding, Amber, our relationship is over and I don't want to see you again. Is that clear?"

Amber said nothing, continuing to sob, and Justin leaned down, exasperated. Amber shrank away. Ella had had enough.

"Justin! Back off *now*, please," she said coldly. "Amber, let me take you to my office and we'll get a cup of tea while you calm down a bit. Justin, I presume you have things to do?"

His eyebrows rose.

"I'm not on the naughty step, Ella. This is none of your business."

"You've said enough, Justin," Lady Susan said, stepping out of the shadows. His eyes widened, and for once, he was lost for words. Lady Susan said to Amber, "Come in here, my dear. It's nearer than Ella's office. Justin, be good enough to send more tea."

Justin stomped away and Ella led the weeping Amber into the drawing room.

~

Ella had just put her key into the lock of her cottage when she heard Justin call her name.

"What the fuck do you mean by getting involved in my life, Ella?" he snarled as he walked down the path towards her. She realised that he must have been waiting for her to come home. She shivered but stiffened her spine.

"*Did* I get involved, Justin? Or did you just enact a soap opera in full view and I just happened to be there?" she replied.

"What's all this about tea? Or did you want to pull all the juicy details out of her?"

"For God's sake, Justin! The girl was in hysterics!" Ella stared at him. "You can't possibly imagine anyone with any humanity would have let her drive home in that state?"

"And now I'm lacking in humanity, am I?" The door of the cottage was hard against her back as he leaned towards her. "Have you any idea what my life has been like this past two months? First she's clinging like a bad smell, despite my best efforts to finish the relationship, and then she tries to trap me into marriage by getting pregnant! It's been a nightmare!"

Ella looked at him coldly.

"It's not all about you, Justin. Have you considered how she must feel?"

"Don't be ridiculous! Of course I have! I'm not a monster! But it was impossible! I kept telling her I wasn't the marrying kind – she didn't accept it!"

"Of course she didn't – she's too young, if you hadn't noticed! She still believes in fairy tales! Or at least she might have done until this afternoon. What were you thinking to go out with someone that age? She would naturally fall very hard for someone as polished as you, Justin."

His handsome face was sullen, and she wondered how she could have ever considered him good looking.

"Or were you thinking with another part of your anatomy?" Ella added unwisely. Angrily Justin leaned close to her, and she realised that while the key was in the lock, she hadn't yet turned it. She was trapped and vulnerable as Justin's face went red with rage. And then she saw Connor, barrelling towards them at speed. A moment later, his big hand on Justin's shoulder wrenched him away, and she was free.

"You okay, Ella?" Connor's glorious Irish tones could not have been more welcome.

"Yes," she breathed, putting her hands on her knees to slow her thumping heart.

"I should take yourself off, Justin. Before I truly lose my rag."

Connor's blue eyes were furious slits and Justin turned on his heel and stalked off. There was a lengthy pause before Ella straightened.

"Thank you." Her voice sounded cracked and scratchy.

"You could do with a drink. Where's your key?" She gestured to it still in the lock, Connor turned it, and she walked unsteadily in.

"Sit."

Ella seemed glad to collapse onto the sofa; she stared into space and began to shake.

Connor clicked on the kettle and found crockery. After a brief time, he thrust a mug at her.

"Drink," he commanded, and she took a deep swallow of the tea. Gradually, he noticed that she stopped shaking. A tabby cat slinked into the room and jumped onto Ella's lap. Ella seemed to calm as she stroked it. After a few minutes, Connor leaned across and tickled its ear.

"Gorgeous creature," he commented, and she gave a slight smile.

"This is Monty."

"How long have you had him?"

"Seven and a half years in July," she said promptly, and he laughed.

"Very precise!"

"I had him as a three-month-old kitten when I came here."

There was something else, he thought, but didn't press it, instead handing her a glass with half an inch of whisky in it.

"What was *that* all about then?" he said as she took a sip and sighed in pleasure.

"Justin? There was a bit of a to-do at the house earlier this afternoon." Connor listened as she told the sorry story of a teenage barmaid and lost innocence. His jaw clenched as he heard what she didn't say – that a sophisticated, older man had unthinkingly caused pain to someone almost young enough to be his daughter to have his ego stroked. Disgust welled up in him.

"Jeanette warned me about him, but I found it hard to believe," Ella finished. "It seemed so... so unlike the Justin I knew."

"Were you in a relationship with him too?" Connor asked, aware how tense he was waiting for the answer. Ella laughed.

"Oh no! I thought we were friends... we had the odd meal out, you know – occasional drinks, a movie. I wondered if he was becoming a little more pointed in his attention to me recently, but while I found him good company, we never clicked that way."

The relief washed through him.

"I'm glad," he said. She looked at him quizzically, and he hesitated.

"I'm glad he hasn't hurt you," he said at last. Her dark grey eyes flashed silver at him.

"Why?"

"Because you're too nice to be hurt?"

This time it was Ella's time to hesitate.

"I'm not sure how you know I'm nice," she asked slowly. "I've not exactly been welcoming or helpful to you, have I?"

He swallowed and reached for his mug. Taking a sip of tea gave him time to think.

"Monty obviously adores you, so you can't be all bad, even if your taste in garden design is execrable." She laughed and then gave a deep sigh.

"I'm sorry. Regardless of my personal views, I've not been very professional. I've been worried about the costs and how that will impact the estate's finances. And worried about the tenants, they don't react well to change."

"Nor you?"

She stiffened and then, as he tweaked an eyebrow, relaxed.

"No, fair point. Nor me. I like order and purpose," she said, trailing her finger around the edge of her mug. "Your garden design didn't give me that – it made little sense to me, from the knowledge I had about gardens and garden history. It never occurred to me that I didn't understand enough to trace its origins. It doesn't make total sense to me, even now, but I'm getting my head around it."

Her honesty floored Connor who was unsure what to say for a second.

"All you had to do was ask, Ella," he said in a low voice. "I'd have told you whatever you wanted to know."

"Yes. I might have been too proud to ask."

He stared at her.

"This is another reason you're too nice to hurt." She looked up at him, startled. "You're honest, Ella. Honest when you don't like something, honest when you've made a mistake."

She gazed at him, and he reflected that her eyes could appear silver at times. After a few more minutes, she politely thanked him again and hustled him out of the door.

He dreamed of her that night.

25

Ella had been expecting the news, but her heart sank anyway when Lady Susan spoke to her a week after Justin had doorstepped her.

"I suggested to Justin that he resign and he has agreed that this is best," Lady Susan said crisply. "I'm relieved, if I'm honest, even if it *is* a tremendous inconvenience. I think the scene with that young girl opened my eyes to a side of Justin's character I never suspected. He'll be leaving at the end of the week."

Ella hid a sigh. She'd been with Lady Susan while Amber had sobbed out her sorry tale in the drawing room, and Emma had rarely seen her employer more angry. There was no need to tell of his threatening behaviour towards her, she thought.

"Which leaves us with the matter of the wedding," continued Lady Susan, and Ella's eyes snapped to her face. "I know you'd rather not, but I'd like you to take over the arrangements."

"Me? I'm no wedding planner!"

"I know, but even if I place the advertisement this week and get some responses, it may be months before Justin's replacement can start work."

Ella wound her ponytail around her fingers, thinking. A dozen ideas flew around her head, all eventually discarded.

"Isn't there another way?" she asked, knowing there wasn't.

"My dear, if there had have been, we wouldn't be having this conversation," Lady Susan said a little testily. "But really, Ella – I thought you'd moved on. Haven't you?"

Ella stared, conscious of an intense mix of shame and betrayal. She wondered if her reaction to weddings was real, or just a Pavlovian response. She grasped for something practical, ignoring her screaming nerves.

"I'll need some administrative help with the Friends' Scheme, I'm losing track with it. Could you find someone for me, please? Perhaps Lord Ralph can spare someone from his office?"

"Of course."

"Very well. I'll look at the file and speak to Justin before he leaves," Ella said without expression and left.

∼

Connor was laughing at Jonas' description of one of Magda's hapless boyfriends when Ella opened the door. The smile on her face faltered a little as she saw him and then slipped back into place. Connor, however, had been expecting to meet her – had been waiting for her.

"Ella, how are you?" he asked, as he rose to his feet, giving her the warmest smile he could. She blinked at him.

"Erm... I'm well, thank you. Yes, fine. Thanks for asking." She seemed slightly knocked off track, and Sam cleared her throat. Collecting herself, Ella turned to Jonas and Sam. "Hello – lovely to see you again. I hope Lady Susan has explained that Justin has left Ashton Manor and you have me in his place?"

"Yes, she phoned," Sam said sunnily. "I'm sure you're as incredibly organised as Justin was!"

Connor watched Ella closely. She was stressed, he thought. Damn, he should know, he could spot the signs a mile away.

Love in a Mist

"Yes, well, he gave me the file and I'm now very familiar with it, so I hope I won't miss anything."

Connor saw Sam's eyes flick to Jonas and a tiny communication pass between them. Jonas complimented Ella on the smooth running of the auction and the amount of money it had raised. Ella smiled and Connor noticed that her spine softened slightly.

"From what I saw, that went off with no problems at all so we're completely relaxed about you handling our celebration. Now, can we talk about the wine? I know that Justin was having problems getting the label I requested..."

Connor inwardly applauded Jonas' skill in moving past the potentially awkward change of staff and onto the task itself, which would automatically trigger Ella's superb administrative and planning skills. He slipped out of the room, mouthing to Sam that he'd meet them later. He returned to the project office feeling slightly better, to find Mike beaming over the fact that one part of the arbour would complete a week earlier than expected.

At five thirty, Connor returned to the project office from the Rainbow Walk and discussions with the structural engineer over the huge steel tubs which would contain the roots of the trees. It had been a positive conversation, Connor mused, and he opened his laptop to update the project plan, feeling better than he had done for a while. Mike shrugged on his jacket and reminded him about the health and safety visit the following day. Connor grunted, his eyes still on the plan.

"Are you off soon?" Mike asked at the door. Connor shot him a glance.

"Stop your fussing, Mike," he replied without heat. "Jonas and Sam are visiting and we're off out to the pub this evening, so relax, I won't be here all night."

Mike simply grinned.

"It's my wedding anniversary tomorrow and I'm taking a day off. So the health and safety visit will be down to you, unless you give it to one of the crew. It's at ten o'clock and the guy we're dealing with from the council is a real one for the detail. Just wanted to remind you." Then he left.

Connor sighed and took out his phone to enter the appointment and was about to press 'save' on the entry when Lady Susan's words floated through his head.

"There are some things you absolutely should do, and some that really, you need to delegate."

"Okay – but who?" he muttered. He listed the crew in his head. Craig would be a disaster. He had no head for detail. Tony and Aadesh were too busy with the Rainbow Walk. Jayne... actually Jayne was perfect. He deleted the calendar entry, found the email from the council and forwarded it to Jayne with a brief note asking her to cover the meeting. He spent five minutes wondering if he ought to be there and sent another email telling Jayne to ring him if she had any concerns. A minute later, he received a text from Jayne, suggesting that he should chill and she'd be fine.

He sat back in his chair with mixed feelings of relief – who on earth *liked* health and safety? – and a tiny sliver of guilt. He shook it off. He was a *designer*, for the love of God! During this, Jonas and Sam sent him a text, telling him they were waiting outside, and when was he coming, for heaven's sake?

"Thought you were never getting out of there, Con!" Jonas grinned.

"Enough of your cackle," Connor replied, striding towards him. "I'll change and we can head off to the pub. How'd the meeting go?"

"Interesting," Sam said carefully.

"'Interesting'?" Connor frowned.

"Mmm. We'll tell you all about it in the pub."

∾

"I like this place," Sam mused, looking around the pub.

"They keep the beer very well and I think there's a new chef," Connor said, scanning the menu. Jonas went to the bar to order the food and eventually returned with a table number. He took a long swig of beer and smacked his lips in appreciation.

"You're right, Connor – this place keeps some grand barrels. I'm surprised you're not joining us." He nodded at Connor's sparkling water.

"Health and safety meeting tomorrow – need a very clear head," Connor responded. Jonas nodded in understanding, and Connor wondered when lying had crept into his skill set. "Anyway, how was the meeting with Ella Sanderson?"

"She's a strange girl, isn't she?" Jonas said thoughtfully. "The meeting was fine, she's completely on top of all the wedding arrangements, even stuff we hadn't thought about—"

"Like confetti – or rose petals as it will be," put in Sam. Jonas nodded.

"But she was so tense. At first I put it down to nerves, but eventually I decided that it's because she really didn't want to be there."

"Absolutely! I thought it would be fine because we sat with her at the ball, but it was almost as though that never happened!" Sam added.

Connor remembered Sam's abrupt change of attitude as Ella had arrived at the table, shaken up by her meeting with the ex-boyfriend.

"Yeah, what was that all about?" he asked. "One moment I thought I might need to ask you to go easy on her and the next, you said something about her dress." Sam rolled her eyes.

"Well, I didn't know who the smoothie with the blonde female was, but even I could see that it was a tough conversation before she came over! And then you went off to rescue her and bring her to the table, didn't you?"

Connor was silent. He supposed it might have looked like that. And yes, she had been upset, hadn't she? "I thought she might cry when she walked over. So I decided that I could forgive her for being a complete pain in the arse to you while we ate dinner," Sam continued blithely. Jonas stretched an arm along the top of the booth seat where they were and gently stroked his fiancée's shoulder.

"I thought your table looked fun," Connor mused, wistfully. "I wished I'd have been with you, to be honest, rather than making polite conversation with Cathy Mason."

Sam punched him lightly on the shoulder.

"Pah! Some people don't know they're born! We *did* have a good time. But today was just..."

"...very uncomfortable," finished Jonas.

"With you and Sam?"

"At first, I thought it was that, and that we'd completely misread the dinner. But as things went on, I thought it might be the topic."

Connor digested this information.

"What? I know she's not a wedding kind of person. Hell, Lady Susan told me that months ago! And I remember a conversation at Christmas when she suggested not everyone swooned over white lace and confetti, or some such thing. But truly, she wasn't comfortable talking about your wedding?"

The food arrived at that moment, and there was a pause in the conversation as they settled again.

Sam took a mouthful of burger and chewed it thoughtfully.

"No. And I think it would have been *any* wedding. It wasn't personal to us. It was almost as though she was treading on broken glass in bare feet."

Connor and Jonas both paused at that. Jonas nodded and put his hand over Sam's.

"Yes, that's it exactly. It was painful for her."

"Has she ever been married?" Sam asked Connor, who shrugged.

"No idea, although she went out with the jerk on our table and he hurt her. Lady Susan told me that. We've been too busy sniping at one another to share personal history. I've been in her cottage, but at the time she'd had a bit of an upset and I was focused on getting her tea rather than taking in her surroundings."

Sam's eyes gleamed.

"Upset? What's this?"

Connor dug his fork into a piece of steak.

"Justin was being an arse. And way too forceful. Luckily, I was on hand to intervene."

Love in a Mist

"Oh." Sam looked shocked.

"Aye. I should have thumped him," Connor muttered.

"So perhaps she hates weddings because she's never had one?" Jonas suggested.

Sam wrinkled her nose.

"That doesn't sound right to me, but who knows? It seems a great shame if she's so unhappy about doing this that she has to. Isn't there anyone else?"

Connor shook his head, trailing his fingers up the side of his glass.

"She's the most qualified person and has the most authority on the estate though I'm sure she'd rather be doing something else in wellies!"

"From what she said, that's definitely the case," Jonas said. "When we'd finished the meeting, she talked about the estate and that this is a busy time of year on the farms, what with cleaning the livestock buildings and muck spreading. Not to mention the fundraising for the garden... I think she's worried about what will happen to her plans for the rest of the estate."

Connor was silent. He knew Ella was worried about the garden being a drain on the estate's finances but hadn't realised that Ella was handling so much responsibility alone.

"Yeah, but strangely all that doesn't seem to faze her, does it, Jonas?" Sam said. "She's more concerned about the reputation of the house with the media and how the tenants might go to town on Lady Susan if the garden isn't a success – sorry, Con, didn't mean to add to the pressure, but she *is* worried. The traditionalists – led by the National Conservation Trust, but there are a lot of others – are starting to make a bit of a noise. I read about it in one of my trade mags."

Connor scowled, thinking about the letter referring the garden to the Historical Commission.

"Journalists are hardly my favourite people, but currently they're being helpful, she says – more positive than negative stories. But Ella's worried the balance might change," Jonas said. "I told her that my media officer would be in touch with her to think about a strategy, and I left her my card."

"What did she say?"

"It was the most human I saw her throughout the whole meeting," Jonas said thoughtfully. "I thought she was going to hug me. She's very keen to hear from Claudia."

"Claudia?" Connor asked.

"My press officer. If anyone can make a difference to your media coverage, Claudia Moretti can."

26

Connor groaned as he turned over and thumped the pillows. Again.

His night had started well; he'd watched some TV and sipped his disgusting chamomile tea. He'd listened to the meditation on the app of his phone and when his eyelids had drooped, he'd stretched to turn it off and fallen into blessed, blessed sleep. That had been about eleven o'clock. He couldn't remember whether it was a good thing to look at the clock when you were suffering from insomnia, or whether you should just let time drift. He lay in bed, feeling almost paralysed. Eventually, he glanced at the clock. It was four in the morning.

Unwanted memories from the last few days trampled through his brain – looking from the cereal box to the bread bin as he tried to decide whether to have toast or cornflakes for breakfast. How he had eaten neither. The way his stomach grumbled until lunchtime. Mike looking at him strangely when Connor had asked him to bring him a sandwich from the café, leaving the choice open. It was easier. Looking at the empty page in his sketchbook and wondering where the afternoon had disappeared.

Then there was the message from Jonas, sounding urgent...

Connor couldn't quite remember what it was about, but he'd get back to his best friend today. He ought to write that down.

Connor reached for the pad at the side of the bed, but couldn't find a pen. No matter, he'd remember. Wouldn't he? No, he was forgetting quite a lot lately; he needed to write a reminder. Now wide awake, he switched on the light and searched for the pen. It lay on the floor and, swearing, he picked it up and scribbled a note, 'JONAS'. Would he remember what that meant? He added 'return call' and then, with a sigh, put the pen on the bedside table and turned off the light.

Some time later, he was still awake, and as always happened, his thoughts turned to the garden. Really, he should be sleeping better, because the work was finally progressing well. They'd almost finished the multi-level fountains, and Ceinion's amazing sculptures were now in place. And the sculptures looked stunning. The photos for the National Contemporary Art Award would look fantastic. Next week they'd plant the trees on the Rainbow Walk; once the cranes had hoisted them into place, the heavy machinery could leave the site and he could see what he was doing. Really, it had been difficult to work out what to do with so much kit on site, and he'd been a bit testy with the crew. Actually, quite a *lot* testy with the crew. Jayne had left the project office in tears the previous day.

He sighed. Jayne just needed to toughen up, although Mike had really bent his ear about that argument, and the rest of the crew had been a bit stand-offish. Not that he minded; he was getting to the stage where he preferred his own company, anyway. He knew they were just trying to help, but having them flapping about him, suggesting that he needed to take a break, was just irritating. Not that taking a break was something he'd turn down. His mouth twisted in the darkness.

God, yes, he'd like to take a break. Somewhere far, far away where no one had ever heard about the garden at bloody Ashton Manor. Or bloody Ella Sanderson. She was a real thorn in his side, criticising his plans, poking her nose into his working habits and getting into his hair. Didn't she have enough to do? He'd caught her looking at him lately, and it seemed she was always around to see him screw something up. Judging him and then pretending to be understanding. He shook his head in the dark. That was ridiculous. He shouldn't be thinking like that. Whatever Ella was, she was upfront. And after all, she was focused on protecting Lady Susan's investment; she was desperate for the garden to be a success.

He changed his position in bed. Lord above, he didn't remember the bed being this lumpy...

His mind drifted idly over the idea of going away. How he longed to just forget all about this project! He wondered what it would be like to get up in the morning and not be thinking about earth moving, structural engineering, and plants. Or the blasted budget. Or Ella, who always seemed to haunt his thoughts. He would like to see her again with her hair loose, like she'd been at Christmas rather than tied back in that damned ponytail. He wondered if she ever *really* let her hair down, literally or figuratively.

An owl hooted in the twilight and reluctantly, pushing away images of white beaches by turquoise seas, he focused again. He knew he couldn't just up and leave, Jonas was his oldest friend and he was counting on him to finish this garden so he could marry Sam in style. His garden was part of their special day. Goddammit, Jonas was *depending* on him, and so was Sam. And what would Magda say? He'd never hear the end of it. And his family... no, let's not go there, he thought.

He'd just have to double down on the work. Not that it was all his responsibility, a rational part of his brain said. He was, after all, just the designer. But he was a designer with a reputation to protect, hadn't he said that? Yes, he was sure that he'd had that conversation. But he would not panic. No, the last time he'd panicked he'd made himself ill. His recovery had taken a while, months even. And that was another reason he couldn't let Jonas down. No, he definitely didn't want to go through that again. He'd reinvented himself after that illness, grown stronger and more resilient. He had a list of international clients as long as his arm. And he'd built that client list from the ground up. He smiled at his unintentional pun. No one helped. He had no titled sponsors, knew only the bare minimum about how the industry worked. But he had talent; some people said he had genius. And he'd worked like a dog to build his company of specialist landscape contractors and horticulturists. What was happening now was just part of the effort.

He wondered what time it was. He raised his head from the pillow to peer at his alarm. Five thirty. God, had he been awake all that time? Surely not. His head thumped back on the pillow and five minutes later he thrust his legs from under the duvet. It wouldn't be long before the alarm went off, so he may as well get up and go for a run. Groaning softly, he reached for sweats and a tee shirt.

Exercise was good, he reminded himself as he crept downstairs. At least it wasn't bloody raining. He was about to slam the front door when he remembered his neighbour and instead, shut the door with a quiet click.

~

Ella yawned. Something had woken her, she didn't know what, but it was probably Monty. She sighed and raised her head. Monty was fast asleep at the foot of her bed, his body impossibly heavy and long in sleep. She lay back and watched as the sun's light prised through the crack in the curtains. It would be a gorgeous day, and really, she ought to make the most of it. But lassitude sucked her back into the pillow and she remained where she was, snuggled into the bedcovers. The alarm would come on in a minute or two. And for God's sake, she deserved an extra five minutes in bed. She'd been so tired last night, she'd found her eyes closing as she watched TV.

But, a minor triumph, she had finished the brief for her new administrator. She'd have gone insane if she'd had to develop the database of Friends for the garden alone – she just didn't have the time, what with all the work on the estate farms, and keeping the house up to scratch and open to visitors. That reminded her, she needed to talk to someone about compiling a fact sheet for the garden, people were always asking. She sighed. Damn Justin for landing her with all this.

She shifted against the mattress and Monty opened one eye, unimpressed.

"Sorry. But I'll give you breakfast!" she said to him apologetically. He stretched and arched his back as he stalked up the bed for his morning scratch behind the ears. Then he paddled the quilt. "Oh, all right," she grumbled as she hopped out of bed and reached for her robe. She slept naked, inspired by Marilyn Monroe, who only wore Chanel No. 5 in bed. That was at least one thing that hadn't changed since Stephen. Which reminded her, she needed to put a stop to his calls, which were becoming a pain. Tightening the belt, she pushed her feet into slippers and padded downstairs.

The sun was shining through the leaves of the trees, dappling the light through the kitchen window. Ella ran through her normal routine; hot, strong tea, cat food for Monty and thinking about the day ahead from the comfort of the huge armchair in the sitting room. She was mentally going through a list of meetings and tasks when she heard the front door close in Daffodil Cottage. She glanced at the clock: five past six. Was that Connor going? Or coming back? If he was coming back, that was even earlier than usual. She skipped to the window and peeked out. Nothing, he wasn't on the path.

"Coming back then," she murmured. God, did the man never sleep? She could have sworn she heard the radio before she retired to bed and that was at eleven – no, midnight last night. She tutted to herself, and gripping her mug, she ran upstairs to shower.

She wasn't sure why she could hear him through walls that were eighteenth century and at least a foot thick – but she could. Well, unless her imagination was running riot. Their bathrooms were adjacent, so she heard a faint echo of the shower running as she brushed her hair in the mirror. She smirked. She herself was tall, and the bathroom in the cottage was a little cramped; Connor stood a good six inches taller than her. He must have to duck every time he took a shower. She giggled and then the image of Connor wet and naked tapped at her consciousness, and she could see from her reflection that a flush was starting in her cheeks.

"Good grief, Ella! Get a grip!" she mumbled and dived into the shower. She hummed as she washed, and ran the water a little cooler than normal to give herself something else to think about than Connor's hard body.

She was just towelling herself dry when she heard the crunch of gravel outside the cottages. Snatching up her robe, she pulled it on and padded over to the window to see Connor striding away towards the manor. It wasn't even seven o'clock yet. Even from this distance, she thought his shoulders looked stiff, and she pulled her own shoulders down, as if willing him to relax.

Ella stared out of the window, concern lapping around her thoughts.

She knew there were people who could function perfectly well on four or five hours sleep a night, but given the bags under his eyes, she was fairly certain that Connor wasn't one of them. And yesterday, she'd thought he'd seemed lost in the project office, not connecting with people around him. He'd looked rather blankly at her when she'd asked him when he would hang the dragon nests, as if she was speaking a foreign language. Then he'd stood up and knocked a mug of tea over the desk, almost as though he'd lost coordination of his limbs. When people had rushed to help him save papers and plans, he'd barked at them to leave him alone to do it. She'd been shocked. And then, when the papers had been salvaged, and the tea wiped up, he'd made a joke and apologised ruefully, saying something about taking more water with his drink. The crew had smiled, and the atmosphere had eased, but she'd seen from their faces that his behaviour was unusual, not what they were used to.

And she realised that the energetic, joyous, Connor McPherson from six months ago, while not disappearing, had changed in the last six weeks. His temper, while still fiery, had erupted for the things that warranted it. Now it seemed it flared up over nothing. She pursed her lips and Monty protested as she stopped stroking him.

"I know, I'm sorry. But I'm worried, Monty. Very worried."

27

It was a mixture of good and bad news.

The bad news was that the Historical Commission, acknowledging that the first phase of the garden didn't need anyone's permission, nevertheless wanted to look at the work, particularly the second phase of the build. The result of their consultation would be passed on to the local authority and would be taken into consideration when Lady Susan sought planning permission for phase two of the build.

"Interfering busybodies!" Lady Susan ground out through clenched teeth. "We may need to get Clayton involved in phase two."

Ella made a note, although she had already been in contact with the manor's lawyer.

"When are they coming to see us?" Lady Susan asked, cross. Ella glanced at the letter.

"To be confirmed, they say. I've drafted a letter saying that we'd like to focus on completing the garden and that Connor won't be available to answer their questions until that's happened. I hope that will shut them up for the foreseeable future, at least."

Lady Susan nodded vigorously.

"In the meantime, I'll write to our Member of Parliament to invite them to the launch and get them on side," Ella continued. "Nothing like a bit of MP involvement to put the wind up the local authority..."

"Excellent. Right, enough of these minor irritants, what's else is happening?"

Ella told her.

"But, Ella, that's wonderful!" Lady Susan beamed at her. "Two *thousand* Friends?"

Ella nodded, barely able to believe it herself. Tamsin, her new administration assistant, had gone through the task like a controlled tornado, entering data and putting Friends into groups, sorting out subscriptions and developing a short, chatty welcome email and letter to send to them.

"Excellent, excellent!" Lady Susan clapped her hands in excitement, just as Lord Ralph walked in.

"Hey-ho! Unbridled joy? What's that about?"

"Not quite unbridled joy, dear," replied Lady Susan wryly. As she explained about the Historical Commission, Ella reflected her employer was recovering well, but she was still a little skinny, in Ella's view. Still, the doctors had said it would take six months, and they were still five weeks off that.

"What do you think, Ella?" Lady Susan said, making Ella start.

"Hmm? Sorry, I was thinking about something else. What was that again?"

Lord Ralph peered at her.

"You look a bit tired, Ella. Isn't it about time you had a break?"

No chance of that, given where we are with the garden build and the opening date coming towards us like a train, and the sheep shearing on the farms, not to mention the potato crops, Ella thought wryly.

"I'm fine," she replied easily. "Now Tamsin's in place, my workload is more manageable and to be fair to Justin, the house runs almost by itself. But how are the applications for the new manager coming along? Do you have a lot of interest?"

Lady Susan sighed, a little gloomy.

"Not as much interest as we'd hoped, but we thought we'd re-advertise."

"How many applicants?" Ella asked, hiding her dismay.

"Only two, and they don't have quite the experience that this house demands," Lady Susan said. "I'd be a little nervous about appointing either of them, given how important it is that the house runs like clockwork when the garden opens. Can you carry on a little longer?"

"I daresay a week here or there won't make that much difference, but as long as you know I won't be able to do this indefinitely?"

"No, of course not! Now, what can we ask our Friends to do, other than come and visit and get ten per cent off when they visit the café?" Lord Ralph asked her.

"Well, I wondered if they could help with planting after the garden opens?" Ella said thoughtfully. "We could give them a hands-on experience of being part of the estate's gardening team? I thought it would be really interesting for those with a passion for gardening."

"That's a wonderful idea! Connor mentioned that we ought to recruit the head gardener now, although I thought we'd get through phase one of the build before we started thinking about that," said Lord Ralph.

Yes, thought Ella. Also, better for the budget to do it later rather than sooner... She caught herself on a sigh and instead smiled brightly and went to tackle her enormous to-do list.

～

"Ella Sanderson," she said crisply as she picked up the phone.

"Miss Sanderson? My name is Vincenzo Mazzi," said a cultured voice that immediately brought to mind rich, melting toffee. Ella's mouth dropped a little, and then she shut it with a snap.

"Good afternoon, Signor Mazzi. How can I help you?"

"I received your details from Sam Winterson, who told me you were looking for sponsors for the garden that you are building. My company, Mazzi Solare, wants to increase its visibility in the UK and we may be interested in looking at the garden and the plans for the next phase."

Ella tucked the phone under her chin as she scrabbled for a pen and her notebook.

"I see. Well, Signore, what would be a suitable starting point? We created a basic pack of information I could email to you, if you wish? I presume you're in Italy, rather than the UK?"

"The basic information would be useful to see, but I will be in England in the next few weeks and if we take things further, I will want to see the garden. Would late June be convenient?"

The sooner the better, thought Ella, quickly leafing through her diary.

"Of course. We're hosting an event mid-August -"

"Jonas' wedding? Yes, I am aware of this and I shall be attending."

"You will?" Ella caught herself. "I'm sorry, I didn't know..."

"How could you?" purred the voice down the phone. "I don't think I would expect you to memorise all the guests. Yet."

Ella couldn't decide whether she liked his tone and eventually ignored it.

"Quite so," she said blandly. "If you could just give me your email, I'll send over the pack – or should I send it to your marketing agency?"

He snorted.

"I make my own decisions, Miss Sanderson." He gave his email address, and she repeated it carefully. "I look forward to it and to speaking with you again," he said.

"Yes, me too," said Ella, not sure if she was being truthful or not. Then the line went dead.

~

The lights blinked out suddenly and Connor raised his head from the papers he was studying. After a few seconds, it was clear that the lights weren't coming on again. He swore under his breath, and rose from the table, stumbling over the chair leg and catching a knee.

Love in a Mist

"Feck!" he said, fumbling in the dark to reach his phone in the kitchen. The tiny light spread eerie shadows over the pots and pans.

He groped about for a minute or two before he heard knocking at the door. Ella was standing there with a torch. His eyes slid over her. Out of her suit, in jeans and a sloppy joe sweater, she looked much younger. She gave him a tentative smile.

"Hi. Are you okay?"

"Stumbling about a bit," he grinned, rubbing his knee.

"I'm off to the manor to see if they've lost power too. Coming?"

They walked to the manor with Ella's torch providing a circle of light by their feet. Connor's long legs ate up the distance, and he shortened his stride so that Ella could keep up. When she tripped over a tree root protruding slightly from the path, he grabbed her arm to keep her upright. She gasped a little as he hauled her closer to him. He could smell her, musky and sweet, and his senses switched to full alert.

"Sorry! Missed my footing..."

"It's very dark," he agreed, gently removing his grasp when he was sure she was steady.

"I wonder what the problem is," she said a minute or two later. "We overhauled the manor's electricity supply last year, linking it to the solar panels on the roof."

"You have solar energy? Impressive."

"Yes, seemed to be a sensible investment – save the planet and some money at the same time." He could see her teeth flash in the dim light as she smiled.

"I wish everyone was so enlightened. Pardon the pun,"

She laughed softly, and the sound ignited a tingle down his spine. As they drew nearer to the manor, he stopped and listened, fear coiling in his stomach. Ella paused.

"What's up?"

"Listen."

"I don't hear anything."

"Me neither. But we *should* hear the fountains running. We left them on for a trial period, remember?"

"Shit," Ella said under her breath and walked faster towards the house, looming black against dark skies. Connor followed, his heart pounding.

He saw the front door of Ashton Manor open and someone scampered out, the beam of the torch bouncing with their steps.

"Theresa! Is that you?" called Ella.

"Oh, Ella, all the electrics have blown!" Theresa said, almost in tears. "I was just going to check the generator."

"Right," Ella said. "Connor, I know nothing about electrics…" She looked at him expectantly. He shook his head.

"Me neither. I'll ring Mike." He saw her glance at her watch but ignored it as he punched in the number. Mike was grumpy but said he'd be there in thirty minutes. Connor turned to see Lady Susan and Lord Ralph in the doorway, with full candelabras. He thought they looked like a pair from an old masters' painting, and for a moment, the bustle faded, as though he was sinking under water. He turned to see Ella watching him, and he forced himself to concentrate.

"I think," Ella said carefully, "that as the fountains aren't working, and everything was fine before, our blowout is connected to them."

Yep. Is this blasted garden completely *cursed*? thought Connor bitterly. Then a light flashed on in his brain.

"I think it's safe to assume that, but I'd still like Mike to have a look," was what came out of his mouth. She nodded and then went to see Lord Ralph. Connor gritted his teeth and waited for Mike to arrive.

∼

Connor stared into the distance. The lights were on, at least.

Mike had been astounded at the cabling job and appalled that it hadn't been checked; someone would get a rocket in the morning. Well, later this morning, it was one thirty.

Ella had packed Lord Ralph and Lady Susan off to bed some time ago when Mike had done enough to put the power on inside the house. There was time enough to sort things out later, she'd said. Mike wasn't so sanguine.

"I can't believe the mess that the contractors left," he said quietly to Connor. "It's a bloody miracle they didn't set the place alight, given the state of the wiring they left!" Connor gulped, and Mike belatedly patted him on the shoulder.

"Not that it can't be fixed," he added. "But we can't risk running the fountains until we've got this all sorted. I'll call Dave Henshaw to sort it out, he's incredibly reliable, and he owes me a favour."

"Who signed off the work?" Connor asked, tonelessly.

"Some guy Ella always uses," Mike said in a grim voice. "The idea was that this way, she could include it in the house expenses rather than put against the garden. She was trying to be helpful, but I should've known that this would need a specialist. I should have checked, I've been so busy—"

"I know, we all have," Connor cut across him. He saw Ella turn and walk towards them.

"I screwed up," she said in a rush before Connor could speak. "I used Sedgeley's, the electricians we use for the house, and they were patently out of their depth here. I think this is their fault, and also mine, for suggesting them."

Connor could barely make his mouth work, but he forced the words out. "Did you do this on purpose?"

Mike gasped, and Ella stood very still.

"What?" she said, her voice breaking.

"Do this. Sabotage us. You've always hated the garden, never wanted us to succeed, put lots of *little* irritations in my path," Connor snarled. Ella shook her head.

"No! How – how can you think that?"

"How can I think that?" Connor drawled, watching her gulp. "How do you imagine?"

"Now, hold on a minute," Mike said. "Connor, shut up, you're being an idiot. Ella, ignore him."

Ella seemed to gather herself. She skewered Connor with a silver look from hard eyes and spoke in a voice that could have frozen water.

"If you think, after Lady Susan became ill, after the conversation I had with Lord Ralph, I would *deliberately* screw this up, you've even less intelligence than I thought possible. Not to mention all the work I did to raise money for this bloody project, the *hours* I've spent rustling up favours from our suppliers *on top of* my other full-time job!" She drew a breath. "You're not the only person who's worked hard on this garden, Connor! But no one else counts, do they? Because you're the genius designer and it's all about *you*!"

She stepped forward with clenched fists, and Mike stepped forward.

"That's enough from the pair of you!" he said, exasperated. "We can have this argument another time when we've got this mess sorted out!"

Connor rolled his eyes, and Ella seemed to calm down with an effort.

"What can I do?" she asked and Connor exploded.

"I think you've done enough, don't you?"

"I've already sent a message to someone and hope to hear in the morning. It'll be fine," Mike said, ignoring him. Connor stared at Ella and realised that her eyes were bright because they were filled with tears. His stomach lurched and then his jaw tensed. Could he have got it wrong? His mind flashed over conversations, what had happened during the build, even the discussions when he thought she was on his side.

Yes. He might be wrong. But he'd wait until he was sure he *was* wrong before he made the apologies. Ella's chin rose, and she swung away, presumably to return to the cottage.

He thanked Mike for coming out, but his project manager scowled at him.

"Not that I expect this to change your mind, but I think you're an idiot and wrong. As if we needed any more enemies!"

"We'll see. Let me know when Henshaw is coming."

28

Naturally, thought Ella, everything was *not* fine. Mike's electrical contractor, Dave Henshaw, who was as broad as he was tall, blew out his cheeks when he saw the cabling.

"Frankly, I don't know how you didn't burn the place down!" he whistled as he struggled to his feet after peering at the fuses, cables and switchgear. "It's been complicated by the solar panels, but... well, I think you'll need to check the lot, if not re-install it all."

"*All* of it?" Mike said sharply. Dave shrugged as he dusted off his hands.

"Well, given the state of the work here, let's just say *I* would. It's your choice." His voice trailed off, leaving Ella in no doubt that only an idiot wouldn't do exactly as he'd suggested.

"How long will that take?" she asked, dreading the answer.

"About two weeks to do it properly, I would say."

Ella closed her eyes in despair. It was too much; first that oaf suggesting that she did this deliberately, and now the humiliation of having suggested something that had gone *so* wrong. But she had only been trying to help!

"There, there!" Dave soothed. "Give me access and me and one of my lads will go over it all with a microscope. We might manage it in ten days, you never know. But the sooner we start, the better."

"How much?" Ella asked before Mike could say anything.

Dave wrinkled his nose and looked at Mike.

"Well... mate's rates?" Mike nodded vigorously. Dave sucked his teeth and then gave what Ella considered a reasonable figure. God alone knows what it would have been outside of mate's rates.

"Deal," she said swiftly. "Let me have your card and I'll send a confirmatory email. Can you start today?"

The brown eyes in his face gleamed at her with approval.

"A lass of action! Grand, just what I like. Here's my card. If you let me see the original spec, Mike, we'll make a start."

The pair walked away, deep in conversation. Ella sighed and tried to ignore the sick feeling in her stomach. The additional cost was a blow. That, and the fact that after all her effort, Connor thought her capable of such an underhand, despicable act of treachery had left her bruised, and even weepy. And angry – God! – she was furious. She brushed aside the fairness in her nature which pointed out that in fact, at the beginning of the build, she'd been somewhat less than helpful. But this... *this*... wasn't her. Goddamn it, didn't he know that?

She clung on to that feeling of anger; it seemed to be the only thing keeping her upright. Something in the back of her mind whispered that the cost, surely, should be the thing which made her angry. Not what Connor thought about her.

She glanced at the business card in her hand, just as Connor barrelled around the corner. She straightened her spine and looked past him, before turning on her heel and marching towards her office.

"Ella, where's Mike?" he called after her.

"Find him yourself!" she responded childishly while she continued to walk away. She heard him curse behind her and smiled tightly. He thought she'd been unhelpful before that ridiculous outburst last night.

"Well, you ain't seen nothing yet!" she muttered.

"Tell me again," Connor said to Dave Henshaw. Dave sighed heavily and started his explanation from the beginning. There was another man there too, from Sedgeley's, the electricians that Ella had suggested, looking incredibly uncomfortable.

As he listened, he started to feel a cold lump in the centre of his chest grow, until he found it difficult to speak.

"We did what we thought was right," said the man from Sedgeley's, when Dave had finished. "But I've not been easy since the job finished so I rang this morning and Ms Sanderson told me about the problems. I came straight away."

Dave glanced at his fellow electrician, shuffling and uneasy.

"When Simon arrived, we were just about to pull out the lot – so he's actually saved us a bit of time, explaining the thought processes behind the work," added Dave. Connor looked up hopefully and Dave rapidly shook his head. "Not that this will knock much time off the rewiring, but maybe a day?"

Connor straightened his shoulders and thought hard. What could they do while Dave sorted out this mess? His mind skimmed over the plans which he knew off by heart now, and inwardly he groaned. The fountains were the last piece of engineering work before they moved onto the planting in that area of the garden. If they were digging up the cables to check at each stage of the cascade, that would mean they couldn't do anything to either of the banks.

Mike pursed his lips, obviously thinking along similar lines.

"We could sort out some of the wet weather structure in the arbour, but after that, we'll be twiddling our thumbs. The trees for the Rainbow Walk won't arrive for another two weeks, I can see if we can bring them forward..."

"I can't apologise enough," Simon said awkwardly. "Ashton Manor is one of our biggest customers and we should have turned the work down. But I thought we could handle it. And Ms Sanderson seemed so anxious about it, I really wanted to help."

"How did she ask you to help?" Connor asked casually, ignoring Mike's glare.

Simon thought a little, his sandy eyebrows furrowed as he recollected.

"She asked if I'd worked on outdoor electrics, which we had. She told me about the fountains and in my mind, I just imagined they were a lot, lot smaller than they were. When we arrived and saw the scale of it – well, I nearly said something then."

"Why didn't you?" Connor's voice was hard.

"I wish I had!" Simon said, hanging his head. "But I really wanted to help, and I thought, how hard can it be...?"

Connor was silent.

"You've every right to be furious, but truly, we were trying to help. Sedgeley's will happily pay for the rewiring and anything else that's within our capabilities, we'll give you a discount for," Simon added.

"That won't be necessary, Simon," Ella's cool voice floated from behind Connor. "Mr McPherson will be arranging all his own works from here on in. And you work, if you recall, for Ashton Manor."

Simon swivelled from Connor to Ella's expressionless face, clearly confused, until Dave drew him away to get on with the job in hand. Mike, seeing storm clouds gathering, also excused himself. Connor regarded Ella's still figure and thought she looked all angles, all spikiness.

"Couldn't you have let him make the offer?" Connor asked quietly. "He obviously feels bad. We wouldn't have taken him up on it, obviously."

"Still thinking I'd be sabotaging your efforts, Mr McPherson?"

"No – because his firm, however well-meaning, doesn't deal with the type of work we do. Look, I'm sorry. You look awful."

Her mouth dropped open, and she gasped in outrage.

"Your insults just go on and on, don't they? First my integrity, now my appearance!"

He shook his head.

"No, no, I meant that I've caused you pain, and I can see it on your face," Connor said and wondered how deep he could dig himself before he threw the shovel away. Ella glared at him and put her hands on her hips.

"You have *irritated* me. I don't give a damn what you think of me personally, but strangely, I object to you calling me a saboteur, a liar, or devious, or... or... or anything else which fits with your small-minded view of the enormous efforts I've put into this bloody garden."

"Ella—"

"What has Simon told you?" she demanded.

He told her.

"So unless the next words out of your mouth are an apology, you can raise the rest of the money alone."

"I'm very, very sorry."

Silence.

"I'm very sorry. I'm an idiot. I should have known you wouldn't do such a thing," he said. She stared at him, her mouth a firm line.

"Why didn't you?" she asked at last.

"What?"

"Why didn't you know I wouldn't sabotage the *one* thing my employer wants to achieve this year?"

This time, Connor was mute.

"*Why*, Connor? What had you seen that would imply that I was capable of wrecking Lady Susan's hopes and dreams? And if you think you're getting away *without* this conversation, you arrogant little shit, you have another think coming!"

Connor's head reared up and his lips folded together firmly. Her silver gaze skewered him and she folded her arms, as if she was indeed prepared to wait all day for his answer.

"All right. I was wrong, very wrong. I jumped to the wrong conclusion," he finally said. "It seemed as if everything was starting to go well, that we were finally on top of it. And then this..."

She glared at him, and he saw that this conversation was not over.

"We've been working together for at least a couple of months now, and honest to God, I thought you knew me better than that! This was an attempt to be helpful that backfired," she said.

"I know," he muttered to the floor. Then he looked her full in the eyes. "I do know you better than that. It was just – everything was getting on top of me. This was just one more thing."

She said nothing. And then she sighed and that awful frigid expression left her face.

"Right."

Were they friends? He didn't know. But perhaps it was a start.

"I'll just have a quick word with Simon," she said.

He stood back to let her go ahead of him and watched her ponytail sway from side to side as she walked towards the electricians, her slender figure graceful and elegant. He felt a bit of lump beside her, truth be told. But the conversation, although acutely uncomfortable, had lightened his mood a little, and the sense of being wrong in the world had receded slightly. He shook his head, amazed. Who'd have thought her good opinion of him would be so important?

∽

Ella kept her mind a careful blank while they spoke to the electricians. She'd wasn't afraid of conflict, never had been. But with Connor, the rift had felt like having a whole body plaster pulled off. She'd not eaten all day, feeling too queasy this morning to sit down and have breakfast. She'd managed half a cup of tea.

As the electricians started to describe what had to be done, she understood enough to know that her attempt to be helpful was going to cost them in both budget and time, but more concerning was the impact on the *rest* of the build. She bit her lip, feeling the guilt swamp her. Connor looked side-swiped, she thought, which made her feel even worse.

Dave pulled Simon aside, and they began to gently pull at wires and look at them intently.

"Can you continue around the cabling work?" she asked Connor, and he seemed to start.

"The rewiring? I don't know... No, I don't think so. They'll need to dig up the housing for the cables. I'm not sure yet what we'll do instead."

His shoulders sagged.

Her earlier anger forgotten, Ella said, "It's all my fault, I don't know what to say."

He gazed at her for a moment.

"You were trying to save us some money," he said finally.

"I know, and my intentions truly were honourable, but this – this is awful!" she said, her throat tight.

Connor turned to her, taking her by the shoulders and for a wild moment, she wondered if he would shake her. Really, he had enough to deal with, without her personal guilt trip. Ella gazed into his blue eyes and wondered idly if he knew just how beautiful they were.

"You were trying to help, as you said. We are where we are, we'll just have to be creative," he said fiercely.

She tried to speak and failed, her voice clogged with distress and was astonished as he hugged her, pulling her into his arms suddenly. The length of his long, hard body pressed against her. Then his arms dropped from her. She blinked, registering the loss of his warmth. She stared at him wordlessly and then blindly walked away.

•

29

Connor stared at the bottles of booze on his shelf. He couldn't remember the last time he'd taken a drink. He picked up a bottle of whisky and put it down again. Actually, yes he could remember, he'd drunk one glass of champagne at that ridiculous Halloween event. And another at Jonas' house at Christmas. And another at the auction. He realised suddenly that every time, Ella had dominated his thoughts. His gaze swept around his living room for the moon-gazing hare, and to his surprise, a sense of peace lapped gently at his mood. Maybe a drink would also help.

He was desperate for sleep, and against all his instincts wanted to take a sleeping pill. And he had a banging headache. Dave Henshaw and his small, wiry assistant would be on site tomorrow to finish the wiring and check and double-check the power to the water features so they would not be plunged into darkness again, but they'd still lost time from the build.

He closed his eyes. God, yes, he did indeed need a drink, and he would have one, but first – what could he take for his headache? The bathroom cabinet didn't hold much, but his washbag yielded some powerful painkillers that he'd taken for a sprained ankle some years ago, which he'd never thrown out. He peered at the instructions. *Take only four in any eight-hour period.* He'd take two tablets now, which would sort out his head. If he still had the headache in the morning, he could take another two with his breakfast.

The tablets went down with tap water, which cooled his throat. He rinsed the glass, dried it and put it away. He sighed, toying with the idea of food and just as quickly rejecting it. He rubbed his chin, his beard rough against his fingers. He would need to trim it again soon. A flash of memory lit his consciousness. He'd been sixteen, and his sisters, led by Caitlin, had teased him mercilessly at the result of his trip to the Turkish barber.

"Oh my God, it's *so* matinee idol!" giggled Caitlin.

"We'll have no blaspheming in this house, I'll thank you!" came his father's voice and Caitlin had disappeared like mist. When his father had seen him, he'd smirked at Connor's goatee too. Just one more thing his father had laughed at in the long, long list throughout Connor's life.

He blinked, and he was back at the cottage at the kitchen sink. He reached for a glass and a bottle of red wine. The cork came out with a satisfying pop, and Connor sniffed the neck. Smelled like wine. He poured a generous measure and took a tentative sip. He wasn't even sure if he'd like it, it had been so long... But yes; it tasted plummy and smooth and he took a bigger mouthful. He grabbed the bottle and headed for the sofa.

His thoughts flicked over the events of the past few weeks. The fountains had been the last straw for the schedule, stopping any planting nearby while the electricians checked the cabling. All week, he had focused on damage limitation. Even before this, he'd worked with the crew from dawn until dusk, planting, and building. But it wouldn't be enough. The arbour would be ready, but it would be in a wasteland of half-finished earthworks and landscaping. He knew now that to finish the first phase as he'd planned it would be impossible with the size of crew and budget they had, no matter how many hours they put in. He'd failed, battered by the weather, unbending officials, fickle sponsors and an over-ambitious schedule.

To mitigate the sinking of his heart, he poured more wine. He'd failed before – or at least he had in the eyes of his unforgiving father – but this time it mattered. His failure was crucial to one of the most important people in his life: Jonas. He took a deep drink and unbidden, memories from ten years ago flooded his mind.

"Connor, what has happened to you?" He could hear his father in his head, berating him. "It's no good sitting here and feeling sorry for yourself! People are counting on you to deliver! And it's your responsibility isn't it, you're the money man, aren't you?" Connor could see his father using his bony fingers to put quotation marks around the word 'money man' and say them with as much distaste as he might say the word pornography. Connor had hidden his head in his hands. His mother had come into the room to drag his father away, muttering as he went. "What kind of son have I raised?" The words rattled Connor's brain, blocking the soft, soothing words of Caitlin who pulled him into her arms.

Connor reached again for the bottle and found it empty. He stood too quickly and swayed against the low arm of the leather sofa.

"Damn," he said, and concentrated on putting one foot in front of the other. He'd have some coffee, sober up a bit. Actually, screw that. He searched for another bottle of the red and smiled broadly when he found it. It was a good job Jonas drank red wine, or he'd have none in the cottage. After pulling out the cork, he walked carefully back to the sofa and fell into it. He stared blankly at the fireplace, now empty with the arrival of June.

Connor had long forgiven his father for his words but he couldn't forget them – they stuck like burrs to his memory, pricking him at times like this.

He poured more wine and wondered if this was the action of a weak man – getting drunk. Nah, it was about relaxing him. He looked again at the hare. As his eyes slid over its graceful lines, some tension drained from him. Although that damned headache was still there. Where had he put those pills? Ah yes, they were sitting on the kitchen counter, ready for him to take when he went to bed. He frowned. Had he taken some already? No, he didn't recall that. He'd have another glass of wine first and then head up to bed.

Really, he thought, as he sloshed the wine into the glass, he ought to drink more often. It had been a promise to himself to help him stay sane, to stop him falling... falling wherever it was he fell when he got ill. But by God, this was helping him relax in a way he hadn't relaxed in months. Of course the other way had been with sex, but even that had lost its appeal. Although Ella Sanderson had intrigued him, with her chilliness blowing – well, cold and then warm and then, the other day in the office, *very* warm indeed. Who knew she was passionate about sculpture? Although maybe the hare should have given him a clue, but he'd missed it. He wondered in what other ways she could be passionate. And then that hug over the fountains... He could still feel the imprint of her against him, before she'd marched off. He assumed she still hadn't forgiven him.

His temples throbbed, and cursing, he made his way over to the pills, kicking a chair or two en route.

"Oops," he said absently.

The pills needed water, so he carefully filled a glass and took two pills. No more, the instructions were clear. He staggered back to the sofa and sipped his wine, his eyes focused on the hare again. It was lovely, long-limbed, elegant and cool. Like the woman, he realised.

Well, the wine certainly was relaxing him, he thought woozily. Perhaps he ought to get into bed. And then, just as he was getting to his feet, it all went black.

～

Ella put the book down, having read the same paragraph three times. Monty glared at her.

"Yes, I *know* I'm fidgeting. And I'm sorry, but I don't know what's the matter with me!" Ella protested. Sighing, she rose and made tea. She picked up the book again. Ten minutes later, she threw it across the room. Monty gave her a haughty look and slinked away with delicate steps.

"Thanks for the support there!" she muttered towards his rear end as he flicked his tail at her and disappeared around the corner. She sighed. She'd tried distracting herself with a variety of media tonight – TV, the radio, even a selection of CDs. Nothing held her interest for more than five or ten minutes. She'd eaten and then cleaned up, then cleaned out the cutlery drawer, then taken out the bin. She'd forced herself to sit down and relax – and how successful had that been?

The pile of papers on the coffee table called to her, and she took them onto her lap, sorting through odd pieces of junk mail, her bank statement, a flyer for a barn dance next month in the next village – and Jonas Keane's card. She contemplated it, her fingertips tracing the logo for Halcyon Enterprises, embossed no less, and the plain black letters that made up his name. She'd spoken to Claudia Moretti, his press officer, and had wondered after the call if she was as elegant as she sounded. But regardless, she'd been a goldmine of excellent advice, and Ella had scribbled three pages of notes about how to handle negative press coverage during their forty-five-minute call. She would need it for the bloody Historical Commission...

Ella slumped back on her squishy sofa, wondering if her growing sense of unease was warranted. No noise from next door. Although Connor might be sleeping. As she'd advised him. She tutted to herself.

"For heavens' sake, be rational!" she muttered and got a glass of whisky. As she regarded the half-inch of golden liquid, she came to the reluctant conclusion that she was drinking too much lately. Still, she had a bloody good excuse – two jobs, deadlines piling on top of her, and trying to create money out of thin air.

And keep an eye on Connor McPherson. She sighed gustily.

It wasn't as though he wanted help. She'd done everything she could to offer it and been firmly rejected. Hell, he thought her capable of deliberately messing up his wiring. And Mike, Lady Susan had both tried, without success. He just ignored them, working all hours, and becoming a proper grumpy bastard in the process. But now – *now* she was concerned. When they'd had the news about the fountain cabling, she thought something had died in Connor's eyes. The guilt of her actions gnawed away at her. If only she'd not tried to cut corners!

Love in a Mist

And what on earth had she thought she was doing, allowing him to hug her? She could still feel his strong thighs against her body, and the muscles in his arms.

She heard a thump from next door, and froze, listening intently.

There was silence. Could he be in bed? He certainly could do with the rest. She'd been up in the small hours herself to get a drink the night before and noticed the light from the cottage windows shining on the front lawn. And she had noticed him up and out earlier and earlier lately.

Their relationship had been tense since the fountain debacle. As though they both expected the other to break a precarious truce. But it wasn't just with her; he seemed to be jovial and joking one moment, terse and monosyllabic the next with everyone. And he had... withdrawn. No, she decided, Connor McPherson was certainly not 'right'.

Her eye caught sight of Jonas' card on the table. Before she could think twice, she grabbed her phone and dialled the number.

"Keane."

"Hello, Mr Keane, this is Ella Sanderson."

Pause.

"What can I do for you, Ms Sanderson?"

Ella opened her mouth and then shut it again.

"Hello?"

"Hello, I'm sorry, I'm not sure how to start this conversation," she said in a rush. "It's about Mr McPher... it's about Connor."

"What about Connor?" the voice on the end of the phone became razor sharp.

"I'm worried. I don't know him very well, but I think he's working too hard and today we had another setback." It suddenly occurred to her that Jonas was a customer, and she clammed up, suddenly doubting the wisdom of the call.

"How did he take that?" Jonas asked, ignoring that piece of information to focus on Connor.

"Not well," Ella said and then told him about the mood swings, the distance he seemed to keep. "He seemed to, like, withdraw. His face closed up. If you know what I mean?"

"Oh, I know," Jonas said grimly. "Where is he?"

"He's in the cottage next door, but I... I don't know, I'm concerned for him. I heard a thump a while back and then... nothing. No TV, radio, nothing. The walls are thick, but even so, I can usually tell if he's in there."

"Hang on. Sam?" Jonas Keane called to Sam. There was a muffled response. "I think Con may be in trouble, can you please call him? I want to know how he sounds."

Dimly, Ella could hear a ringtone next door. It went on and on. A moment later, Jonas came back on the phone.

"There's no answer. Can you give him a knock?"

Ella was already moving, and within a minute was banging on Connor's door. After two minutes, she peered through the window.

"I don't understand, he might not even be in, the place looks emp — Oh! Oh, my God!"

"What?" barked Jonas.

"He's on the floor, I can see his foot..."

"Can you break in?"

"No, I'll call an ambulance and run and get the spare key to get in." Ella disconnected the call and dialled emergency services. Once she knew they were coming, she turned and ran to the manor, clattering into the estate office to get a spare key. Four minutes later she was back, fumbling with the lock, her chest heaving.

She darted inside the cottage and her head swam as she saw blood on the carpet. Then she realised it was wine, and her mind computed two nearly empty bottles and then...

"Oh, no!" she breathed as she caught sight of the packet of evil-looking pills. "Oh God, Connor, what have you done?"

In the distance, she heard the sirens, and she knelt by him and held his hand, waiting for the ambulance to arrive.

30

"Ella!"

Ella turned to see Sam Winterson rushing towards her, arms outstretched. Without a thought, Ella walked into her hug and burst into tears.

"There, there," soothed Sam, gently drawing her to one side to sit on a hard plastic chair. "He'll be fine. He's a big strong lad." Ella nodded, unable to speak.

"Thanks for your text," Jonas said, looking sombre. "I can barely believe it."

"We should wait until we hear what the doctors have to say before we jump to any conclusions," Sam said firmly, rubbing Ella's back as she would do a baby. Ella closed her eyes for a moment, soothed by the motion. She sniffed, and wiping her eyes with her sleeve, pulled herself together.

"Lady Susan and Lord Ralph have been here, but I sent them home," she said, her throat feeling scratchy. "I said I'd call in the morning. Or later," she amended, looking at the clock.

"I bet you're wrecked, aren't you?" Sam said, looking around the dull turquoise walls. "Is there anywhere we can get a drink?"

"The café closed at ten thirty, so we're reduced to vending machines, I'm afraid," Ella said.

"Ella?"

Ella stood up to greet Jeanette, very different and efficient in her nurse's uniform.

"Jeanette! How is he?"

"I can't tell you, you're not family. But strictly between us, he's doing better." Ella closed her eyes, unprepared for the wave of relief which washed through her.

"Is his family coming?" Jonas asked.

"Yes, I understand one of his sisters is on her way – luckily, she was in London, rather than Ireland."

"Caitlin?" Jeanette nodded and cast an eye up the corridor. "But I can't really tell you anything else, you need to get it from the doctor." Ella nodded and squeezed Jeanette's hand. As if on cue, the doctor, frowning at a flip chart, walked towards them. She introduced herself as Dr Khan.

"I brought in Connor McPherson," Ella said. "I know you can't tell us much – but is he okay?" The doctor raised her eyes to Ella's tear-stained face.

"Are you a close friend, or a relative?" Ella shook her head. Jonas stepped forwards.

"I'm a close friend. He's going to be my best man in about two months, I hope."

"Well, I can only tell you he's stable, and we're doing some toxicology tests on him at the moment. He's unconscious and likely to remain that way for a while."

"Can we stay?" Sam asked.

"Visiting hours are definitely over so I suggest you come back tomorrow. You'll just get in the way of the nursing staff." And with that, Dr Khan bustled away. As soon as the doctor disappeared around the corner, Jeanette grinned.

"Not known for her bedside manner, but she *is* right. I'm on duty tonight. I've got Ella's number and if you give me yours, I'll include you in a group message if there's any change."

"I'll wait to see Caitlin and we'll get a cab back to the cottage. Is it okay if we land ourselves on you for the night, Ella?" Jonas asked.

"Of course," Ella said, automatically starting to plan sleeping arrangements. "Will Caitlin need a bed? Connor's cottage also has a spare room, so she could stay there. If that's all right?"

Sam beamed at her.

"Yes, that would be great – she won't have had time to arrange anything. I'll help get things organised." Sam went on tiptoe to kiss Jonas. "See you later, sweetie."

～

Ella was giving Connor a stern talking to while the machines beeped and the oxygen canister wheezed. Jonas would soon bring Caitlin, who'd finally arrived at the cottage at three in the morning. Jeanette had sent a precious text saying that Connor had been comfortable all night and was still stable. Ella had arrived at the hospital at nine o'clock and, fortified by the worst cup of tea ever to pass her lips and some soggy toast from the canteen, she'd been at Connor's bedside for an hour. She shifted on the uncomfortable chair and glared at him.

"Honest to God, Connor, *nothing* would ever be worth this!" she told his unconscious form firmly. "I understand you were worried about the garden, but really – a bit of bare earth here and there would hardly be the end of the world, would it?"

She watched his face, the skin beneath the beard pale and translucent. Those thick dark eyelashes would not be out of place on a model.

"Goddamn you – if you only knew about the *shock* I had. Seeing you on the floor, thinking you were bleeding when actually, it was the sodding wine! Frankly..." she leaned closer to his ear, feeling his warmth brush her skin. "You're a complete idiot and if you ever give me a scare like that again, I'll kill you myself!"

"Ah, you might have to get in line, love!" said a lilting voice behind her and she twisted around so fast she almost hurt her neck. A dark, curvy woman who could only be Connor's sister was leaning against the door frame, her blue eyes twinkling. Ella scrambled to her feet.

"Caitlin, is it? I'm Ella, I live in the cottage next door. I couldn't sleep, so I decided to come over."

Caitlin's gaze sharpened as she examined Ella, and Ella asked her in a rush if she'd been comfortable in Daffodil Cottage. The previous night, Ella had tidied up a bit while Sam put fresh bedclothes on the guest bed. Ella had thought the cottage considerably changed from when she'd had supper. Not dirty, or a mess, but somehow uncared for. At supper, there had been flowers, a faint scent of wood polish, a sense of warmth and homeliness. Now it reminded her of a hotel room with the bare minimum of housekeeping.

"I think I'd have had to sleep in the car if it hadn't been for you! So, thank you." Caitlin moved over to peer down at her brother. Her soft mouth tightened slightly. "Have you seen any doctors?"

Ella hadn't. "Shall I ask?" she offered. "You stay here with Connor." Caitlin murmured her thanks, and Ella walked to the nurses at their station. She returned ten minutes later.

"Apparently, they'll be doing rounds in about an hour, so I'll get off," Ella said briskly. Caitlin nodded at her, and Ella could see the smudge of mascara which might have come from tears. Ella immediately went down on her haunches by her chair. "My friend works here as a nurse and she sent me a text – she shouldn't have – but she told me he'd had a good night. I don't know if that helps?"

Caitlin smiled tremulously. Once again, the likeness between brother and sister struck Ella, and it struck a chord in her heart.

"Can I get you a drink? Although I would avoid the tea, which resembles industrial waste. Not that I drink a lot of industrial waste." Caitlin laughed out loud, and Ella smiled in response.

"Coffee then?" Caitlin said.

"Probably safer."

When she returned, Caitlin was outside Connor's room, talking to the doctor that had dismissed Ella the previous night. Ella apologised and backed away, but Caitlin waved her forward.

"Ella, Dr Khan says that Connor is out of danger!"

Ella carefully put the coffee down on a nearby table, gathering her thoughts as quickly as she could and clamping down on the wild elation rising in her.

"That's marvellous news! What a relief!" she said.

"I know! Isn't it?"

Ella's eyes swivelled to the doctor who was already walking away but paused long enough to add, "It's likely he'll recover. He's a healthy man and appears to have the traditional luck of the Irish."

Ella closed her eyes briefly and opened them to find Caitlin watching her.

"I must get off," she said hastily. "Give him my..." she was just about to say, "my love" but she stopped herself and said, "Give him my best wishes."

Caitlin said that she would, with a speculative look in her eye, and Ella fled.

~

He was surfacing from deep water. Voices swirled above his head, but he couldn't work out the words. Perhaps he should sleep again...

"Con?" Caitlin's voice pierced his fug. "Look, big brother, ma's on her way so *truly* you need to be on your game. Please wake up."

Connor's eyes fluttered open, and he sighed. Sam and Caitlin came into view and he saw the smile stretch across Sam's lovely face.

"*There* you are," she said softly. "Glad to have you back, Connor." Someone grabbed his hand, and he realised it was Caitlin.

"Cait? God, was I dying? Is that why you're here?" His voice rasped through a dry throat and Sam pressed a glass to his lips, lifting him off the pillow as best she could.

"Jonas! Help me lift him, will you?" she called, and he recognised Jonas' strong arms hoist him up. He took a sip of water, and then another.

"Slowly," Sam commanded. "Don't want you choking now you're back with us."

Connor lay back, gasping a little. As his breathing steadied, he looked at the three faces above him. Then a nurse came in, someone he thought he recognised. Whisking the curtain across to cut off the rest of the room, she checked his blood pressure, the drip in his hand and took a blood sample. She worked quickly and gently, and only five minutes later she pulled back the curtain again with a grin and marched off.

"Well..." he said into the sudden quiet.

"Good to see you, bro," Caitlin whispered, and drew Connor into a hug. He could feel the tears splash onto the back of his gown and pushed his sister gently away from him.

"Caitlin? What's this?"

"We thought..." Caitlin couldn't speak and Jonas stepped forward.

"We thought you'd done something stupid."

Connor was perplexed for a moment, and the events of the previous evening formed shapes in his head. A picture of the kitchen worktop came into his memory. Oh God, he thought suddenly. The bloody pills! How many did I take? He closed his eyes, shaking his head in disbelief.

"What did you assume I did?" he said. No one spoke, and then Caitlin said hesitantly,

"We thought you'd taken an overdose."

He nodded. Yes, that's what he'd thought they thought. Shit. He opened his eyes.

"So everyone is clear – I didn't try to take my own life. I had a drink for the first time in months, took tablets for my head, and then forgot I'd taken them, which was the drink. I might be stupid, but I'm not *that* stupid."

He saw Sam's shoulders relax, and Jonas drew a huge breath. Caitlin's eyes shone with tears.

"Thank the Lord for that," Sam said and hugged him. Then they all talked at once – asking him if he knew what day it was, then talking about the dreadful catering at the hospital, and whether he needed the bathroom. He responded, but a little mechanically, appalled that his sister and his two best friends would judge him capable of suicide. Especially after... How could they even *consider* that?

While they chattered around him, he thought back over the last months. He picked out a pattern in the memories and it became more obvious how it started – not sleeping, no quiet time, driving himself into the ground, losing his temper, shutting himself off. The clearer it became, the more determined he grew. Something needed to change. When he got out of here, he'd be doing something about that.

∽

Lady Susan sagged with relief.

"That's marvellous news, Ella! Thank goodness! A complete recovery, you say?"

Ella nodded, looking at more missed calls on her phone. More bloody journalists, she thought gloomily. Taking advice from Halcyon's press officer, Claudia Moretti, she'd kept her comments honest and short. She did the same with Lady Susan.

Vincenzo Mazzi's office had called to ask about visiting the gardens. After a bit of dithering on Ella's part, a date was now in the diary. She'd just have to keep her fingers crossed that Connor would be out of hospital and fit.

"Well, that's three bits of good news today! I've found an interim housekeeper!"

Now it was Ella's turn to be delighted.

"Oh, that's brilliant! Who are they?"

"Joanne Jones," Lady Susan beamed. "And the best news for you, Ella, is that her background is in wedding planning! So she can take over the Keane celebration!"

Ella wasn't sure how she felt about that, suddenly. Over the past couple of days, she'd shared Sam and Jonas' concern, growing closer to them. Suddenly, the wedding was no longer an event that would torture her, but something in which she wanted to be involved. How strange.

"Is that all right?" Lady Susan asked, her face concerned. "I thought you had so much to do with the garden, that you'd be glad to get rid of it!"

Ella forced a smile.

"Yes. I am! When does she start? I must do a handover. And obviously, we'll need to check with Sam and Jonas that they're happy with us playing pass the parcel with their event..."

"Actually, I took the liberty of calling Sam and she recognises that you've had a massive workload and just wants you to do a handover," Lady Susan said. Ella was robbed of breath momentarily and astonished at the pain from the stab of hurt. She'd imagined she and Sam and Jonas had developed a bit of a bond. Well, how wrong could you be?

She murmured something about needing to talk to Mike and left Lady Susan looking puzzled.

31

Connor was tiring a little. But that wasn't surprising, given that his mother had just left in tears of relief. Caitlin and Magda were keeping him company, and that was even more exhausting. At last Caitlin left to take a phone call from another member of the family, and Magda fell silent.

After a few minutes, Magda said calmly, "You did it again, didn't you? And don't pretend to be asleep, I know you're not."

Connor reluctantly opened his eyes.

"What?"

"The Superman thing. Think everything depends on you and try to do it alone."

Connor opened his mouth to deny it and then remembered the conversations with Mike, Lady Susan, and Ella and abruptly closed it again. Magda nodded.

"Mmm. Guessed as much."

Connor hesitated while he formed the sentences in his head.

"People tried to help. But either I didn't think I needed it, or I was too stubborn to accept," he admitted. "Or maybe I didn't see how they *could* help?"

"Who offered?"

He shrugged, starting to feel slightly ashamed.

"Mike, for one. But he had enough on his plate. Lady Susan, and I truly didn't think she should try to help me – she's my client. And..."

He paused.

"And?" prompted Magda.

"Ella Sanderson. She tried a couple of times."

"She lives in the cottage next door, doesn't she? Is she the lady who wouldn't know a good garden design if she fell over it?"

Connor nodded, smiling.

"And she found you? And rang Dad on the night you were taken ill?"

Connor nodded again. He knew Ella had been in the ambulance and had visited him when he'd been unconscious. Caitlin had mentioned it. But she'd not come since, and he was upset about that. He frowned and found his god-daughter watching him intently.

"Caitlin told me Ella was sitting by your bed giving you a *right* earful when she arrived from London."

"Was she?"

"Yeah... have you seduced her yet?"

Connor laughed.

"I wish! No, Ella Sanderson is not the seducing kind."

Magda regarded him with her head on one side.

"No? Have to say, Connor, someone who's in hospital at two in the morning and back six hours later telling you off for taking an overdose doesn't sound like someone who doesn't give a damn."

"It wasn't an overdose, it was an accident."

"Yeah, but she didn't know that, did she?"

Connor kept quiet. Magda continued.

"All these offers of help and you end up getting drunk and almost coming to a sticky end with pills, Connor?" Her green eyes, so like her father's, glared at him. "As my godfather, is this any example to set?"

Connor stared, surprised at her harsh tone.

"I know, I know," he replied after a pause. "I've not been thinking straight. But the garden's been cursed with problems from the beginning and I should have known in February we couldn't finish it. Truly, it is my responsibility."

"And you're *still* not thinking straight! It might have been your responsibility to have a conversation with the client about it – but not to *build* it!" Magda sounded exasperated. "For God's sake get a grip, Connor! Who knows what could be done if you'd just *talk* to a few more people about it, rather than carry it all yourself!"

Connor couldn't think of a thing to say in response. Magda suddenly looked contrite.

"Shit, have I shot my mouth off? I'm sorry, Connor-"

"No, you're right," he interrupted. "Ella said as much to me too."

There was a pause.

"Did she? Hmm. Despite what Sam says about her taste in gardens, I think I might like her," Magda said, thoughtfully. "I think she's an original."

Connor was thoughtful. Yes, Magda was right. Ella was an original. Was she worried about him? A snatch of memory teased at him and he wondered whether he was imagining it, or whether he had heard her voice?

"You're a complete idiot and if you ever give me a scare like that again, I'll kill you myself!"

Connor said nothing but hope, slim but persistent, grew in his mind. An original? That had given him an idea.

∼

"You know our position, Ella! I can't work miracles!" Mike snapped at Ella as she sat down opposite him and then immediately apologised. She waved away his words.

"What about volunteers? We have tenants who have a little time on their hands until mid-July and I've spoken with Lady Susan about approaching them to ask if they would help. And I'm certain some of them will."

She *was* certain. Some tenants were angry Lady Susan's garden might be the target of hostility from the National Conservation Trust, not their favourite establishment body in normal times. They'd also seen some less than complimentary press coverage in one of the county magazines. Their dander, thought Ella, was well and truly up.

"Not everyone can help," she continued. "Our arable farmers are busy with potato spraying and cereal crops but our livestock farmers can lend a hand. What you need to work out is what can they do?"

It was like lighting a fuse. Mike suddenly stood up and called into the adjoining office.

"Jayne! Aadesh! Can you come in here?"

The crew members arrived and Mike quickly repeated Ella's suggestion of using the tenants. Jayne scribbled furiously on a pad, and the conversation was suddenly rapid, backwards and forwards. They talked about Connor's reaction and thought about ways to make the extra help palatable to him. They thought that Connor had been involved in an accident and Ella didn't correct them by telling them about the pills. After all, it was none of their business, she reasoned. In the middle of this, her phone rang, and glancing at it, she saw it was Sam. Ella tensed and moved away from the noisy table to the window.

"Ella Sanderson."

"Hi Ella, it's Sam!"

"Hello. What can I do for you?"

"Erm... well, is everything okay?"

"Fine. Has Joanne been in contact?"

"Yes, and we're coming in next week. But I know that the garden build is behind and I've had an idea. Are you able to talk to me now?"

"As a matter of fact, I'm in with Mike now, working out how we can use willing estate tenants to help with the garden." Ella's voice sounded cool, even to her.

"Ella, are you sure you're okay? You seem a bit distant."

"I have a lot on my mind."

"Right... well, the idea I had was to offer my group of twenty apprentices for a month. They work for me and on the gardens of the developments Jonas builds. They're at college, so they're not novices in landscaping and basic horticulture. I thought Mike could set them on and they'd more or less organise themselves and frankly, they'll be champing at the bit to work on a garden for Connor McPherson... and I thought I might lend a hand too... Hello? Are you still there?"

Ella pulled herself together.

"I'm sorry, you've just taken my breath away. That sounds like a *fantastic* idea. Just let me hand the phone to Mike so you can tell him – he'll worship you forever!"

Sam's protest stopped her.

"Hang on! Before you pass me over, I wanted to ask you if Vincenzo had called?"

"Was that you too? Yes, he's coming at the end of the week. It's so kind of you to give us an introduction." Ella grabbed the side of the desk, slightly dizzy. She was so used to bad news, she was unsure how to handle good news. Sam's merry laugh floated over the phone.

"Oh, don't thank me yet! He's a stickler for detail, is Vincenzo Mazzi! And if the garden hadn't been perfect for his business, he wouldn't be coming to see you! He's only been in a business a short time, but he's very careful with his cash, Vincenzo! I think he gets it from his father."

"Hang on – does his father run Mazzi Industries?" Ella said, suddenly recognising the massive energy firm and its owner, Cesare Mazzi, who'd been through more wives than she'd had hot dinners, it seemed.

"The very same."

"Thanks for the heads-up," Ella murmured. "I'll make sure we're all on point."

"He's a clever man, so keep it simple. Don't sell to him, just show things as they are. He appreciates a straight talker. And don't give the sponsorship away – he really wants to improve his profile in the UK and if this is right for him, he'll give you a fair price so make sure you drive for one."

"Right."

"And the last thing..."

Ella waited.

"We're sorry that you're not going to handle our wedding, but when Lady Susan called and explained about how much you had on your plate, we thought it might help you if we worked with Joanne, who sounds very professional. But after all you've done to help our celebration and Connor, we wondered if you could join us on the day?"

For the second time in five minutes, Ella couldn't speak.

"Me? But – but you don't know me!"

"Don't we?" Sam's voice was dry. "After the past few days, Ella? Look, I don't want to force you, because you won't really know anyone else other than Lady Susan and Lord Ralph – well, besides us and Con, obviously – but his family will talk to anyone and I'd be chuffed to bits if you would come. Will you?"

To her horror, tears flooded Ella's eyes and her voice cracked. She hated weddings and hadn't been to one since her own was so abruptly cancelled. And suddenly, in a second, that seemed like ancient history.

"I'd love to," she choked out.

"Oh God, please don't start me off too!" came Sam's watery chuckle in her ear. "It's been quite a few days, hasn't it? And I bet Jonas hasn't said thank you for saving his best friend and best man, has he?"

"I imagine he's been busy," Ella managed. Sam gave an unladylike snort.

"Pah. Bloody men. Anyway, you'd better hand me to Mike and hopefully I'll make his day."

∽

Connor's release from hospital was more kindly than he deserved; nurses smiled and wished him well, particularly Jeanette, who he had finally identified as Ella's netball teammate. No one at the hospital had scolded him for wasting their time, although Dr Khan had gently suggested that downing nearly two bottles of wine after an abstinence of more than a year was to be avoided. She'd made him promise to throw away the pills.

Love in a Mist

Caitlin had hugged him and shepherded his mother away when she wrung her hands too much. He'd had a text from his father, nominating his only son as a complete idiot, and only then adding that he was pleased Connor was on the mend. His other sisters had bombarded him with texts, and nieces and nephews sent videos saying they were looking forward to seeing him in Donegal soon and would he bring his fiddle? He *was* coming home soon, wasn't he?

He was a lucky, lucky man, he mused, as he unlocked the door to his cottage. Lucky to have people who cared about him. Lucky to be alive. Did she but know it, Ella was approaching sainthood in his family as the person who'd been aware enough to worry about him, smart enough to phone Jonas, and caring enough to stay with him in hospital.

The cottage smelled of lavender, as though someone had been in to air and clean it. There were fresh flowers on the kitchen table, which made his throat tight, and the fridge was stocked with milk, butter and cheese. He shook his head and dropped the overnight bag that Sam had packed for him. He took a deep breath and picked up the note by the flowers. It was Ella's neat hand.

Could you come to the project office when you're settled? We've got some suggestions about the garden. We'll expect you about noon, but let me know if this is too early. Ella Sanderson.

He frowned. What was that about? He had spoken briefly with Mike and told him about his hospitalisation and been pleased at Mike's no-fuss response. Mike had told him he was planning a much-reduced schedule.

But this sounded like things had changed. He waited for the tide of panic to rise in him. This time, the tide was tempered by curiosity about what Ella would say. He knew that without an army of contractors (which they couldn't afford) the first phase couldn't be finished, and although he'd been round and round the problem in his head, he hadn't found a solution. But what had Magda said to him – he ought to try not to be Superman? Okay, let's see what the collective hive mind could suggest.

32

Connor opened the door to the project office. There was a second's pause as a dozen pairs of eyes turned his way and then there was bedlam – cheers and whoops, Mike pushing forwards to shake his hand, Jayne beaming at him and Aadesh and Craig slapping him on the back, welcoming him. For the second time that day, his throat constricted and, as if looking for an anchor, he searched for Ella, standing quietly at the side of the room. His breath caught at the fierce flare of emotion in her face before her normal calm descended. He grabbed the back of a chair to steady himself. After the noise subsided, he smiled ruefully.

"Sorry to leave you to deal with it all," he said. "I've been indisposed."

He heard chuckles and gentle comments of 'idiot' and 'skiver'. When the joshing subsided, Mike cleared his throat.

"It's good to have you back! But we haven't been idle. We wondered what your opinion would be about this!" He pushed a schedule towards Connor. Connor ran his eyes over the plans.

"How?" he asked. "This will take a crew of about seventy people, even more! Last time I looked there were only ten of us. Unless you've robbed a bank?"

"That's next week. Meanwhile, Sam's lent us twenty apprentices for a month, we have another twenty tenants – and I have a small army of Friends who can't wait to get stuck in, if you tell them what to do," said Ella's cool voice. He gave her a long look, her dark grey eyes glinting silver. Waiting, expectant.

"If we briefed the apprentices, then gave them ten or so of the volunteers, we could crack through the planting fairly smartly, leaving our crew to focus on the structural work that we still need to do," Mike added, tapping his pen nervously on the pad in front of him. "What do you think?"

Connor was silent, feeling as if he'd just been taught the biggest lesson of his adult life. He glanced up and saw the expectant faces.

"I think it's brilliant," he said finally and felt the room exhale.

"Right, I'll start bringing people in on Friday to work on the arbour, so the plants have time to settle," Ella said crisply. People started talking all at once, and that, Connor thought, was that.

∼

Connor smiled as Ella scurried across the path towards the manor. She looked very focused and, as today Vincenzo Mazzi was visiting the garden, she would need to be. He knew Vincenzo's father, Cesare, better than his son, and mused on the very mixed personal reputation of Cesare Mazzi, who was on his fourth or fifth marriage. Vincenzo was a different character altogether, almost monklike compared with his father. Connor was aware of Vincenzo's growing reputation as a very astute businessman and a straight talker. Pleasant, simply-spoken – but ruthless. Silently, he wished her luck and then turned towards the newly-named Dragon's Den. The simple name had been submitted by a host of children from several schools and what was good enough for them, was good enough for Connor.

The plan for today was to hoist the willow nests into position and trial run the special effects. The light was perhaps too bright this morning, but the test would show the technician from the AV company the best location to place the projectors and speakers. And for the first time in ages, a lick of excitement flared through Connor's veins.

Half an hour later, Niels, a jovial Dutchman who was almost as tall as Connor, twinkled at him.

"We're ready to go, yes?"

Connor nodded eagerly, and Niels flicked a switch to begin the visual display. He talked in rapid, excellent English as the images flickered among the trees. "We've programmed the computers so that the dragons' movements are in random patterns; you'd need to watch for two weeks, twenty-four hours a day before any of the images repeated. It's the same for the sound tapes. We thought about adding music but thought it would be more naturalistic if we just kept it to the noise of the creatures."

Connor jumped as a dragon, a glorious animation in green and gold, roared and spit out a flame at a tree branch. He was impressed. And that was in the light of morning. In the dusk, the images would be spectacular.

"Do they land in the nests?" he asked, because after all, that was why the nests were in place.

"We might need to adjust some projectors slightly, but yes, I believe there's a small dragon coming out of the nest at the back – do you see it?"

Connor's gaze fixed on the nest, and the projection of a dragon, shyly edging its head from the small hole in the wicker structure. Connor's mouth dropped open in delight, and he turned, beaming, to Niels.

"Good God, that's amazing! You've done a brilliant job!"

Niels smiled, and then both men heard someone clapping. Connor turned to see Vincenzo Mazzi, cool and elegant, walking towards them with Ella close behind him, looking slightly flushed.

"Bravo!" the Italian said, his pale brown eyes dancing as he followed the circling dragons.

"Hello. I presume you're Cesare's son, Vincenzo?" Connor said.

"I am Vincenzo Mazzi," he said, without acknowledging his father.

"And you are Connor McPherson?" Vincenzo smiled briefly and Connor put out a hand.

"For my sins. How are you?"

"Very pleased to be here to witness this!" Vincenzo responded quietly. "Magnifico!"

Connor made introductions, wondering all the time why Ella was flushed and quiet. As Vincenzo spoke eagerly to Niels, he edged closer to her. "All okay?" he murmured. She smiled.

"He's quiet, but to the point. Good job I'm not an impressionable teenager, given how handsome he is."

"Hope he's not overstepped the mark?" Connor said, surprised at her words and tensing up. She glanced at him and smiled again.

"Not his style, I think. He's scrupulously polite. He's certainly not patted my bottom."

He'd better not! Connor thought and wondered if he'd spoken that aloud.

"I wonder if you could join us when you're finished, Connor? To talk Signor Mazzi through the plans for the next phase?"

"Sure. Will you be at the manor?"

"Yes, I have a small delegation coming around later today. Perhaps Signor Mazzi could join with the journalists?" Ella looked as though there was an unpleasant smell under her nose as she said the words. Vincenzo laughed softly, and it transformed his face.

"We share a common dislike of the media, I see! Mr McPherson, we need to speak about how you're powering that water feature..."

"It's powered from the solar panels from the manor roof," Ella said firmly. "However, in phase two, we're planning a new visitor centre and the power for this will need to complement our green credentials, if you're interested."

Vincenzo fell silent for a moment.

"Interesting. Yes, by all means, let us go to the manor. I'm looking forward to meeting Lady Susan. Ciao, Connor."

Ella gestured him in front of her and as he walked away, she turned briefly back to Connor to give him a thumbs up.

Thank God the weather had held, Ella thought as she gathered the press packs from the office. Tamsin, with pink hair and a nose ring, chewed the end of her pen. "Is Adam here with his grandfather?" Ella asked.

"Yeah, waiting at the manor – said he wanted to call in on Lady Susan," Tamsin said. "Ceinion Bryant called to say he'd be about half an hour late, he's been held up on the M4."

"That's a nuisance, but never mind," Ella said, mentally re-planning her route to visit the key sculptures at the end. "If he calls again, tell him to text me when he gets here. What with Vincenzo Mazzi, the technicians, the sculptor and the journalists, it's like Piccadilly Circus at the moment – or a soap, I can't work out which."

"Is Mr Mazzi still here?" Tamsin asked, pretending to swoon on the desk. "Cor, what a gorgeous looking man! And he's only twenty-six, so footloose and fancy-free! Ooh, that accent! Makes me go all wobbly on the inside! Do all Italian men look like that?"

"No, I understand he's a particularly luscious specimen," Ella said dryly.

"Do you need me to take anything to the manor?" Tamsin said hopefully.

"Sadly not, but I do need a list of volunteers to work in the garden on Friday."

Tamsin stuck out her tongue.

"Spoilsport. And yes, I've got about forty people, and I'm waiting to get responses from about..." she checked her list. "... about a dozen more. If I haven't heard by tomorrow morning, I'll call them all."

"A star is what you are," Ella grinned.

"And don't forget to call that bloke back," Tamsin added. "He called the office again this morning. He's beginning to sound desperate!"

Stephen, thought Ella. The grovelling letter she'd received from him that week had been particularly infuriating. All kinds of slimy excuses for his behaviour – and she thought he was probably still engaged to the pneumatic Juliet, too. What a bastard.

"Frankly, my dear, I don't give a damn," Ella said, rolling her eyes when Tamsin looked puzzled and didn't get the reference. She'd have to introduce her to Rhett Butler before long… "Right, I'll call him this afternoon and hopefully that will be the end of it, I can't have him hassling you as well as me. As if I didn't have enough to do…"

Ella was still muttering as she headed to the manor. Once the journalists were with Lady Susan, she'd ring him – and let him have it with both barrels. A grin lifted her lips and as she walked across the courtyard, the sun was shining, and her step lightened. God, what a difference a week made. Last week… well, she'd rather not think about last week.

Adam was eating a chocolate biscuit with Lady Susan and his grandfather Cedric when she arrived. And Vincenzo Mazzi was still there, looking as darkly handsome as ever. Ella pondered briefly why she didn't find him irresistible, and as a picture of Connor flashed through her head, she moved her thoughts firmly on. Vincenzo was also a bit of a cold fish, she thought; very restrained.

"Are you ready to talk to the journalists, Adam?" she asked.

He nodded, his mouth still full of biscuit, and Cedric heaved himself to his feet. Lady Susan looked on, amused.

"I hope you're up for this, Cedric," she said. "Journalists can be very demanding creatures."

He winked at her.

"But then again, we have Adam as our secret weapon. I bet they blink first."

Looking at the little boy, Ella thought Cedric was right. It would take a concrete-hard heart to dismiss this bright five-year-old. She couldn't wait to show him the Dragon's Den.

"I'll bring the press back at about two, Lady Susan and you can have a conversation with them over tea – or something stronger." Ella held out her hand to Adam. "Shall we go then?"

∼

Cedric had been bang on, Ella thought, half an hour later. Adam *was* a secret weapon, talking to journalists about what they'd finally called the Dragon's Den and how to cater for mythical creatures and the average dragon. Connor had listened intently, as had Vincenzo Mazzi.

"And what do you think of the Dragon's Den now it's built, Adam?" one journalist asked.

Adam tipped his head back and said simply, "I like it. The nests look like I thought they would."

Ella breathed a little easier.

"Well, Adam, I'm relieved about that, but would you like to see the dragons themselves?" asked another journalist. Adam shot him a scornful look.

"They don't come out in the day. And you might scare them," he added, looking askance at the journalist's bright green sweater. Ella saw Connor suppress a smile and step forward.

"Well, it so happens that they've just moved in, Adam, and they're a little restless, so they might come out. Would you like to see?"

Adam turned, his eyes wide, and nodded.

Connor nodded to Niels, and even the journalists fell silent. Seconds later, Adam raised his eyes to Cedric.

"I can hear them!" he whispered. Everyone could. The sound of wings beating the air, some strange unearthly calls and whistles. And then a large blue and violet dragon poked her head from a nest and Adam squeaked in excitement. Above the group in the tree canopy, dragons suddenly swooped in the air, small ones, gold ones, green and red ones, and Adam sighed in appreciation. As a tiny orange dragon appeared to dive-bomb the group, Adam laughed and clapped his hands as one or two of the reporters ducked. Ella, who had flinched away instinctively, also laughed at her foolishness and then marvelled at how realistic the animation was. Then, suddenly, the dragons landed on their nests and disappeared. All was quiet.

"Whoa!" Adam breathed. "That was *awesome*! Granddad, did you *see* them? Can I come again at night?"

"We'll have to wait until it opens, Adam," Cedric said, his face split by a wide smile at his grandson's pleasure. The reporters peppered Connor with questions, and he introduced Niels, who talked quietly to a few reporters about the technology. Ella was relieved to see him draw them out of Adam's earshot to keep his dreams alive.

"I'm so sorry I'm late!" A stocky, mop-haired man jogged up to the group and Connor hailed him.

"Ceinion! Brilliant – you made it!"

Ella watched as Connor introduced the sculptor, and she hid her surprise. He seemed too ordinary to have created the glorious sculptures she had seen – he reminded her of an overgrown teenager.

"And this is Ella Sanderson, who runs the estate," Connor said as he drew the Welshman over to her.

"It's wonderful to meet the person who created those amazing pieces!" she said sincerely and was surprised to see Ceinion blush.

"Th-thank you," he stuttered a little in response.

"You're entering the gardens into the National Contemporary Art Award, aren't you?" someone asked. Connor nodded and raised his voice to address all the journalists.

"Yes, this will be the debut of our outstanding sculptor, Ceinion Bryant, and although we're keeping some pieces a secret, we have a couple to show you." And Connor, effortlessly taking over from Ella, led the way into another part of the garden.

Ella smiled. It was going well. Fingers crossed they'd have some positive coverage from all this effort.

An hour later, it was all over, and Ella led the group to the manor. Once the journalists were in the genteel hands of Lady Susan and Lord Ralph, she ducked out of the room and picked up the phone in the cavernous hallway. She dialled the number and tapped her foot until Stephen answered.

"Finally!" Stephen announced when she gave her name. "I thought you might be avoiding me! I've been thinking about you non-stop—"

"I've been too busy to think about you, Stephen, and the only reason I'm ringing now is to tell you not to ring again – we've got a lot on and I can't have you hassling me or my staff."

"Oh, hang on—"

"No, Stephen. It's over. It was over from the moment the weaselly letter landed on my doormat, telling me you'd changed your mind. *Two weeks* before the wedding. It was over when I had to contact everyone to tell them it was off, and when I had to return all the bloody wedding gifts! Alone," Ella interrupted. "It was over seven years ago, and it's certainly all over now. Don't ring me again." And she put the phone down, feeling breathless, elated and as light as thistledown. She wheeled around at the noise behind her to find Connor looking thunderstruck.

"He stood you up?" he said quietly. She nodded, raising her chin.

"Arsehole. I should've decked him when I had the chance."

A slow smile spread across his face, making his blue eyes twinkle. "But perhaps you've done a better job?"

"*I* think so."

He chuckled, a soft sound that ran up and down her spine. She needed to join the press group, she thought.

"So you're footloose and fancy-free?" he asked, blocking her way into the room.

The minutes seemed to slow, and she looked into blue eyes and the world tilted as she was sucked into a vortex. The clatter of crockery tore the atmosphere, and she stepped to one side, peeping at him from under her lashes.

"I always was, Connor." And she swept back into the room.

33

Connor stretched his arms and straightened the crick in his neck. He glanced at the bright blue sky through the window and smiled wryly at the change in his fortunes. Now, apparently, the weathermen were prophesying a drought.

An elderly man poked his head around the door to the project office, apologised for disturbing Connor, and asked if he'd seen Steve or Luke, two of Sam's employees.

"They headed out to the rose garden about fifteen minutes ago," Connor said, standing up. "Do you know where that is?"

The newcomer nodded and disappeared. Connor thought the old man was so thin a powerful wind would break him in half. He wondered what Steve and Luke would do with him.

He asked as much of Sam when she breezed into the office a few minutes later.

"Archie? By God, there's nothing that man doesn't know about roses! If he were ten years younger, I'd be offering him a job!" she said, searching through some papers on the desk. She shot him a glance.

"You didn't really explain the rose garden, I'd like to know more. Do you have time before I go back to the crew?"

Connor immediately dug out the plans and began to explain.

"When I was pushing my grandmother around in her wheelchair before she died, she told me she loved to sit and smell the flowers. When she'd been walking with her frame, they were always too low or too high for her. So I've got three levels – the pergolas high up, the big pots at chest height and the planted roses at knee height."

Sam nodded and Connor described how he'd used a colour wheel to put clashing colours next to one another.

"So here I've got the purple rose William Lobb mixed with the Buttercup rose – both shrubs, both scented. They'll be glorious. And in the next section, we have orange amongst a choisya, which will have bright green leaves when the rose is in bloom..."

"Wow. Very modern!" murmured Sam.

He laughed.

"I imagine the traditionalists will hate it, but I have some soft, romantic planting with the usual pinks and reds a little further along."

"Yes, you've been having trouble with the traditionalists, haven't you?" Sam grinned.

"The National Conservation Trust? And the Historical Commission? Aye, they've been a royal pain in the rear."

"And nearer to home?"

Connor looked straight at Sam.

"Ella? Yes, we didn't see eye to eye at all when we met. I think she's thawing a bit."

"Have you explained this to her?"

Connor shook his head. "No, she hasn't had time to stop by lately. Unsurprising, given the number of volunteers she's juggling. She's been amazing..." His voice trailed off.

"She doesn't seem like the type of woman who you'd get on with, if I'm honest. Well, thinking back to Birgitta..." Sam paused delicately.

Connor groaned.

"Don't remind me of Birgitta!" Reluctantly, Birgitta came to mind – glamorous, curvy and flirtatious. In the early stages of their relationship, he'd wondered if they'd ever make it out of bed.

"No, she didn't seem quite... right for you," Sam said tactfully.

Connor chuckled. It seemed a long time ago now. He folded the plans and while he was putting them in a drawer, asked Sam casually what she thought of Ella.

"I think she's great," Sam said at once. "Smart, focused, great sense of humour. She was amazing when you were recovering. Caitlin practically thinks she walks on water."

"Caitlin would think *anyone* who wasn't Birgitta walked on water!"

"She may have saved your life, Connor. I think you should at least buy her dinner. Magda certainly thinks you should."

"And how is Magda?" Connor asked, changing the subject.

Sam sighed heavily.

"Changing courses. I'm not happy about it, but it seems she's made her mind up. I wanted her to have a wider sphere of expertise..."

"But she knows what she wants, Sam."

"She knows what she *thinks* she wants! I don't know if she'll enjoy it for an entire year, come rain or shine!"

"She can come and work for me," Connor said easily. "Don't look so surprised! I think she'll be brilliant and you can be sure she won't get special treatment."

"Are you sure? God, she'd be thrilled! Will you tell her when she arrives?"

"Tell me what?" asked Magda, barrelling through the door.

"God, talk of the devil!" Sam said, looking with exasperation at her soon-to-be stepdaughter. "You have ears like a bat, I swear."

"How would you like to spend your internship with me?" Connor said and watched as Magda went pink with pleasure and hugged him.

"You'll need to behave!" Sam said. "No special treatment, Connor says!"

"Don't sweat it, Step-mama," the irrepressible Magda said, recovering her poise. Sam spluttered and gave Magda a thump on the arm.

"Well?" Connor demanded.

"Yes, I *would* like!" Magda said, grinning widely.

When Ella walked into the project office, she thought for a moment it was empty. She hesitated and then a sigh and the sound of scuffling came from under a desk and a teenager rose from the floor, blowing her cheeks out.

"Oh!" the girl said. Ella realised that the teenager was a young woman of about twenty and wondered what she was doing in the project office. The girl narrowed her eyes and strode forward, holding out her hand.

"Hi! You must be Ella. I'm Magda Keane."

She took in Magda's glossy dark hair and green eyes, which she'd undoubtedly inherited from her father, and automatically shook her hand. Her mind was wondering how Magda Keane knew who she was.

"Yes, I'm Ella Sanderson, estate manager for the manor. Are you waiting for Sam?"

"She's looking at the rose garden with Con, I was looking for my earring," she explained, holding out a delicate gold stud. Ella reflected on how very assured Magda was. "Can I help you?" Magda added, and Ella's eyebrows rose.

"I was looking for Connor, rather than Sam," she responded. This slender girl had settled in confidently, she thought, trying to clamp down on her irritation and ashamed that she *was* irritated. It was hardly Magda's fault that she oozed poise.

"Can I give him a message?"

"No, it's fine. I'll catch him later," Ella said, thinking the schedule of volunteers could wait. If she was honest with herself, it was more of an excuse to see him... She turned to go.

"Thank you for finding him – for saving him, I should say," Magda said in a rush and Ella paused, unsure what to say to her. Attempted suicide was a bit of a tricky topic to include in conversation, and Ella wasn't sure how she could avoid it.

"I was delighted to help," she said at last. "It was lucky I was there."

Magda gazed at her, and Ella thought the young girl was trying to read her thoughts.

"Yeah, although he's such a lightweight, isn't he?"

Ella frowned. Whatever she had thought Magda would say, that wasn't it. Lightweight wasn't how she would have described Connor's burden over the past few months.

"What do you mean?"

Magda flapped her hand.

"You know – staying off the booze for twelve months and then necking two bottles so he didn't know what he was doing."

Her words, said so nonchalantly, caught Ella's attention.

"Didn't know what he was doing?" she repeated.

"Yeah, he was so sozzled by the drink, he didn't realise he'd taken the pills, so he took more. According to the doctor, that was what made him pass out. Otherwise, he'd just have had the hangover from hell..."

Ella's face cleared as relief flooded through her. He hadn't attempted suicide; it had been an accident.

"How incredibly stupid," she said, almost to herself. Magda was watching her closely.

"Yeah, what an idiot! Talk about irresponsible! I'll be reminding him of that for years!" Magda gurgled with glee.

"Why had he given up drinking?" It flashed through Ella's mind that whenever she'd seen Connor with a drink, it was just *one* drink, followed by water.

"I think..." Magda paused. Had Magda confided too much? Ella wondered. She waited. "I think he just wanted more control," Magda said finally.

"Mmm. I know the authorities have driven him to distraction by all the red tape that comes with designing a garden for a historic house."

"Yes, he's mentioned it a couple of times."

Both of them laughed at Magda's wry tone.

"Anyway, I'll tell my hopeless godfather that you're looking for him."

"Thanks. It's been lovely to meet you," Ella said with perfect sincerity. Magda grinned.

"Ditto."

Ella left, her mood lifted.

∼

From the window of her office, Ella smiled with satisfaction at the dozens of people wearing brown Ashton Manor gardening aprons, scattered all over the grounds. She had agreed with Lady Susan and Lord Ralph to give everyone who worked on the garden a credit towards a year-long pass when the gardens were open to the public; work six times on the garden, get a year-long pass. A few enthusiastic gardeners had already earned their pass and yet carried on coming.

The sunshine glinted off tools and shears, and for a moment she closed her eyes her contentment bone deep, basking with the warmth on her face. After months of broken sleep and a sense of running on empty, it was a joy to breathe, to know her energy levels had risen and that she could cope with the minor hassles that running an estate of this size naturally threw at her.

From a distance, she could make out the figure of Tony Smyth, talking with Sam Winterson. As a livestock farmer, Tony didn't have too heavy a workload this month, although she wanted to know how the vaccination of his lambs was going, and she made a mental note. He threw back his head and laughed with Sam, who was charming him as she seemed to charm everyone.

Even her, Ella thought wryly. Her invitation to the wedding had been so unexpected, so surprising, it still stunned Ella. She ought to dig out a dress soon, although Jeanette was nagging her to buy something new. Ella's mouth twisted; Jeanette was a dab hand at spending other people's money. Although if the comments on the dress for the auction were anything to judge by, she had a talent for dressing Ella.

Decided, she sent a text to Jeanette to ask if she was free on Saturday to go shopping. A few minutes later, she had a response.

About time too! C U at 10.30, Brooks? J x.

Love in a Mist

If they were starting at Brooks, the posh department store in the nearby town, she'd better bring her credit card, thought Ella, trying not to panic.

"You look lost in thought," said Connor, appearing by her side. Ella pressed a hand to her throat.

"Oh! You made me jump!"

"Sorry." His blue eyes sparkled, not looking sorry at all. He followed her gaze towards the gardens. "It's starting to look a lot better," he said.

"It is. Sam's apprentices have been a godsend."

"As have your small army of volunteers."

"Well, we will complete the arbour and the first phase in time for the wedding, which is what's important."

His gaze settled on her face.

"Yes – but it's not the only important thing," Connor said softly, watching her intently. She raised her eyebrows, questioning. "I think what's important is that we're working together. Finally. With no misunderstandings." He took a step towards her.

Ella's couldn't breathe very well. He was too close, but she didn't move. Her mouth was dry.

"I'm glad too," she choked out. They were frozen for a second, then his head bent towards her. She thought she might have stopped breathing altogether.

"Con, I wanted to ask... oh!"

Ella jerked backwards as Magda's bright tones shattered the moment. She saw Connor close his eyes, draw a deep breath and turn to face his god-daughter.

"I'll be there in a moment."

Magda backed out of the room, looking pink. His strong fingers curled around Ella's shoulders. "I must go. But we're not finished talking. Not by a long chalk."

Then he strode, whistling, out of the room.

34

"What's happened?" demanded Jeanette as Ella strolled over to her by Brooks' impressive glass entrance. "You're different."

Ella blinked.

"Er... well, I have been getting some sleep lately, so you probably don't recognise me without bags under my eyes!"

Jeanette shook her head.

"Nope, although you look better, thank heavens. No, it's not that. What else?"

"We got an email saying the garden has made the final of the National Contemporary Art Awards this morning," Ella said, looking into the display window. "What about that colour?"

Jeanette glanced at the model in a cerise suit and shook her head.

"Too middle-aged and don't change the subject. Splendid news on the award. But what *else* has happened?"

Ella wondered about the almost-kiss with Connor, replayed on a loop in technicolour since yesterday. She fixed an innocent expression on her face.

"Nothing. And I agree, not that colour."

Jeanette peered at her face.

"Hmm... *something* has happened, even if you don't know it." Jeanette focused. "Okay, what are we looking for? What do you want?"

"That I look nice for a wedding where there will be lots of business people who earn ten times what I do?"

Jeanette scoffed.

"A bit limited, Ells-bells!" Ella grinned at the nickname. "Think bigger, more ambitious!"

"Like what?"

"How about – I want to have everyone whispering behind their hands, wondering who this glorious, mysterious creature is?" Jeanette pushed open the heavy doors of the department store with a flourish.

"God, no!" Ella was appalled.

"Or how about – I want to have every man within a ten-foot radius laying down at my feet and declaring eternal love?"

Ella giggled and shook her head.

"No, I've come to buy a dress, not a miracle."

"Okay, how about – I'd like Connor McPherson to apologise for every moment of stress he's given me in the past year?"

Despite herself, Ella's colour rose.

"Aha!" Jeanette said triumphantly. "I thought so! So... something sexy and alluring and—"

"Red," added Ella, inspiration suddenly striking. Jeanette stopped mid-step.

"Red?"

"Well, flame red might be a better description," she amended. "I want to wear something a bit different."

"Right." Jeanette looked at her, slightly baffled. "We'd better get on with it. Thank God you don't want a hat."

~

There were many people in the great hall for the informal launch of the garden, and Lady Susan and Lord Ralph greeted them all one by one. Connor was beginning to feel nervous that his speech wouldn't do the occasion justice, but there wasn't time to revisit it now.

The arbour, rose garden, and waterfalls were completed and the last tree of the Rainbow Walk would be planted tomorrow. He could breathe.

He idly ran his fingers over his beard and his gaze flicked over to Ella, who was standing by Lady Susan announcing the names of the people who were coming into the hall. Elegant and composed in a cream sleeveless blouse and a red skirt, her ebony hair was folded into a French plait. He looked over her slender arms and narrow waist and fire licked his belly. She appeared in her element among all these people, flowing around the room, smiling and talking. In comparison, he felt too big, a little coarse. He flexed his shoulders under the jacket and wished it was all over.

"Hi Connor, are you okay?" Sam suddenly appeared at his elbow. He turned and kissed her cheek.

"Yes, although I'll be better when I've delivered this speech."

She laughed.

"Well, it will give you some practice for your best man gig." She giggled more when he sucked in a horrified breath, remembering. He shook his head ruefully.

"Don't remind me, Magda's instructed me to hand it over to her for final additions."

It was Sam's turn to look horrified, and Connor grinned. There was laughter from the main door, and Connor turned to see Vincenzo kiss Ella on both cheeks. He stiffened.

"I see Vincenzo has arrived," Sam said dryly. "Thank God he's too young for most of the women here, otherwise it would be carnage!"

"He's a bit... remote for an Italian. Although he's made an exception for Ella," Connor said sourly.

Sam put her head on one side, regarding him.

"You look a bit fierce... If I didn't know better, Con, I'd say you were jealous, but that can't be right, can it?"

"Don't be ridiculous," he growled. She laughed.

"I think Ella's perfectly safe – he's had so many stepmothers courtesy of his father, I think Vincenzo leaves the women well alone."

Connor humphed, and dug in his pocket for his speech notes to scan them without seeing what he'd written. Then he thrust them back and turned to Sam. "Let's go and say hello."

A few minutes later, Connor was shaking hands with Vincenzo Mazzi. Prodded by Sam, Vincenzo talked intensely about his company's development of photo-voltaic panels and his search for a more effective way of storing solar energy. Eventually, Ella, glanced at her watch and said,

"Connor, I need to warn you, the journalist from *Today!* is here. Lady Susan thought it would be useful to invite them to see the community support we've developed for the garden."

Connor and Vincenzo tensed simultaneously, and recognising this, Vincenzo gave a brief laugh.

"The press again! They are, as you would say, a pain in the rear, no?"

"Aye," said Connor. "But I do need to set some records straight, so currently, they're a necessary evil."

"So...?" Ella asked. "Do I hide you, or shove you in front of them?" He smiled warmly at her and was interested to see a flush of pink appear in her cheeks. He rubbed his chin thoughtfully.

"I suppose I'd better do the pretty with the woman – what's her name?"

"Tonya le Clair," Ella said dryly. "You marched off in the opposite direction the last time she was here, so I should have a vaguely credible explanation for that. This time, I don't have Alex Versay to distract her." Connor nodded. Neither Cathy Mason nor Alex had been available this evening, but had sent best wishes. At least that was one handsome man less, thought Connor, distractedly. Sam pursed her lips.

"Connor are you sure? Are you prepared for this? They can be tricky, journalists. And frankly, Ms Le Clair is a bit of a vulture."

"I know that," he said. "I'm not planning to do it now, but offer a future date."

"What if she turns down your suggestion?" Ella asked, eyebrows raised.

He turned to her and gave her his most melting smile.

"I don't think she will."

～

Connor breathed deeply and nodded to the cheering audience. Thank God that was over. He beamed at Lady Susan, who was bustling towards him, her hands outstretched.

"Connor, that was wonderful! Inspirational!" She shook her head as if to gather her composure and grasped his hands. "But Ella's told me about the interview – are you *sure* you want to talk to that awful woman about your illness?"

Connor *wasn't* sure he wanted to talk to Tonya le Clair about his breakdown, but he thought it would serve as closure. His illness was the reason he'd turned to gardening, and he was proud of what he'd achieved. He had plenty of time to prepare. The date they'd settled on was in September. Tonya's heavily made-up brown eyes had gleamed as he'd offered her the interview, and once he'd reminded her she would be the first journalist to interview him in ten years, she would have walked over hot coals to write the piece.

"It's fine," he soothed Lady Susan. "I should have spoken about it years ago, but hey, I'm a bloke. We don't do feelings."

She smiled uncertainly, just as Sam and Ella came over.

"Way to go, Con!" said Sam, giving him a hug. "That was a *mega* speech, as your god-daughter would have said. Brilliant, not a dry eye in the house!"

Connor looked at Ella. Nope, he thought. Mascara perfectly in place.

"Are you sure this piece with Tonya le Clair will be okay?" Ella said seriously. "I'd hate to see her mangle what you say."

"Claudia is going to coach me," he said, referring to Jonas' super-efficient press officer. Ella's brow cleared.

"That's good, now I'm a lot less worried! And it's a hot topic, how gardening is good for your mental health."

He nodded and almost didn't catch her next comment.

"And it will do you good to exorcise your demons."

His looked sharply at her and a slight smile lifted her lips. It was as if she had opened his soul and he could not speak.

He pulled himself together.

"Yeah, Claudia will sort me out, I'll be fine."

They watched the volunteers and Sam's apprentices gradually trickling out of the great hall a bit the worse for wear. Vincenzo Mazzi strolled over to the group, his dark, expressive gaze flicking between them.

"Thank you for that generous welcome to the Ashton Manor family," he said to Connor. "I'm delighted that we could announce the sponsorship tonight."

Ella was thoughtful.

"Yes, I'd like to iron out a few details with you, Signor—"

"Vincenzo," he corrected smoothly. "And what is this – ironing?"

"You need to sort out the small print," Sam explained.

"Ah, I see. *Tutto bene*, I expect your call, Ella. I will look forward to it." He threw a challenging glance at Connor, then kissed her hand, and that of Lady Susan, and gave Sam a hug.

Connor, feeling a rush of emotion he couldn't – or wouldn't – name, fixed a smile and watched the tall, young Italian leave. He turned to Ella.

"If you're going back to the cottage, shall we walk together?"

∽

Conversation on the way to the cottage was sparse. Connor could feel tension nibble at his nerves. As the cottages came into view in the twilight, Connor wondered if she'd like his surprise. It had certainly taken some organising.

Her front garden was tiny, but plenty big enough for the statuette of the ugly goblin looking into the lily pool.

"Oh!" she said, catching sight of it. Then her voice seemed to fail.

"You said it was one of your favourite pieces," Connor said, watching her closely in the still, warm night. "I asked Lady Susan if she would sell it to me when we began to remodel the formal gardens. She was surprised, but agreed."

Silence, and then he thought he heard her sniff.

"How...?" she cleared her throat. "How did you get it here? It looks like it weighs a ton!"

He laughed softly. "I asked Gregory if he would move it with one of his small tractors. I knew you'd be up at the house early for this evening, and he and his son unloaded it. I put it in the position I thought best. Is it okay where it is? I can move it if you want it elsewhere."

"No! No, it's perfect where it is. Thank you so much."

Silence fell and Connor shuffled a bit.

"Would you like a coffee?" Ella said, abruptly. He nodded, and she opened the door. "Take a seat. I have ground coffee unless you'd like instant?"

"Proper coffee? I haven't had that for ages," he said, ducking his head just in time to avoid the beam as he came through the door. She nodded, dropping her bag on the dresser, and surreptitiously wiping her eyes.

"Make yourself comfortable."

He dithered about where to sit and eventually settled onto the sofa. Monty leapt onto his lap.

"Hello, you," he said, fondling Monty's ears. Monty approved wholeheartedly of this treatment and settled down. He heard Ella blow her nose.

"I can hear him purring from here!" she called from the kitchen after a moment. "Are you okay with cats?"

"I'm okay with most animals. Just never owned one."

Ella walked in with a tray and put two mugs, sugar and a small jug of milk on the coffee table and then returned to the kitchen.

"Why ever not?" she called.

"Dad was in the Irish army – we were always moving around. Ma didn't think it fair to be dragging pets around every six months."

"Ah... Did you want a whisky with your coffee, or are you sworn off alcohol for life?"

Love in a Mist

He grimaced. Her tone had been light, but there was a serious intent behind the question.

"I'll just stick with the coffee for the time being. I'll never live it down when I go home – an Irishman who doesn't drink."

The sound of her laughter feathered down his veins. She finally returned with a big cafetiere of coffee.

"I met Caitlin briefly," she said as she put it down with a thump. "God, that's heavy! Could you pour, please?" and she went to pour herself a whisky.

"She mentioned you," Connor said, pouring two cups. "Thanks for sorting out the place so she could stay."

"Your mum came over, didn't she? She must have been so relieved. Did she want you at home?"

Connor concentrated on filling his cup and reached for the milk jug before he responded.

"Not really. But when the wedding's over, I may go back to Ireland."

Ella was quiet, and he found her dark grey eyes fixed on him. He took a sip of coffee, and still she said nothing.

"What?" he asked finally.

"Connor, I found you lying in a pool of red liquid that I thought was blood. I saw the pills and – well, I thought the worst. Like your sister and Jonas. I think I'd like to know how you became a gardener, and why people think you might have committed suicide. And why, after abstaining from booze for a year, you drank not one, but *two* bottles. Will you tell me? Before you tell Tonya le Clair?"

He leaned back, his face stiff.

"Why I drank two bottles is easy enough to explain," he began slowly. "I hadn't slept properly for months and after I heard about the wiring, it got worse. There were some nights I didn't even bother getting into bed. I was desperate. I'd tried chamomile tea, relaxation tapes, reading boring books. It was the last resort."

She stared at him, and under her patient gaze, the knots gradually slipped from his shoulders. He took a slug of coffee and continued.

"As for the rest – I was a finance director, one of the youngest for a

FTSE 100 company. I took a decision on a poor deal, and although everyone was cool with it – these things happen, they said – I thought everyone was laughing at me behind my back. I was the young Turk, the whizz kid. And I'd fallen flat on my face. My confidence plummeted and pretty soon, I couldn't even get out of bed. Then one morning, I snapped – and I took an overdose. Jonas found me."

Ella's eyes were wide.

"So that's why everyone thought I might have topped myself," he said brusquely. "I had form."

"But this was an accident! Magda told me," she added as he looked sharply at her.

"Yes. And I'd sworn that I'd never do anything like that again. But they didn't believe me." He breathed deeply. "My parents didn't understand, particularly my dad."

Ella considered.

"Army man, stiff upper lip, all that bollocks?" she asked, watching him closely. She surprised a snort of laughter out of him, and he nodded.

"Yeah. Yeah, he's never really understood." He sipped his coffee. "But I believe that you can recover from a breakdown. What I didn't know until recently is that you really have to *learn* from it too."

Ella pursed her lips together. He thought she'd probably seen all the signals for his stress he had missed. But then she smiled.

"Shame you're not drinking. This whisky is spectacular."

"Another time? In a few months?"

"Sounds good."

He saw the mischief in her eyes and a fizz ran along his nerves.

An hour later, he paused at the door, the air of the night still warm. He turned towards her and saw her watchful gaze. Unable to stop himself, he dipped his head to kiss her, and her mouth softened underneath his gentle touch. She tasted of whisky and coffee. Desire swamped his body and he forced himself to step away. Ella's mouth dropped open in surprise, and then, relief. It was too soon, he thought.

"Good night. Thanks for the coffee," he said roughly, stroking his finger down her cheek. Her skin was smooth, like velvet.

"And thank you for the statue," she said in a low voice. "It means a lot to me."

"I got it on instinct. Was I right?"

Her eyes wide in the porch light, she stared at him, and then a smile curled her lips.

"Spot on."

35

Ella was pleased she hadn't bothered with a hat. It would be hot. She gazed through the window at an endless blue sky and a bright sun and checked the ties on the back of her neck. She'd never worn a halterneck before and wanted to double-*double*-check the bow. The knot felt firm under her fingers and she looked at herself in the mirror.

"Well, it's not as if your boobs are straining this at the seams, are they?" she muttered.

Still, she looked nice, she decided. The red-orange dress did something wonderful to her skin, and she loved the full skirt that ended mid-calf. The dark grey heels would have her knees protesting before the end of the day, but she had a pair of flats in her handbag and she'd cope. A spray of Chanel perfume, another coat of mascara and her lip gloss and she was ready. The alarm clock by her bed said eleven. She needed to get a move on if she was going to arrive at the arbour cool and un-flustered.

She grabbed the dark grey wrap, checked she had the box of rose petals and the congratulations card, and then took a deep breath.

"No sweat, Nigella," she murmured, using her full name as she always did when she was giving herself a stern talking to. "This is not your wedding, it's someone else's. And I'm sure it would take a world war to keep Jonas Keane from marrying Sam, so chill."

The walk to the arbour was only ten minutes ordinarily, but with heels this high, it took another ten to navigate the uneven paths. She gasped at the arbour's cool, green beauty and the delicate twining of the flowers overhead. She could smell the white roses, which held a special meaning for Sam, apparently. They adorned the pergolas and the ends of the rows of seats. She saw Joanne Jones, unobtrusive in a navy suit, and waved at her. Joanne rolled her eyes and Ella grinned, suddenly enormously pleased not to be in charge of today.

A man approached her to ask if she was on the bride's side or the groom's.

"Um... Sam, I suppose. I work here, Sam invited me a couple of weeks ago."

"Nice to meet you, I'm Fraser, Sam's brother-in-law," the man smiled faintly.

"Ella Sanderson," she murmured. Courteous but efficient, he gave her an order of service and pointed to a seat; she sank into it. After putting her handbag on the floor, she peered over the rest of the congregation to the front of the space, where the ceremony would take place. She spotted Jonas, glancing nervously over his shoulder, and Connor's broad back. And had he had his hair trimmed at last?

"The wild man of garden design," she thought, amused. Then he turned around and looked straight at her, and she gasped, dropping her order of service. She stared, drinking in the sight of him.

He'd shaved his beard, leaving his firm jaw now clearly visible, drawing even more attention to those sapphire eyes. Ella almost forgot to breathe. He was the most beautiful man she'd ever laid eyes on, she thought wildly. Jonas said something to him and she wrenched her eyes away, scrabbling on the floor for the order of service. As she sat up, his eyes were still fixed on her. She suddenly felt naked, his eyes trailing heat over her bare shoulders and loose hair. Her skin prickled, as if she might go up in flames.

"Excuse me?" said a tall, blond, bearded man who was waiting to sit down in the row. She apologised and moved her knees to one side so he and his companion could pass. She tried to re-order her whirling mind, drawing a few deep breaths, and waited for her hammering pulse to subside.

The man who'd just taken his seat eyed her curiously, and Ella smiled weakly.

"Hi, I'm Ella," she said helplessly.

"Hi! I'm Greg and this," he tapped the arm of the Viking, "is Andy. He's in partnership with Sam."

"Nice to meet you," she murmured. "I'm the estate manager here." Andy leaned over and shook her hand, and she could feel the callouses; yes he definitely was a gardener. A stray thought crossed her mind – would Connor's hands feel like this? And then the wave of heat flowed over her face again.

"Are you all right?" Greg asked. "You look a bit flushed."

"Yes, it's very warm, isn't it?" she breathed, wafting the order of service in front of her. For God's sake, get a grip! she told herself.

"Hey, Connor's shaved!" Andy observed.

"Hmm, he's looking a bit of a dish, isn't he?" Greg commented and laughed as Andy hit his knee playfully. Desperate to appear at ease, Ella jumped in.

"I almost didn't recognise him! I've only ever seen him bearded."

Andy glanced at her knowingly.

"Makes quite a difference, doesn't it?"

Ella wished she'd held her tongue and wondered if her face would ever cool down. Thankfully, another couple arrived, introduced as Amanda and Luke. Ella's responses were mechanical but seemed to satisfy all but Andy, whose glance was speculative. Thankfully, the music began, and they stood to receive the bride.

∼

Sam looked stunning, Ella thought wistfully. Leaning against a stone pillar in the great hall later that night, she cradled a glass of champagne as she gazed her fill at the simple pale gold silk dress which skimmed Sam's small, slender figure. Her blonde, short curly hair was adorned only by a circlet of white roses. Ella sighed, just enjoying the sight of her.

"She looks amazing, doesn't she?" Connor said in her ear. "Sorry, didn't mean to make you jump."

She breathed, clamping down on her racing pulse, and risked a glance at him.

"She does. I know that you're supposed to look radiant on your wedding day, but Sam really *does*."

"Jonas looks stunned," commented Jonas' best friend.

Ella giggled.

"Yes, like he can't believe his luck!"

"You should ask him to tell you how he proposed. It was a complete disaster. He was in such a foul mood it was a wonder Sam said yes."

Ella grinned and then waved at Magda, who was with a very pretty girl.

"I think your god-daughter is about to join us," she murmured. Connor groaned under his breath.

"Thank God!" Magda said as she reached them. "I'm so glad you're here! Protect us! This is Lisbeth, my best friend and Sam's niece."

Lisbeth, with delicate red-gold colouring and a sparkling pair of intelligent hazel eyes, smiled and rolled her eyes at Magda's comment.

"For heaven's sake," she said, shaking her head at Magda. "You're overreacting as usual."

"Protect you from what?" Connor asked.

"More like *who* from," Magda said, pulling a face. "The great Vincenzo Mazzi has been boring us all to death over his *amazing* company! God, I never met a man with such an ego!"

Lisbeth hooted, protesting that Magda was exaggerating, again.

"Really? I didn't find him a bore, I thought he was charming." Two pairs of hostile eyes, one male and one female, swivelled to Ella, and she took a hasty drink of champagne. Lisbeth grinned.

"Magda's not used to being told she knows nothing about a topic! I thought he was charming too, if a bit quiet. He's not at all like some

Italians I've met, trying to paw you at the first opportunity," Lisbeth said. "He's got some brilliant ideas about how to use solar power to save the planet – I thought he was inspiring! In an understated kind of way."

"He was so rude! I was only trying to engage in the conversation!" Magda was incredulous. Ella exchanged a glance with Lisbeth and she hid a smile. Connor's confident god-daughter would not appreciate being silenced in any conversation.

"Well, presumably you'll be on the top table for dinner so you'll escape him," she said soothingly. "You both look lovely, by the way."

Magda ran a hand down her deep lemon dress, edged with white lace, nodding to herself as she settled its simple lines.

"It was the least they could do, to make us bridesmaids. You could say we brought them together."

"You did?" Ella was all ears.

Connor smirked.

"I think they were finding their way without your meddling," he said. This time, both Magda and Lisbeth were indignant.

"Don't be ridiculous!" Magda protested. "Do you *know* what happened? Well..."

Ella made a good show of listening to Magda as she told the story, with Lisbeth correcting her friend's exaggerations. In truth, she was acutely aware of Connor's warm body beside her and his spicy cologne. As Magda was hitting her stride, he leaned in to bring his lips close to her ear and his breath caused the goosebumps to rise on Ella's arms.

"Sam's not the only one who looks amazing. Promise me a dance later?"

She nodded, excitement flooding her body. Magda paused mid-sentence and as Connor walked away, Ella glanced up to see green eyes fixed on her.

Lisbeth's gaze flicked between Ella and Magda, and a slight smile lifted her generous mouth. It was like they were both making some calculations, thought Ella, suddenly nervous about what they were reading from her. Magda's face cleared, and she grinned mischievously.

"Come and say hi to Sam, she's asked after you." Magda linked arms, and with Lisbeth, pulled Ella into the crowd. "We can also tease Con about his speech."

∽

Ella was unsure if she'd drunk too much; the room glittered and swam a little. Sam and Jonas had climbed into a low-slung sports car and roared away to start their honeymoon. The rose petals would take days to brush out of their clothes, she reflected. Given the way they looked at one another, Ella thought they wouldn't care. The memory of that warmed her as the evening air turned cool. As Ella watched, Magda had brushed away a tear as the car disappeared, and turning, fell into the arms of Vincenzo Mazzi. He was perfectly still and then pulled her close and dropped a kiss onto her forehead.

Magda stayed perfectly still and then pulled back, and they exchanged a long, still look. Then Magda turned to Lisbeth. Ten minutes later, she was sufficiently recovered to pull Connor into the great hall to dance. Interesting, thought Ella.

Connor had not asked her to dance yet, and she clamped down on her disappointment. She loved to dance. She'd moved around the dance floor with other partners and when she glanced his way, he'd been watching her hungrily. But still no invitation. And she was damned if she'd ask.

She slipped into a chair at an empty table and hidden by the tablecloth, eased off her shoes. Her watch told her it was nearly midnight. She ought to give her thanks to Jonas' mum and dad and be away to her bed. Scanning the group of people on the dance floor she thought that Magda looked a little the worse for wear, clinging surprisingly to Vincenzo Mazzi. Frowning, her eyes searched for Lisbeth, and finding her, she relaxed a little. Magda's wonderful, grounded best friend would watch over her.

She fished out the flat pumps from her handbag and put them on, cursing slightly as her cramped toes, once released, protested at being forced into shoes again.

"Did you want that dance?" said a voice she'd longed to hear all night. Connor, handsome as an angel, his bow tie hanging loose, towered over her. She looked up.

"I thought you'd forgotten me," she said, and then cursed herself. Did that sound whiny? He grinned, his teeth gleaming in the light of the mirror ball.

"You're joking, right? Are you ready to go? Good. So am I."

She was confused. What about her dance? Ella stood up and Connor put his hand in the small of her back; she could feel the hardness of his palm on her bare flesh. His touch made her shiver with anticipation as he guided her towards the exit. They walked in silence along the path that led to the cottages.

"Hang on," he said, as they reached a clearing. "Dance?"

She laughed.

"What to? Is there a band in the hedge?"

He said nothing, just pulled out his phone and pressed a button. Gentle music filled the air and Ella heard Neil Young's *Harvest Moon* float through the still, starlit air. Connor held out his arms, and she walked into them. His lean, hard body pressed against hers and Ella closed her eyes as their bodies fitted together. She sighed in pure pleasure as they danced and she knew that whatever happened, she would never forget this moment.

Neither of them spoke as the song played. When it came to an end, Connor leaned back and looked at her, careful, waiting for a sign. He looped a lock of hair behind her ear, and his fingers trailed feather-light along her neck. Ella stared at his mouth, and then pressed her lips to his. His arms tightened and she heard his breath deepen.

She couldn't pinpoint when it changed from a sweet kiss into something more urgent. But suddenly his hardness jutted against her belly through the thin cotton of her dress, and her breasts ached. She arched her back with a sigh, and thought, at last, they were both speaking the truth.

As the thought crossed her mind, he seemed to draw back, and his mouth gentled. She gave a little moan of disappointment, but he swept his hands over her, rough against her smooth back as though to soothe her.

A few moments later, she murmured against his ear.

"I suddenly feel that I've been waiting for that for weeks."

"Good. Because I think I've been waiting for that for *months!*" He laughed then kissed her palm, and they walked towards the cottages. He paused on her porch. Ella was suddenly lost, not knowing what to do. She paused.

His lips curled in a warm smile and he took her face in his hands and kissed her until she was breathing hard and shaking.

"And *because* I've been waiting for months, I can wait a little longer. Goodnight, sweet Ella. I don't know what I'd have done without you. Thank you."

And with that, he left her standing on her doorstep, again feeling a mix of relief and crushing disappointment.

36

The next evening, Ella was on Connor's doorstep with a bottle of wine and a bunch of flowers. There was no reason a woman shouldn't buy a man flowers, she reasoned. She rang the bell and pushed her nose into the heady lilies, pure white and glowing in the rosy twilight.

A few minutes later, she was still waiting for the door to open and she peered through the window. She gasped, seeing Connor's leg stretched out in front of the sofa. He wasn't moving.

Her thoughts racing, she banged on the door in a panic, and sagged with relief as Connor rose from the floor, looking startled.

"I wondered what had happened!" she exclaimed as he opened the door. "I thought you'd had an accident or something!"

He looked puzzled, and then his expression cleared.

"Oh! No, I was doing some yoga, and I lost track of the time! Is the doorbell not working? No, come in, don't leave. I'll just have a quick sluice in the shower – I'll be five minutes, tops."

Ella stood undecided and then walked in, handing over the wine and the flowers. He thanked her and kissed her lips hard, sending her head reeling.

"There's a vase in the cupboard under the sink, if you want to put them in water."

Trying very hard not to imagine Connor in the shower, Ella cut half an inch from the stems and plonked them into the vase. Looking at them critically, she acknowledged she'd never make a florist.

She placed the flowers on the windowsill. The smell from the oven was wafting through the kitchen, and she heard her stomach rumble. How ladylike. She saw the breadsticks on the table that was laid for dinner and grabbed one, crunching it as she sank into the cushions of the sofa.

She heard the shower running and to distract herself from thoughts of Connor, wet and naked, she picked up a book at the side of the big leather armchair at the side of the fireplace.

"*Mindfulness for Beginners,*" she murmured and chuckled softly at the title. She wondered if Connor would ever find calm – it might be a shame if his energy and passion were dampened by yoga and meditation. A thump and a short, effective swear word came from above her. His voice floated down the stairs.

"Sorry! Stubbed my toe! I'll be down in a minute if I've not crippled myself!"

She giggled and put the book down. No, probably no danger of Connor being at one with the universe quite yet.

She sat down and rested her head on the back of the squishy sofa, letting the tiredness and stress from the previous day wash through her. Although she'd slept in until eight thirty, she could still feel the fatigue in her legs and back from standing in heels for most of the day.

"Serves you right," she said beneath her breath, regarding her feet in flat Grecian sandals. Her eyes closed as memories from the wedding flickered like a movie in her head. Sam's entrance to the arbour and the joy and love on Jonas' face; the pride of Niamh and Friedrich, his parents, Jonas dancing with Magda, and Connor's speech. After a stumble at the beginning, Connor told how he met Jonas at university, and their first steps into the business world. Connor had talked openly about the debt he owed to his best friend while he was ill – and then lightened the mood by saying that he considered that debt completely paid off, given the hassle he'd had with the garden. Connor and Jonas had embraced like brothers. The guests had clapped and cheered and wiped their eyes. It had been a perfect speech. And that moonlit dance. Remembering, she smiled, and then her eyes flew open as Connor said, "And what kind of dream were *you* having?"

She smiled, taking in wet hair slicked back from his glorious face.

"I was just thinking back to your speech," she said, not quite truthfully, and he groaned.

"Don't remind me! God, I was petrified! I can't tell you how pleased I was when it was over!" His eyes flicked over her and her temperature rose a notch. "What can I get you to drink?"

They chatted while he put a roasted chicken on one side to rest and prepared the vegetables. Ella watched with interest. She didn't cook much, just the basics, so she was impressed. Her stomach rumbled again in anticipation. She burst into giggles.

"I'd be thrown out of boarding school for that!"

Connor looked up from his chopping.

"Boarding school? Sounds posh."

"I hated it," she replied lightly. "I wasn't cut out for communal living and we weren't rich or posh enough for the school – I had a scholarship. I was miserable and I couldn't wait to get to university."

He nodded but said nothing. After a moment or two of silence, she continued.

"That was where I met Stephen. My dad had died and Stephen was everything my mother wanted – rich, well-connected and a lawyer to boot – I mean, you rarely see a lawyer out of work, do you? Anyway, she thought he was wonderful and when I announced that we were getting married when we graduated, she was over the moon."

She paused, remembering her mother's face at the news.

"So what happened?" Connor asked gently.

Ella didn't reply at once. Her recollection of that time seemed to have faded into sepia, like an old film.

"Mum put every spare penny she had into the wedding – not that we had a lot to start with. I didn't want a big wedding, but everyone seemed to expect it. So she spent a fortune on a proper country wedding, with a horse and carriage, a bloody meringue of a dress for me I secretly hated, and all sorts of stuff... it cost the earth. And then..." she stopped.

"He pulled out, you said."

"Tosser," she said, shaking her head. "A week before what should have been my wedding day, he was abroad with someone else."

He put down the knife he was using to cut vegetables and wrapped her in his arms. She took a deep breath in, his fresh lemon scent filling her nose. His lips kissed her neck, and for a second, she gloried in the feel. Then she pulled back, forcing a smile.

"Afterward, just the thought of a wedding – *anyone's* wedding – brought me out in hives!" She sobered. "But it was a terrible time in my life. Six months after the wedding fiasco, Mum was killed in a motorway accident."

Connor looked stunned.

"My God, Ella!"

"Yes. That was a grim time, I wondered if I'd caused the accident? She was so distracted, trying to keep my spirits up..."

"Don't think that way. You said yourself it was an accident," Connor warned. She nodded, deep in thought. Yes, sometime in the past seven years, she'd absolved herself of blame for the accident. Taking a sip of wine, she continued.

"After the funeral, I just wanted to get as far away as I could from my home town. Someone told me about Ashton Manor. I applied and, thank God, they gave me the job," she recalled. "They've been incredibly supportive."

His shrewd gaze rested on her, but he was silent. Ella was grateful; she'd overshared. She shuffled, and taking her cue, he picked up his knife again.

"Quite a tale, that. But here I am, listening to you instead of feeding you! Pour yourself more wine, it'll be five minutes. Then I'll tell you a bit about me."

～

She looked amazing, Connor thought, with her casual summer dress and sandals and all that glossy ebony hair tumbling over her shoulders. He stood up and began to gather the plates.

"No, let me," she said, putting her hand on his arm. "You cooked, I'll clear the table."

"Just stack them on the side. You can come again," he smiled. Her eyebrow tweaked, and his pulse leapt in response. Then the phone rang. He frowned, expecting a cold caller. So he was astounded when his father's gruff voice rang out through the answerphone. He jumped up to answer before his father said much more.

"Connor? I thought you were out."

"No, Dad, just took a bit of time getting to the phone."

"Ah. Well, your mother thought it would be a good idea to see how the wedding went."

"Well, I didn't screw up the speech, which was a major plus."

"Didn't you?" his father sounded a little surprised. "You never used to enjoy performing in front of people, you were always hopeless at school..."

Connor sighed.

"I made a special effort because it was Jonas, Dad. It went fine."

"Excellent, excellent..."

Connor waited. When his father seemed disinclined to speak he said, "Is Mum okay?"

"God, yes, your mother's as strong as a horse, never anything wrong with your mother."

"It was nice to see her at the hospital."

"Um... yes."

"Thanks for the call while I was there," Connor said, suddenly determined to discuss it.

His father huffed a bit and then said, "Not a problem, not a problem." There was a lengthy pause. "So... how are you now? All okay?"

Connor could feel the tension building in his shoulders. Would his father completely ruin his evening? Probably. But then, there were things that he needed to say and now was as good a time as any.

"Yes, I'm fine, Dad. But it *was* an accident."

"What? Oh yes, your mother mentioned that. Well..."

"Not like the previous time," Connor ploughed on before his father could skitter away from the topic. "This time it was an accident. The time before, I was ill, Dad."

"Well, I know that. Obviously, I knew that."

"Do you? Because ten years ago you said I needed to pull myself together. Which you wouldn't do to someone who was ill, normally."

There was a silence.

"Dad? Are you still there?"

"Yes, son. I'm still here. I know this time was an accident, your mother told me."

"And has she also told you I was *ill* ten years ago? And do you believe her?"

"Yes. And yes, I believe her." His father was so quiet, Connor could barely hear the words.

"Good," Connor said. His voice softened. "I love you, Dad."

His father cleared his throat.

"We love you too, Connor. And," more throat clearing, "we're proud of you. I saw photos of Ashton Manor's garden in one of your mother's magazines. It looks *galánta*."

Galánta. Wonderful, Connor translated in his head. There was an awkward pause.

"Thanks, Dad." Connor's voice was rusty. Another pause.

"Right, well, keep in touch!"

His dad put the phone down and Connor stared at the receiver for a moment and then turned to find Ella thoughtfully watching him with a tea towel in her hands.

"Well," she said, her contralto voice soft. "Even hearing only half of that makes things clearer."

He nodded, and she reached him before he could move, to pull his head towards her and kiss him. A while later, Connor said throatily,

"Are you dessert?"

She laughed, shaking her head, and she moved away to sit on the sofa.

"So that was your dad?"

"It was."

"You've never discussed the breakdown with him, have you?"

"I tried. He thought I was lacking in moral fibre, or something similar. Told me I was weak. Ma told me he was worried sick, which made him behave like an eejit, but I found it hard to forgive him for a long time."

"Yes, I can imagine. But did you plan to speak to him tonight?"

He shook his head.

"No. But it seemed the right time. And you'd just been incredibly brave telling me your story. You inspired me."

She hooted.

"Inspiring, eh? I've never been called that before! Can this inspiration get some coffee?"

He grinned and followed her into the kitchen.

37

Ella's eyelids fluttered up, and she felt the familiar weight of Monty against her legs. She stretched and sighed. What on earth am I doing here, she thought. An unfamiliar ache in her loins nagged at her, and she shifted restlessly as the flare of desire licked her.

They'd talked into the small hours, until Connor pointed out the time. She'd scrambled to her feet.

"I had no idea! You must be knackered! Where did I put my bag?"

"You don't have to go, Ella." His words had sounded gravelly, rough. She had stared. "Unless you'd rather go, of course."

Lying in bed, the heat rushed once again to her cheeks as she remembered her stuttering reaction.

"I-I'd better get back. You know... Monty... and well, I'm not sure what I'm doing tomorrow – God, where did I put my shoes?"

How naïve she'd sounded! How incredibly uncool! She had stumbled to her feet, searched for the sandals which had been lost under the sofa, and rushed out, barely stopping to thank him for a lovely evening, and then turned around to plant a firm kiss on his mouth before bolting out of the door.

Why had she done that? If the gnawing ache in her body was anything to go by, she wanted him! She wanted his lean body against hers and to have him do all kinds of wicked things to her... Her mind went into overdrive at the havoc that those blue eyes might wreak in her, let alone those big, clever hands.

"Aargh!" she growled to herself and Monty blinked a bleary eye in disapproval. She huffed and stared at the ceiling and then peered at the clock. Ten to eight. Would he be awake?

Tossing aside the bedclothes, she opened her underwear drawer. She stopped, changed her mind and grabbed her robe instead.

She skipped down the stairs and poured food into Monty's bowl, her mind a careful blank. Then she pushed her feet into the sandals she'd kicked off the night before and left the cottage, crossing her fingers as she locked up.

The statue leered at her as she closed her front door.

"Wish me luck," she muttered, and if she was fanciful, she might have sworn the goblin winked at her. She hopped over the tiny dividing picket fence between the cottages and banged on Connor's door. And then she banged again. And again.

Five minutes later, Connor poked his head out of the bedroom window.

"What the hell? Ella, is everything all right?"

She threw back her head and took in his tousled hair and unshaven face. He looked delicious, she thought.

"I need to speak to you," she said, and dragged her fingers through her hair as Connor disappeared back into the cottage.

He threw open the door a minute later, wearing tracksuit bottoms, his chest bare. She glanced away from the muscles in his shoulders and the flatness of his belly. And that arrow of dark hair disappearing below his waistband.

"What's wrong? Ella, for the love of God, what's wrong?"

She took a deep breath and focused on his face.

"What's wrong is that I left last night. I woke up alone this morning and I should have been with you!"

He stared at her and then his eyes slipped down her body.

"I didn't want to rush you," he said, and pulled her into the cottage. Absently, she noticed all traces of their meal had disappeared, washing-up done, and she could smell the polish on the dining table.

"You cleared up. At three in the morning?"

He looked bemused, and then his face cleared.

"I was too het up to sleep," he admitted. "I scrubbed the oven, too."

She stared and then laughed.

"Ella, are you wearing anything under that robe?"

"Nope."

"That's fairly unequivocal," he commented, passing his tongue over his lips.

"I certainly hope so. Oh, for God's sake!" Unable to say more, she put her arms around his neck and kissed him.

He hoisted her into his arms and climbed the stairs, placed her on the bed as if she was a precious package and then continued to kiss her. Ella could feel herself beginning to pant, her body moistening, yearning.

"Sure?" he said, a few minutes later, as he nuzzled her neck.

"Never surer," she said, untying the belt of her robe and sighing with satisfaction as his hungry gaze swept over her. She hooked her fingers into his waistband and pushed his tracksuit bottoms and boxers down his strong thighs. The feel of his naked skin against hers made her head swim, and she moaned as he kissed and stroked her. Ella tossed her head from side to side. It had been a long time, but had she truly forgotten this feeling of tension, of anticipation, of being almost liquid? Or had she just never had it before? And that noise – it was her!

When he gently parted her thighs, Ella thought she'd explode, and gasped as his mouth licked a delicate path across her stomach. His length nudged her and she squirmed beneath him, hearing Connor hiss.

"God, Ella! You're amazing..."

And while he hesitated, she gripped his hips and pulled him down, loving the feel of him filling her. He groaned and moved, and she thought she might die from the pleasure. The ache built and sooner than she knew, she was falling through space, boneless, her head spinning.

Mere moments later, he reared up above her, his eyes closed. She held him tight.

"Ah, Ella, you're a joy," he said after he'd caught his breath and kissed her gently. Then he lay back.

Ella smiled in deep contentment, listening to her heart thundering in her chest. After a few moments, she rolled to face him.

"I hope this won't prejudice our professional relationship," she said demurely and giggled as he looked at her, appalled. He sank back on the pillow.

"God, *now* she shows me she has a sense of humour!" he muttered. "Indeed, you do have hidden depths."

Ella stretched against the smooth sheets like a cat, sleek and satisfied. His eyes ranged over her body, and she smirked.

"I'm a woman of mystery." He kissed her again, seemingly unable to keep his hands off her.

"But truly, how are we going to handle this?" she said when she could speak. "This is very unprofessional..."

"Tell you what, I could resign?"

"Don't you dare! There's phase two to build yet!"

"In which case, I suggest we take it as it comes," he commented, tracing patterns on her stomach.

"I... I... Connor, stop that, I'm trying to think!"

His blue eyes gleamed.

"Make me, Ms Sanderson," he said, and kissed her again. While she still had brain cells working, Ella thought that this was so wonderful, it couldn't last. But she'd make the most of it while she could.

~

"I presume you've read the plans?" Connor asked the investigator from the Historical Commission, who bristled with outrage at Connor's tone. Ella held her breath as Patrick Grayling looked down his nose at Connor. Or rather looked up, down his nose, thought Ella, hiding a giggle; Connor towered over the diminutive Mr Grayling.

"What do you take me for, Mr McPherson? Of course I've studied your plans. Those *plans* are the reason we're interested in the development."

This won't do, thought Ella, stepping forward.

"Connor, Mr Grayling – or can I call you Patrick? Connor, Patrick is *eminently* qualified to discuss the garden and your ideas for phase two. Perhaps we could join Lady Susan in the rose garden?"

"Thank you, Miss Sanderson," Patrick said graciously.

Connor glared at her, and for a split second, Ella thought the past few weeks might never have happened between them. Then he winked, and she pressed her lips together in exasperated amusement.

"Connor can explain the vision for the garden, show you how it links to the history of the house," Ella added carefully.

Connor was stubbornly silent as they walked to the rose garden, and Ella kept up a flow of inconsequential conversation with the increasingly grumpy Patrick Grayling. Lady Susan was waiting in the rose garden, dressed in a white shirt with the collar turned up, beige chinos and flat boots, and she looked twenty years younger than she was. She greeted Patrick Grayling like a long-lost friend and before Ella's fascinated eyes his stiffness melted a degree or two as she charmed him.

Then to her surprise, instead of Connor talking through the garden design, Lady Susan began to talk, smoothly, effortlessly.

"We've noticed a decided shift in demographic in our visitors," she started. "We realised that if we didn't do something significant, our visitor numbers would literally die off. So we designed a garden to attract younger people, fascinate them and keep them returning. In the Dragon's Den, we've developed a magical computer graphic display that references the creatures featured in the Arcadian style, winged mythical beasts."

Did it make reference like that? Ella thought of Adam's initial ideas and then realised how Connor had made them less cartoon, more classical. She glanced at Connor and saw him nod at Lady Susan's words.

"But although we've kept the bones of the Arcadian gardens, we've done away with the temples and monuments they normally featured, and in line with Lancelot 'Capability' Brown's views, replaced them with natural focal points. Such as our fountains, which are solar powered and emerge out of local limestone." Lady Susan pointed to the fountains, now rewired and working perfectly.

Patrick Grayling nodded sagely and made a note in minuscule writing in his notebook, so small that even Ella's sharp eyes couldn't decipher the words.

"Ceinion Bryant's sculptures provide a perfect modern twist on the Roman and Greek statues that featured in the Arcadian style. The soft and simple planting complements them, rather than fighting for attention," Lady Susan said, smiling sweetly at the man from the Historical Commission.

Ella was watching his body language, cautiously optimistic that he was softening. Lady Susan drew attention to the broad paths, a nod to Capability Brown's habit of putting drives in his gardens and something, she said, that would continue in phase two of the garden.

"If we're able to proceed," Ella added quickly.

Connor eventually led them to the arbour and Patrick Grayling stopped short as he entered it, so that Ella cannoned into him. She apologised, but he wasn't listening, he was staring at the garlands that decked the space.

"I recall something similar being created in the original Georgian garden at Brighton…" Grayling said in awed tones. Ella nearly punched the air in triumph. They'd done it. He was sold.

The visit to the Rainbow Walk was just as successful. Grayling commented how Capability Brown was renowned for the speed of his work and use of machinery to transplant trees – much as Connor had done. At last Connor joined the discussion, describing the huge metal tubs for the tree roots to give each of them the perfect conditions. Grayling nodded, with the fervour of the true horticulturist.

"You should return in autumn when the display will be at its best," Lady Susan twinkled at him.

"Hmm. Yes, I would like that," he responded.

Twenty minutes later, Lady Susan was shaking his hand, and walking him to his car.

"Why didn't you lead the conversation?" Ella asked Connor, watching from the door of the manor.

"Ah well, we decided that he would be prejudiced against me. It was better Lady Susan talked through the details and soothed his battered ego."

"Battered by you?"

Connor grinned and her pulse kicked up at the mischief in his eyes.

"Well, if he was going to criticise my garden, I wanted to know he was worthy!"

Ella sighed. "Well, now we'll just have to wait."

～

Ella groaned. Her feet were killing her. She took the gin and tonic offered to her by Lord Ralph with a weary smile. Lady Susan was euphoric.

"*How* many visitors today?"

Ella told her for the third time, and Lady Susan clapped her hands. Someone knocked peremptorily at the drawing room door and Connor strode in, radiating energy. Looking at him, Ella revived slightly and greeted him with a smile.

"Connor! Come in, dear boy, and join us!"

Lord Ralph shook his hand, and Connor curled his large frame into an armchair.

"Well now, they seemed to like it a lock," he said.

"Don't tell me!" said Lady Susan quickly. "A lock means – a little bit?"

"I'll make a Donegal native of you yet, Lady Susan." Connor beamed at her.

The talk was general; about what needed doing the following week to repair the ravages of so many visitors to phase one of Ashton Manor's garden. Ella tried hard to concentrate, but her eyelids drooped. Behind them were images of the day which had dawned bright and not too hot, visitors exclaiming with pleasure at the arbour, children squealing with delight at the fountains and, as the light faded, the winged creatures from Dragons' Den. The hundred volunteers, coached by the garden crew on the planting and the design, had smiled and welcomed all their visitors, and kept them from climbing on the sculptures and from falling into the fountains. It would all happen again tomorrow, but it was less scary now the first day was over.

They'd even had word from the Historical Commission who'd declared that the design was a work of genius and completely in keeping with the house, and that Patrick Grayling would be pleased to write to the local authority to support their application for planning permission. Mr Grayling would enjoy a second visit to the gardens, the letter said, if an invitation were extended.

"Ella? Are you still with us?" She heard Lord Ralph's amused voice. Her eyes flew open, and she blushed.

"Sorry... I was thinking about today. It's been a bit of ride." She stifled a yawn.

"You were up at some godforsaken hour, weren't you?" Lady Susan said kindly. "Then I suggest we raise a toast and then you and Connor can get off to bed."

Ella's eyes flew to her employer's face, but it remained bland and innocent, with no trace of the double entendre Ella had feared.

Connor chuckled, slanting a wicked glance towards Ella. "I feel I could stay in bed for a week."

Lady Susan looked demure, and it was then that Ella knew that her employer had clocked them.

"Erm..." she began, and Lady Susan stood up.

"I think we should talk tomorrow, or even Monday," she said firmly. "In the meantime, shall we raise a toast?"

They stood.

"To the Ashton Manor garden, and the brilliant team who brought it together," Lady Susan said, looking squarely at the pair of them.

"To Ashton Manor garden!"

Ella swallowed, a lump in her throat. They'd done it. Against the weather, the establishment, the corporations, the finances, God above, even above Connor's accident.

And soon, he'd be on his way back to London.

She'd known this from the beginning of their love affair. He'd go back to London and his international clientele, and she'd stay here. Sick at heart, she drew a deep breath and saw Connor frown at her.

"I suppose you'll be heading back to London, Connor," commented Lord Ralph, who must have read her mind. Even as his words caused her pain, Ella smiled at the likelihood that Lord Ralph didn't realise she and Connor were an item.

"Well, yes. Eventually," Connor said. It was the first time she'd heard him uncertain, and she stared into her glass.

"But you'll be back for the second phase of the build?" Lady Susan insisted.

"Ah, yes, I'm planning to be."

Ella stood suddenly.

"I need to go to bed," she announced, unable to listen any longer. "No, I can find my way back, Connor, it's fine. You finish your drink."

She got out of the door before the tears came.

Two hours later, she was lying in bed, staring at the ceiling, tear stains still on her cheeks. Monty had curled up on her legs, sensing she needed comfort, and she idly stroked his ears. There wasn't a way around it; Connor had offices in London. She loved her job. Ashton Manor was her home, her life; she couldn't leave it. And even if he had time, Connor was unlikely to drive a nearly four-hundred mile round trip every weekend. It was impossible. Still, they'd only been together a short time, she'd survive. She'd need to enjoy their time together and prepare to say goodbye. Something twisted in her gut, and she almost groaned in pain. Then she heard the thumping.

"What?" she lifted Monty to one side and grabbed her robe.

Thrusting open the window, she leaned out. Connor had his head thrown back, peering up at her in the dark.

"Connor, it's nearly two in the morning!"

"I know what time it is, woman!" he roared. "Open the bloody door! We need to talk!"

Muttering, Ella padded downstairs.

"Connor, really," Ella remonstrated, but Connor stepped into the cottage, kicked the door shut and wrapped her in his arms. She stiffened, but then his expert mouth stifled her complaints and she threaded her fingers through his thick hair to hold him closer.

Finally, he broke the kiss and rested his forehead against hers.

"We need to talk about what's going to happen," he said. She nodded and walked to the sofa, then decided that to be sitting next to him would make thinking difficult. So she sat in the armchair.

"I always knew you would go back to London," she said in a low voice.

"Did you? What drew you to that conclusion?"

He sounded harsh.

"But... I thought that was where your business was," she said quickly, confused.

"It's where my office is. But I also have offices in Berlin and Amsterdam. I don't have to be where the offices are, Ella."

"Oh."

"I think the pertinent question is – where would you *like* me to live, Ella?"

She nearly rushed into speech and then shut her mouth.

"I... I... I don't know. It's up to you."

"Is it?"

"Of course!"

"Then what would you say if I said I wanted to be wherever you are?"

She stared.

"What?" she whispered.

"I've spent the past hour thinking about this, Ella. What would you say if I said I wanted to be wherever you are?" Connor repeated with exaggerated patience. "Would it make you happy? Or were you just looking for a fling and an excuse to wave goodbye?"

"No!" The word burst from Ella's lips.

"No, it wouldn't make you happy?"

"No! I wasn't looking for a fling! Or an excuse to say goodbye!" Ella said hotly.

"Now we're getting somewhere," Connor said. "So shall I ask again? What would you say if I just wanted to be with you? Wherever that was?"

"Is it possible?"

"Answer the bloody question, woman!" he scowled. "God above, it's like drawing teeth!" He came and pulled her to her feet. "Ella, I know it's probably too soon, but the thought of going back to London – without you – appals me. But I don't know how *you* feel."

His hands gripped her shoulders, warm through the silk of her robe.

"The thought of you going back to London without me appals me too," she whispered. "I've been dreading it. But I can't leave my job here, and I can't imagine what it would be like to commute that far regularly. It would put us both under incredible stress and that's no way to run a relationship..." She could feel the tears welling up and blinked them away.

He sighed and wrapped her in his arms and she nestled there, hearing the thump of his heartbeat.

"I thought I might buy a house in the village," he said conversationally and she stilled at his words. "One that's big enough for lots of guests..."

She stared at him.

"Do you *want* to buy a house in the village?"

"If it means I can continue to see you – yes, very much. Lady Susan and Lord Ralph think it's a splendid idea. Would that be okay with you?"

Ella thought her face might split in two, she was smiling so hard. And crying too.

"Yes, I'd love that."

There was a silence as he kissed her thoroughly.

"Don't you think phase one of the garden is like phase one of our relationship?" he asked when he raised his head. "I wonder what phase two will bring?"

Ella pressed her body against him and felt his response.

"Don't rush it. I've still got lots of exploring to do to, you know, really *get used to* phase one. I could do with some help."

"At your command, Ms Sanderson," he said, and she led him up to bed.

ALSO BY SARA SARTAGNE

Sometimes love needs a plan...

A feisty garden designer with a green conscience. A successful, ruthless property magnate. A match-making teenager. What could possibly go wrong?

Desperate to keep her garden design company afloat, Sam doesn't need a relationship – she needs business! All that stands between her and the commission that might save her company is reclusive businessman Jonas Keane.

Jonas Keane is not interested in the kind of woman who puts her career before her home and family. Been there, done that. Ordered to stay home to recuperate from illness is frustrating as hell – but it allows him to oversee the renovation of his own garden while staying a silent partner in a housing development. What he doesn't expect is to run headlong into a budding romance with a blonde, pixie-faced gardener intent on upending his plans.

Jonas' daughter Magda is fed up with her dad's long hours and picture perfect girlfriends, and believes bright, petite Sam is the perfect solution. When tension between Sam and Jonas mounts with the summer temperature, she's thrilled. But a proposed housing development threatens Sam's beloved countryside, and suddenly, Magda's match-making plans hang in the balance.

Can Sam save the beauty spot from the bulldozers? Can Jonas put pleasure before business? And will Magda get her happy ever after?

Readers of Jill Mansell will love Sara Sartagne's debut novel, Book 1 in the **English Garden Romance** series! Click here to buy in the UK! Click here to buy in the US!

AFTERWORD

Thank you for buying the second book in the **English Garden Romance** series and thank you for supporting independent authors. Writing can often be a bit of an echo chamber ...scribbling away, but no-one is reading! So - if you liked *Love in a Mist*, please leave me a review.

It's an enormous help to authors just starting out! And if you'd like to know when I'm releasing the third book in the English Garden Romance Series, sign up to my mailing list on my website – www.sarasartagne.com

I won't send endless emails, but enough to say hello, tell you news and offer some freebies.

Talking of which, if you sign up to the mailing list, I'll send you a **free** novella called *A Bouquet of White Roses*, which tells how the story all began.

You can get this, and other freebies, by signing up to my mailing list. Alternatively, if you'd like to connect on Twitter, say hello to me on @SSartagnewriter.

Arranging wedding flowers is no fun when you're in love with the groom...

Afterword

Florist Dawn Andrews' business is to create beautiful bouquets, not to break up relationships. But when she's asked to arrange the flowers for the wedding of an old school friend, it's hard to ignore her budding feelings.

Dawn is the loveliest woman that landscape gardener Sam Winterson has ever seen. But as an engaged man, he dismisses the growing chemistry between them.

Until, that is, Sam has to rescue Dawn from an assault outside a nightclub. While he's only doing what any honourable man would, Sam finds himself caring rather too much about the florist with the heart-shaped face and sherry-brown eyes.

With the wedding only five months away, can they dismiss their mutual attraction and carry on as 'just friends'?

Printed in Great Britain
by Amazon